D1487595

THE WITCH HOAX

THOMAS J. KOLODZIEJSKI

The Witch Hoax
Written by: Thomas J. Kolodziejski
Copy editing by: Amber Richberger

www.facebook.com/tjkolodziejski

ACKNOWLEDGEMENTS

Special thanks to my family and friends for their unwavering support.

CHAPTER 1

KILL THE CZAR

The FM stations didn't play oldies anymore. Static and hissing on the AM frequencies disturbed the deep silence. Darkness, but for the soft glow of a desk lamp, surrounded him in his dorm. Everyone was at the Carnegie Village party that night. Breathing heavy, he observed an envelope with a broken wax seal and his name in golden calligraphy: *Johnathan Hallman*. He adjusted his collar. From the sleeve of his tuxedo jacket he pulled a hangtag. Next to a bottle of whiskey, a crumpled paperback Friedrich Nietzsche book sat, liberated, once hidden beneath a mattress he'd vowed never to sleep on again.

~~

John leaned against an old Victorian lamppost in front of Francesca Hall, counting the walkway lights around the university's quad. Steam from his breath was the smoke from an imaginary cigarette. Marcus and two graduate students joined him. Kasey had not yet arrived. John complained that it was only him and three other students waiting outside. He had envisioned a wealth of scholars assembling out in front of the hall, embarking upon a glorious convoy to an "intellectual mafia summit". The other society members and esteemed guests had alternative transportation to the dinner. Marcus stalled the chauffeur for as long as he could, but the driver would not compromise the schedule for Kasey. A short walk along a cobblestone path led them to their stylish limousine.

During the drive to Lafayette, John endured small talk with the grad students while Marcus fidgeted, repeatedly mentioning

Kasey and her absenteeism. John grumbled with a heavy sigh. He opened a compartment along the interior and fixed himself a drink. The others refused his offer. Marcus reminded him, more than once, that perfect behavior was expected and to "take it easy with the drinks". Marcus was, however, more concerned with Kasey. By the time the limo had arrived, he'd spoken her name twenty-seven times.

The Lafayette Banquet Hall was not an especially large venue, but its luxurious ambiance and lush amenities frequently drew high-class patronage, mostly for upscale weddings. This night, Lafayette welcomed the Avalonti Society's illustrious, annual Thanksgiving charity gala. John pressed his wide eyes against the window as they pulled into the secluded parking lot. Men in tuxedos walked by the courtyard's triple-tiered fountain with elegant women dressed in the height of fashion. Valet attendants in three-piece suits hustled for tips. Luxury vehicles, limousines and fully restored vintage cars transformed the parking lot into a showroom. Classical music could be heard from within the banquet hall each time the doors swung open.

Inside, Don Vandacheler coordinated, showing guests to their assigned seats. John and Marcus faced the doorway, a few rows behind the head table. Tapping his fingers nervously, Marcus looked past John to the empty chair next to him. The sound of impatient clocks ticked away in his mind. With an unbreakable focus, John surveyed the head table, reserved for honored guests. Respectfully, members of the Avalonti Society did not sit at the head table. John recognized the CEO of Congriata Enterprises—Victor J. Villalobos, Bishop Darius E. Armstrong, Delegate Kendra Devoux and Senator William Sebastian Croffley.

At 6:59 p.m., Marcus sighed victoriously; Kasey had arrived just in time.

John gazed upon the entryway as Don Vandacheler took her by the hand.

Kasey Chong, a twenty-year-old sophomore at the university, wore a petite, burgundy, Alexandre Vauthier bell-sleeve satin dress. Two curled strands of her shiny black hair dangled over her soft, pale cheeks. Diamond earrings, a gift from her grandmother in Seoul, mirrored the sparkling in her eyes under the dazzling chandeliers.

"*Ahem*. John, you're staring," Marcus whispered.

"I wasn't," John protested, beginning to blush.

Marcus Williams, a twenty-two-year-old economics student, wore a slim-fit, black Dolce & Gabbana tuxedo, white Ferragamo loafers and his father's platinum-ice Rolex. Complimenting his smooth, dark complexion was an ear-to-ear smile, greeting her warmly as they approached.

"You look ravishing, my dear," Marcus said, feigning a British accent, bowing, kissing her hand.

"Thank you, milord," Kasey replied as she curtsied, indulging in the roleplay.

Don Vandacheler, the society's thirty-eight-year-old British mentor, smirked as he walked away to meet other guests. His eager steps gently ruffled his voluminous dark-brown hair that rested cordially on the collar of his faille-trimmed black suede jacket. With his novelty cane, white cotton gloves and fluent grace, he radiated an aura of class and sophistication.

Marcus showed Kasey to her seat. John fixed his attention on the chandeliers. Marcus glared, silently admonishing him for his refusal to stand and pull out her chair. Kasey scoffed, rolling her eyes.

"John," she coldly spoke, taking her seat next to him.

"Kasey," he retaliated.

Ruggedly handsome, John Hallman's chiseled features distracted from the faded scars on his face; memories of yesteryear's violence. He frequently adjusted his generic tuxedo and occasionally removed his polished leather slip-on shoes under the chair. Threads of his dirty-blond hair fell just before his dark blue eyes as he carelessly rested his elbows on the table.

"Elbows," Kasey chided, tapping his arm.

John huffed, placing his hands in his lap, slouching.

"Posture," she instructed, demonstrating in her chair.

John gritted his teeth and sat up straight.

Feedback from the microphone silenced the audience. The violinists withdrew from playing. The dinner guests situated themselves and focused their attention on the podium for the opening speech. Dr. George Verner, chairman of the Avalonti

Board of Trustees, presided. John listened attentively as Dr. Verner spoke for nearly half an hour on the ethics of philanthropy and their charity missions to the disenfranchised. The smell of filet mignon and lobster teased their appetites.

"We humbly thank our esteemed guests and members for your generous contributions and most worthy attendance. Please enjoy your dinner which will be served momentarily. Thank you," Dr. Verner concluded.

Piloted by an army of waiters, serving carts strolled down the aisles and between the long rectangular tables, offering hungry guests the cuisine of their choice. Silverware against the porcelain dinner plates clanked together in a hypnotizing synchrony. The string ensemble played while the banquet hall filled with indecipherable chatter.

John's inhibitions had weakened, and his voice grew louder with each glass of champagne. Discovering that Marcus had also played football in high school, he and the other students engaged in casual sports trivia. John ignored Marcus's recommendation to moderate his drinking. For dessert, he ordered a slice of chocolate cake and another refill of his Dom Pérignon.

Reaching for a utensil, John clumsily knocked over a glass of water, splashing the older gentleman sitting across from Kasey. A hush fell over the nearby guests. Kasey quickly threw a cloth napkin on the spillage as the old man turned around to investigate.

"Sorry! I'm so embarrassed," she coyly confessed.

"*Oh,* don't worry about it, sweetie," the old man reassured, adding his napkin, "it's only water. It's only water."

The old man resumed his conversation with a group sitting at the next table.

Kasey leaned towards John. "Don't screw this up," she whispered sternly, nonchalantly taking his glass of champagne away.

Every head turned toward the entrance.

"What the fuck!" John shouted, dropping to the floor.

Screams erupted from the guests as gunshots from a semiautomatic rifle rang out in the parking lot. They simultaneously took cover. Four stout security guards drew pistols from under their tuxedo jackets and advanced to the entranceway. Shivering, one of the grad students clung to John while they hid under the table. Marcus was nearby, shielding Kasey. No one spoke a word. An engine roared, decreasing in volume as a car sped away from the banquet hall. John freed himself from the terrified grad student and peeked out from under the tablecloth. With a furrowed brow, he noticed Don Vandacheler sitting in a chair with his legs crossed, sipping tea, having a relaxed conversation with a man wearing a tweed blazer.

"Son of a bitch!" a man near the entryway shouted, looking out the window.

John cautiously extended his neck to see that it was Senator William Sebastian Croffley.

"Get down, John," Marcus ordered.

John crouched down again. Reaching up, he carefully grabbed the glass of champagne Kasey had taken from him and resumed his hiding. He took a sip.

"Seriously?" Kasey whispered.

John shrugged, taking another sip.

Sirens in the distance alleviated some of the tension. Guests gradually emerged from under the tables. With murmurs, the indecipherable chatter had returned.

When the police arrived, one of the security guards nodded at Dr. George Verner.

"Ladies and gentlemen," Dr. Verner calmly announced over the microphone, "we do humbly apologize for this unexpected inconvenience. We're working with police to secure the perimeter for the safety of our guests. At this time, we ask that you all please retake your seats. Waiters are coming around shortly to take drink orders. Please be advised that, while this appears to be an isolated incident, guests should remain seated and stay within the building for the time being. I will make further announcements as more information becomes available. Again, we do humbly apologize for this inconvenience and appreciate your patience until this matter is resolved. Thank you."

Stepping out into the crisp air, John saw Senator Croffley's Maserati Quattroporte being loaded on a tow truck. Pebbles of glass blanketed the empty parking space. A couple of vehicles were collaterally damaged from the hailstorm of bullets, but there were no injuries. Police directed foot traffic as a courtesy. The students learned that the assailants were not interested in harming the guests. The attack against Senator Croffley's car was an intimidation tactic. Specific details on the shooter's motives were unknown to the Avalonti Society. With aid from the open bar, most of the guests had regained their cheerful disposition. The rest of the evening had gone off without a hitch. John, Kasey and Marcus received instruction to join Don Vandacheler at Francesca Hall on Sunday at 2 p.m. for their next meeting. John, Marcus and the grad students piled into the limousine while Kasey waited for her Uber.

∿

Francesca Hall, the society's clubhouse, stood as one of the most magnificent structures at the university; located outside of Washington D.C. in the state of Maryland. The Avalonti family spared no expense during the hall's construction in 1941. Romanesque stone stairs climbed to meet a wraparound porch adorned with towering Corinthian columns. Intricate carvings lined the massive cherry wood double doors of the main entranceway, complete with Victorian-styled wrought-iron handles. Overlooking the quad, a spacious veranda was visited by the intrusive ivy that encompassed the outer red-brick walls. Located on the eastern border of the campus, the hall was surrounded by Yoshino cherry trees, Gothic stone fountains, rose bushes and meticulously manicured evergreen hedges. A series of blue stained-glass windows accentuated the high ceiling; littered with ornate cornices and exquisitely detailed moldings. Polished marble floors accommodated a Beha grandfather clock and a Steinway baby grand piano. An oversized crystal chandelier dangled above the finely crafted furniture near the wood-burning fireplace. Above the mantelpiece, the Avalonti coat of arms proudly displayed the Latin words for Reason, Knowledge and Progress as their motto. A liquor bar and three Brunswick billiard tables to the right of the grand foyer offered members entertainment. Home to many antiques and artifacts, the left wing of the hall included a priceless three-hundred-year-old book collection gifted by Dr. Simon Avalonti. Oil paintings encased in golden frames hung from the interior walls; anniversary presents to Phineas Avalonti, the late founder, from his beloved artist wife, Francesca.

~~~

Sunlight crept through the soaring stained-glass windows of Francesca Hall. On an antique red velvet couch near the grand fireplace, the three students sat, eagerly awaiting their second orientation. The butler opened one of the massive cherry wood double doors. Dress shoes tapping in long strides across the polished marble floors echoed throughout the cavernous hall as Don Vandacheler approached. In quiet anticipation, the students watched as he prepared the meeting.

"Gentlemen—and lady," Vandacheler addressed the students, "congratulations are in order; you've passed your first assignment. On behalf of the Avalonti Society, I would like to thank you all for your attendance at the Lafayette charity fundraiser, and for your scrupulous behavior. Aside from the obvious unpleasantries, we hope that you all enjoyed your evening."

"Absolutely," Kasey assured.

"Yes, sir," Marcus said.

John nodded.

"I had a wondrous time myself," Vandacheler confessed as he walked over and stood in front of John. "I was particularly fond of the champagne. Very tasty, wouldn't you say, John?"

Kasey smirked delightfully.

John looked at the floor with slumped posture.

"You'll be pleased to know that you're famous," Vandacheler sarcastically announced, tossing in front of them the Sunday edition of a local newspaper, folded to the *Arts & Humanities* section. The photograph featured, among others, John, Kasey and Marcus.

Marcus and Kasey gushed over their picture in the paper.

John wasn't sure if he wanted to look.

"As you may know," Vandacheler theatrically spoke, "the Avalonti Society is a vanguard university society committed to the noble pursuit of knowledge. Here, we chase truths with the scimitar of doubt and rigorously question until all uncertainty is vanquished. The process is recorded and—much like in the olden days of the Great Library of Alexandria—archived in these journals."

The students leaned forward, observing copies of the *Avalonti Journal* that he tossed onto the coffee table.

"Knowledge and understanding are the fulcrum upon which our civilization turns. Which brings us to your next assignment." Vandacheler walked a few steps to the grand fireplace, retrieved three envelopes from the mantelpiece and returned to the antique red velvet couch. "As probationary members of the Avalonti Society, you will be required to complete a few more tasks before your formal induction—to demonstrate your worthiness." He handed each student an envelope. "Your next assignment will be to *kill* the Russian czar."

The students scrunched their faces.

"I'm only joking, of course. The last czar died over a hundred years ago—poor Nicholas. Your next assignment," he continued in a serious tone, "will be one of self-analysis. Before one can understand obscure things, one must understand themselves. You shall write an essay. In this essay you will delve into your own mind; documenting your beliefs, your fears, your hopes and your dreams. You will include your strengths, your weaknesses, your loves and your hatreds. You will not withhold any detail and you will not tell any lies. Once you finish writing the essay, you are to read it. You will read it out loud and *only* to yourselves. Then, you will destroy it. Your words will fall upon no other ears but your own."

"Cool," Kasey commented in a dreamy tone.

"What?" Marcus puzzled. "How will you know that we did the assignment?"

"We won't," Vandacheler answered, pacing in front of the students, "but *you* will."

Kasey stared with a mesmerized gaze.

"What's in the envelopes?" John asked.

"The envelopes contain a brief history of our society, who we are and what we represent. Also, a list of our rules. Please carefully examine our guidelines and take into consideration that failure to obey them will result in your slow and rather painful death. I'm kidding, sort of. It will, however, justify your permanent removal from the society. So, please be wise."

John grinned.

Kasey and Marcus nodded obediently.

Having other matters to attend to, Vandacheler gathered his belongings. "We shall meet here again on Saturday, December the 5th, 2 p.m. sharp. We have a little surprise for you. Until then, get some rest and enjoy the holiday break. Mr. Budwin will show you out when you are ready, of course. Goodbye, all, and be safe in your travels."

Bowing deeply with subtle indifference, Vandacheler excused himself. The tapping of his red and black lizard-skin dress shoes echoed once more as he gracefully exited the hall.

"Great champagne, huh, John?" Kasey chuckled, wasting no time to dig into him.

"You're lucky, John," Marcus added.

"Alright, alright," John pleaded, standing from the couch. "Let me see that article."

Kasey offered John the newspaper. He quickly snatched it out of her hand. Walking towards the grand fireplace, he grimaced at his picture in the paper, seeing that the photograph had captured his gaudy, inebriated smile.

"So, how come you didn't ride with us in the limo?" Marcus asked Kasey.

"No particular reason," she answered, glaring at John behind his back.

Marcus smiled. "*Oh*, well, I'm glad you made it."

John stared at the newspaper for a minute then began flipping the pages.

Marcus and Kasey raised an eyebrow as he continued fervently.

"What are you doing?" Kasey begged.

"It's not in here!" John shouted, continuing to flip through the pages.

"What's not in there?" Marcus asked.

"The—the senator's car. They didn't mention anything about it. There's nothing in here but some stupid soft news story about the society dinner," John informed with increasing panic.

"Well, I saw the reporter leave before it happened," Marcus calmly explained, standing from the couch.

"Dude, that doesn't matter," John argued. "We're talking about a senator getting his car shot full of fucking bullets. This is something that should be national news. Why isn't it in here?"

Marcus snickered. "This isn't small-town Missouri, John. The Lafayette Banquet Hall is right outside of Washington D.C. You'd be surprised at what doesn't make the newspaper around here."

"Yeah, but like I said, we're talking about a U.S. senator."

Marcus shrugged.

"Maybe they'll put it in tomorrow's paper," Kasey suggested, throwing her backpack over her shoulder.

John rolled his eyes, shaking his head at her.

"They probably will," Marcus assured.

"You guys are acting like this is no big deal or something," John ridiculed. "I saw you two cowering under the table."

"Yeah, when I thought they were coming inside," Marcus defended. "Once I knew they were just there for Croffley's car, I couldn't have possibly cared less. Also, I wasn't cowering, I was being smart."

"Yeah, right," John objected.

"What happened at the Lafayette dinner is definitely an example of why we need more gun control in this country," Kasey opined.

With a quick turn of his head, Marcus peered at Kasey. "Let me tell you about these democrats."

"Oh gosh," Kasey snickered.

"Nah, I'm serious. Whatever reason they were threatening Croffley, it was probably something he brought onto himself. Democrats are always doing shady shit; taking bribes, hanging around the Mafia and shit," Marcus explained.

"Oh, and the Republicans are any better?" John huffed.

Kasey inhaled sharply. "Well, I have a ton of things I need to get done before I leave for Cincy tomorrow, so I'm gonna head out."

"*Oh*, okay. Goodbye, Kasey," Marcus saluted, changing his demeanor, smiling. "Have a wonderful Thanksgiving with your family."

"Goodbye, Marcus. Have a safe Thanksgiving," she said, courteously hugging him.

Turning to John, she said, in a less enthusiastic tone, "Goodbye, John."

John didn't speak.

"Goodbye, John," she repeated.

He continued to ignore her.

"Okay," she scoffed, "whatever."

Exiting the hall, she paused momentarily to wish Mr. Budwin a safe and happy Thanksgiving as well.

Marcus looked at his wristwatch. "Well, buddy, I too have to get going. You have a great Thanksgiving, John."

John shook his hand. "Goodbye, Marcus."

"Oh," Marcus taunted, "you say 'goodbye' to me."

"Of course."

Marcus chuckled, patting him on the shoulder. "Later, John."

"Later."

~~~

Kasey took a flight to Cincinnati and Marcus returned to his parents' house in Bethesda. John was one of the few students who stayed at the university during the Thanksgiving break. Bo Zhang, his roommate, brought him curried fish and sticky rice on a paper plate wrapped in tinfoil that his mother had sympathetically prepared. When Bo surprised John by returning early on Thanksgiving, he found him asleep at 5 p.m. with a half-smoked joint laying on his chest. Empty alcohol bottles and a trail of opened philosophy books riddled the dorm. Before waking him,

Bo shut off John's new radio, blaring '50s music so loud it could be heard at the other end of the hallway. After the meeting at Francesca Hall, John fruitlessly searched for days to see if any mainstream media outlets were covering the story of the gunfire at the society dinner. The only story he found was from a tabloid-grade blog citing the incident in near-perfect detail. The writers even had a photograph of Croffley's demolished Maserati, presumably leaked by the tow truck driver. To John's dismay, the visitor commentary on the blog was largely negative. Many of the commenters dubbed the story as "fake news".

CHAPTER 2
THE MARQUIS

Ominous clouds loomed over the horizon. Cheering and chanting resounded from a rally outside of the university auditorium. Confetti bombs, vintage noisemakers, sirens and bullhorns were all used to discourage patrons from attending a controversial guest lecture. John watched from across the quad, standing on the kingly stone stairs of Francesca Hall. Something caught his eye in the distance. Marching toward the demonstration was a group of black-clad protesters, concealing their identities with bandanas and balaclavas. Hoisted at the front of their formation was the red and black anarcho-syndicalist flag. Misty rain began to fall.

Along the cobblestone pathway, Don Vandacheler advanced toward the hall, unimpeded by the spectacle across the quad. Wearing an executive leather handbag over his black suede jacket, he walked with focused determination.

"Johnathan," he greeted, sprinting up the stone stairs, "how do you do?"

"I'm good," John said, distracted by the protest.

"Joining us?" Vandacheler asked, impatiently holding open one of the double doors.

"Yes, sir."

Entering the hall, John found Marcus and Kasey dressed in semi-formal attire, talking casually on the antique furniture near the grand fireplace. He glanced down at his blue jeans then joined them on the couch. The old butler took Vandacheler's jacket.

"Will you be taking tea, sir?" Mr. Budwin courteously asked in his low, scratchy voice.

"No," Vandacheler sighed, "I don't believe we shall."

Mr. Budwin nodded, bowing slightly.

Vandacheler sourly gazed upon him as he returned to his post, commenting in an unobserved whisper, "My goodness, do we really need a butler?"

The skies were darkening.

Joining the students, Vandacheler prepared the meeting.

"I didn't see any mention of Croffley's car in the news," John said softly, leaning towards Marcus.

Marcus shrugged. "It just wasn't that big of a story."

John scoffed, shaking his head.

"I'm just glad nobody got hurt," Kasey added.

Vandacheler stood from a red velvet parlor chair.

"What's going on over at the auditorium?" John asked.

"Never mind," Vandacheler urged, "we've more important things to discuss. You'll be pleased to know that I have some auspicious news for you."

Vandacheler took three brochures from his satchel and handed one to each student. "Kasey, my darling, university records show that you live off campus. This may not be so appealing to you, but you will be given the same offer. John and Marcus—you should find this an adequate upgrade from your current living arrangements."

John and Marcus gaped at the pamphlet: *The Avalonti Marquis Hotel & Suites.*

"The society is offering generous accommodation during your probationary period. The Marquis is an Avalonti Holdings property, open, free of charge, to all students who are current members. Your stay is optional, of course. Should you elect to upgrade, we have arranged with the university to prorate you or your family for your dormitory fees. Kasey, unfortunately, we cannot help you in that regard."

John snarled his face. "Where do you live?"

"My folks bought me a house a few blocks from the school," Kasey shyly admitted.

"Your folks bought you a house!" John scowled.

"What do you care? You just got a free upgrade to a freaking five-star resort," she fired back.

"I'll take that as you'll be staying put then?" Vandacheler asked, attempting to quell the tension between her and John.

"It's really tempting, believe me. I'm very thankful for the offer but I should decline," she humbly rejected, handing back the brochure.

"Understood," Vandacheler accepted. "John, Marcus?"

"I'm in," Marcus responded without hesitation.

"John?" Vandacheler nudged.

Gentle rain percussed against the stained-glass windows.

"I'm in," John declared.

"Brilliant," Vandacheler stated, rapidly informing, "your suites will be fully furnished. You will enjoy amenities such as free Wi-Fi, laundry service, indoor swimming pool, gym—which I know you lads will make good use of—tennis courts, spa, access to the restaurant and bar, room service, free shuttle service which runs every forty minutes to the university only a couple of miles away. Let's see, I'm sure I'm forgetting something. *Ah,* front desk will be happy to do what they can to satisfy your requests within their power to do so. I can't guarantee they'll be able to fetch you a glass of zebra milk at 3 o'clock in the morning, but by God they'll try."

John smirked at Kasey, adding a little shimmy to rub it in. "I'm sure your house is nice though, *Kase.*"

Kasey scoffed.

"It's all good, Kasey," Marcus teased, "you can come play tennis with us." He motioned as if swinging a tennis racket.

She crossed her arms. "I ha—really don't like you guys."

Marcus chuckled, turning to Vandacheler. "So, how many society students live there?"

"Of the 986 rooms at The Marquis, there are roughly 22 occupied by Avalonti members," Vandacheler answered.

"How many members does the society have in total?" Marcus asked.

"Including inactive alumni, 733 living members. Typically, there are around fifteen new members inducted per year. But, as you know, Caesar wants to expand the society."

"Where is this Caesar guy? We ever gonna meet him?" Marcus asked.

"Unlikely," Vandacheler answered. "Caesar lives in New York now. He's the CEO of the Avalonti holdings corporation. He manages the society remotely, although most of the work is done by the High Council."

"What's the High Council?" John asked.

Vandacheler squinted. "They're mentioned quite a lot in your orientation packet."

"Oh, yeah, I remember now," John assured.

"So, how come I never see any other members in here?" Marcus asked.

"Francesca Hall is mostly used for special events these days— and orientations," Vandacheler informed.

"Y'all better start using it more, or the university will find a better use for it," Marcus surmised. "It's all economics; the allocation of scarce resources, supply and demand."

"That can't happen," Vandacheler asserted.

"Does the university even own this building?" Kasey asked.

"No," Vandacheler answered. "This building, along with the quarter-acre plot of land surrounding it, is owned by the Avalonti Trust Association, even though it's a part of the university's campus. The Avalonti Foundation contributes generously to this university and has been a partnership for decades. The cobblestone pathways that surround the quad, for example, were donated by the Avalonti family and installed the same year this building was constructed."

Kasey nodded slowly. "Interesting."

"So, I hate to ask this," John said, tapping his fingers, "but why wasn't the shooting at the Lafayette dinner covered in any of the mainstream newspapers?"

Marcus sighed, rolling his eyes.

"I'm afraid I don't have an answer for that," Vandacheler replied.

"Why hasn't Avalonti published anything about it in the journal?" John interrogated.

"Dude, come on," Marcus reprimanded, shaking his head at John.

"The submission deadline for the December issue was before the incident took place," Vandacheler explained. "Should any of our contributors feel the desire to write about Lafayette, they will do so, and their articles will be published in the January edition, which comes out later this month."

"Do you think anyone will write about it?" John inquired.

"I couldn't say," Vandacheler answered. "Remember, Avalonti is a scholarly journal, not a newspaper."

"Why don't *you* write something about it?" John asked. "Why not inform the public? We're supposed to be all about truth-seeking, right?"

Marcus and Kasey cringed.

"That we are," Vandacheler agreed. "Unfortunately, I am not a journalist," he joked.

"I'm curious about something else—and I don't mean to offend," John said, confronting Marcus and Kasey's bewildered staring. "Why didn't you take cover after the gunshots went off? You just sat there like nothing was happening."

"Alright, come on, John, that's enough!" Marcus interfered.

"No, no," Vandacheler said, holding a hand up to Marcus. "John's curiosity is perfectly natural. It's a matter of logical deduction, John. I was managing guests all night. I was aware that none of them were outside during the gunfire. Had the assailants been interested in harming any of our guests, there would've been bullets flying through the windows, I imagine. Instead, they emptied an entire thirty-round magazine in a steady, isolated succession, indicating that there was a *singular* target; quite discernibly a vehicle as the shooting took place in the parking lot. After hearing a car speeding away from the building, I was able to quickly determine that their rampage—for whatever reason they had to enact it—was over. With the addition of the four burly security guards present, I found no reason to throw myself to the floor. Did you have any other questions, John?"

Kasey smirked at John.

"No, sir," John said, looking at the polished marble floors.

"Jolly good," Vandacheler remarked.

Marcus's attention was stolen away by a faintly heard ruckus coming from across the quad. "What's happening out there?"

Springing to their feet, the students raced to the main entranceway to investigate. Marcus propped one of the doors open with an antique oriental brass doorstop. The students watched from a distance. Undeterred by the rain, a scuffle had broken out between the demonstrators and patrons of the lecture. As campus security rushed to intervene, they witnessed an uproarious commotion accompanying the vandalistic shattering of an auditorium window.

"Tolerant liberals at it again," Marcus hissed.

"They're just standing up for what they believe in," Kasey defended.

Marcus's eyes widened. "By breaking windows?"

John scoffed. "And who are they protesting this time, Dr. Martin Luther King, Jr.?"

Kasey raised an eyebrow. "Why do you say that?"

"Because last time they were out there protesting William Zodeger," John answered.

"Well, yeah," Kasey insisted, "Zodeger is a homophobe."

"Is he now?" John groaned. "And how much do you know about Dr. William Zodeger?"

"Enough to know he's a homophobe," she snarled.

"Yeah, Kasey? Is that your assessment or the hivemind's?"

"The *hivemind's?* What the heck are you talking about, John?" she implored.

"You don't know shit about William Zodeger. You know how I know that? Because I actually researched the guy. Yep. Read both his books, too. The guy is ultra-progressive."

"Are you kidding me? I saw the video, John," Kasey sneered.

"*Oh* yeah, *that* video. The propaganda piece that was edited by Zeda Flame, the alt-right troll doll. You got suckered, Kasey," John insisted. "They made that video to see if they could get progressives to turn on a fellow progressive—and you fell for it!"

Marcus stood next to John, showing solidarity by quietly nodding.

"See, that's the problem with people!" John erupted. "They don't ever look at all the facts—they just believe what everyone else believes! I saw the unedited interview with William Zodeger and Kurt Wilson. The edited video clearly took him out of context. Zodeger has vehemently supported adoption rights for homosexual partners since 1979. He was an early social justice crusader, that's why the alt-right wanted to destroy him. And they used people like you to get the job done. Great job, Kasey!"

"Yeah, Kasey, it was a witch hunt," Marcus added. "The Progressive Student Rights Coalition rescinded the protest once they realized they had blundered. People still showed up to shut him down, though. It was crazy."

"Oh, *great*, you guys are teaming up on me now," Kasey said, crossing her arms.

"I can't believe this society even picked you, Kasey!" John shouted in her face. "You're not a freethinker, you're a fucking troglodyte!"

"That's enough, gentlemen!" Vandacheler scolded, loosely putting his arm around her. "We're here to enlighten, not to vilify," he decreed, patting her on the shoulder.

"Thanks, Don," Kasey uttered.

"I'm sorry, Kasey," Marcus swiftly apologized.

John didn't speak.

"Okay," she softly spoke, grabbing her jacket from the coatrack, "I'll see you guys later."

Vandacheler peered intently at John.

"Bye, Kasey," Marcus pouted. "Sorry again."

Kasey somberly left the hall, stopping briefly to say goodbye to Mr. Budwin on her way out.

"I'm sorry, sir. I guess I got carried away," John offered.

"I'm sorry, too," Marcus moped, "even though I didn't really do anything."

A clap of thunder rumbled with a downpour of rain. Vandacheler stood by the doorway, tongue-in-cheek, looking beyond Francesca Hall's meticulously manicured evergreen hedges. "Thunderstorms in December," he poetically spoke. "This unpredictable Maryland weather shall never win my heart."

John and Marcus studied each other's look of shame.

Contemplating what had just transpired, Vandacheler hoped to find departing words of wisdom. "There'll be some paperwork, of course—and hopefully we can get you lads moved into your new rooms before the winter break."

CHAPTER 3
EXIT STAGE LEFT

Don Vandacheler studied performing arts at Juilliard in his younger years, then quit theater to pursue a doctorate in chemistry at the university. Born of wealth in London to a family with ties to the aristocracy, Vandacheler had attended the finest schools and was reading at a college level before his tenth birthday. His father, while unconditionally supportive, chuckled softly at his son's refusal to go by Dr. Vandacheler. When he wasn't detained by societal duties, Vandacheler was conducting research at the university's chemistry lab, or patronizing one of the local dinner theaters. Neophytes, which were probationary members, reported to Don Vandacheler for orientations, meetings, guidance and support.

Typically, the prestigious Avalonti Society did not induct at the undergraduate level. Publishing a reputable scholarly journal, the society's members were usually tenured professors, scientists, philosophers, economists, researchers and grad students. Caesar Avalonti, the Godfather, sought to expand the society by allowing sophomores, juniors and seniors to apply for membership. Once the decision was democratically voted in, the Avalonti High Council posted a bulletin seeking three undergraduates for a trial run of the idea. Of the 400 students at the university who submitted applications, John, Kasey and Marcus were selected as protégés. Don Vandacheler accepted the task to manage the experiment, placing him officially in charge of, and responsible for, all three of the students.

Utilizing his theater skill, Vandacheler organized a short, intimate production at Francesca Hall for the students. After witnessing the chaotic argument days earlier, Vandacheler understood the necessity to expedite proper debate training. This evening, he brought in two society members: astrophysicist Chad Wilcox and Professor of Philosophy, Dr. Thaddeus Arnold. The men would take part in a staged discussion; a play. Vandacheler marked the event as one of the students' mandatory tasks. The purpose of the production was to demonstrate proper discourse etiquette, starting with *discussion* and *informal debating*. It would be easier to show how civilized people argued, Vandacheler thought, rather than attempting to explain it.

"Lady and gentlemen," Vandacheler theatrically announced, "please welcome Mr. Chad Wilcox and Dr. Thaddeus Arnold."

The students applauded softly, watching from the Victorian couch.

"I present to you an exclusive Vandacheler Production: The Physicist and the Theologian."

The students applauded once more.

Francesca Hall's main lights dimmed, and a floor-level spotlight shined on a pair of antique red velvet parlor chairs. Dr. Thaddeus Arnold, playing the established theologian, sat by the crackling fire reading a newspaper. He would be joined momentarily by Mr. Chad Wilcox, playing the young physicist. Their names would not be changed.

Physicist: "Good evening, Dr. Arnold."

Theologian: "*Ah*, Mr. Wilcox, won't you join me for a drink?"

Physicist: "Certainly."

Mr. Wilcox retrieved a glass decanter of brandy from the mantelpiece.

Physicist: "May I?"

Theologian: "Please."

Mr. Wilcox topped off Dr. Arnold then poured himself a glass. Dr. Arnold folded his newspaper as Mr. Wilcox took his seat.

Theologian: "I read your recent journal papers. With great interest, I might add."

Physicist: "And did it find you well, sir?"

Theologian: "You're a credit to your field, young Mr. Wilcox. Your intrepid dedication does not elude my admiration. I do, however, find your closing statement to be a bit troubling."

Physicist: "Thank you for your kind words, sir. May I ask what you find troubling?"

Theologian: "Certainly. You conclude that 'with mounting evidence, The Big Bang has drifted away from theory and is now steadily traversing into the realm of incontrovertible science'. I'm afraid I quarrel with your choosing of the word *incontrovertible*. A bit provocative, wouldn't you say?"

Physicist: "I accept your criticism. Perhaps I was a bit careless in my choice of words. It is, nevertheless, not entirely bereft of truth."

Theologian: *"Truth you say*, Mr. Wilcox?"

Physicist: "We stand on the shoulders of our great predecessors, Dr. Arnold. In 1929, a critical discovery was made by Edwin Hubble. Dr. Hubble gazed into our cosmic sea and, through a new perspective, saw that our universe was expanding in all directions. Through his telescope, he confirmed that our galaxy was not alone, disrupting the archaic perception of our place in the cosmos. In 2001, the Wilkinson Microwave Anisotropy Probe was launched. The team successfully imaged the Cosmic Microwave Background, allowing a unique glimpse into the early life of our universe. The WMAP data and emerging research favors our theory, quite strongly, I'm afraid."

Theologian: "Thank you for your eloquent explanation, Mr. Wilcox. Might I ask what your fundamental objection to the idea of God is?"

Physicist: "An omniscient, omnipotent, omnipresent entity being responsible for the creation of the universe seems highly unlikely."

Theologian: "Thank you. May I now ask what preceded this cataclysmic explosion that we call The Big Bang?"

Physicist: "Certainly, Dr. Arnold. It stands to reason that the creation and expansion of the universe was indeed the result of a cataclysmic explosion from whence all matter was condensed into a single point of infinite density. We call this the singularity."

Theologian: "Thank you. And may I ask what came before this proposed singularity?"

Physicist: "Well, sir, there are other theories on this matter. It is, however, a widely held belief within the scientific community that nothing predates the singularity of The Big Bang. It is the origin of our cosmic birth, if you will."

Theologian: "A single point where all space, all matter, all life, all knowledge and all of time emerges?"

Physicist: "Yes."

Theologian: "Wouldn't you say then, Mr. Wilcox, that the universe itself is omniscient, omnipotent and omnipresent?"

Mr. Wilcox contemplated, swirling the brandy in his glass.

Theologian: "What ignited, if I may ask, this cataclysmic explosion that thrust all things into existence from the point of singularity? What ignited The Big Bang?"

Physicist: "As Stephen Hawking and Leonard Mlodinow profess in *The Grand Design*, the spontaneous creation of a universe does not require a sentient being to light the torch. Our only honest answer, however, is that we do not yet know *precisely* what caused it."

Theologian: "Then wouldn't you agree, Mr. Wilcox, that *some* level of faith is required for your belief in The Big Bang, as it is for my belief that God created the universe? They are both theories, after all."

Physicist: "I suppose I could agree—for now, anyway."

Theologian: "For now."

Dr. Arnold smiled warmly at the young physicist then stood from his chair.

Mr. Wilcox followed his lead.

Physicist: "It has been a pleasure to speak with you, Dr. Arnold. I appreciate your thought-provoking insight—even though we fundamentally disagree on the origin of the universe."

Theologian: "The pleasure has been all mine, young sir. Might I add that science and God need not be such bitter rivals in the end?"

Physicist: "Perhaps, you may. Goodnight, Dr. Arnold."

Theologian: "Goodnight, Mr. Wilcox. Give my best to your family."

Physicist: "Will do, sir. Likewise."

The men shook hands.

Vandacheler approached the "stage", signaling that the play had concluded.

The students applauded as the two men bowed.

"Thank you to Mr. Chad Wilcox and Dr. Thaddeus Arnold for their lovely performance," Vandacheler said as the main lights in the hall returned, courtesy of Mr. Budwin.

～

The seasoned society members did not rush off after their performance. It would be the first time John, Kasey and Marcus enjoyed an intimate discussion with higher-ranking members of the society, known as Sages. The men stayed for a little over an hour after the performance. John repeatedly thanked them. Mr. Budwin showed them out when the time came for their departure. John and Marcus would soon follow.

"Hey, Kasey, got a second?" John asked, putting on his coat by the door.

"I suppose," Kasey responded.

"Look, I'm not good at meaningful apologies, but the way I acted toward you the other day is not who I want to be. You have every right to be upset with me, and I can't expect that to go away in the blink of an eye, but I want you to know that I truly am sorry for how I made you feel."

Kasey smiled. "I think you're better at meaningful apologies than you think you are. I accept your apology, John."

"Thanks," he said, nodding gratefully.

"Sure thing."

John studied her eyes for a moment. "Goodnight, Kasey."

She smiled bashfully. "Goodnight, John."

John pulled open one of the massive cherry wood double doors.

"Hold that door!" Marcus shouted, rushing over.

John held the door.

"Goodnight, Marcus," Kasey saluted.

"Goodnight, Kasey," Marcus said, giving her a quick hug. "Come on, John, I'll walk back with you. I'm not finished with your ass yet."

Kasey grabbed the door, taking John's place.

"Alright," John snickered, walking out, "but I'm telling you, Marcus, the system of capitalism is fundamentally flawed."

Marcus shook his head. "Don't worry," he said, winking at Kasey, "I'll fix him."

Kasey giggled. "See you guys."

Their voices faded, walking between the old Victorian lampposts of Francesca Hall. She closed the door behind them, stepping backwards through the foyer with a pensive smile. Near the grand fireplace, Vandacheler observed Mr. Budwin standing over a stage light, searching for its power switch.

"Good gracious, it's right here," Vandacheler said, kneeling down, flipping the switch. "*Oh*, that's right," he joked, "they didn't have electricity in *your* day."

Mr. Budwin chuckled politely.

Vandacheler unplugged his stage light from the extension cord and took it under his arm. In the left wing of the hall, Kasey meandered, humming to herself while skimming the library.

"*Ah*, Kasey, good, you're still here," Vandacheler said as he hurried by, carrying his stage light. "I was wondering if I might have a word with you if you could spare a moment."

"Sure," Kasey agreed.

Vandacheler set the light by the entrance and motioned for Kasey to follow him. They walked toward the antique red velvet couch while Mr. Budwin returned to his post near the door.

"How are you, Kasey?" he asked, taking a seat, crossing his legs.

"I'm good," she answered.

~~

Vandacheler expressed a few concerns and offered Kasey encouragement. They talked for a while about the challenges she would likely face during her tenure as an Avalonti member and beyond. She assured him she would not be so easily deterred. The hour grew late. Patting her on the knee, he stood from the couch. Kasey and Vandacheler helped Mr. Budwin close for the night then walked out together. Mr. Budwin advanced toward the nearby faculty parking lot while Vandacheler and Kasey remained on the hall's porch.

"It's quite cold. Could I offer you a ride?" Vandacheler asked.

"It's only a ten-minute walk. I'll be fine," Kasey politely rejected, buttoning her pea coat.

Vandacheler smiled, wrapping up in his fashionable scarf. "Alright then."

"Thanks for everything, Don. I really appreciate it."

"Of course. Goodnight, Kasey," Vandacheler said, picking up his stage light. "You take care of yourself."

She smiled. "I will. Goodnight."

~~

Devonshire Heights was connected to the university via a path that cut through a wooded area on the eastern border of the campus behind Francesca Hall. Despite its proximity to the university, the community consisted predominately of middle-class families, aside from the occasional group of grad students who lived in one of the single-family homes. Kasey was the only undergraduate who owned a piece of real estate at Devonshire, courtesy of her loving parents. Most of the students who lived off campus rented at the more favorably priced Carnegie Village on the southwest side of the university near the happening business district. Devonshire Heights was a "lame" place for a university student to live, according to many of the undergraduates on campus. There was an elementary school, a middle school and a high school about four miles northeast of the university, assuring that Devonshire Heights would be nothing short of a typical American suburb. A plot of green space and a guardrail between the university property and the community made the area an ideal hangout spot for teenagers. Kasey's house was on that dead-end street, about a five-minute walk from the guardrail.

Emerging from the wooded area into her neighborhood that evening, she noticed a parked car running on the other side of the street with no headlights on. The driver taunted her by revving his engine twice. She removed her hands from her jacket pockets and crossed her arms, taking a deep breath as she continued down the sidewalk. Smoke escaped as the driver rolled down his window, revealing two Caucasian men about her age.

"Sup, baby. Can I get your number?" the glossy-eyed driver asked.

The passenger chuckled, flaunting a bottle of beer.

"Sorry, I have a boyfriend," Kasey replied.

"Oh yeah? What's his name?" the driver probed.

"*Uh*—John," she blurted out.

Smirking, the driver put his car in reverse and drifted backwards. "It's okay, baby, he doesn't have to know about us. It'll be our little secret."

"Sorry," she repeated, walking a little faster.

"Come on, bitch, you know you want this dick," the driver declared.

The passenger laughed. "Yeah, she does."

Kasey huffed, keeping her pace down the quiet suburban street. The driver stopped. She jumped as she heard his car door slam. When she turned to look, he was walking aggressively toward her. She bolted.

"Get back here, you fucking whore!" he shouted, chasing after her.

The streetlights illuminated the empty sidewalks. Living rooms shined blue with a TV sedation. Kasey ran feverishly, calling out for help. Her heart pounded. She could see her house, but she knew she wasn't going to make it.

"Help!" she screamed, running into a neighbor's yard. "Help!"

"Come here, you fucking bitch!" he roared, reaching out to grab her.

Kasey tumbled to the ground, rolling through the grass. The man tripped over her, falling forward to his hands. Kasey quickly stood. The man lunged, tackling her as she darted by.

"Why you fucking running, bitch?" he barked, climbing on top of her, holding down her arms. "I ain't gonna hurt you."

With labored breathing, he lowered his face down to her neck. Sweat beads gathered on his forehead. Alcohol was heavy on his breath. Kasey screamed in desperation, struggling with all her might to break away. He cupped his skinny hand and covered her mouth. "Shut the fuck up, bitch," he whispered in her ear.

Her bloodcurdling screams had alerted a group of young grad students who were having a small party a few houses down. Two students leapt from the porch and ran ferociously towards him, shouting, "Leave her the fuck alone!"

The attacker sprang to his feet, fleeing to his car. The two grad students kept after him. Kasey sprinted toward their house. "I don't know him! I don't know him!" she cried, running to the porch.

A frazzled young woman jumped out to catch her. Kasey collapsed in her arms. Another student stood at the edge of the yard, looking down the street. Tires screeched in the distance. The engine roared as their vehicle approached. "Fucking assholes!" the grad student yelled, hurling a bottle of beer. The bottle smacked against the speeding car, shattering through the air. Glass particles glistened like confetti under the streetlight's luminosity. The attacker and his friend escaped into the night.

The three grad students rejoined the others on the porch. Kasey sat, trembling and hyperventilating, with her back against the house. Two women sat on either side of her, stroking her in a futile attempt to calm her down.

"Are you okay?" one of the grad students asked, catching his breath.

Kasey stopped panting for a moment and looked around at all the people surrounding her.

She broke down and started to cry.

"Brian, did you call the police?" the homeowner asked his friend.

"They're on their way," Brian assured.

Two rookie officers arrived promptly on the scene; a male and a female officer. Paramedics arrived shortly after to make sure there were no injuries sustained. They wrapped Kasey in a warm blanket and brought her hot tea. Neighbors, drawn by flashing lights, offered to help but were asked by police to return to their homes. The police drafted a report and assured the students a proper investigation would ensue. Dave and Jennifer, the homeowners, thanked them for their courteous service.

As the paramedics and police were wrapping up, a senior officer arrived on the scene. The first-responding officers briefed him. Huddled on the porch, the students watched his cold reaction to the news. Lights from his cruiser flashed against the house. He sniffed loudly, taking a step towards them. Climbing slowly up the steps, he glared unflinchingly at Kasey.

"So," he grumbled, "what did you do to him to make him chase you?"

The grad students gasped.

The female officer quickly joined them on the porch. "We're all finished here," she said, stepping in front of the senior officer.

"That's ridiculous," Brian scoffed.

Jennifer sat down next to Kasey and put her arm around her.

Kasey's eyes fell into a void.

CHAPTER 4

THE RED PORCUPINE

Thousands of leather-bound books graced the towering shelves in the left wing of Francesca Hall. Rare titles and early edition prints proudly sat behind glass near the entryway. In addition, the library archived the *Avalonti Journal*, offering every issue printed since 1941. The priceless three-hundred-year-old book collection was born long before the Avalonti Society was founded. Passed down through the generations, the last personal owner was Dr. Simon Avalonti, who admirably gifted it to his son's society in 1951. Breaking tradition, Phineas Avalonti never took personal possession of the books. The official owner of the collection was the Avalonti Trust Association, which managed the finances, real estate and personal property of the society. Academics hailed the transfer from personal ownership to general ownership as a philanthropic undertaking, long before the apex of the Digital Revolution. Though some of the titles were off-limits due to their fragility or exceedingly high value, the book donation had offered a greater overall exposure to the knowledge contained within them.

Arriving early at Francesca Hall for their last meeting before the new year, John obtained the latest edition of the *Avalonti Journal*, checking to see if anyone had written about the Lafayette charity dinner. Marcus was standing by the door, talking with Mr. Budwin about The International Butler Academy. While John was reading, sitting in one of the antique red velvet parlor chairs, Vandacheler quietly approached him.

"Johnathan, how are you?" Vandacheler asked, sitting in a chair next to him.

"I'm doing okay," John replied, looking up from the journal. "You?"

"I'm well, thank you."

"That's good."

Vandacheler tapped his fingers, taking a breath. "Listen, I've been meaning to have a little chat with you about something—if you have a moment."

"Sure," John said, closing the journal, using his thumb as a bookmark.

"It is not my position, nor my desire, to judge anyone's clothing," Vandacheler apprehensively spoke, "but I must inform you that there is a dress code at Francesca Hall."

"Oh," John said, glancing down at his worn-out blue jeans, "I'm sorry about that."

"You're fine," Vandacheler reassured. "Just—in the future—business casual or better."

"Sure, no problem."

"Much appreciated," Vandacheler said, standing from the chair, patting him on the shoulder.

"Shit," John said under his breath, looking down at his blue jeans again.

Mr. Budwin opened one of the massive cherry wood double doors.

"Hi, guys!" Kasey shouted, walking into the hall.

Marcus smiled. "Sup, Kasey."

John didn't acknowledge her.

"John, you okay?" she asked, walking towards the grand fireplace.

"I'm fine," he answered, glancing up from the journal.

"*Ah*, Kasey, how are you?" Vandacheler asked.

"I'm good."

"I trust you made it home okay the other night?" Vandacheler pried.

"*Yep*, all good in the hood," she assured.

Vandacheler paused, squinting, studying her mannerisms. "Are you sure you're okay? You seem a little off."

"I'm fine," she said, summoning a gaudy smile. "I've just been studying a lot. Been really busy lately. Just tired, I guess. I have As in all my classes, though."

"Excellent to hear," Vandacheler said, nodding. "Shall we proceed with the meeting, then?"

"You always say that," Marcus joked, impersonating him, *"proceed with the meeting."*

Vandacheler smiled.

Kasey and Marcus took their seats. A moment later, John stood from the parlor chair and sat next to Kasey on the antique red velvet couch. Kasey inconspicuously glanced at her phone while Vandacheler prepared the meeting. She received a text message from her friend, Alyssa: *Meeting at The Red Porcupine 2nite if u r interested.*

"John, Marcus," Vandacheler announced, "your keys." He handed them keys to their new rooms at The Marquis.

"Sweet!" Marcus cheered.

"Hell yeah!" John shouted, high-fiving Marcus above Kasey's head.

Kasey sat with a rigid posture, twisting her mouth to one side, staring blankly at the floor.

Vandacheler raised a hand to them, silently instructing them to reestablish their gentlemanly composure. "Permit me to say that in our short time of knowing one another, I feel you all have demonstrated true Avalonti potential. We shall meet here after the winter break, on Saturday, January the 9th, at 2 p.m. sharp. As we draw closer to your official induction, please be reminded of the rules, guidelines and principles of our great society. During our next meeting, we will discuss your final task as probationary members."

The students looked at each other, smiling and nodding.

Vandacheler ducked behind the bar to retrieve a bottle of Château Lafite, vintage 1996.

"Kasey, are you 21 yet?" Vandacheler asked in jest.

Kasey chuckled. "Not yet."

"It's a good thing that contributing to the delinquency of minors does not contravene any of our bylaws, wouldn't you say?" Vandacheler teased.

"I *would* say that," she said, feigning a smile.

Vandacheler poured the wine and handed a glass to each student. "Since we will not be here for the new year, I thought we might have a little premature toast."

"I hate wine, but I'm down," Marcus griped.

"I thought Republicans liked wine?" John asked in a humorous tone. "*Oh* wait, I was thinking tax cuts for the one percent," he joked.

Kasey giggled.

"I'm surrounded by a bunch of damn liberals," Marcus whispered, shaking his head.

"So long 2020; a year that will never again be," Vandacheler said, raising his glass.

"So long," the students toasted.

They all drank.

Kasey's face contorted with disgust.

"*Ah*, $1600 well spent," Vandacheler remarked.

John's eyes widened.

The students placed their wine glasses on the coffee table coasters. Mr. Budwin immediately proceeded to clean them up. Vandacheler grimaced, slightly curling his lip as he observed the top of Mr. Budwin's balding grey head.

John and Marcus looked at their keys, tapping their feet.

"Now, I suspect you lads have a bit of moving to do," Vandacheler said.

They sprang to their feet, stopping midstep, waiting to be dismissed.

"Carry on," Vandacheler said, bowing deeply.

"Thanks again, Van!" John exclaimed.

"Yeah, thanks a million," Marcus praised, skipping to the door. "Merry Christmas, Kasey!"

"Merry Christmas, Marcus! And you too, John!" she shouted.

Kasey watched John waltz out the door without saying goodbye again; just before the winter break to top it off. "I'm so stupid," she said under her breath. She picked up her phone and texted Alyssa back: *What time?*

~~

The Red Porcupine was a radical, worker-owned bookstore and coffeehouse residing on the corner of a busy street in the business district not far from the university. Their mission was to build community and expand resources to disenfranchised people via funding co-ops and projects centered around grassroots political activism. The café offered only locally sourced, free-range, organic, certified non-GMO food and fair-trade coffee. Working only through independent publishers, The Red Porcupine offered a variety of books atypical to traditional bookstores. The space also functioned as a forum for networking, coordinating and organizing protests, open-mic nights, and for hosting guest speakers; usually of a subversive nature. Despite criticism, The Red Porcupine was modern, hygienic and properly managed.

Kasey arrived at The Red Porcupine to meet her friend, Alyssa, and a few other women for a meeting. Kasey was not yet a member of the women's group but had recently gained an interest in joining. Mel, a twenty-three-year-old senior at the university, was the leader of the women's group, even though she rejected any such title. Mel wore glasses, bohemian-punk clothing and a military green bandana over her short, greyish, light-blonde hair. She carried with her a large, beige handbag made from hemp and recycled cotton. Screen-printed political patches and other pieces of fabric were sewn on the outside of the bag. Mel was educated, principled, astute and never broke character. The only known pictures of her smiling collected dust in her parents' attic.

Alyssa De Luca, a new protégé of Mel's, wanted Kasey to join their group for camaraderie, privately confessing that she felt a little out of place around the other women. Embarrassed by her "former self", Alyssa sought reformation, expressing a newfound interest in activism and social consciousness. Alyssa was short, only a little taller than Kasey, with long, wavy brown hair and a prudish attire. Kasey and Alyssa met during their first year of college in a photography class and had developed an apolitical friendship, rarely discussing controversial subjects.

Tackling various issues, Mel's group worked in tandem with others, like the Progressive Student Rights Coalition, demanding the implementation of new policy at the university that would give a stronger voice to traditionally underrepresented minorities. Their petitions and protests garnered increasing support, including positive sanction from a number of professors.

After purchasing a cup of fair-trade coffee, Alyssa introduced the other women to Kasey. "This is Karen, Joy, Lakesha and Elsa," she said, going around the table.

Alyssa walked her over to Mel. "And this is..."

"I'm Mel," she interrupted, refusing her introduction.

Alyssa forced a smile.

"I'm Kasey. Nice to meet you all," she said, reaching for a chair from the other table.

"Nice to meet you, Kasey," most of the women replied.

Kasey's metal chair dragging across the hardwood floor disrupted the intense quietness of the café. Mel examined her as if she were sizing up a boxing opponent. Kasey noticed.

"Oh, who's this?" Kasey asked, startled, reaching down to pet a dog that was hiding under their table. "You're so cute," she said, petting the dog.

"Sorry," Karen said, pulling him away, "he's a service dog. You can't pet him."

"Oh, I'm sorry," Kasey said, folding her hands in her lap.

"It's okay," Karen assured, "you didn't know."

Kasey took a deep breath, glancing down at the "do not pet" collar on the dog. The women commenced. Their topic that evening was 'the portrayal of women in classic films.' Kasey took out a notebook and situated herself. To break the ice with Mel, she leaned in and whispered to her, "I absolutely love your shirt by the way."

"Thanks," Mel said in a lackluster tone.

Mel's shirt read: *DEAD MEN DON'T RAPE.*

~~

At twenty-one, Bo Zhang was the same age as John. Bo was on the swim team, and, despite his rapacious appetite, he never gained any weight. Averagely tall with ordinary black hair, he presented a relaxed, occasionally feminine demeanor. Kindhearted and thoughtful, Bo had a vast collection of friends. When he wasn't training in the pool, he exercised his online gaming skills and indulged in a secret relationship with K-Pop. John and Bo elected to stay roommates at the start of their sophomore year. When Avalonti posted a bulletin seeking three undergraduates for an experimental expansion of their society, Bo was the one who encouraged John to apply, knowing that he often read the *Avalonti Journal.*

While Kasey accepted her membership into the women's group, Bo helped John move into his new apartment at The Marquis. Having only a few sets of clothes, basic supplies, a laptop and a portable AM/FM stereo, the only challenge was moving John's ample collection of books; the one thing Bo *wouldn't* miss tripping over. The university accepted gently used and slightly damaged books from individuals and booksellers and offered them free of charge to students. John would occasionally stop by the community center and clean out their selection of history and philosophy books. If they didn't have a title he wanted, he would reluctantly venture to a local bookstore and buy a copy with the modest weekly funds his grandmother sent him. Eventually, they finished moving John into his new apartment.

"Dude, this place is so swank," Bo said, pulling back the curtain of the sliding glass door.

"Yep. Recently remodeled. State-of-the-art. 700 square feet. Way more than I'll ever need, but I dig the balcony," John said, leaning up against the office desk in his new living room.

"I'm gonna miss you back at the dorm, man," Bo confessed, gazing out at the bustling town below.

"I'll stop by—and you can visit me anytime you want."

Bo nodded. "Cool."

A moment of silence passed them by.

"I'm proud of you, man," Bo said, turning around. "You've come a long way."

John snickered. "Don't get all sappy on me, man."

Bo chuckled, walking over to the breakfast bar. "You've been a good friend to me, John."

John sighed, rolling his eyes. "Well, you've been my only real friend since I got here—so you win. Everyone else here just thinks I'm an asshole."

"Well, that's because you *are* an asshole, John," Bo teased, standing from the barstool. "But you'll always be a winner in my book."

"*Oh*, Jesus Christ," John said softly. "Thanks, Bo, I appreciate that."

"I wanted to give you this," Bo said, walking over to him.

John looked at his hand, lowering his eyebrows.

"For some new clothes," Bo said, offering him a wad of cash.

"Charity?" John huffed.

"No, no," Bo assured. "I just—I just wanted to do something nice for you. You've worked really hard to get where you're at and I'm proud of you. Also, I don't think the rockabilly look is ever gonna make a comeback, dude."

"Come on, man, you already helped me with the tuxedo. I can't take anything else from you," John said, turning his head.

"Come on, John, I'd really like you to take this."

"I can't."

"Just take it."

"No."

"Dude, I'm not leaving until you take this fucking money," Bo joked.

"Alright." John chuckled, reluctantly accepting. "Fine."

"See? That wasn't so hard, was it?"

"I really appreciate you, Bo," John confessed in a serious tone.

"Likewise," Bo said, extending his hand for a handshake. "You mean a lot to me, John."

"You too, man," John said, dodging his handshake, giving him a hug.

Bo hugged him tightly, patting him on the back.

"So, *uh*, that a 68-inch?" Bo asked, looking at the flat screen television as they disengaged.

"75-inch."

Bo nodded. "This is a really nice apartment. You're gonna be happy here."

CHAPTER 5

THE CARNEGIE VILLAGE BLOWOUT

Carnegie Village was a gated college community just outside of the university near the business district. The New Year's Eve party at Carnegie Village would be held at Liam's house that year. Liam was the captain of the university's swim team but refused to join a fraternity. With his roommates, they rented one of the few single-family homes at Carnegie Village and made their own rules—which were few. Typically, Liam's parties would be in friendly competition with fraternities, but that year was different. Kappa Sigma decided to merge their party with the Village party, which was decidedly unexpected because they usually threw the best parties at their house. At the end of Liam's street was an undeveloped section of Carnegie Village. The collaborated plan was to use the space as concert grounds. Liam's team worked together with the frat, booking bands, hip-hop groups, EDM artists and building a make-shift stage. They even brought in confetti cannons and supplies for an illicit fireworks production.

On the day before the start of the winter break, Bo visited John in his new apartment at The Marquis. Bo invited him to the big New Year's Eve party, even though the first party he attended at Carnegie Village, during his freshman year, ended in disaster. John had managed to offend the largest guy at the party and a vicious fight between them erupted in the parking lot in front of Liam's house. Beyond John's wishes or acknowledgement, Bo used his social connections to secure a truce from Ritchie; the man who beat John unconscious in the parking lot. Bo just needed John to agree to the terms.

"Fuck that guy," John said, refusing the agreement.

"Come on, man, it happened last year," Bo pleaded. "He might've won the fight, but you still got some good shots in. That dude is like *freakishly* large. He's, like, twice your size. Nobody thinks any less of you. There's no reason not to squash it, man. Liam doesn't want any fighting at his place—and not to mention, Avalonti has a strict rule against violence."

"Their rule is against unprovoked violence. I'm allowed to defend myself. But you're right, there's no reason not to squash it if it'll ease your damn mind."

"So, is that your final answer?"

John heaved a sigh. "Yeah. Squash it."

Bo exhaled slowly. "So, how's Kasey doing?" he asked, changing the subject.

John squinted. "Kasey?"

"Yeah, Kasey Chong. She's one of the other probationary members, right?"

"Yeah, what about her?"

"You didn't hear?" Bo puzzled.

"Hear what?"

"*Uh*, she got attacked the other night while walking home. I just found out about it. Sorry, I thought she would've told you."

"What! She didn't say anything to me. What happened?" John demanded.

"Some dude jumped out of his car and chased her down the street. He yelled a bunch of shit at her then knocked her to the ground. He was like—trying to kiss her neck and stuff. These guys at the party chased him away before he could do anything. I'm not sure who they were. My friend Brian was at Dave's party when it happened. Dave lives a few houses down from her, over in Devonshire. Cops and paramedics were there and shit. It was pretty crazy from what I heard."

"Do they know who it was?"

"Nah," Bo answered. "Cops said they would investigate. Don't hold your breath, right?"

John fell into silent contemplation.

Bo studied John's solidified posture for a moment then looked at his phone for the time. "Well," he said, slapping John on the shoulder, breaking his gaze, "I just wanted to stop by and invite you to the party. I gotta get going. You're not going back to Missouri for winter break, right?"

John stared at the floor. "No, I'm staying here."

"Right on. I'll text ya. I don't know about Christmas Eve, but I'll be by on Christmas."

John smiled. "Cool."

"Alright, man, enjoy this sweet fucking pad, you lucky bastard."

John chuckled. "Will do. Take care, bud."

∿

Avalonti, being an academic society with official university endorsement, required their student members to keep a GPA above 3.5. John effortlessly aced his final exams and assignments and maintained a GPA above 4.0. Blazing through his "mediocre schoolwork", he eagerly delved into new books that were not part of his required reading. Included in his leisure reading was the *Avalonti Journal*. Drawing him to the society was their commitment to free inquiry and open discussion, which was routinely stifled within the bulwark of the university. The Avalonti Society encouraged freethinking and the rigorous pursuit of knowledge, having no membership prerequisites based on political or religious affiliation. John noticed a pattern among his peers; they would only read obligatory material or books that fit their beliefs. One of John's favorite hobbies was to read the books of his "enemies". Whenever John found himself in a philosophical or theological argument, he would usually know more about their beliefs than they did. During the first half of winter break, John read for hours upon hours at a time, occasionally anticipating the big New Year's Eve party that was around the corner.

∿

On Christmas Eve, John nursed a bottle of beer at The Marquis restaurant, periodically sneaking a swig of whiskey from his flask in the bathroom. By six o'clock he was the only one sitting at the bar. While vacuum cleaners relentlessly howled, an employee stacked chairs neatly on top of the tables. The bartender offered John a puzzled glare when he asked for another beer. "We're closing up, guy," he scoffed. "Merry Christmas, okay?"

"I have plenty of booze upstairs," John grumbled under his breath, dropping a modest tip.

Instead of returning to his room, John ventured out into the cold, heading downtown toward the business district in search of a bar that would accommodate him and the six dollars that remained in his pocket. He sighed miserably. Almost every building he passed had a closed sign on their door. There was a nightclub he knew of that was open, but they charged seven dollars for one bottle of Bud Light. John meandered for nearly an hour without any luck. The brightly lit, festively decorated town was dead. Giving up hope, he elected to change course to midtown and head back to The Marquis. Halfway back to the hotel, he remembered there being a little bar near the courthouse uptown that didn't close for the holidays. Deciding not to return home, he continued north to the historic district; a picturesque colonial style part of town.

On his way to the City Towne Centre, he passed Heaven's Grace Baptist Church. It was the only building he saw that showed any signs of life. John paused, contemplating, listening to the faint sounds of music through the door. The air outside was a frigid desert. John's socks drowned in freezing sweat. Reluctantly, he pulled open one of the doors and entered. Inside, there were three sections of pews filled with guests. On stage, the pastor gently nodded to the church choir's rendition of "Carol of the Bells", assisted by a local middle school's student orchestra.

Numb from the cold and the artificial warmth of the whiskey, John gazed upon the choir, letting their song flow over him like a calming summer breeze. In the back row of the pews, he spotted a little boy with blond hair sitting next to his older brother and his parents, all dressed in turtleneck sweaters and festive garb. His mind wandered back in time. Observing the little family, an intrusive moisture found his eyes. The older brother turned to look at him. The boy smiled at him for a moment then turned back around in his seat. John lowered his head. In his peripheral vision, he saw one of the deacons on his way over.

"You're welcome to sit and join us," the deacon whispered, patting John on his back.

"Sorry," John said, turning, grabbing the door handle, "I gotta go."

Racing back to midtown, John heard a weak voice calling out to him from around a corner. A man bundled in layers of blankets surrounded by plastic bags and an army duffel sat out on the sidewalk.

"Can you spare any change?" the man asked.

John looked at the man's chapped weathered skin and broken lips. His eyes were desperate and genuine. Atop his weary head was an old, worn-out Vietnam veteran's hat. John reached into his pocket without hesitation.

"Here you go," he said, handing the man his last six dollars.

"Thank you," the man exhaled, beaming appreciation.

"Merry Christmas, sir," John said, kneeling down, shaking his hand.

"God bless you," the man said, squeezing with both hands. "God bless you."

~~~

Reading through the Avalonti guidelines, John observed a strange rule; lower ranking members of the society were not granted access to the veranda. Only members of the High Council climbed the spiral staircase of Francesca Hall. For reasons beyond his comprehension, his desire to sit on the veranda became nearly overwhelming after reading the decree. The other rules were fairly basic, including a dress code at Francesca Hall and a strict rule against violence, in or outside of the university.

Bo stopped by John's on Christmas with a present: Ayn Rand's *Atlas Shrugged*.

"I know you get a boner for mean old bitches," Bo joked.

John chuckled, set the book down and opened a desk drawer. "I totally forgot people gave presents on Christmas, Bo. But I have something I want to give to you."

"It's cool. You don't have to give me anything, John," Bo assured.

"You've been like a brother to me, Bo, and I want you to have this." John handed Bo the beloved silver pocket watch that his father had given him.

"Remember, time is the most precious gift of all," John teased. "In the end, it's all you ever really had."

Bo fought back tears, examining the watch. "John," he said nervously, "I have something I've been meaning to tell you."

John nodded. "Sure, bud, go ahead."

Bo paused for a moment, smiling uneasily. "I'm *uh*—just glad we're friends," he said, retreating from what he truly wanted to tell him. "Thanks for the watch."

"Absolutely."

Bo gave him a hug.

John made coffee in the Verismo and they discussed their plans for the upcoming party. Bo informed him that several of his friends who traveled out of town for the winter break were returning early just to make it. Excitement was growing around the highly anticipated event.

～～

Bo returned to John's apartment a couple of days after Christmas, bearing news of great interest; two other fraternities had joined the roster for the upcoming Carnegie Village party. Additionally, since most of the sororities were forbidden to host parties with alcohol, as decreed by the NPC, many of them were planning to attend as well. The Village party would be an unorthodox amalgamation, but was, nevertheless, poised to go down in university history.

～～

On New Year's Eve, John and Bo rendezvoused at The Marquis and enjoyed a couple of pregame wine spritzers. The big night had arrived. Bo agreed to wear a suit instead of his vintage gamer shirt because John was going in his tuxedo. The first band went on at 8. John and Bo agreed fashionably late was ideal. While they were hanging out in John's apartment, Bo received a text from Liam: *Dude, catch an Uber, no parking spots left.*

John and Bo agreed they better get to the party quickly. They arrived just before 10. The Uber driver dropped them off at the far end of Liam's street, unable to get any closer. John and Bo looked at each other in disbelief. The Village party had gone viral on social media. Hundreds upon hundreds of people showed up with piles more showing up every minute. There was a squad of police cars and emergency vehicles at the end of Liam's street with their lights quietly flashing. Students would walk by them, brandishing beers, mocking them with impunity, asking if they wanted any donuts. The police weren't there to shut the party down; they were only on standby in case the colossal party turned riotous.

John and Bo pushed through the crowds. There were sixteen apartments on each side of the street before reaching the party headquarters at Liam's place. The thirty-two apartments, all rented by students, collectively joined in on the party, opening their homes to the public. The balconies and rooftops were lined with partygoers. As hordes of people continued to show up, new sections of Carnegie Village fell prey to the party. By 11, it was unstoppable. People from neighboring counties as far away as Baltimore County flocked to the spectacle, drawn by social media.

At 11:30, the media arrived with camera crews. Along with them, the police called in backup to install a blockade at the main entrance, refusing to allow any new guests access to the community, even if they lived there. Dispatched to prevent "fence hoppers", foot patrol secured the perimeter. Hundreds upon hundreds had turned into thousands upon thousands. Every time the police helicopter flew overhead, shining their searchlight on the crowd, an uproarious cheering blared from the streets and rooftops. Police patrolled the party grounds lightheartedly. They promised to overlook minor offenses such as pot smoking and underage drinking, hoping to garner cooperation. They were substantially outnumbered.

Outside of Carnegie Village was the heart of the business district. The college town's main boulevard overflowed with people en route to the party, causing a chain-reaction traffic jam on a nearby interstate highway. The turnout was staggering. Even with Liam's crew and the various frats involved, it was difficult to explain exactly how the party had avalanched into something so monumental; so fast and so organically.

John and Bo had managed to get inside of Liam's house, which was oddly less packed than the parking lots. The "real party" was happening out in the cold. Kegs were randomly placed along the sidewalks and kiddie pools were filled with cans of beer. Liam's crew and the frats brought in a professional entertainment company who had setup a PA system and stacks of speakers outside. People danced as the EDM artist spun energetic dubstep. When the DJ dropped heavy bass, Liam's house rumbled, causing picture frames to fall from the walls.

After a game of beer pong and some innocent flirting with a group of sorority sisters, John and Bo found a secluded part of Liam's house to talk. The room was a small sitting area connecting the living room and the kitchen. There was a love seat, a recliner, a lone wooden chair in the corner, a small coffee table and an end table with an unplugged brass lamp sitting on top of it. While they were chatting, four Caucasian men about their age walked into the room. They wore baggy clothes, sideways baseball caps, gaudy jewelry and designer cologne. One of them had a tattoo across his neck that read: *Hard 2 Kill.*

"Sup," John greeted them.

The crew leader spoke with an exaggerated urban accent, "Sup, y'all tryna hit a blunt?"

Bo was about to decline until he heard John answer, "Yeah, man."

Bo, a fan of electronic dance music, nonchalantly attempted to persuade John to leave Liam's house and watch the concert outside. John declined. Bo took a shot of vodka to calm his nerves. He could tell that the four guys were not students. They ritualistically passed the blunt in a circle, to their left, until it was gone. Bo rubbed his eyes as smoke suffocated the little room.

When the blunt burned out, they heard faint moans coming from a couple in the room above them. High from the marijuana, they all snickered in juvenile delight. The faint moaning did not last long, provoking another round of laughter. John and Bo quietly listened to the four guys sharing stories of their romantic conquests. Bo occasionally and inconspicuously nudged John, attempting to leave the little area of Liam's house and return to the party outside. John discreetly flashed his finger, indicating that they would leave in a minute. After the four men had regaled them with tales of their sexual exploits, the skinny crew leader was comfortable in confessing the criminal activity he took part in. They all listened to him talk for a few minutes. The atmosphere changed. Bo saw John's hand clench into a fist as the man continued to brag.

∿

Outside, the music raged on. Thousands of people rang in the new year with an earth-shattering roar. Electricity was in the air. Fireworks exploded in the midnight sky. Drawn like moths to a flame, partygoers swamped the main boulevard, hoping to catch a glimpse of the oddity that had amassed within the walls of Carnegie Village. It was unlike anything the town had ever experienced before. News outlets as far away as Quebec, Canada, would cover the story days later. The Carnegie Village blowout would go down as one of the most spectacular events in university history.

CHAPTER 6

THE FINAL TASK

On Saturday, January 9th, 2021, John stood before the grand cherry wood double doors of Francesca Hall, wearing a long-sleeved polo shirt and a pair of stiff khakis. His sweaty hands clutched the wrought-iron handles. Taking a deep breath, he pushed open one of the doors and apprehensively entered.

"I can explain!" John shouted defensively, walking through the foyer.

Marcus and Kasey stood with gaping mouths. Vandacheler squinted with obvious concern. Mr. Budwin, normally an expressionless old man, appeared horrified.

"What in the *hell* happened to you, John?" Marcus enquired.

John laughed nervously, rapidly shaking his head. "It's not what you think. I'm innocent. I didn't do anything. I swear, I didn't do anything."

Kasey scoffed and walked away. "Stupid macho crap, I bet."

"It wasn't macho crap, Kasey—at least not from me," John defended.

"Alright," Vandacheler suggested, "just relax and tell us what happened."

"We were at the Carnegie Village party on New Year's Eve," John frantically explained. "Bo and me. These guys thought we were someone else, I think. I don't know, they just attacked us for no reason. I swear. Ask Bo, they broke his nose, too. I swear, I didn't punch anyone, I didn't hit anyone. I swear, I'm innocent. They jumped us."

Vandacheler glanced at John's hands, noticing abrasions and small cuts on his knuckles. "We certainly believe you, John. I am dreadfully sorry that you and your dear friend were attacked."

"Thanks," John uttered.

"Come now," Vandacheler insisted, turning sharply toward Kasey and Marcus, "I'm sure John has suffered enough. Let us not exacerbate it. Shall we, instead, proceed with the meeting?" Vandacheler patted John on the back, guiding him toward the Victorian couch.

Kasey took her seat on a parlor chair, across from the couch she normally sat in. With her arms crossed, she shook her head disapprovingly. Though she tried to avoid it, she couldn't help but look. She touched her cheek and frowned, gazing upon John's pitiful black-and-blue face attempting to hide under a baseball cap and a poor makeup job. "No," she whispered to herself as tears began to form. "No."

Vandacheler shuffled some paperwork in preparation for the meeting.

"Lady and gentlemen, I am pleased to announce that your formal induction draws nearer than you may think," Vandacheler proclaimed. "Hopefully, by the end of the school year, you will all be full members of the Avalonti Society. Naturally, before any probationary member is officially inducted, they are issued a final task. Now, for the last 75 years or so, the initiation process has been the same. But, as you all know, you three are a part of a new undergraduate protégé program. As Caesar Avalonti is quite experimental from time to time, he is introducing you all to a very different kind of task; one that has never been tried before within our walls."

Disquietly, the students looked at each other.

"You three shall work together on a social experiment," Vandacheler informed. "The benefit of a social experiment is its unique ability to provoke genuine reaction, and thus, genuine research data—as none of the subjects are aware they are in the experiment. As we are a society that prides itself on the spreading of knowledge and enlightenment, your objective should be congruent to that philosophy. You will document your theme, your hypothesis and the results of your experiment for peer analysis. Though you will be granted a certain level of creative control, we ask that the project be conducted in a professional manner and not include any volunteers unless they are Avalonti members. You may also use hired services if you require them, pending our approval of said expense. During the experiment, friends, family and other cohorts are not to be made aware of the details of the project. After the experiment, however, you'll be at liberty to divulge the details at your leisure. You will have until May 22nd to complete the project. Are there any questions?"

"Yeah, what exactly do we have to do?" Marcus enquired.

"You'll decide that," Vandacheler said.

"It's a little vague," Kasey remarked. "Sorry."

"No, you're right, it is," Vandacheler agreed. "It's Caesar's idea, not mine."

"Social experiment, eh? Alright, I'm trying to figure this out," Marcus vocally pondered. "I saw a video once of this guy pretending he was homeless to show how people would treat him. Some people treated him like crap, but a lot of people treated him good. I found it interesting that so many people were willing to help him, even though they didn't see the cameras. Are you talking about something like that?"

"Yes, something like that," Vandacheler agreed, "but bigger."

Kasey sighed.

"I understand it's a bit daunting," Vandacheler confessed. "It does, however, sound more fun than the usual final task."

"What's the usual final task?" Kasey asked.

"A live debate in front of a panel of society Judges."

"That doesn't sound so bad," Marcus opined. "Or do you have to do it naked or something?"

"The usual final task," Vandacheler divulged, "requires the probationary member to *convincingly* argue the affirmative on an extremely controversial topic; one that the society knows you would not agree with."

"So—they would've made me argue in favor of the Ku Klux Klan because I'm a black atheist?" Marcus conjectured.

57 | P a g e

"Perhaps," Vandacheler agreed.

Marcus shrugged. "Sounds better than a social experiment."

"Dr. Alexander Kirshner nearly collapsed backstage after his initiation debate," Vandacheler informed.

"Backstage?" Marcus questioned.

"Yes, they do it in the auditorium. You stand under a white-hot spotlight and speak into a microphone," Vandacheler explained.

"What did he have to argue in favor of?" Kasey asked.

"Dr. Kirshner's younger brother was born blind. He was asked to argue in favor of mandatory euthanasia of children born with birth defects," Vandacheler answered.

"That's terrible," Kasey winced. "Why would they do that to him?"

"It is designed to scrutinize the prospect's ability to debate, and to gauge their level of tolerance for opposing and objectionable ideas," Vandacheler explained. "It's also a form of hazing, just like any other vanguard society would subject you to."

"*Meh*, that's nothing compared to what I hear some of these fraternities make you do," Marcus insisted.

"Very well then," Vandacheler announced, "you all have your assignment. Should you elect to complete it, you will have until the end of the school year to showcase your grand reveal. May 22nd. I suggest you find your theme before time proves your enemy. I shall take my leave shortly. If you're interested, the famed Avalonti Sage, Dr. Robert Novini, will be here tomorrow afternoon for the final stop on his book tour."

"Who is he?" John asked.

"*Ah*, John, you were so quiet over there I might've thought you were napping," Vandacheler joked. "Dr. Novini is at Oxford now, you'll like him. He heads a team of researchers who, among other things, debunk conspiracy theories. Occasionally, they are even employed by the Ministry of Defense to help clarify UFO sightings."

"What time?" John asked.

Vandacheler smiled. "Three o'clock. Anyhow, good seeing you all again. Happy New Year, Merry Christmas, Happy Hanukkah, yada-yada. Goodbye and farewell."

"See ya, Don," Kasey said.

"Farewell," Marcus said with a British accent.

Vandacheler bowed to Marcus and Kasey then looked at John. "Might you walk out with me?" he requested.

"Yeah, sure," John timidly agreed.

Kasey and Marcus watched Vandacheler and John walk through the doors.

"What do you think he's going to say to him?" Marcus asked Kasey.

"I don't know, but John is so full of it," Kasey grumbled.

CHAPTER 7

DR. NOVINI

When John arrived at Francesca Hall the following day, Dr. Novini was halfway through his speech. The hall was unusually crowded. There were at least fifty people in attendance; many of whom were not Avalonti members. John spotted Vandacheler sitting by the fireplace in a parlor chair near the front row with his legs neatly crossed. John stood by the entryway with his hands in his pockets, shading himself with the bill of his baseball cap. Marcus and Kasey did not attend.

Dr. Novini was known for his passionate, controversial lectures and speeches. Aggressively, he would walk from one side of the audience to the other, speaking fiercely with his hands, occasionally pushing his grey hair away from his face.

Dramatically throwing a newspaper in the air, he shouted, "We can't trust the fucking media! Our governments lie straight to our God damn faces! Scientists are being bought by big corporations and half the doctors are owned by the fucking pharmaceutical industry!"

John crossed his arms and focused on Dr. Novini's words. The crowd listened attentively.

Dr. Novini continued, "So, we ask ourselves, as skeptics, what gives rise to conspiracy theory? Sure, there are often unprovoked *wild* fantasies, but what about the other ones? What about the ones people hear and, on a larger scale, become convinced without proof? What is the catalyst to the birth of conspiracy theory?"

The audience looked around the room, largely remaining quiet.

Dr. Novini stopped pacing for a moment. "Deception. Deceit. Diversion. Sweeping the truth under the rug then forbidding anyone to look under it. *Lies* are the root cause of conspiracy theory. Think of a man who walks into his home at one o'clock in the morning, drunk as a sailor. His wife asks him where the hell he's been. Well, he claims he's been visiting his poor, sick old parents. She knows he's lying, so what does she do? Her mind starts to wander. She convinces herself that her atrocious, repulsive, fat bastard of a husband has just completed having toe-curling, mind-numbing, heart-stopping, unprotected sex with the most gorgeous fucking woman in all of England!"

Laughter and sporadic clapping filled the hall.

Dr. Novini held up his hand and continued softly, "Now can we, in good conscience, blame his dear wife for her paranoia? She's been lied to so many times. If he would've told her the truth—that he was at the local, blowing his paycheck on whiskey and Boddingtons pub ale with a gaggle of other *fat* repulsive bastards—perhaps her mind wouldn't have wandered so. She may have hit him upside his hideous head with a rolling pin, but she probably wouldn't have lent much credibility to other suspicions. It was the *lie* that birthed the theory."

Dr. Novini retrieved one of his books from a fold-out table near the Steinway piano.

"In my book, I attempt to bridge the gap between conspiracy theorists and skeptics. My colleagues and I firmly attest that we are largely cut from the same fabric; that of truth-seekers. Some of them have merely wandered off the path a bit. Though we will surely debunk whatever needs debunking, we do so *not* to condemn—but to enlighten. Our quest, which I cover in the book, is to establish incorruptible scientific authority; objective science that is bereft of special-interest meddling. Our quest is to find the truth; the *real* truth. Thank you all for coming."

The audience clapped. Those who were sitting stood to applaud. Dr. Novini bowed dramatically, causing his hair to flop in front of his face. John navigated through the crowd toward Novini's book distro.

"How much?" John asked, interrupting Dr. Novini who was answering questions from the audience.

Dr. Novini did not answer John directly but proceeded to make a general announcement. "If anyone wants a copy of my book, please take one. I was a penniless college student for a long time, believe me, I understand. If you should like to make a donation, however, there is a jar at the end of the table."

"Thanks," John uttered as he took a book, dropping a ten-dollar bill into the jar.

John's phone vibrated in his pocket. John, Marcus and Kasy had set up a group chat for discussing their social experiment ideas earlier that day. Marcus texted the group: *Think of anything yet?*

No response.

~~

Quickly leaving Francesca Hall, John ventured to the business district not far from the university. Stumbling across The Red Porcupine, he decided to browse their selection of books. As he walked through the door, he heard a faint voice call out his name. He turned to see Kasey sitting at a table in the café area with a group of women and a service dog. Politely, he waved then turned back to the shelves, intrigued by the irregular content of the books.

After purchasing a paperback book and a cup of fair-trade coffee, John briefly visited Kasey and her friends at the table. Kasey introduced John to the women, who were mostly receptive of his intrusion. Mel, who was *not* receptive, coldly introduced herself to John. There was a subtle awkwardness between them though they both pretended to have never met before.

~~

Marcus pestered Kasey and John about choosing a theme for the "vaguely detailed" Avalonti assignment. They agreed to meet at The Marquis that evening, since there was a private celebration for Dr. Novini at Francesca Hall for full members only. John insisted on having the meeting at his apartment because he possessed a wealth of books; books that may have been useful for inspiration.

"*Geez*, is your place this nice, too?" Kasey asked Marcus as they walked into John's apartment together.

"Yep, pretty much the same place," Marcus answered.

63 | P a g e

"I hope you guys brought your thinking caps," John said, tapping his hat.

"I did bring something," Marcus enticed. "I was going to give you guys your presents yesterday, but the mood wasn't quite right. I know y'all didn't get me anything. I'm not offended. I'm way out of line for even doing this, but I *love* Christmas."

He handed John and Kasey each a wrapped present from his backpack.

"Oh my gosh, Marcus, you're so sweet," Kasey boasted. "You'll have to at least let me buy you a coffee at The Red Porcupine sometime."

Marcus scoffed. "Marcus Williams in a communist bookstore? I don't think so, Kasey. Starbucks is as far left as my ass will go."

Kasey chuckled. "Okay, Starbucks it is then."

"Thanks, Marcus," John praised, opening the present. "I never met an atheist who loved Christmas before."

"Come on, *John*, you think Christmas is a religious holiday? It's merely the celebration of materialism and the beautiful free market with all its joyous merriment," Marcus declared.

"I don't know who is worse," John noted, shaking Marcus's hand in thanks, "the filthy communists or the filthy capitalists."

"The filthy capitalists!" Marcus answered proudly. "We're much worse, baby. Hell, we're the devil incarnate!"

John chuckled, looking down at the books Marcus bought him for Christmas. One book was *A History of Witch Trials* and the other was a book on laissez-faire economics. Kasey received a sterling friendship knot pendant on an elegant 18" silver chain.

"I know you like weird history," Marcus said to John, "so I got you that witch book. I threw in one of my guys—Dr. Thomas Sowell. Read that shit before these Marxist fucks brainwash your ass," he said, walking over to Kasey. "Hey, Kasey, let me help you put that on."

"Sure," she said, smiling brightly.

In front of John's dining room mirror, Marcus stood behind her and fastened her necklace.

"Beautiful," Marcus said confidently as their eyes met in the reflection.

"This is so awesome, I love it," Kasey gushed, gently stroking the pendant. "Thank you *so* much, Marcus."

"You're very welcome, my dear," Marcus said, impersonating Vandacheler.

"You guys have any ideas for a theme?" John interrupted.

"No," Marcus answered, returning to the living room, "but I do have *an* idea."

Marcus opened John's laptop on his Belafonte glass coffee table. "Let's watch videos of social experiments for starters."

Kasey and John nodded at each other in agreement. John took out a piece of paper and a pen to jot down any ideas.

～

The social experiment videos they viewed on YouTube were mostly self-promotion pieces from cyber celebrities. Their videos often involved disingenuously giving homeless people money in exchange for viewership and positive feedback on their channels. They watched videos for over an hour, hoping to find something more complex.

Marcus's phone vibrated.

"Shit, I gotta go," Marcus said, looking at his phone.

"What do you mean?" John asked. "We haven't come up with anything yet."

"I know, but my girl is out front," Marcus explained.

"Your—your girl?" John asked with a hint of relief. "Why did you make plans with your girl?" he implored.

Marcus smiled slyly. "I didn't. She, *uh*—just got a little lonely."

"*Awe*, I didn't know you had a girlfriend. What's her name?" Kasey asked.

"She's new. Her name is Ashley. We met at a YAL meeting. But yeah, I gotta go," Marcus said, standing from the couch. He quickly gathered his things and walked to the door. "I'll see you guys later. Let me know if you come up with anything."

"Bye, Marcus," Kasey said.

John glanced at Kasey as the door shut, seemingly louder than before. Twiddling his thumbs, he sat in silence on his brown leather couch, inches away from Kasey, who was scratching the back of her neck, even though she didn't have an itch. After about a minute, they simultaneously attempted to break the cumbersome silence.

"Uh."

"So."

"Go ahead," Kasey offered.

"I was just going to say this social experiment stuff is kind of crazy," John mumbled.

"Yeah."

John tapped his fingers.

Kasey looked around the apartment.

The faint sound of laughter from a group of young bachelors walking down the hallway disrupted the heavy silence for but a moment.

John breathed sharply. "Let's watch another video."

"Yeah, yeah, good idea."

John reached for his glass of water while the video was playing and inched away from her. He played a couple of short videos while they sat in silence. After the last video finished playing, she stood from the couch.

"Well, I should be going, it's getting late."

"Yeah, I was gonna say, I'm getting pretty tired," John assisted.

Kasey gathered her things and walked to the door. "I can just walk out, right?"

"Yeah, of course."

"I mean, I don't need to stop at the front desk or anything?"

"No, no, you should be fine."

She took a deep breath, grabbing the handle. "Okay. See ya, John."

"See ya, Kasey."

The door closed behind her.

"Idiot!" he cried out, slapping himself on the forehead.

CHAPTER 8

GO ASK ALICE

The following week, Kasey, Marcus and John arrived at the inevitable conclusion that they were hopelessly stumped. None of them had come up with anything remotely plausible. Time, as Vandacheler had cautioned, would soon become their enemy. Kasey, despite Marcus's protest, had convinced them to meet her at The Red Porcupine. They ordered coffees and found a table in the café.

"Ashley and I are going ballroom dancing this weekend," Marcus imparted.

"Are you serious? I used to do junior dance competitions. I love dancing!" Kasey exclaimed.

"Why don't you come with us then?"

"Third wheel? I don't know."

"Take John with you," Marcus suggested, nodding in a sideways motion.

"I can't dance," John grumpily divulged.

"That's a shame," Kasey said in a snotty tone.

John squinted at her.

"I gotta say, these commies make some damn good coffee," Marcus said, observing his recycled-paper cup.

"Do you guys want to get started?" John asked. "I can't believe it's this hard to figure out an idea for a stupid social experiment. I would've much rather collapsed backstage after a twenty-minute debate."

Kasey chuckled.

Marcus nodded. "Yeah, let's get started."

"Fire up the laptop," Kasey said.

~~

They watched videos of social experiments on John's laptop for a while. A few nonsensical ideas were blurted out, but they remained fruitless in their effort. On top of their overall lack of productivity, Marcus had become inattentive, distracted by a middle-aged man in the café who wore a red t-shirt with a print resembling a Coca-Cola® logo that read: *Fuck Capitalism*. He grumbled incoherently until he finally left his seat to confront the man.

"*Great*, we lost Marcus," Kasey said.

"He's obsessed with this capitalism crap," John criticized.

Kasey giggled. "Right."

"I'm gonna grab a Chai tea, you want one?" he asked, standing from his chair.

"*Uh*, yeah, sure."

"Cool, I'll be right back," he said, advancing toward the counter.

She smiled, nonchalantly fixing her hair in the café window's reflection.

~~

Marcus was in a friendly argument with the man in the café. Marcus was pursuing a degree in economics and leapt at any opportunity to argue in favor of free market theory. The middle-aged man attested that American capitalism was a perversion of laissez-faire economics, relying on covert slavery, worker exploitation and a carefully orchestrated system of hierarchical oppression, all made possible by the force of government. Though anti-capitalist, the man advocated for free trade, insisting that viable markets could flourish without state intervention and needed neither exploitation nor centralized currency to function. Marcus had met his first anarchist. While they chatted and argued, Kasey and John continued watching YouTube videos, brainstorming social experiment ideas over their Chai teas.

"That dude is crazy as shit, but you know what? I like him," Marcus said, rejoining John and Kasey at their table.

Kasey chuckled.

"You fascinate me, Marcus," John jested.

Marcus smiled and fixed his imaginary tie. "I fascinate me."

Kasey giggled.

"Okay, we're not coming up with anything and I'm getting tired of sitting here," John stated. "What do you guys think? Try again later this week?"

"Alright, sounds good," Kasey agreed.

"I guess so," Marcus said.

∿∿

John and Marcus had arrived at the café together in John's new car; a rustic grey 1989 Buick LeSabre. He begged his grandmother to send more funds, citing his need for mobility. She complied, sparing what she could. They gave Kasey a ride home so she wouldn't have to take another Uber. After they confirmed she was safely inside, Marcus made an announcement.

"That guy in the café gave me something. I told you, he was crazy as shit."

"What did he give you?" John asked.

Marcus investigated his surroundings as John pulled away from Kasey's house then reached into his pocket. "You can have this shit if you want, I don't fuck with it. That dude basically shoved this shit into my pocket."

Marcus revealed a plastic sandwich bag containing an illicit substance.

John continued to drive, glancing in his direction. "Shit, he just *gave* that to you?"

Marcus laughed, handing it over. "I sure as hell didn't buy it."

"Damn, nice," he said, stuffing it into his pocket. "Thanks, man."

"Maybe it'll help you come up with an idea," Marcus joked.

～⌒

John had read extensively about Mesoamerican rituals involving psychoactive substances to induce spiritual trance. Though he had never consumed psychedelics before, he was eager to experiment. The sandwich bag Marcus had given him contained a little over an eighth of an ounce of a Brazilian strain of Psilocybe Cubensis; better known as magic mushrooms. The bag also contained six aborts; tiny blue mushrooms packed with psilocybin. John was unaware that six aborts within a standard eighth of mushrooms could produce wildly different results than what he was expecting.

Heating up two slices of leftover pizza in the microwave then covering them with the entire bag of mushrooms, John was ready to embark upon a psychedelic journey. After his first bite, he quickly realized that the mushrooms were overpowering the once delicious cheese pizza. Thoroughly chewing and gagging in between bites, he decided to cut up an apple for a chaser. Surviving the nauseating consumption of the mushroom-littered pizza, he proceeded to his living room and waited for the drugs to kick in.

Fats Domino's 1955 song "Ain't That a Shame" played through his Atmos speakers while he sat alone on his brown leather couch. Skimming through an old issue of the *Avalonti Journal*, he patiently waited. After fifteen minutes, he sighed, convinced that the mushrooms were fake; not Psilocybe Cubensis but rather *Tubaria Furfuracea*. Setting the journal on the coffee table, he decided to read more about psychedelic mushrooms on his laptop. The psychoactive compounds psilocybin and psilocin, found in almost all psychedelic mushrooms, were isolated and named in 1958 by Swiss chemist Albert Hoffman; the man who first synthesized LSD. Though not as powerful as lysergic acid diethylamide, the mind-altering properties of psilocybin were potent enough for the United States Federal Government to classify it as a Schedule 1 drug. In an infinite cycle, the fungi sporulate, colonize the rich substrate beneath their caps, and from their mycelium sprout new mushrooms.

Magic mushrooms and other psychotropic substances, such as peyote, were ceremonially used by Native American tribes and primitive cultures for thousands of years. Many saw the magic mushroom as sacred and it would only be consumed under guidance of a shaman, a chief or an elder. Recreational use of psychedelics was sacrilegious to many of those who maintained a profound spiritual connection with nature. The trees were said to speak of a deeper wisdom. Chief Seattle said that "man did not weave the web of life; he was merely a strand in it. Whatever he does to the web, he does to himself."

The non-recreational use of psychedelics was not confined to religious ceremonies. Anti-asylum psychiatrists sought to use psychedelics to treat patients with permanent psychosis. Therapists wanted to help patients like the little girl who suffered the delusion that an atomic bomb resided within her. Even after viewing X-rays of her own body, she retained the belief that she would inevitably be, as Oppenheimer had declared for himself, the "destroyer of worlds".

On an end table, a Friedrich Nietzsche book sat. Nietzsche dubbed "truth" as coins that will lose their embossing and once again exist as nothing more than pieces of metal. He claimed that "truths are illusions which we have forgotten are illusions". Though a fan of Nietzsche, John disagreed and maintained that objective truths *must* exist in the universe. He flipped through the pages for a moment then placed it on top of a book entitled *The Myth of Sisyphus* by Albert Camus. Next to the stack, Dr. Novini's book sat, containing within it a critique of the media: "Delicious lies are far easier to consume than bitter truths. The media paints a picture of a reality that does not exist. You're being lied to. We live in a world created by cameras and parlor tricks. All the world's a stage. We're not receiving information anymore; we're being fed propaganda. Journalism is dead." Pausing, John thought about Senator Croffley's car being vandalized. The story was never covered, and few ever spoke of it again.

John picked up the witch book that Marcus had given him and read the closing statement: "These are not just words on pieces of paper. Human beings really did light other human beings on fire. This shame will never be forgotten. When atrocity strikes, it remains a part of the vast human compendium, eternally etched on the timeline of our existence. The scars may fade, but they will last forever." John returned the book to the end table, tingling with a sensation as if he had consumed a mild opiate. Objects in his peripheral vision began disintegrating, and tiny particles slowly floated towards the ceiling.

"What the hell," John said, turning to inspect the disintegrating objects. Observing them head-on, they appeared as normal. Smirking, he lit a joint and took a deep draw. Exhaling, he noticed the sound of his breath was more pronounced than usual. As the smoke cleared, the glass entertainment center in front of him began to glisten with heightened resolution. "Maybe they weren't duds," he said, yawning, rotating his jaw. Though calm, he felt an overwhelming desire to squeeze the plastic orange juice bottle that he was drinking from. Taking another deep drag from the joint, he smiled uncontrollably. "Shit," he giggled, "they're finally working."

"Come on, Let's Go" by Ritchie Valens blared epically through his Atmos speakers. With his mouth hanging open and his eyes wide, he listened keenly. Though he had heard the song many times before, it resonated with a new intensity. The vocals hit him like thunder. The guitar solo surged through his body like lightning. The atmosphere was dancing with the tempo of the music. Lighting the joint that had burned out, he inhaled deeply, leaning back against the couch. "You look different," he said, slowly caressing the leather. "You're my friend," he added. Taking another drag, he stared blankly, contemplating the new world around him. After a few minutes, he flinched, saying, "I figured it out. People are weak because of shoes."

Sitting up, he reached for his bottle of orange juice and twisted off the cap to take a sip. The simple task was immeasurably more difficult than usual. "Orange juice," he said, chuckling, entertained by the label that was becoming strange and alluring. Without taking a drink, he set the bottle down on the center of the glass coffee table. Tiny ripples, like dropping a pebble into a lake, shot towards its edges. "Dude, I am fucked up," he said, tapping the glass repeatedly.

"I gotta take a piss," he mumbled, standing from the couch. On his way to the bathroom, he stopped to analyze the chrome candle sconces that were morphing with an overlay of cartoonish illumination. Distracted by the imagery, the dozen or so steps to the bathroom took nearly twenty minutes to complete. The effects of the magic mushrooms were intensifying with every stride. The walls swayed like palm trees in a gentle breeze. The music was pure energy. The apartment was beautiful beyond fathom.

Standing in front of the toilet, his legs wobbled as he struggled for accuracy. The hexagonal mosaic tiles protruded from the bathroom wall. Intangible specks of blue and red that he occasionally saw in his field of vision were peacefully exploding, like quiet little fireworks. Closing his eyes, he saw the specks transforming into assorted pieces of vintage candy. Intrigued, he closed the bathroom door and shut the lights off. Against the backdrop of darkness, the visual hallucinations amplified, creating a vivid phantasmagoria of colorful geometric patterns, swirling around him in a chaotic harmony.

"This is fucking crazy," he said in a slow declaration. "Where is all this light coming from?"

Linking with a cosmic surrealism, he became one with the universe. He struggled to remember why anything pedestrian mattered to him at all. Alleviated from all his concerns, he approached a level of absolute bliss; something he once viewed as crass and unreachable. Peaking from the drug trip, all the world around him had vanished. Time didn't exist. Matter was fleeting and illogical. There was no up or down or left or right, only an infinite plane of thoughts simultaneously coexisting in a dream world in which he was now a part.

"I think, therefore I am," he said, recalling a thought experiment from René Descartes.

Retrieving a joint from behind his ear, he placed it in his mouth and lit his lighter. The orange glow of the flame cast his mind back to the Stone Age. Imagination was merging with reality. Memories passed down through the generations. And there, under the spell of the magic mushrooms, he caught a glimpse of his ancestors, gazing upon the same stars that still twinkle in the night sky. Ghosts. Ancient wisdom. The Pleiades still flee the mighty Orion.

Toking the joint, he coughed loudly.

The multi-colored geometric patterns turned a chilling red.

"Jesus fucking Christ!" he cried out.

Rattled, he threw the rest of the joint in the toilet and flipped the light switch on. Quickly, he exited the bathroom and returned to the brown leather couch. When he'd coughed, it sounded like his father angrily shouting, "John!"

The music was no longer friendly. The anthropomorphized objects stared into him. His peaceful thoughts shifted to dark thoughts. He thought of the day he told his father of his acceptance into an irreligious east coast university and would not be attending seminary school. He remembered the sound of dishes shattering and chairs being thrown from the living room, causing his grandmother's painting of Jesus Christ to fall from the wall. He remembered how tightly his frail and innocent mother held him while they hid in his bedroom during the rampage. He remembered seeing the grip of a model 19 Smith & Wesson single-action revolver attempting to hide in her waistband. He remembered the last thing his father said before he left his childhood home forever: *Both my sons are dead.*

John raced to the kitchen to splash cold water on his face. Lifting his head from the sink, the entire apartment became saturated. Water dripped from the ceiling. As the faucet ran over his hands, he entertained the thought that there was no way an apartment that nice belonged to him; a small-town boy from Missouri. *Why*, he thought, *would a university society provide lush room and board to a mere probationary member?*

Inspecting the large chef's knife in the sink that he used to cut the apple with, he decided that the people who *really* lived there were butchered in the bedroom, and that he was cleaning up evidence. The water continued to pour from the faucet. He knelt to the floor as he was met with another disturbing thought. "Jump," he uttered, looking at the sliding glass door. "No!" Burying his eyes into the palms of his hands, he squeezed his forehead with punishing force, terminating visions of the pavement rapidly approaching as he plummeted from the 14th story balcony. Moaning, shaking and panting, he reached up, grabbed a bottle of liquor and took a chug.

"Fuck, fuck, fuck, fuck, fuck," he whimpered.

Clarence "Frogman" Henry played in the background. The kitchen breathed, shrinking and expanding. Grotesque imagery flashed before his eyes as if he had two different sets of vision. His hands were rotten and decomposing. On all of the cherry wood cabinets, he saw the face of a dalmatian that he had for a brief period when he was a little boy; a dog he had completely forgotten about. The detail of the dog's face on the cabinets resembled the real dog with stunning accuracy. John was involuntarily opening files from a memory bank hidden deep within his brain. He shook his head violently. Pulling himself up, he leaned over the kitchen sink. Turning off the faucet, he was momentarily convinced that he had been standing there for years.

"They're coming," he said, hyperventilating.

Waiting for an army of hotel security that he believed were on their way to apprehend him, he backed himself against the corner of his kitchen with his eyes locked on the front door. He thought his life was over. Cowering in the corner, a flicker of hope emerged. His lip twitched with a cautious smirk. Looking at the liquor bottles, he made a discovery: the alcohol was neutralizing his paranoia and diminishing the delusions. He quaffed it as an antidote. Two shots. Three. Four. Five. Six. Seven.

Gradually escaping the trip, he envisioned the great philosophers all turning their backs on him. "I'm a coward," he sighed. "A real intellectual would've let it drive him mad." Breathing heavily, he wiped the sweat from his brow. It was his apartment. There was no army of security coming to arrest him. He was innocent. He was free.

The panic had largely disrupted the pleasing visual effects, but they returned in weak formation as he lay on his couch, drunk, staring blankly at the wall. Contemplating deeply while listening to Connie Francis, he arrived at a revelation: all the positivity in his life had come through hardship. Enlightenment, John figured, usually came at a steep price. The Avalonti social experiment, he decided, didn't need to *be* positive to *have* positive results. Marcus was, though not as he had imagined, correct in his comical suggestion that the magic mushrooms would help him figure out an idea for the project.

CHAPTER 9

EUREKA

Stuck somewhere between a tech nerd and a jock, Liam Prescott aspired to become an entrepreneur *and* a professional athlete. People often complained about his overbearing confidence. When he spoke, no matter how serious he was, he sounded sarcastic. Thinly muscular with light brown hair and enduring acne, he was not considered the most attractive among his swim team brethren, even though he was the captain. He purposely listed only his negative qualities and attributes on his online dating profile, including his "unfortunate endowment" that was evident in the florescent pink speedos he proudly wore during competitions. Bemusing to some, Liam had won the hearts of several female students on campus and had a new girlfriend every other week or so.

A couple of days after Kasey's brainstorming session with John and Marcus, Liam spotted her in the hallway walking to class.

"You're Kasey Chong, aren't you?" Liam asked mischievously.

"Yeah, who are you?" Kasey asked, keeping her pace down the crowded hallway.

Liam smirked, walking backwards. "I'm Liam. So, how's your knight in shining armor doing?"

Kasey stopped on a dime. "*Uh*, I have no idea what you're talking about."

Liam rested his elbow against the wall. "I never thought I would be driving somebody's tooth to a hospital. I'm pretty sure my future therapist is going to *love* that story."

"Who—what are you talking about?" Kasey demanded.

"Johnny boy hasn't had much luck at Village parties, I'll tell you that."

"Wait, wait, wait, wait, wait—are you talking about John Hallman?"

Liam nodded. "Yep."

"You were with him that night—at the New Year's Eve party?"

"Indeed, I was," Liam answered theatrically. "It is kind of *my* house. But yeah, he was there. That tuxedo he was wearing was *super* awesome."

"Tell me, Liam—what the heck actually happened that night?"

"What did *he* tell you?"

"John said that he and his friend were attacked for no reason."

Liam snickered. "Not exactly."

"I *knew* he was lying. So, what *really* happened?"

"What am I gonna get for telling you?" Liam asked seductively.

She sighed. "Dude, just tell me."

"Okay, okay." Liam continued in a semi-serious tone, "Johnny and Bo were smoking a blunt with these gangster wannabe piss ants. They were chilling for a bit. Then they heard me upstairs getting it on with some chick, and these guys started bragging about all the girls they banged—but probably never actually banged. Anyway, Johnny and Bo were standing there listening to their bullshit. Then one of the dudes told a story about how he chased a *Chinese girl* down the street over in Devonshire Heights and was laughing about how he made her piss herself."

Kasey focused intently on Liam's story, nervously rubbing her hands together.

Liam continued, "Johnny boy got this idea in his head that they were talking about *you*. Johnny grabbed the fucker out of his chair and slammed him against the wall. I think the dude pissed himself, I'm not sure. Well, naturally, his friends jumped in. One of them smashed a beer bottle over Johnny's head and a pretty fucking crazy fight happened after that. We're still trying to get blood stains out of the carpet."

"Uh..."

"Luckily there were paramedics on standby because the party was so massively large. We throw super nice parties; you should come sometime. I'll give you my number. Anyway, one of those dudes picked up this brass lamp—and I mean, this fucker is a solid brass lamp—and hit Johnny over the head with it. Split his shit wide open. Shitty thing is, they slipped away before I got back downstairs, because I would've kicked all their asses."

Kasey shuddered. "That's so terrible."

"Yeah, poor guy had to get *nine* staples on his dome."

"The hat," Kasey uttered.

"The what?"

"Nothing. *Um*, Liam, do the police happen to know who these guys were?"

"Oh, the police are looking for them, believe me. Bo told them everything. They fucked Bo up pretty bad too. I hope they find them, because that fucker who hit Johnny with the lamp is in serious trouble. Like, attempted murder trouble. I mean, who the fuck would hit someone over the head with a brass lamp? Dude, I pressed a white dish towel against Johnny's head and that fucker turned completely red in two seconds. It was the most fucked up shit I've ever witnessed. And let me tell ya something, *Kasey cakes*, I've seen some fucked up shit in my day."

Kasey cringed. "That's horrible."

"Yeah, and, *uh*—I'm sorry that bastard chased you like that—seriously not cool. The guy Brian you met at Dave's house that night; he told a bunch of people what happened to you, in case you were wondering how Johnny knew that shit. Oh, and sorry that *gangster* dipshit was too stupid to know the difference between Chinese and Korean."

"Yeah."

Liam tore a piece of paper from his notebook and resumed his full sarcastic tone, "*So*, I'm writing down my number with a *pencil*.

81 | P a g e

Yeah, I use a *pencil* because I'm old school like that. I'm really hoping you're going to call because I'm already in love with you and I think our kids would be so fucking cute."

Kasey forced a smile and took the paper. "*Uh*—well, thanks, Liam. I appreciate you telling me what happened. I gotta get to my class. It was nice meeting you. I'll see you around, okay?"

"Sure thing."

～～

Kasey arrived early at Francesca Hall for their next meeting. Since Marcus didn't particularly like The Red Porcupine, and John didn't want people at his apartment anymore, they decided to have their meetings at Francesca Hall, which was typically open and empty during the afternoon. Vandacheler was there, sorting out paperwork over by the grand fireplace. John was already there too, perusing the famous book collection in the left wing.

Kasey quickly snuck up on John between the bookcases.

"John, I'm so sorry about the way I acted toward you."

"What are you talking about, Kasey?" John asked, snarling his face.

"The first meeting back from the winter break. I'm so sorry, John. I ran into your friend, Liam. He told me everything. I feel terrible."

John continued to observe the titles of the leather-bound books as if Kasey hadn't said a word. He took a few steps to his left then unenthusiastically said, "Don't read too much into it, Kasey. I would've kicked that guy's ass no matter who he chased down the street. He was a douchebag."

Kasey held herself, rubbing her bicep with her thumb, staring at her shoes. "Well, I appreciate you standing up for me anyway."

John sharply pushed a book back into its place then turned to look her in the eyes. "I didn't stand up for *you*."

Walking out from between the bookcases, John joined Vandacheler by the fireplace. Kasey stood motionless. She exited the library section of the hall only when she heard Marcus enter.

～～

John announced he had devised a thorough plan for the social experiment project. Vandacheler, intrigued, took John's seat on the couch next to Kasey and let him stand to deliver his thoughts.

"I finished Dr. Novini's book," John began. "Novini writes extensively on Edward Bernays, propaganda, corrupt journalism and the unsubstantiated conspiracy theories that emerge from lies and deceit. I also read the book that Marcus bought me for Christmas. Thanks again, Marcus—the, *uh*, one about witches, not the economics book. I haven't started that one yet."

"Damn, man, you should definitely read that," Marcus suggested.

"I will. Anyhow—the history of witch trials in Europe and America are particularly gruesome. Not only in how they tortured and killed innocent people, but how it came to be in the first place. Minds were corrupted by religion, paranoia, fear, propaganda and conspiracy theory. It is quite disturbing. Janet Horne, 1727, was the last person to be legally executed for witchcraft in the British Isles. This was during the Enlightenment, 18th century; the age of reason—the age of Voltaire. The civilized world at this time was inching toward the hope that reason would annihilate superstition. By the 21st century, the western world unanimously agrees that witch trials are but another scar on the face of their history." He paused for a breath. "Now, I know you guys are tired of hearing me talk about Croffley's car being shot up at the society dinner, but that event truly opened my eyes to a big problem we have in this country. Journalism is dead. People aren't getting information anymore—they're being fed propaganda. Not much different than how it was in 1692 during the Salem witch trials. The worst part is—people don't even know it's happening. They trust the mainstream media far too much. We need to fix this."

"What are you proposing?" Vandacheler asked.

"A witch hoax," John divulged. "We're bringing witches back."

Marcus laughed. "Bringing them back? Dude, you should know this being from a Bible-thumping hick town out in the middle of nowhere. Witches never went anywhere—not to these religious nuts."

"Religious nuts, perhaps," John agreed. "Believe me, I know, my father is a pastor at a Baptist church. Also, witch killings are still happening among primitive cultures around the world. But

I'm talking about something a little more widespread, something modern. This isn't Papua New Guinea; this is the United States."

"*Uh*, witches *are* among us. Don't you know anything about Wicca?" Kasey questioned.

"1954, Gerald Gardner? I'm not talking about them," John argued. "I'm talking about the *servants of the devil*. The sorcery that caused religious history such panic and dismay. Just let me explain."

"So, you want to make witch hunting and witch burnings widespread in America, is that it then?" Kasey antagonized.

"Yes, chaos and pandemonium," John joked. "But no, seriously, I just want to see if we can get people who *don't* believe in witches to fall for a witch hoax. It's an experiment designed to show how easy it is to trick people—which can be highly beneficial for research purposes. If we can show people how they're being tricked, they'll be more likely to think for themselves in the future. We will have another Renaissance."

"And how exactly are we going to create a witch hoax?" Marcus probed.

John, directing his attention to Marcus, answered, "We're going to create a website; an online conservative news publication. This will give us a platform to spread the hoax. First, we'll build up readership with news stories and opinion pieces, using Facebook to promote the website. We'll become legit in their minds. Then, once we have secured substantial readership, we're going to accuse a politician—a democrat—of being a witch and get stupid conservatives to believe it."

"*Hey*, I'm a conservative," Marcus protested.

John sighed. "Not conservatives like you, Marcus. You know the ones I'm talking about."

"I don't like the idea," Kasey stated.

John threw up his hands, exclaiming, "Of course, you don't!"

"John, it's just mean-spirited and crazy and no one would believe it anyway," Kasey said, standing from the couch, walking away.

"People believe the God damn earth is flat, Kasey! They'll believe whatever I fucking tell them to believe!"

Vandacheler sighed. "John, please."

"Sorry," John uttered. "I'm just saying, people *will* believe it. Remember the Michigan relics? Remember what Professor Francis Kelsey said in 1911? He said, 'Men will be ready to believe what they wish to believe and that no hoax will be too preposterous to be without a following.' We can get people to believe whatever we want."

"Have you considered charges of libel, John?" Vandacheler dissuaded.

"We won't actually accuse them of being a witch. We'll theorize it. We'll imply it. Then, we'll let the crowds do the convicting. Don't worry, all of this will be revealed as a hoax. That's where we introduce the enlightening aspect of the project. That part is critical. Everything will be documented. The only people who will be *hurt* are the people stupid enough to believe the hoax. They'll look like the morons that they are, and we'll be celebrated for it. It'll be the *War of the Worlds* broadcast all over again."

"Will it now?" Vandacheler poked.

"Look," John said, "I know it's a little confusing, but I'm telling you, it's a good idea. If we can get people to actually believe some wild story like this, posing as a media publication, we'll be able to demonstrate the power that the media has— and maybe, just maybe, we can weaken their stranglehold over us."

"But aren't there already examples of how the media controls the way people think?" Marcus inquired. "I mean, just look at Kim Jong-un—his people think he's God."

"Yeah, there's a shit ton of examples," John agreed, "but the masses don't care. They've been desensitized. You need something outlandish, something outrageous, to get their attention."

"I guess," Marcus conceded.

"Listen," John pleaded, "we'll start a publication. We'll make it look real. We'll get tons of readers. Then we'll put a story out there that *suggests* that a politician is a witch, and you know damn well there's gonna be people who buy it. When they do, it'll create a buzz. Once everyone is talking about it, we'll come out and say *Gotcha!* —here's how we fooled you. Then everyone will hopefully *think* before they believe something they read in a newspaper. The end result is simple—we're spreading knowledge and enlightenment."

Kasey sighed.

"*Welp*, I'm tired of trying to figure out an idea for this social experiment, so I'm good with convincing dumbasses that witches are back," Marcus said, turning to Kasey. "Come on, *Kasey*, it's not *that* bad of an idea."

"Can I think about this?" she requested.

John nodded. "Absolutely. Take your time. If you come up with something different, let me know. I'm just saying, it's an idea."

"I just don't like the idea," she declared.

"Yeah, I know, you said that already," John grumbled.

"It is not my position," Vandacheler informed, "to approve or deny your theme. If you should choose to pursue an idea like this, you will be granted the resources of the society. I must remind you, *however*, that Caesar is commanding a positive outcome. Your formal induction into this society depends on the reception of your grand reveal."

"You're gonna blow it with this crap, John," Kasey snarled.

"Then come up with something better! You stu—" John restrained himself, feeling Vandacheler's watchful eyes on him.

"The only thing stupid here is this idea of yours," Kasey opined.

"Are you even a freethinker, Kasey?" John accused. "I'm not trying to be a dick, but I just don't get why you want to be in this society."

"Johnathan," Vandacheler cautioned.

"Van, I'm not trying to insult her. I'm genuinely curious. Are you an atheist, Kasey? An agnostic? Deist? Henotheist? Christian? Buddhist? Hindu? Muslim? Taoist? Shintoist? Jew? *Huh? Huh?* Come on, tell us!"

"Why are you like this, John?" Kasey scowled.

"Like what! I'm asking a simple question! I know Marcus is a conservative atheist who is obsessed with capitalism and secretly likes hanging out with communists because he enjoys robust debate. He's pursuing a degree in economics. He plays chess and likes football. He has a girlfriend named Ashley. He doesn't like drugs or alcohol. His father is a doctor, his mother is a lawyer. I could go on and on. You, *Kasey*, we don't know anything about you! Except that your parents forced you into ballroom dancing and you run slow!"

Kasey frowned. Her chin started to tremble slightly.

"John," Marcus said, standing between him and Kasey, "Kasey is getting a physics degree. She wants to work at the LHC in Switzerland someday. If that don't work out, she wants to be a teacher. Her parents are converted Christians. Kasey grew up Christian, but she disavowed and is now an agnostic. Her parents own a real estate business in Cincinnati. Her grandfather is a Buddhist who lives in Seoul. He's a pacifist—like Kasey is—and practices Taekwondo every morning. Kasey doesn't like alcohol or drugs either. She likes dancing, *yes*, and photography, art, Celtic symbols, flowers—especially roses—and making collages from magazine clippings. She's an only child and always wanted a brother. She *really* hates guns. Kasey is liberal but that's okay because she loves people and just wants to do good in this world. So—don't say *we*, John."

Vandacheler and Marcus quietly stared at him.

John nervously swallowed.

The Beha grandfather clock loudly ticked.

The judgmental staring continued.

The clock ticked louder.

John picked up his backpack, glancing at Kasey before storming out of the hall.

"Let's just do his stupid idea. I don't even care anymore," Kasey hissed.

CHAPTER 10
THE DAILY VERANDA

"Starting an online publication and gaining substantial readership in a short period of time is not really that difficult," Zach assured the group. "With the proper resources at your disposal."

Vandacheler summoned two young Avalonti members to help with the project: Zachery Goldstein—an online marketing and advertising expert studying for his master's degree in finance, and Arjun Khatri—a PhD student with a background in graphic design and web development. Vandacheler had green-lighted the project. The witch hoax project would be broken down into three stages:

Stage 1 Infiltration: Create an online conservative news publication and accumulate substantial readership.

Stage 2 Defamation: Select a politician. Write an article suggesting that the politician is a witch and publish it to the online news publication.

Stage 3 Revelation: Record the effects of the hoax. Publish all data on the online news publication for public analysis.

Arjun formatted and designed the website and launched their news publication via a 3rd party web hosting provider. It was online in two days. Inspired by John's fascination with Francesca Hall's forbidden veranda, the publication was called *The Daily Veranda*. To fabricate age and authenticity, Arjun painstakingly published old articles from syndicated news outlets that allowed copying. It was often encouraged for independent publications to copy stories from larger news outlets if they simply credited the source and backlinked the original article. Arjun published hundreds of backdated articles to *The Daily Veranda*.

For original content and opinion pieces, they each submitted their own articles, pending the approval of the group. New content played a significant role in the growth of the online publication. Advertising old news was minimally engaging and yielded low CTR (Click Through Rate). A proper media outlet had to publish several articles per day covering current issues and events. *The Daily Veranda* would be a mix of original pieces and copied articles.

The publication's target audience was average conservative Americans. Marcus and John focused on writing about politics, philosophy and economics while Kasey focused on science, public schooling, art and photography; all from a "conservative" perspective. Zach and Arjun contributed by adding articles about the tech world. Within a couple of weeks, *The Daily Veranda* appeared as a legitimate online news publication.

A legitimate looking publication, however, was nothing without traffic and readership. Although they opened accounts on every popular social media website to promote *The Daily Veranda*, their ideal platform to establish presence was Facebook. Zach was an expert on Facebook metrics and advertising. For perceptibility, readers would need to see a Facebook page with a substantial amount of *likes*. CNN garnered over thirty million, and Fox News over twenty million. For the intended purpose of their publication, they estimated that they would only need roughly two million *likes*. To grow *The Daily Veranda's* Facebook page, Zach posted their original articles and launched a series of advertising campaigns with precision targeting. Sponsored Facebook posts that exhibited high CTR received additional advertising budget to reach a greater audience. Avalonti expense accounts funded the project. Successful ad campaigns awarded them an influx of Facebook page *likes*, and thus increased readership; which was critical for when they launched the defamation article. Zach and Arjun also set up Google AdSense; running other people's advertisements on *The Daily Veranda*. They were not interested

THE WITCH HOAX

in monetizing the publication for profit, only in creating the image of authenticity.

Demonstrating impressive skill, the team's only challenge was remaining patient. It would take time for *The Daily Veranda* to grow large enough for the defamation article to sufficiently circulate and induce a significant public reaction. In between political news and opinion pieces, they would write and pepper in articles that referenced witchcraft and the history of witches. The idea behind the witch-related articles was to prime their audience for the hoax. To assist with the primer articles, Vandacheler called upon two Avalonti Sages: David Oakman, scholar of medieval folklore, and Dr. Winston Douglas, scholar of English monarchs. David Oakman was an expert on witch folklore and Dr. Douglas possessed extensive knowledge on King James VI of Scotland, who subsequently became James I of England in 1603; a notable figure in regard to witch perception. The scholarly aid may have proven beneficial, but upon learning the details of the project, both men refused to offer their assistance. Outranked by the men, Vandacheler was powerless to retain their services.

Kasey, who reluctantly participated in the project, relished spitefully in the scholars' refusal. Both Sages agreed that the disconcerting witch hoax project was an abomination unto the core values and principles of the society. John shrugged off the rejection and eagerly accepted the task of writing the primer articles himself. John read King James's *Demonology*, a dissertation on contemporary necromancy published in 1597, and the *Malleus Maleficarum*, published in 1487 by the discredited Catholic clergyman Heinrich Kramer. Along with the book Marcus had given him, John was handsomely equipped to write the primer articles solo.

~~

Vandacheler reopened the print room, which had not been in use for decades, as an office for the publication team. Up until the emergence of email, society members often wrote for the *Avalonti Journal* within the walls of Francesca Hall. Though called "the print room", the actual printing of the journal occurred in a larger facility managed by the University Press. The print room hid behind the liquor bar and Brunswick billiard tables in the back of the right wing of the hall. It was a secluded area, but it was not enclosed. One could raise their voice a little and speak to a member standing by the main entranceway. John marveled over the room's antiquity. There was a circa 1911 Western Electric Model 317 hand-cranked wooden wall telephone near the corner that once took calls in the Avalonti family's Bethesda mansion. Hanging next to it, an original 1933 *Daily Mirror* newspaper displayed the headline: "Prohibition Ends at Last!" To the left of the framed newspaper, a series of portraits hung as timeless homages to the legendary scholars of the Avalonti Society. Old typewriters and green glass banker lamps still graced the solid wooden desks. Vandacheler had five computers installed; one for each student working on the project. Over the following weeks, the students worked tirelessly, increasing their presence and gaining new readers.

In the print room, Vandacheler talked with Zach and Marcus while the five students worked on their articles.

"So, I don't get the connection between chemistry and acting," Marcus said to Vandacheler. "Like, how does one go from the theater to the chemistry lab? What's the bridge there?"

Zach interrupted, "Whenever a man does something that doesn't make sense, there's always a woman involved."

Vandacheler smirked at Zach then turned to Marcus. "Chemistry is a different kind of theater—one that can potentially unlock profound mysteries of the universe."

"Like I said," Zach joked, "he was chasing a woman."

Vandacheler smiled.

"Where are *you* going?" John asked Kasey.

"I have to go, there's a meeting this evening," Kasey answered, putting on her pea coat.

"What meeting?"

"With Mel and the girls."

"Mel?" John grumbled. "Did you finish your last article?"

"I'll finish it later," she promised.

The other three students looked at John as he stood from his chair.

"Kasey, I'm not trying to be an asshole," John insisted, "but we have a lot of work to do here. We need you on this project."

"I'll get it done, *relax*. We have to prepare for the rally tomorrow."

John peered at her. "The rally? What rally?"

"The women's rally."

John scoffed. "The *women's* rally?"

"It's very important to me, John. Don't start with your crap."

"And what rights don't you have that *I* have?" John implored.

"Reproductive freedom, equal pay, the right to exist free from systemic rape culture and patriarchal oppression. Should I go on?"

"*Oh geez*, you sound like you're reading from a pamphlet. Is this Mel chick teaching you *how* to think or *what* to think?"

"It's not like that, John. You have no idea what kind of crap we still go through. You can't see through your own privilege."

"My *privilege*, huh? So, you cast off the shackles of organized religion to join a feminist cult, is that it, Kasey?"

Vandacheler stood from his chair, rolling his eyes and shaking his head. "Here we go again."

"It's not a cult, John," she argued. "Women have to band together to fight male oppression."

"Male oppression, huh?" John sneered. "Women are treated like royalty in this country and you know it."

"Oh, really?" she snarled. "When was the last time *you* had to worry about being raped walking home from school?"

"W—w—we all have our problems, Kasey," John stammered.

Vandacheler quietly approached them.

"What do you think, Don?" Kasey asked.

Vandacheler stood between them, placing each hand on one of their shoulders. "I think," he slowly spoke, "that you two should have lobster bisque at your wedding reception. It's quite tasty, I assure you."

Arjun snickered. John lowered his head. Kasey giggled.

"It's good shit," Zach added. "Not kosher though."

"Hey, Van," Marcus asked, chuckling, "don't you know that you're inadvertently using your position of authority as our society mentor to reinforce the patriarchal institution of marriage? How dare you downplay valid women's rights issues with a gesture of comic relief. Tsk-tsk."

"Clever," Vandacheler mocked.

Kasey picked up her bag and smirked at John, who was hiding his blushing face.

"I'll see you guys soon," she saluted the rest of the group.

"Bye, Kasey," they said, refocusing on their work.

John made brief eye contact with her before she walked away.

CHAPTER 11

PROPAGANDA

"Propaganda," Professor Diageo explained to the students, "whether it's via radio, television, newspaper, art, literature, film—whatever medium—is designed to change the behavior of people. Not merely the way they think, but the way they act as well."

At Francesca Hall, the students focused on Vandacheler's friend and Avalonti Sage, Professor Lance Diageo, who agreed to offer his assistance. Diageo, at thirty-nine years old, was a recovering Marxist whose ascent to "bourgeois" status nudged him into moderate liberalism. His extensive understanding of unconventional politics and subcultures was a benefit to the witch hoax project. Diageo was brilliant, but he was also a controversial figure among the Avalonti ilk. With equanimity, he praised men like Julian Assange and Edward Snowden. At times, he would shed his tweed blazer and play his acoustic guitar while singing under a tree in the quad. It was not uncommon for students to develop romantic or platonic feelings for him as a result of his political inclinations and laidback teaching style.

"Propaganda is most effective when it's targeted accurately. I've evaluated the project and I think it has potential. Results from a project like this could give us tremendous sociological data. You're off to a good start, but your targeting is a little off," Diageo criticized. "Average conservative Americans are no more likely to believe a witch hoax than average American liberals; contrary to your hypothesis."

"Who must we target then?" Arjun begged.

Professor Diageo grinned ominously.

~~

Since John spent a considerable amount of time on his first primer article, he decided to publish it to *The Daily Veranda,* despite Diageo's theory of mistargeting. The engagement rate on the first primer article was insignificant. For perspective, an article Marcus posted the day before, covering left-wing censorship initiatives against conservative voices on American college campuses, garnered an average CTR; 6200% higher than John's primer article. Diageo was correct. The primer article, "A Century of Witchcraft", although failing to generate any interest, did offer insight; they knew who *not* to target in the future. Zach and Professor Diageo worked together to reconstruct the targeting profile while the others wrote new articles. Diageo convinced Zach to drop "conservative" as a prerequisite for future targeting. Instead, Diageo narrowed their audience down to "conspiracy theorists who are anti-establishment, aged thirty-five and older with no conventional political affiliation". Their new target market would include people who were on the right *and* the left of the political spectrum. On top of legitimate news articles and opinion pieces, they would include content that appealed to their new audiences. The team agreed on adding, from a neutral position, articles about Roswell, The Illuminati, the JFK assassination, the Rothschild family, Operation Paperclip, MK-Ultra, Unit 731, Fukushima, Dulce Base, the moon landing, 9/11, and various other topics of interest, targeted to whom Diageo dubbed as "persuadables".

~~

The new articles and new targeting showed a much higher engagement rate than their previous campaigns. Their Facebook page swelled with new *likes*. Considerably different from the strait-laced conservatives they previously attracted, John began to study the new people liking their page. Other than Mr. Budwin, John, Marcus and Kasey were the only ones at Francesca Hall that evening.

"Hey, guys, check this dude's profile out," John instructed Kasey and Marcus while they worked on articles.

"Let me see," Kasey said excitedly, standing from her chair.

They gathered around John's computer.

"Age 42. Dog lover. Catholic. Anarchist. No king but Christ," Marcus read the man's short bio info from the screen. "Catholic anarchist?"

"Is that even possible?" Kasey enquired.

"I guess so," John answered. "These new people are fucking crazy."

John showed them another person's profile who recently *liked* their Facebook page.

"Age 44. Metalhead. Ufologist. History is a lie," Kasey read from the screen. "Uh, okay."

"Do another," Marcus requested.

"Age 39. Anti-Vaxxer. Tesla killed God. Research HAARP," Kasey read from the screen.

John pulled up another profile. "Let's see what this guy is all about."

"Age 37. SJW. Antifascist genderqueer. 9/11 was an inside job," Marcus read from the screen. "Pull up another."

"Age 43. Flat-Earther. Red-Pilled. MGTOW. IDW," Kasey read from the screen. "What the heck is all this?"

"Are there any women?" Marcus asked.

"Hold on, let me find one," John said, scrolling. "*Ah*, here's one."

"Age 36. Vegan. Animal Liberation Front. E.L.F. Space is not real. Freethinker. Truth-Seeker," Marcus read.

John scoffed. "Wait, does she really call herself a *freethinker*? A *truth-seeker*?"

"*Uh*—it looks that way, John," Marcus informed.

"That fucking audacious, stupid bitch!" John exclaimed. "Space is not real? Fucking idiot!"

"Hey," Kasey scorned, "you shouldn't use the B-word like that."

Marcus snickered. "The B-word?"

"The word has sexist connotations. It's been used as a pejorative term for women since the 15th Century," she explained.

"Kasey. Age 21. Ballroom Dancer. Annoying Feminist," John joked.

Marcus chuckled.

Kasey gently elbowed him. "Shut up, John."

John smiled at her. "I'm just teasing. I won't use it again if it bothers you that much."

"How kind," she jested.

"Happy birthday, by the way," Marcus said.

"Not until next week," Kasey informed.

"Shit," Marcus stated, changing the topic, "we need to figure out who we're going to accuse of being a witch."

"I already figured that out," John divulged.

"Who?" Kasey asked.

"U.S. Representative Anastasia Carval, the darling of the progressive movement," John revealed.

Kasey squinted. "Why her?"

"Well, she's young, not terribly bright, ultra-progressive, controversial, always in the news. Conservatives hate her, that's a given. There's also something I noticed while looking at all these new people liking our page. Even if they look liberal or leftist, they all seem to hate her, too. She's the perfect target because nobody knows how the hell she got a job as a U.S. representative. The only way to explain her rise to power is witchcraft."

"I can't believe I'm about to say this, John, but that's a good idea," Kasey confessed.

"Hell yeah," Marcus agreed. "I hate AC, she's a fucking commie."

John grinned. "All we have to do now is figure out how to convince people she's a witch."

~~

Professor Diageo, who had developed a keen interest in the project, was skeptical that John's primer articles were enough to induce a successful witch hoax. He dubbed them "weak propaganda". Under Diageo's guidance, the team outsourced a video project to an impartial, foreign online advertising company,

Hallstatt Analytica. The video production team at Hallstatt Analytica produced six thirty-second films that featured footage of mass refugee migration, starving children, virus outbreaks, political violence, war and various other real-world ailments. Flashing periodically between the disturbing scenes were images involving witchcraft, sorcery and Satanic rituals, as well as subtext that implied correlation. Hallstatt Analytica advertised, from their own platforms, the six thirty-second propaganda films targeted to the same people the Avalonti team were showcasing their "reputable" online news publication to. According to Diageo, the propaganda videos would influence their audience's subconscious minds. When the time came to publish the defamation article that suggested Anastasia Carval was a witch, he believed, the readers would be much more receptive of the idea.

CHAPTER 12

THE RAVEN

Trapped beneath the ice of doubt was stubborn curiosity, chipping its way through layers of skepticism to emerge onto the surface of plausibility. The first stage of John's social experiment idea was a resounding success. *The Daily Veranda* had gained considerable online readership in a short amount of time, as assured by their advertising strategist, Zachery Goldstein. The team had entered Stage 2; selecting Congresswoman Anastasia Carval to decry as a witch. Considering proper execution, the students argued over *how* they would defame her as a witch, and the project hit a roadblock.

Returning to his apartment a little early that evening, John fixed himself a mint julep and decided to relax on his balcony and enjoy the night view of the bustling town below, despite the cold. With his free hand, he pulled back the curtain of the sliding glass door.

"Jesus Christ!" he shouted, recoiling, dropping his cocktail.

A large black raven had collided with the side of the hotel and landed dead on John's balcony. John forced a laugh to interrupt his nervous panting. He called the front desk and they sent a maintenance man to remove the carcass. John decided he would have his mint julep in the living room that evening.

～～

Before the maintenance man had scooped up the bird carcass, John snapped a few photos with his phone to show Marcus and

Kasey. Taking a break from writing articles, John, Kasey and Marcus gathered around the grand fireplace of Francesca Hall.

"That's some fucked up shit," Marcus said, looking at John's phone.

Kasey cringed. "I don't want to look at that again. That poor bird."

"What are the odds, right?" John rhetorically asked.

Marcus squinted and paused for a moment. "What *are* the odds?"

"Birds fly into shit sometimes, Marcus, don't get weird," John suggested.

"Yeah, but in February?" Marcus doubted.

"Come on," John teased, "I know you're a conservative, but you can't be *that* stupid."

"I don't think I've seen any birds around either, John," Kasey added.

"Oh, *God*, you too?" John griped.

"I'm just saying, it's strange," Kasey defended.

"Listen guys, common ravens don't migrate. Yes, it's unusual for them to be in this area, but there *are* documented sightings of common ravens in this town. They typically build nests high on mountain cliffs, or in tall pine trees. I'm on the 14th floor. This bird probably observed the building as a possible nesting area and had an unfortunate accident."

Marcus chuckled. "Sounds like you did some research."

Kasey shuddered, turning away from John.

"What are you doing?" John asked, observing Kasey's reaction.

"It's just shocking," Kasey said.

John rolled his eyes.

"Isn't it an omen to find a dead bird on your balcony?" Marcus asked.

John turned to Marcus, studying him with a frozen glare. "Omen? *Omen?* Marcus, the rational atheist, asking if a dead bird is an omen? Listen to you two," he scorned. "I feel like I just shared this story with two middle school kids at a bus stop. You're supposed to be men—people of reason."

"Why would you be at a middle school bus stop, John?" Marcus teased.

Kasey's lip twitched with a hidden smirk.

John laughed. "You guys are something else."

~~

Vandacheler entered the hall and interrupted their conversation. He learned that an old friend from his theater days would be performing in New York City in a couple of weeks and asked the students if they wanted to take a trip with him.

"I could definitely use a day or two away from this place," Kasey said.

"Awesome," Marcus added.

"I'll go," John agreed.

"Jolly good," Vandacheler remarked.

"Oh, hey, Van, you gotta check out these pictures," John insisted.

Kasey turned away as John pulled out his phone.

"I think it's an omen," Marcus joked.

"No," John said, chuckling, holding up the phone to Vandacheler, "punishment for drinking a God damn mint julep."

"Hmm, interesting," Vandacheler uttered.

John's smile ran away from his face. "Interesting? That's it?"

"We can't use Avalonti money for the trip," Vandacheler said, breaking his apathetic gaze of the bird picture, "but I'll cover the costs of the rooms and the bus ride."

"You're the man," Marcus boasted, shaking Vandacheler's hand.

"Yeah, you're awesome," Kasey said, giving him a hug. "Thank you so much."

"Sounds great," John said. "We really appreciate it, Van."

Mel scheduled a meeting at The Red Porcupine with the women's group a couple of days later. Since the New York trip was only a few days away, Kasey decided to head in early to buy some books for the long bus ride. Vandacheler, despite growing up among affluence and luxury, loved bus rides, the subway and all things conventional.

Kasey gasped as she walked in front of The Red Porcupine. The storefront had two large windows on either side of the glass door, allowing passersby visibility into the bookstore and café. She pulled out her phone and pretended to text somebody.

"What the heck is he doing?" she said to herself, observing John sitting at a table having coffee with Mel. She stood by a lamppost, spying on them through the window.

John spoke fast and passionately, enthusiastically nodding whenever Mel responded. The only time Kasey saw that kind of behavior from John was after Vandacheler's theater production at Francesca Hall, when he was talking with Dr. Thaddeus Arnold and Mr. Chad Wilcox; men he highly respected. John was too focused on his conversation with Mel to notice Kasey.

"I. Can't. Believe. This," Kasey said to herself, trying not to move her mouth. She huffed and proceeded to walk around the block. By the time she returned, she saw Alyssa getting out of her car, half a block away from The Red Porcupine. When they walked in together, she noticed that John was gone. Before joining the other women, Alyssa and Kasey ordered coffees.

"So, how are things at the *Boys' Club*?" Elsa asked Kasey as she took her seat at the table.

Kasey looked at Mel. "John," she emphasized, "seems to be making progress."

Mel didn't flinch.

"That's good," Alyssa remarked. "I admire you for not leaving the society like you originally planned. It's important that women stand strong in this world. They need you. We need you."

"Thanks, Alyssa," Kasey said, smiling, turning back to Mel. "Guys like *John* just need exposure to educated women. The world—our system—has kept us so much in the shadows that boys simply don't know that intelligent, strong women exist."

"Right," Karen agreed. "Males have been conditioned to perceive women as subservient from an early age. The first thing they usually see is their mother taking orders from their father."

"Exactly," Joy concurred. "Men are neophobic as well. When that perception of female submissiveness is challenged, they often lash out. Masculinity is fragile."

"I'm done with *history*," Lakesha added. "I want to know about *herstory*. Let me hear about that Kathleen Cleaver. Let me hear about that Septima Clark! Let me hear about that Madam C.J. Walker! That Audre Lorde! That Angela Davis! That Sojourner Truth!"

"Right on," Elsa said, nodding. "Right the fuck on."

"Young males are propagators of the patriarchy," Mel asserted. "They carry the torch. The cycle of our oppression is generational and can only be broken if *we* stand up and break it ourselves."

"John comes in here sometimes," Kasey said impatiently. "*Uh*, we could make him an ally. He's very intelligent."

"This is *our* fight, Kasey. We need female allies first," Mel stated.

Kasey took a sip of her coffee and retreated, listening to the other women as they continued to share their thoughts and opinions.

∽

After his conversation with Mel, John returned to his apartment to meet up with Bo and his friend, Pierre.

"No, like this, John, like this," Pierre instructed.

From the brown leather couch, Bo watched, giggling.

"*Ah*, I've had enough practice, I think," John sighed.

"Suit yourself," Pierre stated in a flamboyant tone. "I have to get going anyhow. Watch those videos I sent you, John. Keep practicing."

"I will. Thank you, Pierre."

"You're welcome," Pierre said, sitting next to Bo.

John walked to the kitchen. Pierre gathered his belongings. He whispered something to Bo then stood from the couch. Bo chuckled.

"See you boys later," Pierre saluted, opening the apartment door.

"Later," John said, removing the cap from a bottle of brandy.

"Bye, Pierre," Bo said, inconspicuously winking at him.

Pierre winked back as the door closed behind him.

John fixed himself a drink then joined Bo on the couch.

"It's good to see you again, John," Bo confessed.

"You too, man. How've you been?" John asked.

"*Meh*, I've been okay."

"How's the swim team stuff going?"

"It's going."

"Everything else okay?"

Bo sighed. "Well, these idiot doctors are trying to get me on these new anti-depressants."

John raised an eyebrow. "Anti-depressants?"

"I'm fine. They just try to push that shit on everyone," Bo assured.

"Yeah, I read that there's a lot of corruption surrounding the pharmaceutical industry."

"Bunch of drug-pedaling Nazis if you ask me," Bo joked.

John snickered.

"I miss you, though, John," he said, changing the subject.

"I'm sorry I've been so busy, Bo. We'll hang out when I get back from New York if you want."

Bo smiled. "I'd like that. So, how have *you* been, John?"

"Busy. Stressed. That's college life, right?"

Bo nodded. "Right. Your face is looking much better. How's the tooth?"

"The dentist said the tooth should be good."

"That's good. How's your head?"

"It's okay. I'll have a nasty scar for the rest of my life, though, so I hope I never go bald." He put his drink down. "Did you hear anything? The, *uh*—cops ever going to find these guys?"

"I doubt it. I'm more worried about *you* finding them, John. What's going to happen if you run into them again? I really don't want to see you get kicked out of the society. You've worked so hard to get this chance at Avalonti."

John grabbed his drink, standing from the couch. "I'm not sure what I'd do, Bo. I know what my father would do. Ole Pastor Hallman could have God sitting on his porch, drinking lemonade, begging him not to seek revenge, and he'd still probably kill them."

"I hope it never comes to that, John. You're too good for it. I want you to be remembered as John the Great Philosopher, not John the Murderer."

"Why not both?" John joked.

Bo chuckled.

CHAPTER 13

NEW YORK, NEW YORK

Fantasma Theatre was built during the mid-19th century in SoHo. The small theater was home to legendary vaudeville acts in the 1890s. By the 1930s, after vaudeville declined significantly in popularity, Fantasma attempted to compete with the Metropolitan Opera House by showcasing opera and cabaret singers, with little success. Subsequently, despite the postwar economic boom of 1945, the theater was abandoned until its resurrection in the late 1960s. Wealthy modern art dealers purchased the theater to exhibit bizarre and unusual performances. By the 1970s, Fantasma had become a hipster haven but suffered another abandonment in the early '90s. Ten years later, after a documentary about Fantasma Theatre surfaced at a film festival, the theater received new owners, generous endowments and a series of restorations; preserving most of the original 19th-century architecture and decor. To walk through the doors of Fantasma Theatre was to step backwards in time.

John, Kasey and Marcus sat a few rows back from the stage with Vandacheler. They had enjoyed a brief intermission after the opening act. Vandacheler cautioned the students that his friend's performance could get a little "intense". The lights dimmed again, and a gentle applauding ensued. A spotlight shined on a lightweight chair in the center of the stage. Fog slowly permeated the floor of the stage as foreboding synth music played in the background. Two men in tuxedos, wearing identical goat head masks, walked across the stage and stood perfectly still on either side of the chair. Moments later, the beautiful blonde-haired Nika

Godec emerged on to the stage, wearing a red bikini and a pair of black high-heeled shoes with strips of latex fastened to the bottom, resembling torn human flesh. Vandacheler applauded vigorously for his Slovenian friend.

Nika Godec stood in front of the chair, absorbing the applause, then took her seat. She pulled two straps from the chair and buckled herself to it. One strap over her lap, and one strap across her chest, allowing her arms free movement. The eerie synth music continued as an old, hunched-over man in brown monk's garb crept towards her. The "monk" handed Nika a sleek, black electric violin. The fog intensified. The goat head men remained perfectly still. A violin bow fell from the theater catwalk. She effortlessly caught it while her eyes peered into the audience. John situated himself, sitting firmly in his chair.

The theater filled with the haunting, powerful voice of the electric violin. The sparse crowd cheered as she began to play. Nika opened with a sorrowful adagio piece that she wrote after deliberately spending four weeks in solitary confinement, in a room not larger than a typical bathroom. Nika was not only a skilled musician, she was also a contemporary performance artist. Born into opulence, she would subject herself to strange, often violent, torture to show solidarity with the oppressed, historically mistreated or abused. John, in observing the bizarre spectacle on stage, started to fidget.

"You okay, John?" Kasey whispered.

"Yeah," John assured.

Light fog encompassed the audience. Nika started to play an exquisite allegro piece that reverberated majestically throughout the theater. Nika commanded the bow like a general sending men into an ancient, forgotten battle. Her performances were thunderously loud. A student at the University of Ljubljana described them as "like being viciously assaulted by heavenly angels." Kasey saw John rubbing his shoes together.

"You sure you're okay?" Kasey whispered.

John nodded.

Nika's final piece was a fiery vivacissimo score. The two men in tuxedos and goat head masks remained perfectly still. The synth music could still be heard in the background. The fog continued to permeate the stage. Before the crescendo, two men entered wearing hospital grade facemasks, rubber gloves and pale green surgeon coats riddled with fake blood. They rubbed her upper back with alcohol-soaked cotton balls and plunged two large hooks through her skin, about eight inches apart. Two cables descended from the theater catwalk. The "doctors" attached the cables to the hooks. A strobe light commenced. The skin on her back stretched to its limits as the cables lifted her into the air. She continued to play her violin ferociously, suspended over the stage, strapped to a chair.

John closed his eyes and listened to her wild, wickedly beautiful performance. He fell into deep thought. He thought about his brother. He remembered laughing when he first found his brother lying on the floor that day. His brother was a prankster. He was seventeen; John was fourteen. John would never forget the feel of his brother's cold skin on that day he refused to wake up.

He opened his eyes and exhaled sharply. Nika was still playing. Through his eyes he saw the cables slowly lowering her back to the stage. In his mind, he saw his brother's casket being lowered into the cold dead ground. He remembered the funeral well; it was the only time he ever heard his mother cry.

∼∽

Vandacheler rented Kascy her own room, and John and Marcus agreed to share a double. In their room, John and Marcus briefly discussed the witch hoax project but decided to use the New York trip to unplug for a while. They talked about their days of playing football in high school instead. Marcus expressed distaste for the negative stereotype of football players being branded as intellectually inferior but relished the memories of his popularity. When Marcus regaled him with stories of his exploits and many sexual relationships, John hung his head and confessed that his social life was difficult to keep up as a result of his pious father's oppressively strict rules. Marcus apologized in jest, adding that he was glad he didn't grow up in a "backward small town".

With not much to do, they decided to move a lamp from the wooden nightstand and use it as a platform for an arm-wrestling match. John and Marcus were equal in height, just under six-foot tall. They were both athletic, toned, and exercised often. Occasionally, they would lift weights together in the gym at The Marquis. Though John appeared stronger than Marcus, their arm-wrestling battle deadlocked, with both men refusing to give up.

Interrupting their match was a faint knocking at their door. Suspecting it may have been Vandacheler checking in on them, John quickly pushed the nightstand back up against the wall and replaced the lamp. Marcus opened the door, finding Kasey standing shyly with a blanket and a pillow under her arm. She didn't want to sleep alone. With brief resistance from John, Kasey received permission to stay in their room. Marcus, willing to switch spots, offered Kasey his bed so she wouldn't have to sleep on the floor, but she stubbornly declined. Marcus insisted but she wouldn't budge. Their argument over sleeping arrangements eventually dwindled into casual conversation, poised to last indefinitely. Scheduled to wake up at 8 the next morning, John aggressively shut the lights off and boorishly commanded them to stop talking.

◦◦◦

In the morning, John was the first to rise. Scanning the room, he grumbled and scoffed. Sometime during the night, Kasey had left the floor and climbed into bed with Marcus. John huffed as he saw Kasey asleep, resting her head on Marcus's sculpted chest. Shaking his head disapprovingly, he whispered, "I'm sure Ashley would *love* to see this." Pacing around his bed, he deliberately coughed, trying to wake them. Finally, he threw a heavy pillow at Marcus and said, "Time to get up, guys."

Kasey opened her eyes briefly then closed them again, continuing to lie on Marcus's chest.

Marcus rubbed his eyes and looked down at her.

"*Uh*, Kasey," Marcus said, tapping her on the shoulder.

"What?" she answered sleepily.

"*Uh*, what are you doing, Kasey?" Marcus gently asked.

When she realized she was trespassing, she apologized, rolled over, put her head on her own pillow and quickly fell asleep again.

Marcus sat up on the edge of his bed and looked at John.

They both chuckled.

"*Ah*, man, she probably just had a rough night on that floor," John said relievedly.

Kasey apologized again when she awoke a few minutes later. They lightheartedly teased her. She claimed she didn't remember getting up off the floor. They backed off when they saw how embarrassed she was. To comfort her, John explained that while he and Bo were on the mend after the Carnegie Village incident, they watched movies on his king-sized bed together and reassured her that it wasn't that big of a deal. Marcus raised an eyebrow. Kasey smiled, visibly touched that John was trying to make her feel better.

∿∿

Their bus home didn't leave from Chinatown until 8 that night. Vandacheler, who lived in New York once upon a time, planned a short itinerary. He would take them to various locations, offering a cursory tour of the city. For breakfast, they visited a crowded restaurant at Chelsea Market that served authentic crêpes. Their waiter approached and said, "bonjour." Vandacheler, speaking in French, asked for a coffee and told the waiter that he intended to tip exorbitantly if they received preferential treatment. Kasey surprised Vandacheler by telling him, *in French*, that his pronunciations were perfect, and suggested that they all take a trip to Paris someday. Vandacheler agreed and told her, *in French*, that he left his heart in Saintes-Maries-de-la-Mer. John blinked in amazement, listening to Vandacheler and Kasey carrying on a conversation in French. When Marcus asked Kasey how many languages she spoke fluently, she hung her head and ashamedly answered, "Only four; English, Korean, French and Spanish." Adding, "French is my favorite language."

Marcus told Kasey, *in Spanish*, that he only spoke three languages fluently; English, Spanish and Portuguese. When Kasey asked John how many languages he spoke fluently, he quickly left the table, claiming to have stomach pains. When he finally returned to the table, he steadfastly kept the conversation away from foreign languages. After breakfast, they ordered Jacques Torres hot chocolates and set out to explore Manhattan.

Kasey and Vandacheler walked side by side, talking about the early NYC punk scene, theater, antiques and vintage clothing. John and Marcus followed behind them, talking about gangster movies and the Mafia. John, who rarely left small-town Missouri growing up, spoke fondly of the city, despite what his father would've thought. John's father had warned him long ago to never step foot in New York. According to his father, it was "the city of lost souls". John, unmoved by his father's warnings, took delight in the energetic atmosphere. The streets were bustling. People from all over the world converged, confirming to him New York's reputation as a vibrant, culturally rich metropolis. John wanted to learn as much as he could. Vandacheler jokingly informed the students that the way to tell a tourist from a native was that "only a tourist apologizes when they carelessly bump into you".

They roamed, unhindered by the sharp winter cold, en route to a world-famous pizza joint where Vandacheler had planned their lunch. John was particularly impressed with Lombardi's in Nolita. He thought of Bo and how they used to routinely share pizzas when they lived in the dorm.

They carried on after lunch. John started to walk ahead of the group because Kasey wanted to stop at every single shop along Broadway. Kasey objected to John's impatient behavior, citing that the group waited amiably while he watched a brass band performing vivacious jazz music in the subway for over twenty minutes. John vocally wished she would have stayed home. In retaliation, she wished the same about him, but quickly apologized.

The cold sun sank behind the skyscrapers. On their way to Union Square Park, an old woman wearing sunglasses and a tattered jacket pointed at John from a distance. As he drew closer, the old woman became agitated.

She pointed with her trembling finger and warned, "It's coming for you!"

John investigated his surroundings. The streets were crowded, but she was unmistakably pointing at him. Marcus caught up with him, noticing that he had stopped on the sidewalk, seemingly befuddled. The old woman shook her head rapidly. She continued to point as she issued the prophecy, "Great evil will come for you."

John and Marcus looked at each other with furrowed brows.

"Let's just cross the street," Marcus chuckled.

"Hang on," John said, intrigued by the old woman.

As John approached her, she became frantic and horrified, raising her arms in front of her face defensively. "It's coming. It's coming. It's coming."

"What the fuck are you talking about, lady?" John demanded.

"Dude! Let's just go," Marcus said, grabbing his arm.

"What's coming?" John asked, pulling away from Marcus.

The old woman gurgled and moaned, trembling in terror.

"You better fucking answer me!" John growled, grabbing her shoulders, shaking her.

"John, man, what the fuck are you doing!" Marcus shouted, pulling him away.

The old woman fell to the ground. She stopped trembling and started to laugh diabolically. Her sunglasses fell from her face during the rattle. She was blind.

"Johnathan!" Vandacheler scolded, racing to the scene. He grabbed John by the back of his jacket and pushed him away from the old woman.

Marcus tried to listen to what Vandacheler was saying to John but could only discern one sentence: "You can't do that, John."

Kasey caught up. She picked up the old woman's sunglasses and apologized to her on John's behalf. The old woman started to sob. Kasey put her arm around her, trying to console her.

"It's coming," the old woman softly wept. "It's coming."

Marcus took Kasey by the hand. "I'm sorry, but we gotta get out of here, Kasey."

～～

John didn't say much during the last hour or so of the trip. They boarded an express bus from Chinatown en route to Washington D.C. From there, Vandacheler would drive them back to their homes.

During the quiet bus ride, John finally spoke, "I'm really sorry for ruining the trip, guys. I don't know what got into me."

Vandacheler moved one seat closer to him. "We have to get that under control, my dear Johnathan. There are rules."

"I know, I'm sorry," John said, hanging his head.

"You made an old lady cry, John," Kasey snarled.

"I know, I'm working on it. I'm really sorry," John sobbed.

"We'll work on it," Vandacheler promised, patting him on the shoulder. "We'll work on it."

"I shouldn't have let that old woman get to me," John stated. "She just freaked me out."

Kasey scoffed. "*Oh*, and the dead bird didn't?"

"That's different, Kasey," John insisted.

She rolled her eyes.

"There are," Vandacheler explained, "many eccentric people in New York. Some with less grounding in the real world than others. I'm sure that poor old woman stands there and says that to people all day long."

"Yeah," John agreed, "she was just a lunatic. I should've ignored her."

"Not the preferred nomenclature, but essentially yes," Vandacheler said.

"Damn," Marcus interrupted, displaying his phone, "our Facebook likes are going through the roof!"

Quickly dismissing his remorse for the old woman, John looked at Marcus's phone, saying, "Holy shit, that's awesome. We'll be at two million likes before you know it."

Marcus nodded enthusiastically.

Kasey looked out the bus window, shaking her head.

CHAPTER 14

JACKPOT!

The students readjusted their focus on the witch hoax project. They still needed to figure out how they would convince their readers that Congresswoman Anastasia Carval was a witch. In the meantime, they continued to publish news articles and opinion pieces to keep *The Daily Veranda* vibrant and their audience engaged.

Among a plethora of news articles, John posted his third and fourth primer articles to their rapidly growing Facebook page. The third primer article, "The Rise of Witchcraft in America", highlighted various criminal court cases where witchcraft was allegedly involved. The article performed well. The commentary revealed that their audience was, at least, interested in the topic. It was, however, a mixed reception. Many of the commenters ridiculed the "frivolous charges" and the "overreach of government".

3,287,928 *likes.*

The fourth primer article performed especially well. The article, "Did Hitler and the Nazis Practice Witchcraft?", covered history, theories and allegations revolving around Nazi occultism and the Third Reich. John planned to add two more primer articles to ensure the successful reception of the hoax. Overall, the project was going well, but they were three weeks behind their deadline. John, reminding the team that they had until May 22nd, expressed a newfound level of patience and bumped the deadline back until the end of the month. John wanted to be extra careful in how they wrote the Anastasia Carval defamation article. Everything was riding on that final article.

~~

The vernal equinox, March 20th, 2021. Professor Diageo loudly announced himself as he burst into Francesca Hall, where Don Vandacheler and the five students had gathered.

"Jackpot!" Professor Diageo exclaimed.

"What did you figure out?" John asked inquisitively.

Professor Diageo slammed a piece of paper down on the coffee table in front of the Victorian couch. "I present to you—the answers to your prayers. One of Congresswoman Anastasia Carval's leaked emails, courtesy of KakumeiLeaks."

"What the heck is KakumeiLeaks?" Kasey asked.

"They're a group of anonymous hackers and hacktivists that leak politicians' email correspondences to challenge or uproot their power," Diageo quickly explained.

"Is it legal to have this?" Kasey inquired.

"Absolutely. It's not always legal for them to do what they do, but once it's leaked, it's public domain."

"What does the email say?" John asked impatiently.

The students and Vandacheler gathered around the piece of paper Diageo had placed on the coffee table. It read:

Chocolate Pie, Banana Daiquiri, Banana Daiquiri, Banana Daiquiri.

I sell my soul to the devil tomorrow.

~Anastasia C.

"That's it?" Kasey asked.

"How the hell is this supposed to help us?" Marcus questioned.

John picked up the paper and started to nod. "Yes, yes, this is big!"

Professor Diageo rubbed his hands together in greedy anticipation. "I would forget about the fifth and sixth primer articles, John. You need to act fast on this one, they just leaked this."

"Could you guys please explain this to me?" Marcus requested.

"Marcus, she says 'I sell my soul to the devil tomorrow.' Witches, in exchange for power, were said to have made pacts with the devil," John explained.

"I know *that*," Marcus said, "but..."

"What's all this chocolate pie, banana daiquiri stuff?" Kasey asked, finishing his question.

Marcus sighed. "Thank you."

"It could mean anything to a conspiracy theorist," Zach informed. "They'll *make* it mean something. It could be a spell, or—you know—like code or something."

"Well, obviously she's not *really* a witch, so what the heck is she talking about?" Kasey demanded.

"Her email is a reply," Professor Diageo explained, "to one of her colleagues. In the previous email he asks her what she and her friends had for dessert at the restaurant and when she would announce her sponsorship for a bi-partisan bill that she was reluctant to compromise on."

"*Oh*, okay, I get it," Kasey said. "But aren't people going to be able to see the previous email?"

"We're only showing this one," John declared. "By the time they dig up the rest of the correspondence, Anastasia Carval will already be a witch."

∿∿

Professor Diageo wished John "Godspeed" on writing the article and bid the group farewell. He was leaving for a weeklong trip to the Caribbean with his wife to beat the chill of early spring. Marcus, Kasey, Zach and Arjun gathered around John as he wrote the defamation article on one of the computers in the print room of Francesca Hall. Vandacheler left to take care of something he dubbed urgent but promised to return before they posted the article. After much debate, John and the team finished the article under the nom de plume, Lester Thompson.

"U.S. Representative Anastasia Carval a Witch?"

By: Lester Thompson

March 20ᵗʰ, 2021

U.S. Representative Anastasia Carval is no stranger to controversy. In late 2020, she endorsed an outrageous, unsustainable federal minimum wage hike, drawing criticism from even her most liberal compatriots. Just last month, she pushed a 93 trillion-dollar deficit spending bill for a ten-year plan to tackle climate change and economic inequality; one that would bankrupt the nation.

Congresswoman Anastasia Carval's inflammatory rhetoric reverberates from her district and is felt throughout the nation. She offers little of value to the public. Carval has garnered critique for her unfamiliarity with sound economic policy and her overall political inexperience, prompting many Americans to ask, "How did Anastasia Carval earn a position as an elected U.S. representative?"

Investigations and data from non-partisan sources show that her rise in popularity was the result of an increasing shift in political dynamics and the demand for district representation outside of the status quo. As much of the nation drifts with the progressive tide, it's not difficult to fathom the accuracy of the analysis. Could there be, however, more sinister elements involved?

An email leaked via KakumeiLeaks suggests a possible new insight. Surely, it's next to unimaginable that Congresswoman Anastasia Carval has been, at any level, involved in the practice of witchcraft, but could "sell[ing] my soul to the devil" be wordplay to represent darker dealings? Perhaps with questionable foreign affiliates or her recently uncovered slush fund? Or could it be within the realm of plausibility that she has indeed sold her soul to the devil? Is Anastasia Carval a witch? We highly doubt such a wild fantasy, but, nevertheless, our minds must always be open to any possibility as we rigorously scrutinize our elected representatives.

"It's ready!" John exclaimed. "All we have to do now is publish it to the website, then post it on our Facebook page and wait."

"This is it!" Marcus trumpeted. "This is fucking it! Here we go, baby!"

"Is anyone else about to faint?" Arjun asked. "Because I'm about to faint."

"I might," Zach joked.

"Aren't we going to wait for Don?" Kasey softly asked.

"His name isn't Don, Kasey, it's fucking *Vandacheler*," Marcus declared.

"He'll be here any minute," John promised, proceeding to publish the article on their website for proofreading. "As soon as he gets here, we'll post the article to Facebook and watch the fireworks."

～〜

The students gazed upon the entryway as they heard one of the grand cherry wood double doors open. There was no way to sneak into Francesca Hall; the old doors creaked whenever they were opened.

"Don!" Kasey shouted as Vandacheler walked through the door.

"You mean," Marcus said softly, then shouted, "Vandacheler!"

Vandacheler stopped to bow deeply, then proceeded toward the print room.

"We're ready to post it," John informed.

"Jolly good," Vandacheler said. "The big moment has arrived. How's the article look?"

Zach nodded, brandishing an "okay" hand gesture.

"I trust you all did well," Vandacheler conferred.

"Post that shit, John," Marcus instructed.

Everyone gathered behind John's computer.

John hesitated, stating, "My hands are actually sweating."

"Just click the damn button!" Marcus commanded.

John peered at the computer screen and sighed, standing from his chair. "I can't do it."

"What!" Marcus shouted.

"Just give me a minute," John requested. "This is a big fucking deal."

"Fuck that," Marcus said, sitting in his chair, highlighting the "share now" button with the computer mouse, "I'll post the damn thing."

"Go ahead," John urged.

Click.

CHAPTER 15

THE HUMBLE GODFATHER

Vandacheler received a call at 7:30 the next morning. Dean of Students, Robert Rafalski, an Avalonti high councilman, summoned him urgently to Francesca Hall, refusing to give him any details over the phone. Vandacheler left his estate and drove feverishly to the university. He arrived at 8. Vandacheler's legs trembled as he spotted, from a distance, Dean Robert Rafalski, Joseph Brent Smith and Caesar Avalonti walking to the front porch of Francesca Hall.

"It's a pleasure to finally meet you, sir," Vandacheler said, climbing the stone stairs. "And happy 76th birthday, of course," he added, bowing deeply.

Caesar stood on the front porch near the Corinthian columns, wearing an Italian three-piece suit and a matching white Panama hat. Joseph Brent Smith, the chief operating officer of the Avalonti holdings corporation, supplied Vandacheler with an ominous grin. Caesar shook Vandacheler's hand firmly then motioned, with only a slight nod, for Joseph Brent Smith to open one of the doors.

Caesar's last visit to Francesca Hall was many years prior. The three men obediently followed him as he meandered throughout, rediscovering the supreme beauty of the hall. Caressing the surface of a painting hanging on the wall near the Steinway piano, he touched his face, smiling warmly with his eyes closed.

"I remember when my mother painted this," Caesar said with his husky voice. "*Oh*, how I loved that woman."

"It's beautiful, sir," Vandacheler complimented.

Caesar gently slid his fingers across the keys of the Steinway piano. "My old piano," he said, pulling out the bench. He played a portion of Mozart's piano concerto "No. 27" flawlessly.

"Wonderful, sir," Vandacheler praised.

Caesar sat in silence, adoring his old piano.

"Let's have this tuned," Caesar instructed broadly as he stood from the bench, pushing it back under the piano.

Caesar led the men to a rarely visited corner of the hall. Vandacheler would embark upon a journey to a place he'd never been before. Caesar, and only Caesar, possessed the authority to allow lower-ranking members of the society access to the veranda. Demonstrating the stout physique that he maintained throughout his years, Caesar climbed the wrought-iron spiral staircase without assistance.

A chilly breeze visited them on the spacious veranda. The four men took their seats on the ornately crafted metal patio chairs around the table. Joseph Brent Smith looked out over the railing, admiring the exceptional view of the university. Caesar clasped his hands and tapped his thumbs together slowly, peering intently at Vandacheler, who swallowed in nervous anticipation. From a portable leather case, Caesar removed and prepared two finely wrapped Arturo Fuente cigars for him and Dean Rafalski. The other men kindly refused his offer.

"Tell me, Dr. Vandacheler..." Caesar said, lighting a butane torch lighter.

Vandacheler's heart raced violently as Caesar toasted and puffed the cigar.

"...all about this *witch hoax*."

✎

Later that morning, Vandacheler called upon John, Kasey and Marcus to meet him at Francesca Hall. Caesar and Joseph Brent Smith departed to catch a flight back to New York. Dean Rafalski returned to his office briefly before venturing home. Vandacheler bit his thumbnail as he watched the students cheerfully walk through the double doors. Vandacheler directed them to sit in the Victorian furniture near the grand fireplace.

"I'm afraid I have some upsetting news," Vandacheler spoke.

"What happened?" Kasey asked. "Did somebody get hurt?"

"No one was hurt," Vandacheler assured. "It's about the project."

John's eyes widened. "What about the project?"

"I'm so sorry, my dear Johnathan, it's to be terminated," Vandacheler divulged.

John jumped from the couch, nearly tripping as he scurried backwards. "Wh—what? What are you talking about!"

"I met with Dean Rafalski, Joseph Brent Smith and Caesar Avalonti early this morning."

John squinted. "You met with Caesar?"

Vandacheler paused.

Kasey and Marcus stared from the couch, speechless.

"I'm sorry, John," Vandacheler said, "I know how much this project meant to you. I do have some good news in light of the bad, however."

"Why are they terminating my project?" John demanded. "We just posted the final article. It has over three thousand shares already. Why? Why? Why? Everything was going fucking perfectly!"

"John," Vandacheler pleaded, "I understand this is upsetting, but please remember your composure as a gentleman. I will explain."

John took a deep breath and retook his seat. Kasey patted him on the back.

"Do you all remember the Avalonti Sages Dr. Winston Douglas and David Oakman?" Vandacheler asked.

"Yeah," John said, "they were the guys who thought the witch hoax project was 'potentially disastrous' and refused to help us with the primer articles."

"Yes," Vandacheler said. "Well, I'm afraid they were not the only ones who viewed the project as such. They alerted Dean Robert Rafalski of the High Council, who shared in their dismay."

"They ratted us out?" John moaned.

"They were only doing what they believed was best for the society," Vandacheler defended. "Dean Rafalski contacted Joseph Brent Smith in New York, and he, in turn, relayed the details of our project theme to Caesar Avalonti. After careful contemplation, Caesar thought it best to pull the project."

"But why?" John asked.

"Because the plan included the unsolicited use of a public servant," Vandacheler explained.

"More like public serpent," Marcus sneered.

"They didn't want the project to target anyone high profile," Vandacheler added.

"Well, shouldn't they have told us that in the first place?" John questioned.

"That is where you and I agree, my dear Johnathan. The assignment was ill-conceived," Vandacheler said. "Caesar knows this—which is why he is offering you all full memberships with no further initiation rituals."

Marcus and Kasey were alight with blissful surprise.

"So, no crazy debate in front of the society Judges either?" Marcus asked.

"No. You are all now full members of the Avalonti Society," Vandacheler conferred. "Caesar took responsibility for the duplicitous nature of the assignment and has bestowed upon you a grand conciliation prize."

"Sweet!" Marcus cheered. "We're in!" he shouted, hugging Kasey.

"This is so awesome!" Kasey rejoiced, hugging him back.

"Why did it take so long?" John asked Vandacheler, maintaining a stern look on his face.

"I beg your pardon," Vandacheler requested.

Kasey and Marcus quieted.

"It's March 21st," John said. "Dr. Douglas and David Oakman refused to help us back in late January. That's almost two months. Why now? Why did they wait so long to cancel it?"

"I'm afraid I don't have an answer for that," Vandacheler said. "Bureaucracy, most likely."

John scoffed. "I spent nearly every waking minute of the past two months on this project."

"Yes," Vandacheler calmly spoke, "that is why Caesar awarded you all full memberships. He understands that you all put a great deal of hard work into the project. I do sincerely apologize that this outcome does not satisfy your expectations, but this is how it has to be."

"Come on, man," Marcus said to John, "can't you ever just be happy about anything?"

"We put a lot of work into this," John said with a choke in his voice.

"I'm sorry, John," Kasey said, rubbing his back, "but at least we're full members now."

"Yeah," John uttered.

"I know something that will cheer you up," Vandacheler said, pulling three framed, signed certificates from under his satchel. "Visual confirmation."

Marcus and Kasey gleamed with appreciation.

John lifted his eyes from the floor, slowly taking the certificate from Vandacheler's hands.

"John—everything is going to be okay," Vandacheler promised. "You'll be able to put the project behind you and see the road ahead, I assure you."

"I know. Thanks, Van. I appreciate it," John said, looking at his certificate. "This was all that really mattered anyway."

Vandacheler smiled, patting him on the shoulder. "Good lad."

∾

That night, Marcus finally met Bo. Kasey, paying for the Uber, took Marcus, Bo and John to a sleepy college bar to celebrate their official induction. Kasey and Marcus weren't drinking but granted John diplomatic immunity and promised to look after him. A few seniors gathered around a pool table. Classic rock and '80s pop music played from the jukebox at a moderate volume. John and his friends sat around a small circular table in the corner of the bar near an exit. Bo learned the details of the project. He commented that it was "creepy" then ordered John a Long Island iced tea to complement his beer. John continued to drink with minimum self-restraint.

"The hardest thing," John spoke with a slur in his voice, "was watching all those articles we wrote just being deleted in the blink of an eye. That Facebook page we took from zero to over three million likes, gone, just like that." He attempted to snap his fingers. "They killed my—they killed our fucking project. It's fucking heartbreaking, man."

"I'm really sorry, John," Kasey said, patting him on the shoulder.

He smiled at her.

"If it means anything, I'm here for you," Bo added. "I'll always have your back."

"Thanks, Bo, you're my best buddy," John imparted.

"I love you, John," Bo confessed forthrightly. He swallowed nervously, anticipating John's reaction.

"I love you too, man," John reciprocated, leaning over to hug him.

"I love you, John," Bo repeated, hugging him tightly.

"Awe," Kasey gushed.

"You guys aren't gonna kiss, are you?" Marcus joked.

Kasey turned her head sharply. "Would it be a problem for you if they did?"

"I was joking! Damn! Don't go all *social justice warrior* on my ass," Marcus begged.

Bo giggled, returning from their embrace. "You guys are cool, I'm not offended."

"See, Kasey," Marcus said, "he doesn't even care."

"Nope," Bo assured.

Marcus smiled victoriously as he returned to scrolling through his news feed.

"Marcus, it's rude to have your phone out when you're with company," Kasey scorned.

"Kasey, when did you turn into my seventy-year-old grandmother?" Marcus poked.

John laughed boisterously.

"Well, at least we know how to cheer John up," Kasey said, rolling her eyes.

John's hearty laughter subsided as a heavyset, thirty-four-year-old man approached their table from the bar.

"Now that *had* to have been a funny joke," the man said in a snooty high-pitched tone, chuckling, adjusting his glasses.

"Uh, yeah," Marcus said, rubbing the back of his neck, "it was pretty funny."

"Sorry for just walking over here," the man said confidently. "I'm new to the area. I figured I'd just pop on over and say hi to some new people."

John stared vacantly at the table.

"Uh, hi," Kasey said. "How are you?"

"Oh, I'm good, I'm good," the man answered, moving closer to the table.

Bo smiled uneasily.

"She yours?" the man joked, looking at John, pointing at Kasey.

John didn't answer.

"We're all just friends," Kasey said, chuckling nervously.

"*Oh*, okay, okay," he said with a clicking in his throat. "Well, I'm Kevin. It's nice to meet you all."

Kasey smiled politely. "Nice to meet you."

"And, *uh*, what's *your* name, my lovely lady?" Kevin asked, extending his arm.

"I'm Kasey," she answered, shaking his hand.

John gritted his teeth at the sight of the man's arm directly in front of his face.

"Is that Kasey with a K?" Kevin asked, lowering his arm.

"Yep," Kasey answered.

"Kevin and Kasey. I like that. K and K," Kevin chortled. "Well, *uh*, Kasey with a K—beautiful name by the way—what're you drinking?"

"Oh, just water," Kasey answered.

"Oh, okay, okay," Kevin said, nodding. "How about a Cosmopolitan instead?"

"Um," Kasey said, giggling, "I'm not even sure what that is."

Kevin chuckled. "It's a super girly drink—hardly tastes like alcohol at all—you'll love it."

"Um, no thank you, I'm not having any alcohol tonight."

"Oh, okay, okay," Kevin said, nodding. "How about a Mike's Hard Lemonade?"

"No, thank you," she said. "I don't want anything."

"Oh, okay, okay," Kevin said, nodding. "How about a Smirnoff Ice?"

"Um, no thank you," Kasey said, continuing to smile politely.

"Didn't you hear her, asshole?" John said, tapping the table. "She doesn't want anything."

"Oh, okay, okay," Kevin said, ignoring John. "How about just a beer then?" he asked, smiling at Kasey.

"I think you should fuck off," John muttered, grinding his teeth.

Kevin glanced down at John, smirking.

"I appreciate the offer," Kasey pleaded, "but I'm fine—really. I'm only having water."

"Oh, okay, okay. I'm gonna go ahead and get you a beer," Kevin declared. "You're not allowed to just sit there and drink water all night," he joked.

"I said fuck off!" John shouted, slamming his fist on the table.

Bo flinched. Kasey gasped. Marcus froze.

Silence befell the sleepy little bar. The seniors shooting pool inched toward their table, positioning themselves to break up a fight. John breathed heavily, glowering, clenching his fist.

"Alright," Kevin said, holding his hands defensively at his chest. "I'm gone. I'm gone."

The guests quietly observed Kevin returning to the bar to grab his jacket. He threw some money on the coaster then headed for the door. Once he exited the building, the guests refocused their attention onto John.

Bo put his arm around John in a proud exhibition of solidarity.

"Uh-oh," Marcus said, looking up to see one of the bartenders on her way to their table.

"Hey guys," the middle-aged bartender spoke with a Baltimore accent, smiling. "How we all doing tonight?"

The students on the other side of the bar returned to the pool tables.

"I apologize for that, ma'am," Marcus said, speaking with his hands, "the gentleman approached our table and was being inappropriate to her. My friend, John, here, just reacted a little too aggressively, that's all. He's had a little bit too much to drink—but we have him under control. I can assure you that nothing like that will happen again—and, like I said, I apologize for that disturbance."

John sighed, closing his eyes, shaking his head.

"*Yeah*, he was up there hitting on me too," the bartender said, turning to Kasey. "You okay, sweetie?"

"I'm fine," she said, nodding, glancing at John.

"You okay?" the bartender condescendingly asked, patting John on his back. "Can I get you some water?"

"Uh, no," John said, shaking his empty bottle, "just another beer if you don't mind."

The bartender exhaled slowly. "I'm sorry, hon. I can get you some soda or some food," she spoke delicately, "but I can't serve you any more alcohol tonight."

John clenched his jaws.

Marcus glanced away. Bo swallowed hard. Kasey chewed her bottom lip.

The bartender cringed, awaiting his reply.

"I understand," John said, summoning a smile. "I apologize for my outburst. I didn't mean to cause you any trouble," he said, turning to the group. "What do you say, guys? How about a pizza?"

"Cool," Kasey sighed relievedly, "I'll pay."

"Sounds good to me," Bo said, smiling, patting John on the back.

"Oh, okay, okay," Marcus said, impersonating Kevin, "I'll take some pizza."

John chuckled.

The bartender smiled. "We got cheese or pepperoni."

"Cheese," John ordered.

"That okay with y'all?" the bartender asked.

"Yeah, it's fine," John declared.

"Okey-doke," the bartender said, "y'all just holler if you need anything else."

～～

John issued Kasey, Bo and Marcus each one slice of cheese pizza and kept the rest for himself, even though Kasey paid for it. After John devoured the pizza, he made his way to the bar. Kasey watched him talking and flirting with the bartender who had cut him off. Kasey's jaw hit the floor when she saw him returning to their table with a bottle of beer. John winked puckishly at her, saying, "Told ya I'd get a beer."

John and Marcus took turns playing Arkanoid and Pac-Man near the pinball machine. Kasey and Bo were chatting back at the table. As the hour grew late, students flooded the lonely little bar. John returned to the table, retaking his seat next to Kasey. Marcus finished up his last game of Arkanoid and joined them. Before the kitchen closed, he ordered another pizza, announcing that he was still hungry after John's "rapacious bogarting of the earlier pizza". John sat quietly, listening to Kasey and Bo discuss ballroom dancing and the liberation of Hong Kong. Kasey and Bo got along well, hogging the conversation. John drifted in and out of deep thought while Marcus scrolled through his Facebook news feed on his smart phone. John wondered what his brother would have thought of his induction into the Avalonti Society. He wondered what his father would think. He wondered if his mother would be proud.

"*Uh*—guys," Marcus interrupted.

"Marcus, what is it?" John inquired.

Marcus turned his phone around and showed it to the group.

"U.S. Representative Anastasia Carval a Witch," Kasey slowly read from the screen. "Is that ours?"

"Click into the article, Marcus," John instructed.

"Yep. They copied our article," Marcus calmly stated.

"Who are they?" Kasey asked.

"KNWRZ," Marcus answered, "one of the biggest conspiracy theory publications in the world."

"Fucking *aye*," John cried.

"What are we gonna do?" Kasey asked.

"Wh—what's the problem?" Bo inquired.

"Bo, our publication was deleted," John informed. "The authors of that article, *us*, now have no way to retract it. We have no way to explain everything. It's out of our fucking hands now."

"Alright, let's calm down," Marcus suggested. "So, they got our article—big deal. We knew other publications might've rehashed it, right? Yeah, it sucks we can't retract it now, but it doesn't mean anything. I mean, what's the worst that could happen?"

"Yeah, you're probably right," Kasey said, looking at the clock on the wall. "I'm getting ready to head out in a little while. We're all paid up. Did you guys want to catch an Uber with me or hang out for a bit?"

"What's the name of that publication again?" John asked Marcus.

"KNWRZ," he answered.

"Shit, Lucas is here," Bo said, standing from the table. "You guys are heading out, right?"

"Yeah, I'm heading out," John said. "I'm gonna walk home—get some air."

"Alright, John, be safe, man," Bo said, leaning down for a hug. "I'll see you guys around. I'm gonna hang out for a bit. Nice meeting you, Marcus."

"Yep," Marcus said, shaking his hand, "nice meeting ya. Hey, Kasey, I'm gonna walk back with John."

"Okay," Kasey said to Marcus, turning to Bo. "See ya, Bo."

"See ya guys," Bo said, walking toward Lucas on the other side of the bar.

John and Marcus stood, simultaneously grabbing their jackets from the chairs.

"We're in deep shit," John whispered to Marcus.

"Nah," Marcus uttered.

"*Awe*, you guys are leaving me," Kasey said, wearing a deadpan frown.

"We can wait until your Uber gets here," Marcus offered.

"I'm not fucking waiting," John declared, starting for the exit.

"Hold up, John, damn," Marcus grumbled, shaking his head. "I guess I'll see ya, Kasey."

"See ya, Marcus," Kasey said, accepting a hug. "Bye, John. Thanks for standing up for me earlier. I appreciate it."

"What?" John huffed. "I didn't stand up for anybody," he said, opening the door.

Kasey scoffed, rolling her eyes.

Marcus shrugged, following him out. "See ya, Kasey."

~~

Kasey caught an Uber to her neighbor's house. Bo stayed, running into a group of other friends. John and Marcus returned to The Marquis by foot, discussing the KNWRZ ordeal along the way. Tirelessly, John read comments on the KNWRZ Facebook page, studying reactions from their audience. Many commenters, despite being heavily involved in conspiracy theory, were skeptical. Others were sure of the ominous nature of Anastasia Carval's email, even if they didn't believe that it was in reference to witchcraft. After careful analysis, it appeared that no one believed she was really a witch. Detained by important lab work early that week, Vandacheler agreed to examine the situation and offer an assessment on Wednesday.

~~

By Wednesday afternoon, the KNWRZ post had generated over 21,000 shares. Smaller right-wing news publications and blogs were rehashing the article as well, chiefly under the impression that it was political mudslinging. Facebook memes depicting Carval as the Wicked Witch of the West emerged and were shared among politically inclined humor pages. Most of the well-circulated liberal publications rolled their eyes at the article, refusing to comment or offer refutations. It was four days after the launch of their defamation article, and it appeared that John's witch hoax would go down as a stunning failure.

The students gathered with Vandacheler inside of Francesca Hall as he examined the details.

"It appears the Anastasia article has predominately roused humor and satire. I'm not sure I would invest too much worry," Vandacheler suggested.

Kasey smiled and shrugged. "Well, that's a relief."

"Told you not to worry about it, John," Marcus gloated.

"I don't know," John said skeptically, "there were *some* people buying it."

"John, man, I hate to say this," Marcus contended, "but I think, subconsciously, you want that to be true. You were crazy about this experiment, man. You wanted it to work, but it was destined to fail. With all things considered, it's fortunate that nobody is buying your hoax, bro. You should be happy that Caesar pulled the plug on it and gave you that certificate."

Vandacheler and the others surveyed his reaction.

"Yeah, you might be right," John conceded.

Marcus flinched. "Alright then."

John chuckled. "It sure did get a lot of attention though."

Marcus nodded, smiling with a frown. "It sure did."

John and Marcus returned to their apartments after the meeting. John fixed himself a drink and sat on his brown leather couch. He looked at the brandy glass sitting on his coffee table then back at the clock on his wall. "Fifteen more minutes," he said to himself.

Taking a break from laughing at Anastasia Carval memes on Facebook, he rested his eyes and unintentionally fell into a deep sleep. Twenty-eight minutes later, a loud banging arrived at his door.

"Motherfucker!" John shouted, leaping to his feet.

"John! Let me in!" Marcus yelled through the door.

"I'm coming," John said, taking his time.

John opened the door.

Marcus raced to the living room, picked up the remote and turned on John's flat screen television. "I tried to call, it's all over the news," he explained in a panic.

John rubbed his eyes then focused his attention on the breaking news bulletin.

Female newscaster: "Fortunately, police were able to subdue the armed man before he could harm anyone at the U.S. House of Representatives in Washington this afternoon. We're now learning that the man, identified as 68-year-old Herbert Johnson, is a resident of Fairfax, Virginia. His motives are unclear at this time; however, his target appears to have been Congresswoman Anastasia Carval."

John picked up the remote and turned the television off. Retrieving his brandy from the coffee table, he sat on the couch and held the glass to his lips without sipping.

"John? You heard what she said, didn't you?"

"Marcus, you heard Vandacheler. This doesn't have anything to do with us. You know how many people she's pissed off in the last couple of months?"

"I don't know, John, the timing seems to be a little *too* perfect."

"You're imagining it. Like you said earlier—subconsciously, we wanted to believe the hoax could have been something. It's not, dude. Just let it go."

"Shit, Kasey is calling me," Marcus said, looking at his vibrating smart phone.

John shook his head and took a sip of his brandy.

Marcus answered his phone. "Hey, Kasey, what's up?"

John scoffed.

"What channel?" Marcus asked, picking up the remote. "Okay, I'm on it now. Let me call you back in a minute."

John rolled his eyes.

"John," Marcus said, cramming his phone into his pocket, "they have video of the arrest."

They watched the news coverage until they replayed footage of the arrest. John dropped his drink on the floor. While the police tackled him to the ground, the man repeatedly shouted, "She's a witch, damn it! She's a witch!"

∿∿

The students skipped their classes the following day and met Vandacheler at Francesca Hall at eleven in the morning. They all agreed their involvement in the witch hoax could not be ignored. Kasey and Marcus were sitting on the Victorian couch while Vandacheler sat on the arm of a parlor chair. John arrived shortly after. He stood in front of the couch, slightly wobbling, then carefully took a seat next to Kasey.

"John, are you drunk?" Kasey sneered, waving her hand in front of her nose.

John looked at her through his bloodshot eyes. "I'm fine."

Marcus, sitting on the opposite side of Kasey, stretched his neck to get a good look at John. "Looks drunk to me," he said, nodding.

"I'm *not* drunk, you nerds," John declared.

"Never mind," Vandacheler suggested, "we've more important things to worry about, I'm afraid. It appears my assessment was inaccurate. Unfortunately, the seemingly harmless witch hoax has now reached those who would carelessly act upon its preposterous claims."

"We didn't claim anything," John asserted, "we merely asked a question."

"Yes, John, but it seems *that* question has led others to claim, which was our intention in the original social experiment plan, if you recall," Vandacheler reminded. "With the cancellation of our publication, from whence the original article was published, we now lack the ability to explain to the public the purpose of its creation."

"What about the *Avalonti Journal*?" John asked forthrightly.

"John," Vandacheler dissuaded, "Avalonti is a scholarly journal; it retains an elite readership. I shall remind you also that Caesar has ordered the termination of the project. Our plan to offer resolution in this matter must be discreetly orchestrated."

"Will Professor Diageo help us?" Kasey asked.

"He's scheduled to return this Saturday from his trip to Punta Cana," Vandacheler informed. "I would sincerely hope so."

"It's Thursday. Somebody will get seriously hurt if we don't do something sooner than Saturday," John prophesized.

"I suppose there is *one* thing we could do," Vandacheler offered. "We could contact KNWRZ and request a retraction."

"It's a longshot," John said, "but it's worth a try."

CHAPTER 16

THE DOLLHOUSE MAN

KNWRZ's proprietor agreed to discuss a possible retraction and clarification on the following day, provided the meeting was conducted in person and with only one Avalonti representative. John volunteered. KNWRZ was headquartered just outside of Ranson, West Virginia; not terribly far from the university. Marcus agreed to drive John's car and wait while he met with KNWRZ's owner, Philippe Álvarez.

Expecting an office building, John and Marcus grew apprehensive, driving down a long dirt driveway leading to an old, purple Queen Anne-style house with pink shutters and a white porch.

John took a deep breath before opening the car door.

"Be safe in there, John," Marcus cautioned.

"No shit," John said, exiting the vehicle.

John approached the front door. A metal sign with a vectorized image of an AR-15 rifle accompanied a grim warning: *BREAK IN, YOU WON'T BREAK OUT.*

As John raised his fist to knock on the door, a voice from the intercom addressed him: "Don't knock, just come on in."

John turned the handle, but the door wouldn't open. A remote-controlled locking mechanism sounded, and the door creaked ajar. John pushed the door open and scanned the first floor. Dollhouses, framed paintings of Jesus Christ and a myriad of crucifixes riddled Philippe's dilapidated home. Carefully stepping, he walked onto the unfinished hardwood floors.

"Up here," a voice called from the second floor.

John took a step backwards. "*Uh*, my name is John. I'm looking for a Philippe Álvarez. We spoke about a possible retraction of the Carval article."

"Yes, yes, that's me. You can join me up here, please," Philippe hollered.

John sharply inhaled then took a step forward. Ascending the rickety stairs, he noticed an ample assortment of dollhouses situated in various locations on the second floor as well. The faded pale green wallpaper spoke harshly of the home's age.

"In here," Philippe directed.

John proceeded cautiously down the hallway and entered a small office.

Philippe Álvarez was a stout, muscular man, just under six-foot tall. Combed back with gel, his jet-black hair glistened under the Art Nouveau ceiling lamp. A golden crucifix dangled from his thick, tanned neck. Though shaven, he presented a five o'clock shadow by noon. A magnifying glass headset assisted him while he worked on another dollhouse.

"You're probably wondering about all the dollhouses," Philippe calculated. "Please, have a seat, I'll be with you in a moment."

"Thank you," John said, sitting in an old wooden chair by the door.

"My little sister loved dollhouses," Philippe divulged as he continued to work. "We lost her when I was fourteen years old."

"I'm sorry to hear that," John said. "I lost my brother when I was fourteen years old as well."

"It appears we are *kindred spirits* then, John," Philippe joked. "Perhaps God has brought us together for a reason."

John forced a smile. "They say he works in mysterious ways, right?"

"A drunk driver killed her," Philippe announced suddenly, startling John, "seven in the morning, walking to school."

"That's terrible," John stated, glancing at a cabinet full of rifles in the corner.

Philippe removed his headset and placed a tiny paintbrush into a glass of water. "The last words we spoke to each other were 'I hate you', after I destroyed her dollhouse. I can't even remember why I destroyed it."

John nervously rubbed his hands together. "*Uh*—I'm sorry."

Philippe smiled at John. "We should always remember to say *I love you* to those we care about the most. I'm 56 years old, John. One day, I shall tell her again." Philippe unscrewed the lid from a canteen of water and took a sip. "Now, you're here about this Carval article, correct?"

"That's correct," John answered.

"Do you have any proof that you're Lester Thompson? Any proof at all that you're the author of the article?"

"Unfortunately, our publication was terminated. All proof has been deleted. It's a long story. I can't expect you to believe me, sir, but my conscience leads me to try to fix this before any innocent people get hurt. It's gotten out of control."

"You're with the Avalonti Society, correct?"

"That's correct."

"You know of Francesca Cappellini then?"

John nodded. "I do. Francesca Avalonti."

"Right—the beloved Bloomsbury beatnik wife of Phineas Avalonti. Do you know that she was heiress to an enormous fortune before she disavowed her parents?"

John nodded. "Yes. That was a long time ago. She's been dead for a while."

"You understand that she disavowed them because they were Mussolini supporters who subsequently pledged an allegiance to Adolf Hitler?"

John swallowed. "I've read a little bit about that, yes."

"You're aware, then," Philippe spoke ominously, "that some believe she never actually disavowed them?"

John raised an eyebrow. "*That* I've never heard."

"Do you ever wonder where such extravagant wealth comes from? Wealth that the Avalonti family possess? Do you ever wonder why they're so committed to establishing a presence in academia?"

"They're investors," John defended. "The family tradition can be traced back to 1606, when James I issued a royal charter seeking investors for the joint stock Virginia Company. Avalonti has a ton of professors and philanthropists in their family tree. They're noble people who care about education."

"Would you like to see declassified files from the FBI and the CIA on Francesca Cappellini? Sorry, Francesca *Avalonti*."

"Sir, with all due respect, I don't see how this relates to the Carval article."

"Everything relates to everything."

John shook his head, sighing.

"Are you a religious man, John?"

"I'm an atheist, sir."

"There's no such thing as an atheist—we all believe in something. Was your brother an atheist also?"

John jumped from the chair, nearly knocking it over. "Thank you for your time."

Quickly leaving Philippe's office, John descended the rickety staircase and proceeded to the exit, stopping for but a moment to inspect the dollhouses on the first level.

He raced to the car.

"Shit, John, you scared the fuck out of me!" Marcus bellowed as he opened the car door.

"Drive," John commanded, slamming the door behind him.

Marcus put away his phone and started the engine. "What's going on? What did he say?"

"He's dicking us around. The guy's a fucking lunatic."

~~~

Vandacheler, Kasey and Arjun were waiting for their return at Francesca Hall. Zach, who had completely lost interest in the project before it was ever cancelled, was not in attendance.

"What did they say?" Arjun asked as John and Marcus walked through the doors.

"He's not going to help us," John informed. "It's not a publication team like we thought. It's just one guy, and he's a freaking maniac. *He builds dollhouses.* He has dozens of them scattered all over his shithole house. His house looks like a fucking dollhouse too—it's crazy. And the dude is paranoid as fuck. There was a glass cabinet in his office with a shitload of assault rifles. He has security cameras and shit everywhere. If I didn't leave when I did, I'm sure I'd be buried in his backyard by now."

"Sorry, John, important phone call," Vandacheler said, proceeding to the middle of the grand foyer near the antique floor globe.

"Yuck, I hate guns." Kasey scowled. "I wish they would ban them already."

"Yeah, except we have this thing called *The Constitution*," Marcus protested. "What are you gonna do when someone breaks into your house, Kasey?"

"Call the police," she answered.

"*Oh*, yeah, and what are *they* gonna show up with? Squirt guns?"

"Sorry, Marcus, I'm anti-gun," Kasey imparted. "You're never going to change my mind on that."

"If they ban guns, how is the government going to confiscate them all?" Marcus asked, speaking with his hands. "You think people are just going to give them up willingly?"

"I don't care how they get them," she stated.

"So, then you're not *anti-gun*," Marcus claimed, "you are *pro-gun*. You just want the government to have them all. You want to disarm the people and give the government autocratic control. That's called centralized gun ownership. You know who else shared your belief, Kasey? Mao, Stalin and Hitler!"

She smirked. "So, you think we should be allowed to have tanks and bombs too, huh?"

Marcus nodded. "You're God damn right."

She scoffed. "Sounds like you and the *Dollhouse Man* would get along just fine."

"Guys," John interfered, "come on with this shit, we have to figure out what we're going to do about the witch hoax."

Marcus shook his head. "You go ahead and be unarmed, Kasey. I'll send the burglars over to your house."

"Marcus, come on," John begged.

"Damn liberals," Marcus whispered.

The tapping of Vandacheler's dress shoes echoed as he returned from the middle of the grand foyer.

John's phone buzzed in his pocket. He ignored it.

"I'm afraid I've just received a bit of disturbing news," Vandacheler imparted.

"What happened?" Kasey asked.

"Professor Diageo and his wife were kidnapped from the resort."

"What!" John exclaimed. "Are you fucking kidding me!"

"Is he okay? What's going to happen?" Kasey whimpered.

"That was Dean Robert Rafalski on the line," Vandacheler informed. "They don't have much information at this time, but it appears to be for ransom."

"This could be the hoax at work," Arjun conjectured.

"What did you just say?" John asked, peering at him.

"We've sent negative energy out into the universe," Arjun explained. "Everything is connected in ways we are unable to comprehend."

"Professor Diageo was kidnapped because we sent negative *fucking* energy out into the universe?" John exploded. "I can't believe I'm hearing this shit! I thought this society was supposed to be filled with enlightened, scientific freethinkers!"

"Freethinking is the ability to challenge your own perceptions and assumptions, John," Arjun informed.

"Well, I'm challenging *your* assumption!" John shouted, pointing in his face. "Don't you *dare* try to pin Diageo's kidnapping on me, motherfucker!"

"Johnathan!" Vandacheler scolded. "What will it take for you to learn proper etiquette?"

John quieted, hanging his head. "I'm sorry, Van."

"He'll never learn," Kasey said under her breath.

John pulled out the vibrating phone from his pocket. "Why the fuck is Liam calling me again?" he said, glaring at the screen.

"Listen," Vandacheler spoke diplomatically, "we're all under stress. We feel responsible for the recent event in Washington as a result of our involvement in the hoax's creation, and we fear the worst has yet to come. As esteemed members of the Avalonti Society, we must conduct ourselves with composure while we calculate a plan to aid in the resolution of this matter. As discreet options appear exhausted, I shall make the recommendation to our group to draft a case to the High Council."

"What does that entail?" Kasey asked.

"Caesar must be made aware of the latest outcomes, if he hasn't been already," Vandacheler answered. "I will propose to the council that we confess our involvement to the public, offering an explanation and sincere apology. Avalonti clout will afford us access to the media. We must come clean."

John's head fell into his hands. "This was such a terrible idea from the start. What the hell was I thinking with this stupid witch hoax shit?"

"This isn't your fault, John," Kasey insisted.

"Yeah, it is," John argued.

"No, it's not," she said.

"Kasey, you're an idiot, shut up."

"Don't talk to me like that, John."

"Whatever."

"John, *please*," Vandacheler begged. "The entire assignment was flawed from the beginning. Caesar is very experimental. He took responsibility the day we spoke on the veranda, remember? The Avalonti Society has blundered, but we've been scrupulous for many decades. This will be but a scratch. I assure you; everything will be okay and back to normal soon. With the group's consent, I will draft a case to the High Council."

"I approve," Marcus said.

"Second," Arjun added.

"I consent," Kasey affirmed.

John's phone vibrated in his pocket. "Yeah, I guess, count me in. I'm gonna take this," he said, looking at his phone. "This is the third time Liam has called me. I'll be right back."

John answered the phone as he walked to the middle of the grand foyer. "Liam? What's going on?"

"John, hey man, are you sitting down?"

John looked around. "Uh, yeah, I'm sitting."

"I don't know how to tell you this."

"What's wrong?" John begged.

"He was supposed to be at a swim meet this morning."

"Who?"

Liam sniffled. "Bo. They found him in his dorm room, John. He overdosed."

"Overdosed? Is he...?"

"He's dead, John."

John dropped his phone and collapsed to a knee.

"John!" Kasey shouted from across the room.

The group rushed over to him.

"What's happened, John?" Kasey cried, kneeling beside him.

John grabbed his phone and forced himself to stand. "I gotta go."

"What's wrong?" Marcus demanded.

John, becoming disoriented, spoke frantically, "I gotta go. I gotta go, I gotta go, I gotta go."

Marcus grabbed John by the arm. "John! Talk to me! What happened?"

He pulled away from Marcus and swiftly exited the hall. The group followed him to the doors. Once he made it to the grass, he ran full force across the quad to the other side of the university.

"John!" Kasey called out, stepping onto the porch.

"Stay here," Vandacheler said, gently preventing her from running after him.

The group watched as John disappeared among a crowd on the other side of the quad.

They all took a deep breath.

"Who is Liam?" Marcus asked, breaking the silence.

"Liam Prescott," Kasey replied.

"I think I've heard of him. Swim team dude?" Marcus guessed.

"Yeah, he's one of John's *jock* friends," Kasey answered.

"You say jock like it's a bad thing," Marcus scorned. "I used to play ball. But yeah, *uh*—does anyone have his number? We can find out what happened."

"No," Vandacheler answered.

"Sorry, I do not know him," Arjun said.

"Actually—I do," Kasey said. "I ran into him in the hallway a while ago. John was at his house that night he got attacked. He gave me his number—I think just for emergencies or something. I don't know. He was kind of a jerk. I was never going to call him."

Marcus squinted accusingly.

"I wasn't," she declared.

Marcus smirked.

"I wasn't," she repeated.

Marcus chuckled. "Just call him."

Kasey called Liam, requesting information. After receiving it, she took to sulking face down on the Victorian couch near the grand fireplace. On top of being fond of Bo, she knew how close he and John were. Marcus and Arjun consoled her while Vandacheler prepared a written request to the Avalonti High Council.

∽∾

Avalonti high councilman Dean Robert Rafalski agreed to meet with Vandacheler later that day to discuss the dilemma. Upon arriving, Rafalski's secretary showed Vandacheler to his empty office. Vandacheler stood, practicing what he would say.

Dean Rafalski was a sixty-three-year-old Polish American who was thin everywhere except for his mid-section, which was disproportionately larger than the rest of him. He was shamelessly balding and wore thick glasses that he constantly adjusted. A conservative, short-tempered, no-nonsense war veteran with a wall full of medals, diplomas and certificates, Rafalski was arguably the most intimidating man on campus.

"Sit down, Vandacheler," Dean Rafalski ordered as he entered, closing the office door behind him.

"Thank you for speaking with me, sir," Vandacheler said, sitting in a leather chair.

Rafalski took a seat behind his desk. "Help me understand something, Vandacheler. Were you or were you not given careful instruction to terminate this witch hoax nonsense?"

"*Uh*—sir..."

"Listen to me, Vandacheler. I'm a busy man. You can appreciate that, can't you?"

"Of course."

Rafalski adjusted his tie with mild irritation. "Look, Caesar screwed up with the social experiment. We know this. He knows this. Don't you think he demonstrated *fine character* to come all the way here from New York to address this himself?"

"Yes, sir, but there's been a development."

"I don't want to hear about this nutjob in Washington, okay?" Rafalski grumbled. "We can't be held responsible for that. We don't know where this guy got his ideas. And even if he did get the idea from your kids' article—so what? It's not like he killed her. It's time to move on, Vandacheler."

Vandacheler pleaded, "But the students."

"Look, Vandacheler—Caesar felt bad putting them through that. He's a good man, that's why he came all the way here to deliver them *framed* certificates. The kids got their certificates, just move on from this."

"John will not be pleased to hear this, sir," Vandacheler cautioned.

"*John*, like *all* of our members here," Rafalski stated firmly, "would be wise to follow the rules and obey the orders of their superiors. This bullshit stops now, okay? I don't want to hear another God damn word about this witch hoax nonsense. Can I count on you?"

"Yes, sir," Vandacheler said, looking at the floor.

Rafalski calmed and changed his tone, saying, "Alright. I'll give you a call if we hear anything about Professor Diageo."

"Thank you, sir," Vandacheler said, standing from the leather chair.

CHAPTER 17

AMAZING GRACE

An unseasonably warm and sunny early spring morning welcomed a diverse gathering at a cemetery outside of Bethesda, Maryland. Bo's family were Catholic and had to expedite arrangements. The church would not perform Requiem Mass between Holy Thursday and Easter Sunday. The Avalonti Society provided limousine service to the funeral for their attending members. Kasey stood to John's left, Vandacheler and Marcus to his right. John surveyed the guests in attendance. Liam, Lucas, Pierre and the rest of the swim team stood on the opposite side of the grave. Bo's father clutched his wife. John watched her periodically attempt to escape. Remembering the curried fish and sticky rice she had sent back to the university for him, he was verklempt when he imagined her smiling face sitting around a Thanksgiving table with her son and her loving family.

John peeked sorrowfully at the casket above the empty grave. During the Prayer Vigil, he requested that Bo be buried with the pocket watch he had gifted him. The watch was in there, nestled between Bo and the soft interior lining. After reciting the Lord's Prayer, the priest requested the bereaved to join him in singing "Amazing Grace".

As friends and family commenced, John's body tensed up. Digging his fingernails into the side of his leg with his right hand, he attempted to prevent an emotional exhibition. Out of respect for Bo's family, he struggled to sing. He closed his eyes. Kasey inhaled sharply and slowly took his left hand. He intensely squeezed. The wealth of guests continued to sing as the clouds stole away the sun. John opened his eyes and looked around at the crowd. He envisioned them cheering thunderously as Bo walked across a graduation stage, hoisting his college diploma proudly in the air; a moment of rare jubilation that would never be.

John wouldn't cry at his grandfather's funeral. He wouldn't cry at his brother's funeral. Despite all his effort, all his force, he broke down. Kasey threw her arms around him, hugging him securely. With all her strength she lifted John's crushing weight as he buried his face into her shoulder and wept uncontrollably. Vandacheler assisted her. Marcus followed his lead.

"I'm sorry, guys," John choked out, angrily wiping tears away.

"John, it's okay," Kasey said, rubbing his back.

"It's not okay," John stated, shrugging off the assistance.

Vandacheler stubbornly put his arm around him. "It's okay, Johnathan. Trust me."

As the committal ceremony arrived at its end, John noticed a strange old woman wearing dignified black funeral dress, standing directly opposite the grave. Their eyes locked. John sniffed loudly and scanned the audience, intentionally breaking his gaze. Bo's mother was in shambles. The swim team was consoling Pierre. The elderly priest diplomatically hid his remorse over the tragic loss of another young life. John curiously returned to find the old woman's scrutiny undisturbed. Their eyes locked again. She didn't blink. Forcing his glare from the old woman, John looked at the casket once more; Bo's new home for the ages. John said *goodbye buddy* in his head. He glanced over at the old woman once more. She was talking to somebody, offering him no further attention.

"Don't be paranoid," John muttered to himself.

"What's that, John?" Vandacheler asked.

"Nothing," John assured. "You guys ready to get out of here?"

∽∾

While other students enjoyed their spring break, lounging on Miami beaches or sipping cocktails poolside with their friends at Mexican resorts, John took to seclusion in his lonely apartment. There was no word yet on Professor Diageo's status. The last piece of information they received confirmed that he was being held for ransom. Powerless to help Diageo, John decided to focus his attention on the witch hoax. He sat at his computer listening to '50s music and trapped himself in debate. Explicit command from the Avalonti High Council prohibited his further involvement in the ordeal, prompting him to argue online from phony Facebook accounts. There was a growing number of people subsumed in the hoax after the failed assassination attempt. John reluctantly contacted Philippe Álvarez, begging him to publish a retraction and explain to his KNWRZ readers what Anastasia Carval was really talking about when she facetiously claimed to be selling her soul to the devil. John believed if KNWRZ published an explanation, the hoax would be derailed significantly, and threats of violence would thus be quelled.

John left a half glass of scotch on his kitchen counter and decided to take a drive. Waiting for Philippe Álvarez to return his emails, he contemplated how, if it were possible at all, he would covertly destroy the witch hoax.

~~

John lit a cigarette, took a drag, then quickly put it out. He poured a glass of wine, adjusted his desk chair and delved into researching the hoax he had created. ZzzChan was an anonymous online message board with little, sometimes zero, moderation. The site garnered critique for its controversial content. There, he made a discovery: AradiaGate. Referencing Charles Godfrey Leland's 1899 book, *Aradia, or the Gospel of Witches*, AradiaGate was the name given to the conspiracy theory involving U.S. Representative Anastasia Carval and several others in Washington D.C. accused of being witches. It was also named DaiquiriGate, referencing Anastasia's seemingly bizarre email, by rival factions. In time, it would be ubiquitously known as AradiaGate.

John explored the bottomless depths of the conspiracy theory. He searched everything related to AradiaGate or DaiquiriGate. Most of the publications that covered AradiaGate were amateur, tabloid-grade blogs with limited readership, but there *were* influential talents among them. Inspired by the Hallstatt Analytica ads, a team of conspiracy theorists composed and uploaded a new series of propaganda videos to YouTube and Facebook. Utilizing human image synthesis video technology, they deployed "deepfakes" that exhibited Anastasia Carval confessing to crimes and rituals she had never committed or engaged in. Virtually indistinguishable from reality, the videos were pulled from social media platforms by the administrators. In the unmoderated underbelly of the internet, however, the videos survived, fueling the conspiracy theory.

Along with researching AradiaGate, John decided to see what kind of dirt he could dig up on Philippe Álvarez. He made a shocking discovery: Álvarez was an ex-convict. Shortly after graduating from college, Álvarez tracked down the man who killed his sister. Enraged by the lenient sentence the man had received, he followed him to a shopping mall and beat him to death in the parking lot with his bare hands. He served a twenty-five-year sentence and had only been a free man for the past six years of his life. Digging deeper, John found recent court documents showing that Philippe Álvarez petitioned the State of West Virginia for restoration of his right to purchase and possess firearms. He was denied. The cache of firearms in Philippe's home were illegally acquired and unlawfully kept. Other than that, he could find nothing on Philippe Álvarez, not even a parking ticket.

The mainstream media were no longer covering the story of Herbert Johnson and his failed attempt to assassinate Anastasia Carval. Carval herself refused to comment any further after insisting the entirety of the ordeal was "madness". The only independent media source that retained a substantial readership still covering the story was KNWRZ. KNWRZ, John had learned, was a website project created and maintained solely by Philippe Álvarez. Surviving from revenues he earned from advertisements on his website, he did not have a traditional full-time job. The poor condition of his house might've suggested to an onlooker that he was struggling financially. However, according to website analytics, the monthly traffic to KNWRZ would have generated advertising revenues above two million dollars annually; impressive for a publication under six years old. What Álvarez was doing with the money was unknown to the public.

The popularity of the KNWRZ publication revolved around two key components: its willingness to advocate outrageous conspiracy theories and its overall anti-government sentiment. Solidifying his readership was the occasional confirmation of one of his conspiracy theories; sourcing information from leaked classified documents or showing a more reputable media publication covering the story *after* he published his articles. Many KNWRZ subscribers were drawn solely to Álvarez's frequent exploration of UFO cover-ups, but most of his readers were open to *all* of his claims. Some of his followers took his words as gospel, never displaying the audacity to question him. Gareth Zimone, Editor-in-Chief of the socialist publication *Jacopo-Che*, dubbed KNWRZ's followers as "lemmings".

~~◈~~

When Kasey called on Wednesday, April 7th, John's living room was a disaster. Beer bottles crammed full of cigarette butts sat by the computer, pizza boxes full of crusts piled up on the couch and a blanket of ash covered his desk, the floor, the keyboard and the tuxedo pants that he wore to Bo's funeral several days earlier. Before he answered his phone, he briefly and absentmindedly fixed his hair in the dining room mirror.

John answered the phone. "Hello?"

"Hey, John!"

John smiled gaudily, slightly wobbling in his chair. "Hey, Kasey, it's *really* good to hear from you."

"*Uh*—you too, John. Listen, we just got some great news. Professor Diageo is being released!"

"Oh my God, that's awesome," John slurred.

"Yeah, the society paid his ransom. He'll be home in a day or two. Anyway, I'll let you go, I think Don is about to call you. I just wanted to be the first to tell you."

John spoke with one eye half-closed, "Hey, Kasey—I, I just want to thank you again for coming to the funeral. It means a lot to me that you guys came."

"No problem, John, that's what friends are for. He was a good guy. I'm very sorry for your loss. I'll see you Saturday for the event and we can talk about it then if you want."

"Okay. Thanks so much, Kasey. I really do appreciate it. I'll—I'll see you at the event."

"I'll see ya then. Oh, and, *uh*, John—get some rest, bud."

~~◈~~

John sobered up, enduring a methodic ritual to hasten his recovery from the binge: blueberry and banana smoothies, children's anti-dehydration formula, high protein food, vitamins, intense cardio at the gym, and hot steam baths at The Marquis spa.

Philippe Álvarez had called John a few hours after he spoke with Kasey and asked if he would be available to join him at his residence in a couple of days to discuss a possible project with KNWRZ. He agreed to meet him and continued to punish his body with cardio.

Over spring break, Marcus's father purchased him a brand new 8 series BMW coupe and a professional-grade digital camera for his successful induction into the prestigious Avalonti Society. The BMW was a surprise; the camera was specifically requested. Kasey attended a two-day, women's only camping retreat with Mel and her group. They discussed a range of topics, including, but not limited to gender roles, intersectional feminism, heteronormativity, asexual female bonding, sexism in Marxist theory, the ego, microaggression, male fragility and toxic romance.

CHAPTER 18
REYAL XAOH

In exchange for KNWRZ publishing a retraction on the Anastasia Carval article, John agreed to a written debate series with Philippe Álvarez using his nom de guerre, Reyal Xaoh. John didn't want anything to do with Philippe Álvarez, but he saw that working with him was the only way to derail the witch hoax. Philippe's project was fashioned after the famous Avalonti-Ghazali debates. For years, Professor Hakim Ghazali and Dr. Phineas Avalonti published their philosophical and theological discussions in the *Avalonti Journal*. Ghazali was a controversial, henotheistic Muslim, and Phineas Avalonti was an agnostic atheist. Ghazali and Avalonti maintained a close friendship despite their religious and ideological differences. Hanging above the threshold of Francesca Hall was an iconic, framed black-and-white photograph picturing the two gentlemen shaking hands in their Victorian parlor chairs, circa 1964.

Philippe Álvarez wanted to "revitalize" the debate between believer and non-believer and publish the discussions on the KNWRZ website. He would liken the debates to a 1972 chess tournament between heavyweights Robert Fischer and Boris Spassky. Philippe viewed John as worthy based solely on his Avalonti membership. John arrogantly viewed Philippe Álvarez as an unqualified rabble-rouser whose *raison d'être* was profiting from publishing incendiary rhetoric and wild fantasy. The format of the project would be a series of Q and As. Álvarez would prompt a philosophical or theological question and both he and John would write statements, arguments and rebuttals. They would each carefully examine the opposing content before the discussion was published on the KNWRZ website. Before the debate tournament commenced, Álvarez decided to introduce John to an old college buddy of his: Dr. Shane Ouradnik. They met at Philippe's home in West Virginia. John secretly referred to his home as The Dollhouse.

"Welcome, John. Thanks for making the trip," Philippe greeted him as he walked into the living room of *The Dollhouse*.

"Thanks for having me," John politely stated.

"John, I'd like you to meet an old friend of mine, Dr. Shane Ouradnik."

Dr. Ouradnik pulled his long, frizzy red hair back into a ponytail. "How are you, John?" he asked in a haughty tone, shaking his hand.

"I'm well. Nice to meet you," John said, removing his backpack.

"Could I offer either of you some tea or lemonade?" Philippe asked.

"Lemonade, please," Dr. Ouradnik answered, adjusting his glasses.

"I'm good," John declined, taking a seat by himself on an old, worn-out love seat.

Philippe nodded, walking backwards into the kitchen.

John surveyed the dollhouses that littered the first floor, shaking his head and rolling his eyes. Dr. Ouradnik noticed, sitting in a chair on the other side of the living room.

"The dollhouses are a coping mechanism," Dr. Ouradnik whispered, leaning towards him. "He'll build them until the end of his days; such is the level of his insurmountable grief over the loss of his sister."

"I gathered that," John stated. "What is your area of expertise, Dr. Ouradnik?"

"Theoretical physics, quantum mechanics, string theory—a little psychology."

"Interesting. My friend Kasey would love to meet you."

"Is Kasey a female?"

"*Uh*—yeah—why?"

"When you mentioned her, your mannerism was indicative of reverence or deep affection."

John laughed. "I don't think so."

"Sorry, I shouldn't have assumed you were a heterosexual," he apologized sincerely.

"*Uh*—I'm straight."

"Shane," Philippe said as he returned, handing Dr. Ouradnik a glass of ice-cold lemonade.

"Thank you," Dr. Ouradnik said.

John tapped the arm of the love seat impatiently. "Philippe, will we be discussing the details of your project today?"

Philippe chuckled. "So eager. Yes, John, we shall. First, I thought we might have a friendly discussion about witches."

John sighed. "There is no such thing as witches."

Dr. Ouradnik and Philippe Álvarez smiled at each other.

"Is this something you're certain of, John?" Dr. Ouradnik asked.

"Absolutely," John answered. "Do you believe in witches also, *Dr.* Ouradnik?"

Dr. Ouradnik sipped his lemonade then answered, "Not in the archetypal sense. Religious fables and interpretations tend to distort objectivity, which leads to the brush of pop culture painting over deeper enquiry."

John squinted. "Are you an atheist, Dr. Ouradnik?"

"I'm agnostic, John. As a scientific freethinker, I believe it would be foolhardy to flaunt convictions and assume one's omniscience in a vastly unexplainable universe."

"I would attest that we live in a vastly *explainable* universe," John contented. "You say, 'not in the archetypal sense'. Does that mean you believe in witches?"

"John, are you familiar with quantum mechanics, string theory, the multiverse, Erwin Schrödinger's equation, dark energy, the Higgs boson?" Dr. Ouradnik politely asked.

"I dabble," John shyly confessed.

"It's not a question of whether witches are real or not, per se," Dr. Ouradnik explained. "I don't fear we should ever need to worry about green-faced women flying around on broomsticks. The deeper inquiry is—can we explain, scientifically, what we typically refer to as 'the force of evil'?"

"Good and evil are just words we use to offer assessments after we've implemented our bias," John argued.

"Perhaps," Dr. Ouradnik conceded, "but if evil *is* a force, then it could function in a way like gravity or electromagnetism. The gravitational force of a black hole, for example, could be comparable to the concentration of evil in what we dub as witches, or demons or devils. If the forces of good and evil coexist with intrinsic balance, a *witch* could simply be a disbalance of the forces, like a jet stream that causes a storm. A witch may not be a physical thing at all. If you subtract the religious or folklore concepts and focus on the possible science, then you open up a different kind of discussion."

"But evil isn't an actual force—it's hokum," John insisted.

"We don't really understand the nature of reality. The more you divide the number one in half, the longer it becomes. You have to think outside the box, John."

"Could you do me a favor?" John asked Dr. Ouradnik.

"Certainly."

"Write down some key subjects for me. I want to study some of this in greater depth."

"Absolutely," Dr. Ouradnik said, pulling a piece of blank paper from his briefcase.

"Thank you, sir."

"John, I'm curious," Dr. Ouradnik asked, jotting down the research topics, "has anything unusual happened to you since you started the witch hoax project?"

"Not really," John answered.

"Nothing at all?"

"You strike me as a *learned* man, Dr. Ouradnik," John said, changing the subject. "Why do you consort with dubious characters like Philippe Álvarez here?"

"*Gee*, thanks, John," Philippe stated.

"Transparency is imperative, *False Prophet*. It's best not to conceal my discomfort in working with you. You've left me with little choice in the matter," John criticized.

"We've been friends since we were your age, John. While I disagree with Philippe on many things, I can assure you he's a good man. We all have our flaws, John."

"I don't care about what he did in the past. Philippe publishes blatant, defaming lies and unsubstantiated conspiracy theory as fact," John explained. "He's a propagator of disinformation and deceit. As I've said, good and evil are matters of perspective."

Dr. Ouradnik chuckled, handing John the piece of paper containing the research subjects he requested. "You two have much to discuss, it appears. I'm meeting a friend for lunch in Frederick in a little while. If you have any questions, John, my cell number is on the paper."

"Thank you, sir," John said, taking the paper.

"No problem," he said, walking toward the exit.

Philippe shook Dr. Ouradnik's hand. "It's been a pleasure, Shane."

"Thanks for the lemonade," Dr. Ouradnik said, hugging Philippe. "Good seeing you again. Take care of yourself."

Philippe whispered something into his ear.

Dr. Ouradnik nodded.

"John," Dr. Ouradnik said, standing in the doorway, "remember, think outside the box."

～

John left shortly after Dr. Ouradnik. Álvarez provided him with precise details of the project and issued "Game One". The debate question was, "Is God the Universe?" John immediately suspected that the behemoth pantheistic question was not conceived solely by Álvarez. He discerned that he would be rivaled against Philippe

Álvarez *and* Dr. Shane Ouradnik throughout the series of debates. To strengthen his arguments, John decided to call upon a friend; someone pursuing an eventual career at the LHC. Before he returned to the university, John sent Kasey a text message: *Hey, Kase, I may need a physics tutor soon. I will pay you for your time if you have any you can spare.*

During the drive back to Maryland, John recalled Vandacheler's production at Francesca Hall with Dr. Thaddeus Arnold and Mr. Chad Wilcox. Included in their discussion was the suggestion that the universe itself was potentially sentient. John quickly dismissed the idea of requesting Avalonti Sages for help, fearing he would've been identified as Reyal Xaoh once the debates were published. The Avalonti Society may or may not have pursued disciplinary action against him for his dealings with Álvarez, but John wasn't prepared to risk it. His relationship with Philippe Álvarez would be kept secret.

Becoming antsy, John popped a '50s mixtape into his cassette player. Buddy Holly and the Cricket's 1958 hit song, "Oh Boy", blared through the car speakers. John loudly sang along, speeding down the highway.

"Jesus fuck!" he shouted, swerving, slamming on his brakes, narrowly avoiding a runaway truck tire barreling into his lane from the other side of the interstate. He pulled over to the side of the road to catch his breath. If the truck tire would have struck at such a velocity, it would have wrecked his vehicle and possibly killed him. As he stood next to his car, investigating the highway and regaining his stability, his phone vibrated. Kasey texted him back: *I'll tutor you. You don't have to pay me :P*

～ぬ

John heard giggling around the corner of Francesca Hall the following afternoon as he approached the building for the special event. Kasey was posing in front of a gothic stone fountain under a flowering Yoshino cherry tree near an outside sitting area; once used when society members would have discussions over tea.

"Hey, John!" Marcus greeted. "You gotta check out my new camera."

"Stand together," John suggested, "and I'll get a picture of you guys."

Marcus handed John his camera and gave him brief instructions on how to use it. Kasey and Marcus, who were both dressed formally for the event, stood by the fountain, placed their arms around each other and smiled.

"Say 'John is the smartest man alive,'" John instructed.

Kasey giggled, adjusting her flowy pink dress.

Marcus scoffed. "Cheese, motherfucker."

John directed them and took several pictures. While he was snapping shots, someone approached from behind.

"Why don't you all stand together?" Vandacheler insisted.

"Don! I missed you!" Kasey shouted.

"Lovely to see you all," Vandacheler said. "Kasey, stand in the middle."

They stood together in front of the gothic stone fountain. Vandacheler, concealing his photography skills, snapped a few basic pictures then requested the students to accompany him inside the hall.

"We need to get a picture of all four of us!" Kasey exclaimed.

"There are lots of people inside," Vandacheler informed. "How about a picture of us by the fireplace?"

"That sounds awesome," she said, joining him at his side.

John and Marcus stayed behind for a bit.

"How are you doing, John?" Marcus asked.

"I'm doing pretty good."

"I couldn't help but notice KNWRZ published a retraction of the Carval article. You know anything about that?"

John shrugged, shaking his head. "Nah, I'm over the witch hoax nonsense."

Marcus smirked. "Yeah, it's nonsense alright."

"You ready to go in?"

"Yeah. *Oh*, hey, John, you gotta check out my new ride later. BMW 8 Series coupe, baby."

"Sweet! Damn, man, new camera, new car—what did you do, rob a bank?"

"*Oh*, so a black man gets a new car and a camera and all of a sudden he's a bank robber? Is that it, John?" Marcus asked in a serious tone.

"I—*uh*, no—that's not what I meant."

Marcus laughed. "God damn I love fucking with liberals. You should've seen your face, dude."

John chuckled. "Dick."

"They're presents from my father; he's a very proud man," Marcus said.

"That's awesome. My dad won't talk to me anymore, but I'll save that for the shrink."

Marcus smiled. "You ready to head in?"

John nodded.

As John and Marcus walked through the grand cherry wood double doors, they noticed a large banner above the fireplace that read: *CONGRATULATIONS*. The society members inside began clapping. Kasey rushed over to John and Marcus, joyously laughing.

"Surprise," Vandacheler said.

John smiled. "Jesus Christ, the special event is a party for us."

"How do ya like that?" Marcus asked rhetorically, surveying the guests.

~~~

Dr. George Verner gave a short speech, welcoming the students to the prestigious society, after which he climbed the spiral staircase to the veranda with the editor-in-chief of the *Avalonti Journal* and two other men. John, ignoring their ascent, nursed a glass of wine as he meandered through the hall, talking to several of the esteemed Avalonti members. There, he learned more about the intricate hierarchy of the society.

The society was compartmentalized into three tiers; Novice, Intermediate, and High Council. Each tier had different levels and each level had different classes. The novice tier had two levels: Neophytes and Apprentices. Neophytes were probationary members in the process of obtaining full membership. After at least ninety days and the successful completion of a series of initiation tasks, Neophytes were upgraded to Apprentice: the first level of a full member. Apprentices were required to obediently follow the command of any higher-ranking member, within reason. They would also learn the art of scholarly writing.

The intermediate tier, the largest tier, had three levels: Scribes, Mentors and Sages. Scribes were graduate and PhD students who were required to submit papers to the *Avalonti Journal* to maintain their membership. These included students from various academic disciplines. Mentors, the mid-level management of the society, were tasked with overseeing the Novice tier. They were encouraged, but not required, to submit papers to the journal. Sages, an honored position within the society, were active and alumni members who were considered to be notable academics. These included professors who taught at other universities who were once student members. Their level of participation was generally optional. Don Vandacheler, a Class-A Mentor, was eligible to be promoted to Sage during the next triennial High Council meeting in New York. The classes, a simple grading system, were A, 1 and 2, with A being the highest grade.

The Avalonti High Council had three levels as well: Dukes, Judges and the Excaliburs. Dukes were trusted members who worked in upper-management positions at the university, in notable positions at the Avalonti holdings corporation, on the Board of Trustees or in high-ranking government jobs. Dukes also managed the *Avalonti Journal*, in cooperation with Sages and Judges. Judges were once Avalonti Sages who demonstrated years of active and loyal membership. Judges, usually tenured professors, were the deciding body that voted on new members. The Excaliburs, the few at the top, were on the Board of Directors at Avalonti Holdings Inc. and worked directly with Caesar Avalonti in New York. An Excalibur was once a Duke who demonstrated unsurpassed loyalty to the Avalonti family. The promotion to Excalibur came with a five-million-dollar bonus and a guestroom at the Avalonti mansion in upstate New York, where they were welcome to stay whenever they so desired. Excaliburs did not attend academic symposiums or publish papers in the *Avalonti Journal*. Their function within the society was strictly financial; overseeing the corporation, the Avalonti Trust Association and the Avalonti Foundation. Their privileges were not fully known to lower-ranking members. Caesar Avalonti, of course, was the Godfather: the highest held position that could only be obtained through primogeniture.

The position of Godfather would one day be granted to Nathaniel Avalonti; Caesar's nineteen-year-old grandson. Nathaniel was a tall, skinny young man with long, golden brown hair, high cheek bones and a rigid yet diplomatic posture. He was living testimony to the fact that looks were often deceiving. Trained by a retired IDF specialist in the art of weaponry and Krav Maga, he possessed the skill necessary to incapacitate a man with his bare hands, or to hit a paper target at two thousand yards with a sniper rifle. Although he was aptly trained in the art of combat, Nathaniel was not interested in violence or fighting. Like his fathers before him, his primary interest was academics. He'd recently developed fascinations with neuroscience, psychology and sociology, attending college overseas at the University of Cambridge where his great-grandmother had earned her degree. Nathaniel, despite being separated by the vast expanse of the Atlantic Ocean, kept in frequent contact with his family.

Beyond academics, the Avalonti Society practiced and encouraged philanthropy. In 1969, after Nixon's Tax Reform Act, the Avalonti family established the Avalonti Foundation; a non-profit 501c3. Revenues from the Avalonti holdings corporation funneled through the foundation and were dispersed globally, with substantial funding granted to various developing countries. The establishing of an official charity was only a mere addition to the years of philanthropy demonstrated by the Avalonti family. Their generosity could be traced back through the annals of American history, with their core initiatives revolving around health and education. The Avalonti Society received generous contributions, most notably through their annual Thanksgiving charity gala where some guests opted to pay $50,000 a plate or more. The incentive to make tax-deductible donations during the society dinner was Caesar Avalonti's promise to match contributions, dollar for dollar, from his own piggybank.

John sang praise for the society's philanthropy, but his ears especially perked up when he heard stories of the early years of Francesca Hall; history that was not recorded in the journals. During their heyday after the war in 1945, Francesca Hall became an intellectual landmark. Scholars and academics from all over the world came to debate, discuss, shoot billiards and drink hard liquor. Rambunctious jazz music and cigar smoke filled the hall late into the night. The society's motto was a punkish "Tea in the

Daytime". In 1946, a world-renowned archeologist was famously discovered sleeping on the cobblestone pathway near the hall by an undergraduate walking to a morning class. When the student helped him up, he quickly realized that the man was still heavily intoxicated. The archeologist dusted himself off, groomed his handlebar moustache and returned to the hall for an "eye-opener".

Soirées were standard business up until 1954, when McCarthyism had derailed the party train. Dr. Simon Avalonti, Phineas Avalonti's conservative father, fearing the communist label, reprimanded the society for their late-night reveling. Although Simon was never a member, Phineas Avalonti would not dare to disappoint his father. He complied with his advice to tone the parties down. Guests slowly stopped visiting, and the hall fell into a drab "members only" epoch. But it didn't last forever. Revitalization of Francesca Hall occurred in the late 1970s when Caesar Avalonti returned from living as a beatnik in California and took over management of the society. Inspired by the '60s revolution, Caesar repealed his father's edict that forbade drinking and hallucinogenic drug use and uniquely declared that moderation was "the art of balancing abstinence with hedonism". The soirées returned. Awarded with "diplomatic immunity" from the university, the Avalonti Society became a hidden sanctuary for debauchery, all while impressively maintaining their image of prestige. But the hall's revival was short-lived, and the parties paled in comparison to the early years. By the start of the 1990s, after Caesar's move to New York, the hall had once again become a ghost of its former glory. Matured, and consumed by business, Caesar stopped taking his trips to Maryland altogether, relying on reports from the High Council to assess the society's condition. Months turned to years and years turned to decades. When Caesar visited from New York to cancel the witch hoax project, he was disheartened to learn that Francesca Hall had fallen into obscurity, contrary to the reports that had suggested otherwise. Displeased with the omission of details, Caesar issued a proclamation in the form of a memo to all of their active members, urging participation at the hall.

While John was learning about the hidden history of the society, Marcus was learning more about the *Avalonti Journal*; a periodical that he cherry-picked occasionally for articles on economics. He learned that it was a pillar of the society, circulating a radius larger than he had originally thought. Though there were no other chapters of the club, Avalonti alumni, including Ivy

League professors who were once student members, routinely submitted papers to the journal. Their reach was global.

~~

The hour grew late and members sporadically departed the induction celebration. The remaining members gathered around the Steinway piano near the grand fireplace. One of the older members showcased her extraordinary skill, playing Rachmaninoff's "Piano Concerto No. 3 in D Minor". Kasey was starstruck when she met sixty-five-year-old Avalonti Judge, Professor Diana Luskovo.

The Avalonti Society was officially established in 1941 as a fraternal society. In 1981, a young professor wrote a jarring editorial for the university newspaper on the founder of the Avalonti Society. In her article, she criticized the society for its lack of female representation and mockingly compared Phineas Avalonti to P.T. Barnum, branding Avalonti the less feminist of the two. Young Caesar, who had assumed control of the society by that time, praised the author of the article despite her attacks against his father, whom he loved dearly. Diana Luskovo thus became the first official female member of the Avalonti Society.

Diana Luskovo was highly qualified, brutally intelligent and looked like Coco Chanel. Some Avalonti men confessed that they feared her. She and Kasey talked for a while by the fireplace. As the society was still predominately male, Kasey immediately confided in her. When Kasey told her about the man who attacked her, Luskovo advised her to "get a gun and shoot the fucker next time". Kasey, who would retain her vehement anti-gun views, was empowered by her sentiment nonetheless.

Marcus had left early to attend a fancy dinner at the Bemastra Yacht Club with Ashley, and John stood among a small group of Avalonti physicists, listening quietly and nodding. Eventually, he plucked up the courage to present a question to the group. "So, what do you guys think of theoretical physicists?"

"*Um*—well, I guess they're not all bad," Dr. Sherrell, an experimental physicist, remarked.

The Avalonti physicists chuckled.

"John, how it typically works," astrophysicist Chad Wilcox explained, "is the theoretical physicists construct the mathematical models to explain natural phenomenon, developing theories and abstractions that, in turn, experimental physicists will sometimes evaluate for empirical testing and observational purposes. There's a friendly rivalry between the theorists and the experimental physicists."

"They're also who I buy my drugs from," Dr. Sherrell joked.

"*Ah-ah*. Remember, Einstein was considered a theoretical physicist—so was Hawking," Chad Wilcox defended.

"*Always* defending the theorists. I assure you, John, that Mr. Wilcox isn't always this stiff," Dr. Sherrell teased. "You should see him after a few more snifters of brandy."

Mr. Wilcox smiled.

"Well, I appreciate you guys talking to me," John conferred. "This society is incredible. I could stand here all night and just listen to you guys talk. It really means a lot to me to be here."

"You're one of us now," Dr. Sherrell said. "Stop being so God damn modest."

John grinned, blushing slightly.

"Sorry for the intrusion," Kasey interrupted. "John, do you have a second?"

"Please excuse me, gentlemen," John politely stated, walking away with Kasey.

"I'm getting ready to head out," she informed. "When did you want me to start tutoring?"

"As soon as possible."

"Okay, give me a couple of days and I'll have something prepared."

He smiled at her. "Thank you, Kasey, I really do appreciate it."

She smiled back. "Sure thing, John. I'll give you a call."

"*Oh*, hey, what happened to Professor Diageo?"

"He took a leave of absence. He's not coming back until next school year."

"Oh, okay, that's understandable. See you, *Kase*."

CHAPTER 19

EN PASSANT

Debates, to the academic community, were like world championship boxing matches; spectated far and wide and examined for years. Kasey had analyzed the Bohr-Einstein discussions and the black hole war between Stephen Hawking and Leonard Susskind. Marcus studied the famous clash between economists John Maynard Keynes and Friedrich Hayek. John routinely watched atheists like Hitchens or Dawkins debate live with Christians or other religious advocates on YouTube. Though KNWRZ was not a scholarly journal, John viewed his upcoming debate with its founder, Philippe Álvarez, to be of notable significance. Naturally, he wanted to size him up and study his moves before they started the tournament. One way to glimpse Álvarez, John thought, was through his friend, Dr. Ouradnik.

On Tuesday, John called Dr. Ouradnik and asked if he would be available to sit down with him and discuss the upcoming KNWRZ debates. He agreed. They met at a brewpub later that day on Market Street in downtown Frederick, near Dr. Ouradnik's residence. During their discussion, John extrapolated from Dr. Ouradnik all the information he could on Philippe Álvarez. They sipped microbrews, sitting at a small table in the bar area.

"I'm curious about something, Dr. Ouradnik," John said, changing the subject. "Why did you ask if anything unusual happened to me after we launched the witch hoax project?"

"The Law of Attraction, John," Dr. Ouradnik answered. "You've tampered with forces you don't understand."

"Witches aren't real, though," John insisted.

"Witches—your interpretation of witches that is—probably aren't real. Have you ever heard of Robert the Doll?"

"No," John answered.

"Robert the Doll is an allegedly haunted doll—vexed by voodoo, some say—on exhibit at the Fort East Martello Museum in Florida. Legend has it that, if you offend this doll, *he* will curse you."

"Sounds like more hokum," John suggested.

"A skeptical researcher visited the museum and taunted the doll on display, attempting to show that it was indeed, like you say, hokum. Curiously, the next two weeks of her life were rife with peril. Every move she made was disastrous. She thought she was going insane. So great was her misfortune, she, like many others in the past have done, wrote an apology letter to this doll at the museum. Interestingly, her life returned to normal after she left the letter."

"Purely coincidental," John remarked.

"It's most likely that is *was* a coincidence," Dr. Ouradnik conceded. "Nevertheless, it became an area of interest to those who asked, 'What if it wasn't a coincidence?' Now, John, this is an ordinary doll. It was not born, it has no sentience, it's not alive. How could it *not* be a coincidence, right? The theory, in simplified terms, suggests that a strong collective belief infused this doll with a sort of lifeforce of its own. *The belief itself* is what made it real. I'm not a Catholic, John, but I don't doubt the protective power of the crucifix."

John sighed into his beer glass. "You're telling me that if enough people believe something, it will become reality?" He proceeded to take a sip of his beer.

"That's precisely what I'm telling you, John. Reality doesn't exist without the mind."

John laughed. "*Oh*, shit, you're just as crazy as Álvarez."

Dr. Ouradnik chuckled. "Perhaps. They probably thought Democritus was crazy when he introduced his atomic theory around 400 BCE as well."

THE WITCH HOAX

John signaled the waitress with an upward nod then glared at Dr. Ouradnik. "I'm going to take Álvarez down. Don't underestimate me."

"*Oh*, I encourage you, John."

"But you're helping him, aren't you?"

"I offer my assistance to Philippe, yes, as I will offer it to you. As an educator, knowledge is my only quest, John."

"Let me get the check when you get a chance," John said to the waitress.

"Sure thing, sweetie," the waitress said.

"John, if you hope to be victorious, you're going to have to open your mind and challenge your preconceptions of the universe. Dig deeper into the quantum world."

"*Oh*, I will."

"There's an unexplainable phenomenon in quantum mechanics that will help expand your level of thinking. You'll know it when you find it," Dr. Ouradnik poetically concluded.

John rolled his eyes. "Right."

As John and Dr. Ouradnik finished their beers and waited for the check, a breaking news bulletin came on the television above the bar. They quietly listened to the story as it unfolded. A man was shot and critically injured by police outside of the U.S. Capitol building for brandishing and discharging a firearm.

"Fuck, fuck, fuck, not again," John said, reaching into his pocket. He threw his last twenty-dollar bill on the table then headed for the exit. "Drinks are on me, Dr. Ouradnik. Thanks for coming out. I'll call you soon."

John drove back to his apartment and glued himself to the television. Bradley Hamilton, the gunman who was shot by the Capitol police, was alive but unresponsive. His motives and targets weren't clear. John, suspecting the witch hoax may have been the catalyst, turned to the independent media searching for clues. Upon investigating, John confirmed that KNWRZ's retraction of the Carval article was wholly ineffective. The witch hoax was, to John's dismay, still alive and well.

John's phone vibrated. Marcus was calling to gauge his reaction and to dissuade any possible provocations. John feigned disinterest to ease his mind.

After a few minutes of fidgeting on his couch, John returned to his computer and opened a Google search tab. As he started to type in "String Theory", he received another call, this time from Kasey.

John quickly answered. "Kasey?"

"Hi, John."

"How are you?" John asked.

"I'm doing well. I should have something prepared for you by tomorrow if you want to meet up then."

"Yeah, sure, tomorrow evening around five or six o'clock okay?"

"Yeah, that works. Your place or mine?"

John paused. "*Uh*—I was thinking Francesca."

"Oh, okay, that works for me. Take it easy, John."

"Thanks, Kasey, have a good night."

"You too. Goodbye, John."

John slowly put his phone down. "Your place or mine?" he said to himself, grinning.

～～

The following evening, John met Kasey at Francesca Hall a little after 5 p.m. As John walked across the grand foyer toward Kasey, he noticed two grad students shooting pool on one of the billiard tables in the right wing. John sat next to Kasey on the Victorian couch and retrieved some supplies from his backpack.

"What are these assholes doing in our hall?" John whispered to Kasey.

Kasey giggled. "It's their hall too, John."

"Nobody told me that."

"Okay, I put a lot of work into this," Kasey said, pulling out a large binder from her pack and placing it on the coffee table, "so I hope it's beneficial."

John picked up the binder and flipped through the pages. Kasey had compiled a thorough lesson plan, complete with study guides, word problems, quizzes and an index.

John squinted. "Kasey, this is amazing. You did all this for me?"

"Of course, John, that's what friends do; they help each other."

John smiled for a moment, then lowered his head. "Hey, Kasey."

"Yeah, John?"

John looked at the floor and spoke, "I'm really sorry for treating you poorly all the time. You don't deserve it."

Kasey remained silent, gently taking the binder from him and placing it back onto the coffee table. She took a deep breath. "I'm sorry. I can't accept your apology, John."

"What? Why not?"

Kasey softly spoke, "You feel bad—I get it—but there's more to an apology than that. I accepted an apology from you before and you did nothing to correct your behavior. I'm not trying to be mean, but you hurt me, John."

John hung his head low, glancing at the binder on the coffee table that she had invested so much hard work putting together for him. He nodded slowly. "I understand."

They sat close together on the couch, distantly. John had never experienced a friend rejecting his apology before, on the rare occasion that he offered one. The repudiation would elicit deep introspection. He promised himself he would never hurt her again.

A commotion from the grad students disrupted their intense quietness. Rolling across the marble floors was a cue ball, which leapt from the billiard table from a failed massé shot. The ball lightly struck John's foot and bounced away. He reached down and picked it up.

Kasey leaned toward him and whispered, "Newton's Third Law."

John chuckled.

"Hey, sorry about that," the grad student said, rushing over.

"No worries," John said, handing the ball back.

"Are you ready to start with the first lesson?" Kasey asked.

John smiled at her. "Yeah."

She opened the binder and started to give an overview of their first lesson: Classical Mechanics.

"Kasey," John interrupted.

"Yeah?"

"I'm glad we're friends."

"Me too, John."

~~

Later that evening, John returned to his apartment, slammed a scotch glass on his kitchen countertop and poured his whiskey. He took a gulp and stood in the kitchen, staring at the cabinets. Kasey was 21. She was fluent in four languages. She knew algebra, calculus, geometry, trigonometry, number theory, probability, classical mechanics, quantum mechanics, particle physics, and possessed countless other skills with real world applications. Marcus was fluent in three languages. He was thoroughly educated in Keynesian economics, classical economics, The Austrian School, The Chicago School, socialism, communism, laissez-faire, mercantilism, currency, market theory, stocks, bonds, insurances etc. Like Kasey, he was highly fluent in general mathematics and possessed real world management skills. John, on the other hand, was monolingual, and, nearing the end of his sophomore year, hadn't even decided on a major yet. John assessed himself and declared that he was a troglodyte; a dabbler and a fraud. He saw his hours of studying history, philosophy and religion as largely a waste of time. He no longer viewed himself as qualified to rival established intellectuals, real scientists *or* Philippe Álvarez.

John called Liam and asked if he could get him some cocaine, with the interest of utilizing it to study undeterred by slumber. Liam, who was still mourning the loss of their friend who recently passed away from a drug overdose, was both offended and concerned for John's wellbeing. John begged him, insisting that he had to learn quantum physics within three days. Liam lost his temper and accused John of being an alcoholic. In retaliation, John threw his phone across the room and hurled a full bottle of liquor over his 14th story balcony.

Hiding under the covers, he waited for the cops to show up, but they never did. The hotel management didn't know which balcony the bottle was thrown from. It was 11 p.m., 10 p.m. in Missouri. Drunk, John decided to call his mother. They had not spoken in weeks. When his worried mother asked him why he was calling so late, John uttered, "Sorry, Mom, I was just calling –*en passant*."

CHAPTER 20

THE DANISH GAMBIT

Completing his initial arguments for "Game One" of the KNWRZ debates, John decided to hand deliver his papers that weekend rather than emailing them. For Game One, Philippe would argue that God existed outside of the universe, like a cartoonist overlooking frames of a comic strip. God, according to Philippe, was omnipotent and transcended human understanding. John would argue that the universe contained everything, and that God was only a metaphor, or a delusion, depending on the individual's perception and level of belief. To fortify his argument, he wanted to implement science to back up his claims. Kasey spared John every minute she could to expedite his acquisition of physics knowledge, but he had run out of time. Choosing to bypass a physics-based argument, John issued an aggressive, purely philosophical open that on its surface appeared foolish and clumsy. John's plan was to seemingly sacrifice the opening argument, thereby setting himself up to dominate the middle game.

Philippe and John exchanged papers in the living room of *The Dollhouse* early Saturday morning. Skimming through John's opening arguments, Philippe set the papers on the coffee table discouragingly.

"John—I think maybe you should get some rest," Philippe said, breaking the silence.

"What are you talking about?"

"This was supposed to be a bit of fun, John," Philippe said.

John jumped from the couch as Philippe paced towards the kitchen's threshold. "Fun?"

"Look at yourself, John. You haven't shaved, your eyes are bloodshot—you look as if you haven't slept in a fortnight. I'm starting to worry about you, John."

"What the hell do you mean that this was supposed to be *fun*?"

Philippe chuckled. "Look at this place, John. It looks worse than you do. You and Shane have been the only visitors I've had in years. I—I enjoy having the company is all."

"Forgive my astonishment, but I was under no impression that this debate tournament was supposed to be *fun*. For you retracting the Carval article, I agreed to give you a debate, and a debate is what you're going to get. I'm a man of my word."

"John, come on, this stress is going to kill you. Why don't you take a break from the debate tournament? We can start after the school year. What do you say?"

"I say you're a coward. You know I'm going to slaughter you. The wicked flee when no man pursues him, the righteous man stands bold as a lion—remember?"

"*John*," Philippe said, picking up his papers, "you can do much better than this. Get some rest, come back with something stronger. When we publish these debates, I want them to be something powerful, something profound like the Avalonti-Ghazali debates."

John rubbed his eyes with one hand and rotated his jaw.

Philippe returned to sitting. "John, you're young. I'm old. You have a lot on your plate. Get some rest, go hang out with your friends—go to an arcade or something. Have some fun for crying out loud. You only have one life, John. Don't waste yours like I wasted mine. We can work on this some other time."

John rolled his eyes. "*Hmph*, the last time I went out to have fun, I got a tooth knocked out—and my head smashed open with a brass lamp."

Philippe stood from the couch and walked over to him. "We're only enemies on paper, John. You're my intellectual rival, but you're also a child of God."

Philippe offered him a handshake. John paused, scrutinizing his sincerity. Cautiously, he shook Philippe's hand.

"You know the witch hoax is still alive, right?" John asked.

"Don't worry, John, I'm going to help you kill it."

"Wait, now you want me to kill the hoax? I thought you believed in witches?"

"I do believe in witches, John. They're real. Anastasia Carval, however, is no witch. Kneeling before the feet of Jesus Christ, we shall praise him honestly at his throne. When the great war comes, we will be virtuous, honorable."

"*Philippe*, you know this stuff you publish on your website is all malarkey, right? These conspiracy theories of yours—they're insane."

"Are they now?"

"Yes, they are," John said, nodding enthusiastically. "For example—you were wrong about Dimitri Golovinsk, the Proudhon scholar turned revolutionary who was allegedly routing sensitive information to communist sleeper agents in 1973 after the Christmas bombings of Hanoi and Haiphong. You claimed he was instrumental in the 1984 Cameroonian coup d'état attempt against Paul Biya—but Dimitri Golovinsk died in Sri Lanka during the LTTE insurgency in *1983*. It's pretty hard to be instrumental in something if you're already fucking dead."

"We all make mistakes, John," Philippe said.

"And this bullshit about Francesca Avalonti," John continued. "What was that all about? You were trying to condemn her as a Nazi, but I read those declassified FBI files—they never found anything on Francesca Avalonti. The FBI opened the file in 1944 because of her parents, true, but that doesn't mean *she* was guilty of anything. Lots of people are investigated by the FBI who are innocent."

Philippe flinched. "That's true."

"You're defaming people," John accused. "Francesca Avalonti was a spectacular woman. All the credit was given to her husband, Phineas, but she was the one who came up with the idea to start the society. She wanted it to be like the Bloomsbury Group. And, up until 1941, it was—until Simon Avalonti got involved and urged his son to officially establish it as a fraternal organization. It was just a nameless little group of artsy intellectuals before they branded it as the Avalonti Society. She graciously volunteered to leave the group so she wouldn't cause friction between her husband and his father. Francesca was an awesome lady. She was brilliant far beyond her years. And her paintings—absolutely incredible. When I first walked through the doors of that hall and saw them hanging on the walls, I was almost brought to fucking tears. To me, she was a god damn treasure. But what is she to you, eh? A Nazi? Some villain? Someone to use as a prop to satisfy some conspiracy theory ghost story bullshit? I'll say it again—you're fucking defaming people, man."

Philippe twiddled his thumbs. "And who is Anastasia Carval to you? Some villain? A witch? Someone to use as a prop to satisfy your lust for social status? You charge me with crimes you are no less guilty of yourself."

John's eyes fell to the floor. "You're right," he said, nodding, "I am guilty. But at least I know I am. At least I feel shame. I'd never again publish anything that I knew was false. You think this stuff you're publishing is true just because you got lucky a couple of times? Let me tell you, man, ninety-nine percent of the shit you publish is absolute bullshit."

"I've made mistakes," Philippe said, "and I'm sure I'll make them again. But what I am publishing *is* true."

"It's not true, you can't prove any of it."

"I believe it to be true."

"That doesn't matter," John growled.

"It does matter."

John shook his head. "It doesn't matter. It's not true until it's fucking true, man."

Philippe took a deep breath. "Maybe you're right, maybe you're wrong. Only time will tell. But listen, I don't want to cause you any more stress. Go now, John, live your life a little."

"This *is* my life," John declared. "I am a real truth-seeker. All you conspiracy theorists are just a bunch of fucking posers."

Philippe grinned. "Go have some fun, John. We'll do the debates after the school year. This stress isn't any good for you. There are more important things to life than debating politics and religion, trust me. Live your life a little, John. The debates can wait."

John exhaled slowly. "Alright," he warily agreed, "I'm leaving, but this isn't over."

"I know," Philippe said, nodding.

John opened the front door.

"John, one second," Philippe said, retrieving an object from the bookcase. "Take this."

John looked at Philippe's hand. "I can't take *that*."

"It's a gift."

"No way."

"It's a gift," Philippe insisted.

"Fuck no."

Philippe took a step towards him and whispered something in his ear.

John sighed, reluctantly accepting the item.

Philippe patted him on the shoulder. "Peace be with you, John."

John stared at him and hesitantly spoke, "And with you."

John stuffed the item in his waistband and turned around to exit.

Philippe squinted, rubbing his chin, pondering. "One more thing before you go, John."

"What's that?" John asked, standing in the threshold.

"You're a good writer, John. I've been looking for a skeptic to hire as a contributor. Someone to dissect what I publish and put it under the microscope for checks and balances. Nothing serious like the debates, just short blogs and op-eds."

"You just told me that I needed to start living my life more," John protested.

"It shouldn't take up too much of your time. Couple hours a week. Work at home. Just something to give the website a little flavor. Something to boost readership."

"A gimmick?" John grumbled.

"It pays," Philippe said, shrugging his shoulders. "Also comes with a one-hundred-dollar sign-on bonus. Interested?"

John grinned.

～∾

Wind rolled through his dirty-blond hair as Chuck Berry's "Johnny B. Goode" rang out like a bell through the car speakers. The warm sun shined through the Shenandoah Valley. The diminishing fragrance of the coconut air freshener cast his mind into a daydream. Images of a Polynesian waitress in a grass hula skirt bringing him cocktails on a white sandy beach brought a smile to his face. For a moment, he wasn't John Hallman from small-town Missouri; he was a big-shot executive movie producer en route to lounge poolside at The Kahala, lighting a cigar off a hundred-dollar bill.

Leaving West Virginia, John stopped and perused several antique stores and various little shops along the artery of downtown Frederick. As he browsed, something caught his eye; a shiny bronze apple paperweight. John picked up the bronze apple and held it in the palm of his hand. He flipped it over to see the price. "Damn, 90 bucks," he said, placing it back on the shelf.

John decided to stop off for a pint of ale at a Market Street pub. He ordered a pilsner and watched part of a baseball game on the flat-screen television. Just for kicks, he flirted with women at the bar, collecting phone numbers he would never dial. He regaled bargoers with tales from his not-so-distant glory days as a varsity running back. Buying a round of beers, he engaged in a friendly conversation with a small group of people who were sitting nearby. After a while, his face hurt from smiling so much. Announcing that he was leaving soon, the young bartender made him promise to visit her again. One man gave him a high-five and said that it was good to meet him. As John walked out of the brewpub, he battled a fleeting thought: *The Law of Attraction.*

～∾

John headed back to The Marquis to shave and shower, taking careful precaution not to be derailed by any runaway truck tires along the way. He was scheduled to meet up with Kasey for another study session that evening. Before he left his apartment, he published his first article on KNWRZ, attacking the witch hoax.

By the time he reached the university, he was sharp and ready to delve into the world of physics. When he arrived at Francesca Hall, Marcus and Kasey were talking near the grand fireplace. There were several young members gathered by the billiard tables, shooting pool.

"Is Francesca a pool hall now?" John joked, approaching Marcus and Kasey.

"I know, right," Marcus agreed.

"*Uh*—you're never this happy looking, John. What gives?" Kasey asked.

John shrugged and chuckled a little.

"Oh, *shit*—did John get some ass?" Marcus asked.

Kasey elbowed Marcus playfully.

"Don't talk like that in front of her," John said in a serious tone, removing his backpack.

Kasey and Marcus looked at each other, both raising an eyebrow behind his back.

"It—it doesn't bother me," Kasey confessed.

"No," Marcus said, holding a hand up to her while studying John, "he's right. I shouldn't talk like that."

John plopped on the couch and briskly rubbed his hands together. "Who's ready for some more physics?"

Kasey smiled.

"Welp, I'm gonna let you guys get your *physics* on. I gotta get ready to meet Ashley in a little while. Bemastra Yacht Club again. I'll see you cats later."

"Bye, Marcus, be safe," Kasey saluted.

"Later, bro," John said as they fist-bumped.

Kasey situated herself as Marcus gathered his things and exited the hall.

John handed her the binder.

"Okay," Kasey said, flipping through the pages of her lesson plan, "you seem to have a pretty good grasp of classical mechanics—just keep sharpening up your math. The next chapter is special relativity. Have you ever heard of time dilation?"

"No," John said, shaking his head, smiling.

"Okay. In Newtonian physics, time moves steadily forward in fixed intervals, like on a universal metronome. In Einstein's special relativity, the only true constant is the speed of light, which is about 186,000 miles per second, and time is a relative concept. The closer you travel to the speed of light—that is, the faster you travel through space—the slower time will move for you in respect to stationary objects on earth. If the speed of light is the only constant, then time and other properties must be flexible..."

"*Um*—I know this *should* make sense to me," John interrupted.

"It's okay, John. Think of a man on a train traveling at forty miles per hour..."

~~

John focused on Kasey's explanations and gradually began to comprehend the core of Einstein's Theory of Special Relativity. While Kasey was a strong proponent of mathematics, she viewed conceptualization as the forerunner of physics. If John could grasp the ideas, Kasey thought, the math would follow. They went over the lessons for nearly two hours. The grad students finished their last game of pool and Mr. Budwin, presumably bored, brought them hot Earl Grey tea and chocolate wafers from the small kitchen tucked away in the back.

John stretched and looked at the Beha grandfather clock. "Time is so weird."

Kasey giggled. "Yep, it sure is."

"Four-dimensional continuum. It's a lot to wrap your head around."

"Yep, space-time is quite interesting."

"Speaking of *time*, I should've taken a physics class—I'm eating up a lot of yours."

"*Meh*, it's cool," she said, reaching for her tea. "Now that the probationary period is over and we're full members, all I really have outside of schoolwork is the women's group."

"Yeah? How's that going? Do you hate all men yet?"

Kasey chuckled. "I know the word feminism is like nails on a chalkboard to you, but it's not as bad as you think. Only a small portion of the movement are *man-haters*."

"I'm just messing with you. I really appreciate you helping me, *Kase*—it means a lot to me."

Kasey smiled. "Really?"

"Absolutely. You didn't have to do all this for me, but you did anyway. It's very cool, and I really do thank you."

"You're very welcome, John."

"In fact," he said, picking up his backpack, "I got something for you."

"John, you didn't have to get me anything."

John pulled out the bronze apple paperweight that he went back in and purchased at the antique store in Frederick. He stood from the couch and presented it to her. "I know your dream is to work at the LHC in Switzerland someday, but if you ever ended up teaching, I wanted to be the first student to give you an apple. And this one will stay good forever."

Kasey's eyes watered, taking the bronze apple paperweight. She stood from the couch to give him a hug. "It's beautiful, John. Thank you so much."

"You're welcome."

John hugged her warmly, gently stroking her back. Kasey squeezed him firmly. His heartbeat accelerated. Their eyes met under the quiet luminosity of the lonesome chandelier. John swallowed hard. Kasey trembled softly. Closing their eyes, they inched towards each other in a dangerous, ritualistic dance.

They quickly separated as the hall door opened, just before their lips made contact. Mr. Budwin returned from his rounds of "checking on things outside".

They both laughed.

"Okay, John, keep studying," Kasey said loud enough for Mr. Budwin to hear.

"Yeah, I'll definitely be studying," John said, nervously gathering his belongings.

Mr. Budwin retook his seat near the door, whistling his trademark tune that he believed would somehow cover the smell of his covert cigarette breaks.

"John?"

"Yeah, *Kase*?"

"Thanks again for the paperweight."

John threw his backpack over his shoulder. "You're welcome," he said, smiling. "I'll see ya later."

∿

John returned to his apartment, poured a brandy and reviewed commentary from his recently published KNWRZ article. KNWRZ, courtesy of Philippe Álvarez, announced that they had employed a skeptic to write for the publication for checks and balances. Most of the community was receptive to the idea, but they demonstrated little reprieve. Over the next couple of days, he wrote several articles. They were viciously combated by the conspiracy theorist tribe. When John published an Anastasia Carval gospel, citing her innocence, he received both fiery dissection and a barrage of insults: *Cuck, Statist, Whore, Queer, Nazi, Libtard, Commie, Fag, Moron, Idiot, SJW etc.*

CHAPTER 21

THE UNDERGROUND INTELLIGENTSIA

Kasey requested a hiatus on tutoring John, claiming she was detained by schoolwork and her obligations to the women's group. Since the debate tournament with Philippe Álvarez was postponed until after the school year, John agreed to it, focusing his attention on writing articles for the KNWRZ publication instead.

Philippe's hiring of a skeptic to write for KNWRZ was a response to the multiple allegations of bias and misinformation levied against him over the recent years. Though KNWRZ ranked low on the credibility scale, Philippe believed in the publication and wanted it to be viewed as a reputable source of information. Considering himself a truther and a proponent of free speech, Philippe welcomed dissent, attesting that his articles could withstand any level of scrutiny. To demonstrate his conviction, he hired a genuine skeptic: Reyal Xaoh. Reyal Xaoh became an instant sensation, garnering widespread attention on the underground intellectual circuit within a week. Whenever Philippe published an article, Reyal Xaoh followed up with one of his own, dissecting, correcting, and offering "rational explanations".

Thinking that he would've censored his rebuttals, John smirked in amazement when Philippe started linking Reyal Xaoh's refutations to his articles, unabashedly offering his KNWRZ readers an alternative perspective. Philippe would then write tertiary articles, attempting to dismantle Reyal Xaoh's confutations. Many of KNWRZ's subscribers called their intercourse a gimmick, but it didn't stop them from watching the dance. Some of those who believed that it was a publicity stunt developed the theory that Philippe Álvarez and Reyal Xaoh were the same person. Of course, that wasn't true. Philippe understood the necessity to conceal Reyal Xaoh's true identity and would never reveal John as a ghostwriter, adding to the allure. The publication *Jacopo-Che*, Philippe's archnemesis, published an article about Reyal Xaoh, offering both praise and critique. Gareth Zimone, their ardently socialist editor-in-chief, wrote, "If we should learn that Reyal Xaoh is the alter ego of Philippe Álvarez, then we should at least take solace in the fact that he is capable of summoning rational thought, even if it is a performance. Moreover, if he has indeed hired a resident skeptic for in-house scrutiny, then we must applaud him for his attempts at self-improvement."

Zimone's frequent critiques were the result of a lasting conflict between the socialist atheist subscribers of *Jacopo-Che* and the religious right-wing followers of KNWRZ. Intensifying their rivalry was the witch hoax; pitting skeptics and conspiracy theorists against each other in an ideological war. Paradoxically, some of the *Jacopo-Che* followers were also KNWRZ subscribers. There were atheist conservatives who overlooked Álvarez's offbeat evangelicalism, as well as stalwart Christian leftists who overlooked Zimone's vocal agnosticism. The boundaries were not so neatly established, adding confirmation to the proverbial saying, "politics makes strange bedfellows". There were, however, devout loyalists to every independent publication.

Shortly after the assassination attempt on Anastasia Carval, Gareth Zimone published a scathing article about the witch hoax, branding KNWRZ followers as "lemmings". The personal attack did not go unnoticed. Black hat hackers, loyal to Álvarez, promptly launched a DDoS attack, crashing *Jacopo-Che*'s servers for twenty-two hours. Fearing they would have not been able to withstand a cyber war with KNWRZ loyalists, Zimone reached out to Philippe Álvarez to establish rules of conduct. Surprising to many of *Jacopo-Che*'s followers, Álvarez agreed, allowing the uncensored exchange of critique while discouraging the use of cyberattacks. Álvarez insisted that the hackers acted on their own accord and published a treatise on KNWRZ to demonstrate his sincerity.

Two days after KNWRZ called for a ceasefire, Gareth Zimone awoke at three in the morning to a SWAT team positioned in front of his home, responding to a bomb threat and a hostage situation. Bursting through his door, the police were stunned to find Gareth unarmed and alone. The call was fraudulent. Zimone had been "swatted". Onlooker footage of the raid, along with a steady stream of laughter, circulated throughout the ZzzChan message board. The anonymous user DNTGAFK88 claimed responsibility for swatting Zimone. The hoaxer was later "doxxed" and revealed as KNWRZ supporter Tobias Kindleson. Zimone soon after learned that his side had hackers of their own. Just before his arrest, Kindleson attempted to withdraw funds from an ATM and nearly fainted, discovering that his checking account had been depleted. Hundreds of text messages from various puppet numbers bombarded his phone afterward, all of them reading: *All is fair in love and war.*

After Kindleson fell, war between *Jacopo-Che* and the KNWRZ subscribers intensified. Occasional cyberattacks volleyed as a result. Their feud, however, did not claim a significant percentage of what was happening in the underground intelligentsia. Most of the vast underground intellectual community avoided their conflict. Additionally, most were skeptical of AradiaGate, and followed Reyal Xaoh only because he was besting Álvarez on his own platform. The AradiaGate conspiracy theory was kept alive by a disproportionate insurgence within the underground intelligentsia. Theodora Hamlin, the founder and editor-in-chief of *The Hamlin Post*, brazenly described the conspiracy theory as "ludicrous Dark Web nonsense" and condemned anyone who sought to assert its validity. The conspiracy theorists who endorsed AradiaGate loathed Hamlin, but she did not fear reprisal. Her publication team included a cyber-security force and operated from a high-rise office building in Lower Manhattan. *The Hamlin Post*, emerging in 2005 as an independent, left-wing publication with libertarian leanings, gradually climbed out the subterranean intellectual landscape when they won the Pulitzer Prize in 2012. Hamlin, though her publication received praise from the intelligentsia for its journalistic integrity, maintained connectivity with the *underground* intelligentsia.

The complexity of underground and surface-level politics was often confusing, even to the novice intellectual. John bravely submerged himself into their world to understand what the underground intelligentsia really was. He discovered that the name itself was deliberately oxymoronic, rebelliously mocking "elitist intellectuals" like the ones at the Avalonti Society. He learned that the framework of the underground intelligentsia was anarchistic by default, allowing anyone from any religious or political background to converge on its metaphorical battleground. This was similar to the Avalonti Society's forum, but there was no Godfather or High Council in the underground intelligentsia. There were no owners. It was a loose collection of individuals, online publications, message boards, podcasts, vlogs, blogs and organizations that created an accidental community of unconventional intellectuals, sharing only one commonality: their disdain for the intelligentsia.

The celebrities of the underground intelligentsia were once leading academics themselves. Some came to view higher education as a mechanism that suffocated freethought rather than invigorating it, and defiantly escaped it. Other academics, publicly expressing controversial opinions, were forced underground when they were fired from the universities in which they had taught. In the high-tech framework of the Digital Age, the underground intelligentsia had blossomed into an international metropolis for the free exchange of ideas, heralding it as a new revolution. Without law and order, the conversations were a deep dive into the human experience, sparking discussions and debates rarely heard within the confines of academia.

Though profound, there was a notable drawback to the underground intelligentsia, outside of the myopic and criminal elements that plagued it. Chiefly, the complaint was "rampant misinformation". The scholars and scientists of the Avalonti Society rigorously employed the method of peer review, refusing to publish opinion pieces without disclaimers. There was a clear distinction between what was being published as fact and what was being published as theory. In the anarchistic world of the underground intelligentsia, the unmoderated platform became a playground for deception and mendacity, requiring strident viewer responsibility that was often absent. Some of the independent publications were crowning achievements, acknowledged by the intelligentsia, but many of them were tabloid and blatantly fraudulent. This aspect didn't ubiquitously nullify the value of the underground intelligentsia, but it was, quite naturally, why many academics chose to eschew it and stay on the surface. John found their subterranean world intriguing, though he could not offer his praise and devotion, for it was, to him, the very world that was keeping the witch hoax alive and well.

~~

John, despite his vocal distaste for the underground intelligentsia, was lapping up his newly acquired fame within it, even though only two people knew he was Reyal Xaoh; Philippe Álvarez and Dr. Shane Ouradnik. Spending nearly all of his free time writing articles, joyously attacking the witch hoax and the conspiracy theorist tribe with impunity, John forgot that it was a paying gig. The amount he would be paid was not discussed prior to him taking the job. When he returned to West Virginia later that week for an in-person meeting with Philippe Álvarez, John nearly collapsed when he handed him a twelve-hundred-dollar paycheck. To his greater astonishment, Philippe conferred upon him accolades, telling him to "keep up the good work".

A few hours after receiving his paycheck, a wax-sealed envelope from the Avalonti Trust Association arrived at The Marquis, addressed to him. Breaking the seal and removing the letter, he found, contained within the envelope, a check in the amount of $5000.00. John's jaw hit the floor. Returning to his room, he read the letter with tingling anticipation. He learned that all novice members of the Avalonti Society received a monetary token for advancing from Neophyte to Apprentice. There was, however, a catch. With the check came explicit instructions to deposit the funds into an investment account, forbidding the members to spend it for at least 730 days. Marcus deposited his into his brokerage account and Kasey deposited hers into her MMA. John only had a checking account, so he reached out to Don Vandacheler for guidance. Vandacheler assisted him with opening a tax-deferred IRA, concealing his thought that it was a safer option for John than having an easily accessible money market account.

John kicked his feet up on his brown leather couch, looked around at his luxurious suite and began smiling, laughing and cheering uncontrollably. Unable to sit still, he ventured to the local shopping mall and purchased a new set of clothes. Promising himself that he would be responsible, he took out two hundred dollars in cash from his paycheck to spend and left one thousand dollars in his checking account to save; to later deposit in his IRA.

Parking his car in the hotel garage, John decided to celebrate that Friday by catching an Uber for a night out on the town. Before he left his apartment, he ordered a bottle of rum via room service and tipped the attendant twenty dollars. After some reefer and a bit of pregaming, he set out for an evening of bar hopping in the business district. The loud music pulsed through his body. His unfamiliar laughter resonated within him. Beers turned to shots and memories turned to blurs. He awoke Monday morning to a trashed apartment, an empty bag of cocaine on his floor, and a flashing alert on his mobile banking app showing that his checking account was overdrawn by $138.00. John struggled to recall the events that had transpired. Trepidatiously, he viewed his online banking statement, confirming a vague recollection of buying numerous shots of top-shelf liquor for a bunch of random strangers at a trendy nightclub; one he had previously denounced as an establishment he would've never been caught dead in.

Collecting himself, he reluctantly called Philippe and confessed to him that he had "fallen off the deep end", requesting an advance for the following week's paycheck. After a length of gentle lecturing, Philippe complied, issuing the check with a warning that he would not agree to any future advances. John returned to his apartment, attempting to write articles, but he couldn't summon the attention span to complete a single one of them. Instead, he lounged around, battling regrets and the looming suspicion that Kasey was ignoring him. Knowing that the debate tournament with Philippe Álvarez was around the corner, he texted her to find out when they could resume their physics lessons.

John: *Hey Kasey. How are you?* (Delivered 6:47 p.m.)

John: *Haven't heard from you. All good?* (Delivered 7:15 p.m.)

John: *Just wanted to see how you were doing.* (Delivered 7:22 p.m.)

John: *Are you getting my texts?* (Delivered 7:27 p.m.)

John: *Hope all is well.* (Delivered 7:31 p.m.)

John: *I guess you're busy. I'll text you later. Sorry to bother.* (Delivered 7:35 p.m.)

John: *When do you think you'd be able to tutor again?* (Delivered 8:43 p.m.)

Kasey: *Soon.* (Delivered 9:16 p.m.)

∼∽

Change wasn't only happening at KNWRZ. The Avalonti Dukes, fearing Caesar's memo alone would not be enough to usher in a revival of Francesca Hall, implemented a new policy: two Saturdays per month, active members were required to attend luncheons for networking and discussion. Caesar, upon assessing the society further, noticed an increasing divide between academic disciplines. They were unknowingly building echo chambers. Caesar wanted the physicists to have discussions with the economists, the theologians to have discussions with the mathematicians, the anthropologists to have discussions with the chemists, and so on. Beyond that, Caesar encouraged members to actively seek out those whom they disagreed with. During his father's reign, it was common to see fruitful debates between liberals and socialists, atheists and Christians, conservatives and progressives, or any opposing factions. After their "clashes", they would examine the leftover debris in order to build new ideas from the wreckage, fortify their stances, or at least become aware of alternative viewpoints. That is what Francesca and Phineas Avalonti wanted the society to be, and Caesar aimed to uphold his parents' vision.

Don Vandacheler was enthusiastic about the luncheons. He agreed with Caesar's assessment. Professor Diana Luskovo, who admired Vandacheler, spoke privately with him for a while during the first luncheon. They maintained a close friendship since he was an undergraduate. She made him promise to attend her 66th birthday celebration the following day at Francesca Hall and kissed him on the cheek before leaving. Vandacheler lovingly referred to her as the "matriarch of the Avalonti Society".

As the Saturday afternoon luncheon neared its end, Kasey received an unpleasant call from her friend, Mel.

"Is everything okay?" Marcus asked.

Kasey sighed, hanging up. "That was Mel. She was supposed to be giving me a ride to the show tonight. She just cancelled on me."

"Damn, that sucks. What show? Where's it at?" Marcus asked.

"It's in Baltimore. There's like these amazing punk and ska bands playing tonight. It's going to be the biggest show of the year."

"Well, if you start walking now," Marcus joked. "Sorry," he quickly apologized, seeing that she was not in the mood.

"Don, you like punk, want to go to a show?" Kasey asked.

"I'm dreadfully sorry your evening has been compromised, my dear. I would offer to take you myself if I hadn't already made plans," Vandacheler said.

"Don't worry about it," she said.

"I could pay for your transportation if you'll allow me," Vandacheler offered.

"No," she replied. "Thanks, Don, but I can't let you do that."

She looked around at the group. "Marcus, *come on*, you got a new car, feel like taking the BMW for a spin?"

"*Ooh*, I would, Kasey, but I already have plans with Ashley. What about your girl, Alyssa?"

"She's too prudish for punk."

"And you're not?" Marcus joked.

She rolled her eyes.

"Zach?" she begged.

"Nope."

"*Ugh*. Thanks anyway, *Zach*," she said, turning to Arjun.

"Sorry, I do not have a car," Arjun said before she could ask.

She heaved a sigh. "It's okay, I'll figure something out."

John watched her searching on her phone. Their last study session was several days earlier. To him, it seemed like she had deliberately forgotten about it. During the luncheon, she was overtly mechanical, inconspicuously positioning herself to avoid any private conversation with him. He gritted his teeth, attempting to conceal his frustration. The others talked softly amongst themselves.

"Kasey!" John snapped, hopping off the arm of a chair. "How come you didn't ask me?"

Kasey looked up at him, scoffed, then returned to searching on her phone.

John peered at her. "Well?"

The others fell silent, awaiting her reply.

"John," Kasey huffed, looking around at the group, "I know you. You're not going to drive me to a punk rock show in Baltimore. I didn't want to make myself look like more of a fool than I already have."

"I'll take you," John invited.

Kasey paused. "What?"

"I said I'll take you. What time should I pick you up?"

Kasey smiled cautiously. "Are you serious, John?"

"*Uh*—yeah, I'm serious," John declared. "As long as I'm not out super late. I have an appointment in the morning."

"Alright," Kasey said, "doors open at 8. We should be back by midnight."

John smiled. "I'll be by around 7 then."

Kasey put her phone in her pocket. "Thanks, John, I really appreciate it."

"No sweat, Kasey. That's what friends do; they help each other."

CHAPTER 22

NEVER MIND THE BOLLOCKS

John arrived at Kasey's house a little before 7 and beeped his horn. Kasey ran to the car, wearing black jeans, low-top Converse sneakers, a Velvet Underground t-shirt and a studded leather wristband she bought at the mall. John wore relaxed, casual clothing that he recently purchased from the Banana Republic.

"Nice look," John said, shifting his car into drive.

"Thanks," Kasey said confidently, closing the door behind her.

∾

Mel and her friends at The Red Porcupine introduced Kasey to punk rock. That night would be Kasey's 2nd show. Shows were to new punks as merit badges were to the Boy Scouts of America. Older punks with numerous shows under their belt were often highly respected by newcomers. Although it was contrary to punkdom to idolize anyone or anything, an old-school punk who attended shows in the '70s, '80s or early '90s, or saw any number of iconic bands in their heyday, were usually treated with special reverence. Kasey did her best to learn the ins-and-outs over the preceding months. During the drive to Baltimore, Kasey offered John a crash course on what to expect at the show. He wasn't that interested, prompting her to talk about physics instead. She jokingly excoriated him for assuming that Asian students had no interests beyond academics and lectured him about "positive stereotyping".

~~

The sun was dozing off on the horizon. Baltimore's Inner Harbor was alive with pedestrians and boats. Merriment outside of the bars and restaurants spoke of tourist delight. Stuck in a traffic jam on Pratt Street, John cracked his window to listen to a homeless man who was drumming with enormous talent on a series of plastic buckets on the sidewalk. While listening to the busker, John did a double take, amazed by six children riding wheelies on ordinary bicycles in the middle of the street between the cars. Kasey smiled enthusiastically at him, sharing in the awe of the moment. The punk club was a few blocks north of the harbor on the corner of Lexington and Guilford Ave.

Arriving at their destination, John parked his car near the Calvert Street Courthouse and walked a couple blocks over to the club. John followed Kasey closely as they approached a spikey-haired, middle-aged man with tattoos and piercings taking money in exchange for an entry stamp at the door. John surveyed the inside of the club, which was not larger than a typical bar. A plethora of band stickers and graffiti littered every inch of the walls and the bathroom doors. Young women wearing plaid skirts, bondage belts and fishnet stockings were among guys with tight patched-up jeans, combat boots, studded leather jackets, bullet belts and mohawks. There was a distinct smell of hairspray, leather and cheap beer. A faint fragrance of patchouli and stale tobacco lingered as an aftertaste. Kasey and John stood near the entrance.

"You good, John?"

"Yeah, I'm great."

A young man with disheveled blond hair wearing an Aus-Rotten t-shirt stopped in front of them on his way to the bathroom. He wore a six-pack of beer around his wrist like a bracelet; minus one. Looking back and forth at John and Kasey's empty hands, he removed two cans from his remaining six-pack, handed them each a beer, and, without saying anything, proceeded to the bathroom. John shrugged happily, opening his beer, taking a chug. Kasey giggled and opened hers too, taking a baby sip.

The crowd herded to the front of the stage as loud guitars and a steady "bass-snare-bass-snare" percussion filled the club. The first band was a popular street punk band. Veins popped from the singer's neck and forehead as he sang and screamed into the microphone. Kasey cheered from the back corner near the bathrooms. Having no experience with concerts, John stood next to her and studied his surroundings. He saw an unusual relationship between the audience and the band. There were no bouncers or barricades guarding the stage. At any given time, several punks would jump onto the stage and sing into the microphone with the lead singer. Conversely, the frontman would often jump off the stage into the crowd and continue to sing while in the pit. There was a unique sense of camaraderie in the mosh pit. Punks would pogo or intentionally slam into each other, but if anyone fell, rather than being trampled, several other punks would immediately pick them back up.

"A little different from ballroom dancing, aye?" John asked, raising his voice over the music.

"A little," Kasey shouted.

"You gonna go out there?"

"*Uh*—maybe next song."

Kasey and John remained in the back during the rest of their set. She hadn't worked up the courage to enter the pit. Most of the spectators left the club for smoke breaks or to get some fresh air in the parking lot while the next band set up. The parking lot was only ten spaces, nestled between other buildings and an alleyway. Throughout the show, the parking lot was a hangout spot, even while bands were playing. John saw an opportunity to go to the bar for another beer, which was virtually impossible to get to during a set because of its proximity to the stage. Kasey was still working on her first one.

The band setting up was a ska-punk band. Along with drums and guitars, they had members playing trumpets and trombones. They would perform their own songs as well as covers from bands like Against All Authority. John and Kasey returned to their corner as people reentered. As they chatted, two Caucasian men with shaved heads, cuffed blue jeans and combat boots walked past. John looked at Kasey and raised a concerned eyebrow.

"Aren't they skinheads?" John whispered to Kasey.

"Yep," Kasey answered agreeably.

"*Uh*—and you're okay with that?"

Kasey nodded. "They're trad skins, not *boneheads*."

"Sorry, *what* are they?"

"Boneheads are what the Nazi skins are called. Traditional skinheads are the trad skins; they're not racist. Trad skins are white, black, Asian, Mexican, gay, straight, boy, girl..."

As Kasey was explaining to him the difference between traditional skinheads and neo-Nazi skinheads, two Hispanic trad skins walked by.

"*Oh*—I see," John said.

The mosh pit fired back up as the band commenced to play a fast, melodic ska-punk number. The brass instruments roared with the guitars. Kasey clenched her fists with excitement. They were the band she wanted to see the most. The mosh pit, although maintaining its earlier courtesies, was a bit different when ska bands played. The audience pogoed and moshed, but also engaged in a dance called skanking. While the previous band brought the street punks to the frontlines, ska bands typically brought out the skinheads, "Rudies" and ska-punks. John wished he would have taken Kasey's crash course on the ride down because he was thoroughly confused by all the different sub-genres, and it was even more confusing with her trying to explain it all while the bands were playing. At any rate, he was only there to make sure she was having a good time.

"Are you going out there this time?" John shouted to Kasey, smiling.

"I'm working up to it!"

John finished his can of beer, threw it in the trash, then grabbed her by the arm. "Come on, let's go!"

John, copying how he saw others dancing, put his arm around Kasey, pushed their way to the front and started hopping around. While in the pit, a large skinhead bumped into them and knocked them both over. Within seconds, five people picked them up off the floor and pushed them back into the center of the pit. They laughed together and continued to dance while the band raged on.

During the next song, one of the ska-punks jumped on the stage, fell backwards and accidentally hit John on the top of his head. John, realizing it was an accident, wasn't mad, but he became concerned. He pulled Kasey to the sideline near the amps, pointed to his head and shouted close to her ear, "I'm going to sit this one out. I don't want to reinjure my head."

Kasey nodded and, with a newly acquired sense of adventure, jumped back into the pit by herself. Kasey was petite and barely weighed 100 pounds, but she handled herself well. She fell or was knocked over several times but returned to dancing each time she was picked up. John went back to the corner of the club near the bathrooms and watched her. He shook his head, smiling and chuckling. Before the end of their set, he managed to push his way to the bar. Kasey returned to their corner after the band finished their last song, sweating and pumped full of energy.

"That was so awesome!" she exclaimed.

John chuckled. "You're quite the dancer—a lot tougher than you look."

"Darn right I am," Kasey said, flexing her arm.

"I thought you might need this," John said, handing her a bottle of cool water.

Kasey took the bottle and smiled at him.

Their eyes locked for a moment.

She sipped the water. "I really appreciate you doing this for me, John."

"No problem, *Kase*, I'm glad you're having fun."

While the second-to-last band set up, Kasey suggested that they go outside and get some fresh air. The small club was like a sauna. With vocal relief, she breathed in the late April air, which felt much cooler to her than it really was. Together, they scanned the ample gathering of people in the parking lot, seeing if they spotted anyone from the university. Kasey saw a guy she met at her first show, but he didn't go to their school.

"Clint!" Kasey shouted, abruptly walking away from John.

John furrowed his brow.

Clint sported a 1982 Brit-punk fashion, complete with an Angelic Upstarts logo painted on the back of his studded leather jacket. Under his jacket was a t-shirt that read: *I'm not old, I'm just ugly*. Hairspray, cooked with a hairdryer, held up his faded blue mohawk; which was about eight inches tall. He wore a studded belt *and* a bullet belt over a pair of red Dogpile plaid pants. Zippers and screen-printed band patches were sewn on randomly with dental floss. He sat on a beach chair in the back of his rusty blue 1991 Chevy S-10 pickup truck, smoking a cigarette next to a cooler full of beer.

"Hey, Clint!" Kasey exclaimed, skipping toward his truck.

John followed her over.

Clint looked down at Kasey, snapping his fingers. "*Uh*—Kelly, right?"

"Kasey."

"Oh, *right on*. I was close," Clint said in his weaselly voice.

John smirked.

"*Heh*. Nice bracelet, poser," Clint criticized, looking at Kasey's flimsy studded wristband that she purchased at the mall.

Kasey forced a smile but was visibly offended.

"I'm just fucking with you," Clint said, tossing her a beer. "Don't go crying on me."

"So, how do you get it up like that?" John asked in reference to his mohawk.

Clint exhaled a cloud of cigarette smoke toward John, then snidely said, "Viagra."

Kasey giggled. "*Uh*—Clint, this is my friend, John."

"John? I thought he was *Brad Pitt*."

John chuckled. "Yeah, I'm a little underdressed."

Clint reached into his cooler and handed John a beer. "Dress however you want, my man. You're cool with me, as long as you're not a fascist."

"Thanks," John said, taking the can of National Bohemian.

Clint dramatically cracked open another beer, sat back in his chair and took a sip. "So, what are you *fuck wads* up to tonight?"

"*Uh*—just here watching the concert," Kasey answered.

"The *concert*?" Clint laughed boisterously. "Jesus Christ, you're fucking lame."

"I meant to say *show*," Kasey said, correcting herself.

Clint scoffed. "Yeah right, dork."

"Hey!" John said, clenching his fist.

Clint snickered. "*Relax.* I'm just fucking with your girlfriend, dude. Save your hate for the real enemy."

"She's *not* my girlfriend," John stated boldly.

Kasey quickly turned her head, staring at John for a moment in mild disgust.

"Whatever," Clint said, flicking his cigarette against the nearby brick wall.

John surveyed Clint's apparel and noticed a sewn-on black and green rectangular patch, similar to the red and black anarcho-syndicalist flag that he saw at the campus demonstration.

Clint guzzled his beer then belched.

"So, Clint, what's that patch represent?" John asked, pointing.

"This? Anarcho-primitivism," Clint answered.

"Anarcho-primitivism?"

Clint tilted his head back, finishing the rest of his beer, then grabbed another one. "Anarcho-primitivism," he explained, "unlike anarcho-capitalism or anarcho-communism, is a philosophy that looks *beyond* economic systems to identify the root cause of our worldly ills."

John perked up. "Which is?"

"Human civilization itself," Clint answered.

John squinted. "Embellish?"

Clint took a sip of his beer. "Anarcho-primitivism is a philosophy that suggests we should revert to hunter-gatherers. Overpopulation, famine, disease, plague, technology, government, totalitarianism, war, pollution—all the ills of the planet are a result of our deviation from nature. The plague that wiped out over forty percent of Europe's population in the 14th century, for example, was brought by disease carried along the Silk Road. Why was there a Silk Road? Farming and erecting cities increased the geo-population, thus creating more supply and demand. International trade boomed, which in turn sped up civilization even more. Not only did goods blaze over the borders, but so did knowledge. Ideas started fucking like jackrabbits, which would later give birth to the Industrial Revolution. That supercharged advancement wrought disastrous effects."

"So, capitalism is the problem?" John asked, visibly impressed with Clint.

"Trade is not synonymous with capitalism. Currency and trade are practical and even harmless on a very small scale. But, if you exponentially increase the population and its civilization's technology, then any economic system derails. Capitalism? Dog shit. Socialism? Dog shit wrapped in a rainbow. In order to save humankind, the technological progress we've made must be obliterated. Technologically, we need to go backward, not forward. Stop breeding. Depopulate. Erase all borders. Destroy all government. Live wild and free."

"Marcus would love this guy," John said to Kasey.

"*Oh* yeah, he would," Kasey said, smiling at Clint.

"It's an interesting idea, but it would never work. Not these days, anyway," John declared.

"Well, sometimes you gotta *think outside the box*," Clint suggested.

John paused for a moment, remembering Dr. Ouradnik saying the same thing.

"Say, Clint, did you go to college to learn all this?" John asked, looking at the expired Texas license plate on his truck.

"Nope," Clint answered, "I'm an uneducated vagabond."

"*Hmm*, well, you seem fairly educated to me..."

∿

John and Clint talked for a bit. He learned that Clint was from a middle-class suburb of Houston, Texas. Dropping out at the age of eighteen, Clint abandoned suburbia and took to the open road in a Chevy pickup truck that he inherited from his aunt. Clint explained to John the intricate world of punk rock. Punks like Clint could travel to practically any city in the world, find the local punk scene and be offered housing, food and beer; usually in exchange for modest chores like doing dishes and cleaning up after parties. Clint would crash a city for a while, make friends, party, enjoy his youth, then panhandle for gas money at interstate truck stops to fuel up for the next town. Periodically, he would return home to Texas. At the age of twenty-five, Clint had visited many towns and nearly every major city in the United States. Punks from Oakland to Philadelphia and everywhere in between knew and were friends with Clint. When he wasn't partying, Clint would put on his glasses and quietly read for hours straight.

A couple of Clint's friends gathered around his truck and joined the conversation. John shyly retreated into deep thought. Kasey attempted to showcase herself as a real punk, without much success. While he was contemplating the witch hoax, John noticed fifteen people marching up the sidewalk on the opposite side of the club; twelve large, muscular men with shaved heads, and three women with Chelsea haircuts. Walking in a military-style formation, they all wore combat boots and black t shirts with identical logos on the front.

"*Oh*, look—more skinheads," John said lackadaisically, interrupting their conversation.

They all turned to look.

"Motherfucker!" Clint shouted, jumping out of his lawn chair.

John stood, befuddled, watching Clint's empty pickup truck bob up and down.

The group marching up the sidewalk were a gang of neo-Nazi skinheads looking for a rumble. With war cries, the full parking lot had emptied. Car horns blared as a stampede of violence erupted in the middle of the street. At least fifty people were involved in the clash. Clint was lost among the fury. Spectating in shock from a distance, John and Kasey saw the lead singer of the street punk band swinging his fists wildly. One of the neo-Nazi skinheads executed a 360-spinning hook kick, knocking him unconscious with his heavy boot. Blood sprayed from his face when his head smacked against the pavement. John empathetically cringed. The spikey-haired doorman ran up behind the neo-Nazi skinhead and struck him across his upper back with a wooden baseball bat that he kept behind his chair. The trad skins, who were inside watching a ska band when the fight began, emerged from the club and rushed to the front lines. Although the neo-Nazi skinheads hated the punks, the trad skins were their primary target. The feud between trad skins and neo-Nazi skins had endured for decades. An explosion of fisticuffs raged between the two rival factions.

"Clint!" Kasey shouted desperately, inching toward the brawl.

"Kasey, what the fuck are you doing!" John shouted, grabbing her arm. "*Kase*, we can't be involved in this!"

With screaming and shouting, the explosive battle traveled toward the parking lot. A beer bottle shattered on the ground, nearly striking Kasey. She jumped backwards. As the rampage neared them, a skinny, teenaged punk wearing a white t-shirt lurched out from the frenzy, bleeding from his abdomen. He had been stabbed. Kasey threw her hands up, screaming in horror.

John pulled her, shouting, "We gotta get the fuck out of here, Kasey!"

A combination lock struck John on the shoulder.

It was hurled by one of the neo-Nazi women.

"Come here, cunt!" the woman yelled, charging towards Kasey.

A woman with a purple mohawk kicked her in the face, knocking her to the ground just before she reached Kasey.

"Jesus fucking Christ," John whimpered, guarding Kasey, backing away.

John and Kasey quickly escaped through the alleyway behind the parking lot. They ran full force to his car near the courthouse. The vicious fight could be heard from two blocks away. Three police cruisers raced by with their lights flashing. Kasey hyperventilated, putting on her seatbelt. John's trembling hand dropped the keys as he attempted to engage the ignition. He picked up the keys, started the car and sped off in a panic.

CHAPTER 23

LOST

John's erratic driving had gotten them lost in Baltimore. They drove around for nearly twenty minutes before Kasey was able to calm herself down. She took a deep breath and stared quietly out the window while John struggled to locate signs to the interstate.

"I really hope Clint is okay," Kasey uttered.

"I'm sure he'll be fine; the police were on their way to break it up," John assured.

"That poor kid got stabbed. I hope he's okay too," she cried.

"Yeah, that was, *uh*—pretty terrible—but they all signed up for it."

She turned and peered at him. "What do you mean they all signed up for it? Are you victim blaming?"

"He wasn't a victim, Kasey. He made a choice to jump in the middle of something he should have stayed away from. I watched him do it."

"John, he was like fifteen years old!"

"It doesn't matter," John said, turning down a dimly lit inner-city street in West Baltimore. "I've been in enough fights to know that it was my own stupid ass who signed the check. You write a check; your ass better be ready to cash it. The real world is a tough place."

"*Oh*, listen to you. You're really something else sometimes, you know that, John?"

"It's just the way the world is, *Kase*. It's reality. You better get used to it."

She scoffed. "Or try to change it."

"Yeah, good luck with that," he said, rolling his eyes.

"Where are you going? You know we both have GPS on our phones, right?"

"I don't need it; I know where I'm at."

Kasey chortled. "Yeah, okay."

Kasey resumed looking out the window in silence. John drove on for another twenty minutes, pretending to know a city he had never been to before.

Kasey fidgeted. "I should have gotten Clint's number. I really hope he's okay."

"He's fine," John sighed.

"I really hope so."

John chuckled imprudently. "Don't worry, you'll see him again. You guys can meet up and go live in the woods together and eat bugs off the trees."

She squinted at him. "Are you jeal—what do you care what I do?"

John shrugged. "Do whatever you want. I don't care what you do."

"What about you? Where are you and *Mel* going to live?"

John scrunched his face. "Mel? What the hell are you talking about?"

Kasey scoffed. "*Oh*, please, I saw you two in the café together. You looked like you met your hero."

"So, you're like spying on me or something?"

"*Pff*, no, I had a meeting at The Red Porcupine that day. I showed up a little early to get some books for the NYC trip, and I saw you guys in there chumming it up. I thought you hated her?"

John smirked. "Why do you care if I talked to Mel?"

"I just think it's weird that you pretend to hate her when you obviously don't."

"Listen, *Kase*, I met Mel during my first month at the university outside of the student center. Apparently, she doesn't like Wayne Fontana and the Mindbenders. She came at me with all this bullshit about me being a homophobe for listening to '50s music. I had no idea what the hell she was talking about. Instead of helping me understand her point of view, she decided it would be justifiable to destroy my radio. She righteously pushed it off a ledge, sending it falling to its doom. Motherfucker crashed at the bottom of the stairwell. My grandfather gave me that radio when I was seven." He digressed, "That's the only reason my dad let me keep it all those years; because my grandfather gave it to me. Of course, I was only allowed to listen to gospel stations. My grandfather was cool though; he'd take me out for milkshakes, and we'd listen to oldies in his car."

"I'm sorry she broke your radio," Kasey said.

"Me too. When I saw that you were friends, I knew me and her had to resolve our issues."

"Why is that exactly?"

"Because I needed your help with the witch hoax project. I didn't want her turning you against me more than you already were."

Kasey scoffed, shaking her head.

"Plus," John added, "I wanted you and I to be on better terms so we could have *some* kind of friendship."

"Yeah, right, just admit you like her, John. I know you guys have some kind of secret relationship going on. Isn't that why you were so happy the other day? You *get some* from Mel?" She paused, cringing. "I'm sorry, that's none of my business."

"What the fuck are you talking about, Kasey? I just wanted her and me to resolve our issues. Excuse me for trying to be *diplo-fucking-matic* once in a God damn while. And what about you and Clint, huh? What did you do, fuck him in the back of his pickup truck? *Pff*, he didn't even remember your name."

Kasey crossed her arms, looking out the window, refusing to affirm or deny his allegation.

John gritted his teeth behind her back.

They drove past the corner store they saw fifteen minutes earlier.

"So, are you ever going to get us out of this city, or what?"

"I'm working on it, chill."

She pulled her phone out. "I'm just going to GPS it."

"Just put the damn phone away, I know what I'm doing."

She sighed. "Why are men so stubborn? What's the harm in just admitting that you don't know where you're going? You're in a city you've never been to before, just GPS it, dude."

"*Oh great*, here we go with the man-bashing feminist bullshit. Listen, all we have to do is find the main road."

Kasey laughed at him. "The main road? You're incredible, John. You have no idea what you're talking about. And, for your information, it's not man-bashing feminist bull crap, it's an observation of sexist behavior. You feel threatened, anxious because you're not in control of the situation. You view asking for directions as vulnerability and submissiveness; behavior that you think only women can exhibit. It probably drives you crazy that the GPS voice is female—doesn't it?"

John popped a mixed tape into the cassette player and turned up the volume.

"See," Kasey criticized over the music, "you don't even want to acknowledge it as a possibility. It's an example of the fragile male ego!"

John turned the stereo up louder.

Kasey huffed and raised her voice more, "*Oh*, I'm *John*, Mr. *freethinker* extraordinaire. *Ooh*, I'm so enlightened, but I freeze up any time I have to face legitimate criticism, or anything remotely related to emotion."

John turned the music down slightly. "You women act like you're so God damn oppressed. You have no idea how good you have it. And *you*, Kasey? *Oh*, the rich trust-fund kid that will never have to face any real problems in her sheltered little fucking life. Millionaire trust fund money, your own house at twenty-one, lavish European excursions, the finest fucking schooling money can buy—such a terrible, horrible form of oppression."

"No," Kasey snarled, shaking her head. "That's the thing, John, you're conflating economic privilege with gender privilege. You're forgetting that you're in a position of power as a male—and that isn't nullified because of your economic standing. You're never going to have to worry about being raped and impregnated by your attacker. You're never going to have to worry about being forced to carry a pregnancy to term. You're never going to know what it's like to be treated as a second-class citizen. You can do pretty much anything you want. This world belongs to you, not me."

John pointed dramatically at a row of abandoned houses. "And economic inequality is what? Nothing? It just means nothing if you're a man, right? My grandparents saved their entire lives to be able to pitch in for me to go to a good school. Even with the scholarship, I'll be in fucking debt for a long fucking time. How'd you get to university, huh? With some of Daddy's money that Mommy found in the washing machine?"

"Great, John, *more* sexist stereotypes. The woman washes the clothes while the man is making all the money, right? You'll never see just how sexist you really are."

John aggressively pulled over to the side of the street, parked the car and unbuckled his seatbelt. "It's only about *gender* with you, isn't it? Nothing else fucking matters in your brainwashed little mind, does it?"

Kasey looked around nervously. "John, maybe we should keep driving, this doesn't look like the best of neighborhoods."

John gritted his teeth. "Oh, and why is that, Kasey? Because poor fucks live around here? You think poor is synonymous with criminal, huh? You rich kids make me fucking sick! You think you have it so bad in this world because you're a woman? Try being a man—better yet, try being a poor man. All I ever hear about is *male privilege* this and *male privilege* that—but did you ever stop to think about your own fucking privilege? You women have it fucking made in this country. You want equality? You want to be like a man? Then stop fucking crying about everything; because real men don't fucking cry! And news flash, you already got your fucking equality."

"You are *so* wrong, John, it's unbelievable. I mean, you study history, don't you? What did you do, skip all the chapters on the endless struggle of women? *Oh*, yeah, we can *vote*, and we passed some laws, so that makes everything equal now, right? It doesn't work that way, John. The fight isn't over. There is systemic and institutionalized sexism in this country that you choose not to see because of your privilege. You don't *have* to see it. You don't *have* to care! Do you know where I slept for weeks and weeks after I was chased down the street and called a *whore* in my own neighborhood, not knowing if I was going to be raped or killed by my attacker? Do you know what the cop said to me while I was shivering in fear on my neighbor's front porch? I had to sleep on Dave and Jennifer's couch for a long time—because I was too afraid to be alone in my own home. A couple weeks ago was the first time I've slept in my own bed in months. Every time I hear a car door slam, or someone talking outside, I am in absolute panic. I can't sleep at night. I live in *constant fear*." She paused for a breath. "And the cop—that bitter old man—he looked me right in my face and asked me what *I* did to make the guy chase me down the street. That's the world *I* live in, John."

"That was *one* fucking guy, Kasey. So, every man is guilty because that cop is a fucking asshole? Who saved your ass that night, eh? I *know* what happened at that party. Did the girls jump off the porch and chase the guy away? *Or*, maybe it was someone else?" He chuckled derisively. "Feminism isn't about equality; it's about hating men. You just don't have the balls to admit it."

"You really just don't get it, do you?" Kasey criticized, crossing her arms, looking out the window. "You *really* just don't get it."

"This is fucking pointless," John declared. "Let's just get the fuck out of here. You can tell me what a horrible person I am on the way home. How does that sound? And after I drop you off, that'll be that. The project is finished; there's no reason for us to be hanging around each other anymore. There are a million fucking assholes at that school that'll be willing to tutor me. We don't have to be friends just because we're in the same God damn social club."

"Whatever," she said, shaking her head, "just take me home."

"It was a big fucking mistake taking you out tonight."

She scoffed, rolling her eyes.

Turning up the music, he watched her as she activated the GPS on her smart phone. Thoughts raced through his mind. Gazing upon her sunken expression, he was bitterly reminded of all the times he saw her smiling, all the times he heard her laughing. He thought about the bronze apple paperweight and his promise that he would never hurt her again. Removing his hand from the shifter, he left the car in park. He rolled down the window and lit a cigarette.

John looked in his side-view mirror to the left-hand side of the block. In the distance, there was a carryout Chinese restaurant that served their guests through a window behind bulletproof glass like a bank teller. Below the backlit yellow sign, four old black men in their late eighties sat on plastic chairs in a circle out on the sidewalk. They wore suits, polished dress shoes and spiffy fedoras. Their time was almost over, but they refused to yield; they refused to be run off by the harsh reality of crime, gang violence, and the ravages of the Baltimore city heroin epidemic. Every evening, like clockwork, they would sit until midnight and reminisce about the old days; the hard times and the good. They were the last four men on their block. All the other row homes were boarded up, blighted and condemned by the city. John studied the men with awe and curiosity through the mirror. If Kasey wasn't with him, he would've backed his car up, parked it and joined them out on the sidewalk. There, he would've heard Mr. Jenkins' tales of working at a slaughterhouse in the Jim Crow south before landing a job at the B&O railroad, or Mr. Miller's stories of Hollins Market and Poppleton in the late 1940s after the war, or Mr. Johnson's humble narration of the peace rallies that he attended with his church during the 1968 Baltimore riots, or Mr. Walker's recollection of his first Orioles game he watched at Memorial Stadium, long before Camden Yards was ever thought of. They used to call Memorial Stadium "the Old Grey Lady of 33rd Street". John would've listened with keen interest to the rich history they had to offer; to their epic stories the Digital Age no longer had the ears to hear.

"I didn't know that you smoked," Kasey uttered, breaking his concentration.

"I don't," John said, tapping ash from the cigarette out onto the street.

Kasey's phone shined bright with GPS directions back home.

"It's not good for you," she said.

John snickered. "Yeah, I know. That's what my father used to tell me."

"He's right."

John took a drag, staring at the stoops in front of the old row houses. "I got caught smoking at school when I was fourteen. One of my teammates called me a dumbass because I smoked the cigarette in the middle of the hallway while I was walking to a class."

Kasey squinted. "Why did you do that?"

John took a deep, focused draw from the cigarette. "My grandfather and brother died in the same year. After my brother died, I kind of—went astray for a little while."

Kasey slowly returned her phone to her purse.

"I had to do some stupid after-school smoking class," he imparted. "I got suspended for three days. My father didn't talk to me all day. When he finally knocked on my bedroom door, I thought he was just coming in to lecture me."

"What'd he do?"

John chuckled. "We had a *friendly* boxing match. He won."

"Oh my gosh."

John smirked. "I thought he was strict *before* my brother died. He went full Gestapo afterward. I don't blame him, though. He's a good man. We all have our flaws. After that, I didn't smoke a cigarette again until Bo died. I'm not even sure why I bought 'em. I just can't believe he's really gone."

"I'm so sorry, John."

John turned his head, glancing down at her hand that was resting on top of his. "Kasey—I didn't mean to yell at you and say those awful things. I didn't mean 'em."

"It's uh..." Kasey looked in the rearview mirror, distracted by two men in their early twenties approaching their vehicle. John followed her eyes to the mirror. "Maybe we should go," Kasey suggested.

"Nah. Just be cool," John urged, taking another puff of his cigarette. He blew the smoke out of the window. A droplet of rain fell on his hand.

John nodded to the music that was playing on the stereo. He turned it up a little louder. Kasey clutched her purse as the two men drew near. John peeked down at her hands.

"Don't do that," John discouraged, shaking his head.

"Do what?"

"Just put the purse down and be cool," John whispered.

One of the men walked up and stood perfectly still outside of the passenger-side door. The other man placed his hand on the roof of the car, leaning down to meet John face-to-face.

"Car trouble?" the man said, smiling.

"Nah. We're just talking. Been a long night," John explained.

"I gotcha," the man said. "You know, there's a toll for parking your car here."

"A toll," John said, raising his eyebrows with a smirk.

The man nodded. "Yeah, a motherfucking toll, motherfucker."

Kasey's hands started to tremble.

"What kind of toll?" John asked.

"Fifty dollars," the man declared.

"Fifty dollars," John snickered. "Fuck off."

"John, don't," Kasey whimpered.

The man removed his hand from the roof of the car, stood up straight and turned away. With a sharp twist of his body, he launched a fist, cracking it hard against John's jaw.

"What the fuck!" John shouted, covering his head.

The passenger-side window shattered with a brick.

Kasey *shrieked*.

"Jesus fucking Christ!" John cried out.

The men drew pistols.

"Your money, motherfucker!" the robber demanded, pushing the gun against his cheek.

"I—I—what—I," John stammered, glancing down at the barrel of the gun.

"Now, motherfucker!" he commanded, jamming the pistol harder against his face.

"Fucking take it," John groaned, pulling out his money clip. "That's all I got!"

"Thanks for my money," the man said, stuffing the cash in his pocket, "fucking little bitch."

Kasey struggled to hold on to her purse.

"Kasey, just let him have it!" John begged.

The second man jabbed her in the face. Kasey grunted, stunned, still holding on to her purse. John's eyes widened and his nostrils flared. In one swift motion, he reached into his glovebox, pulled out a double-action, six-shot, .357 Magnum revolver, cocked the gun and pointed it at the man who punched Kasey in the face. "Fuck you!" John screamed with all his breath, all his rage.

Time slowed against the racing of his heart. The next song on the cassette tape started to play Otis Redding's version of "That's How Strong My Love Is". Intense stillness encompassed the standoff. John struggled to steady his trembling hand; like trying to bend a spoon with his mind. Kasey forced herself against the backrest; like suffering the rickety climb on an old wooden rollercoaster, peeking over the edge just before the steep plunge into the unknown.

The barrel of the robber's gun caressed the back of John's head.

Help me, God, just this once.

Kasey's chin mirrored the shivering of John's hand. She tightly closed her eyes.

John gripped the trigger.

Goodbye, Mom. I love you, Dad.

Rain sprinkled under the soft glow of a nearby streetlight. The haunting voice of Otis Redding echoed throughout the night sky. Aiming his revolver, John locked eyes on the man who struck Kasey.

Under the backlit Chinese food sign, Mr. Walker stood from his chair, cupped his hands around his mouth and hollered, "Hey! Knock it off, you knuckleheads!"

The young robbers turned their heads to see the four old men standing down on the corner. Inside the car, John and Kasey were too close to the stereo speakers to hear Mr. Walker shouting in the distance. Over the roof of the car, the robbers returned to look at each other.

"Let's go," the man instructed his partner, walking away from the car.

Still aiming his gun, John watched the second man fade from his vision.

The robbers turned down an alleyway. John lowered his gun. Kasey looked at him through the corner of her eye. Simultaneously, they exhaled. Unaware of Mr. Walker's intervention, John viewed their retreat as a lucky fold in a bet-all hand of Texas Hold 'em.

❧

John took the revolver with his left hand and threw the car into drive. Tires screeched as the pedal hit the floor. Kasey stuffed her purse behind the seat. John handed her the gun. She grinned then carefully returned it to the glovebox. They didn't speak. Signs to the interstate welcomed them to their second chance at life. Wind and misty rain blew through their hair as they soared down the open highway. Their hands met at the center console as they rode off into the early morning darkness.

❧

Midnight was the memory of a pipe dream. Shaken up by the robbery, Kasey had asked John to spend the night on her couch. With the sleeping bag that she'd purchased for Mel's camping trip, she would join him in the living room. She unlocked the front door and welcomed him into her home. Scanning the first floor, he apprehensively entered.

"Nice place," John complimented, almost in a whisper.

"Thanks."

"Home sweet home, right?" he said, chuckling nervously.

"Yeah," she said, giggling softly, "no more hanging out in the hood for me."

The smile ran away from his face. "That robbery could've happened anywhere, *Kase*. There's a lot of good, hardworking people living in that neighborhood."

"I know," she said, looking at the floor. "I didn't mean anything by it."

John nodded. "I know. It's cool," he said, putting his hands in his pockets. "You, *uh*, ready to call it a night? I need to be up in a few hours."

"You mind if I grab a quick shower first? I feel disgusting."

John shrugged. "*Eh*, you don't need my permission."

"Cool, give me ten."

John began investigating her living room as she sprinted up the stairs. At a cursory glance, he thought Marcus may have been accurate in his assessment that Kasey had turned into his seventy-year-old grandmother. The carpet was freshly scented, bearing the recent markings of a determined vacuum cleaner. Crafts and knickknacks cluttered the walls and shelves. Flowers were neatly arranged in glass bubble vases on each of the end tables. The furniture appeared to have never been sat upon. Looking around the room, he paused. He noticed the bronze apple paperweight he had given her, proudly sitting on top of a small bookcase. Next to it was a framed picture of all of them at Francesca Hall. Marcus had prints made for her, presumably by request. John smiled as he touched the apple. Continuing his inspection, he walked over to the big screen television on the opposite side of the room. Squinting, he noticed something odd sitting on a shelf behind a glass door in the entertainment center. He shrugged his shoulders and proceeded to the couch.

Plopping on the plush, light brown sofa, John put his hands behind his head and kicked up his feet. He heard the shower turn on from upstairs and began unenthusiastically whistling Mozart's "Eine Kleine Nachtmusik". His eyes wandered. Kasey had a record player and two crates of vinyl LPs in the corner near the entrance. After a few minutes of lounging, he stood from the couch and skimmed through her albums. Most of her records were sub-genre indie music that he never heard of. Flipping through the second crate, he paused and smiled for a moment, revealing a Johnny Cash album in the middle of the stack.

A noise through the pipe indicated that the water had stopped. John resisted the urge to rummage through her purse that she left sitting near the door, but his curiosity prevailed. He wanted to know why she had risked her life to hold on to it during the robbery. John powered up the stereo and moved the tonearm to the first song of Tom Waits' *Mule Variations* record. Under cloak of the music, he searched through her purse, discovering a canister of pepper spray, eight dollars in cash and an Ohio driver's license.

"She drives?" he whispered to himself. "Dude, you're an asshole," he declared, zipping the purse back up.

Retreating from his unethical searching of her property, he returned to looking through her vinyl records. His superficial hunting through her purse had offered no insight as to why she was so protective of it. Perhaps, John thought, it was merely out of instinct or principle.

"Don't you just love vinyl?" Kasey asked, descending the stairs.

John turned to see Kasey drying her hair, wearing an oversized t-shirt and a pair of pink pajama pants. "At the risk of sounding like a hipster, I prefer the sound of vinyl."

"Me too," she said, draping the towel over the banister.

"You got some cool records. I didn't know you liked Johnny Cash."

"Who doesn't?"

"*Yeah*, all the hipsters like him these days," John said, glancing at the television. "Did, *uh*—Marcus leave his camera here?"

"No," she said, shaking her head.

"Oh, right on," he said, "yours just looks a lot like his."

She turned her head towards the entertainment center. "Well—he gave me his, actually. He said he didn't want it anymore. I think he just felt bad that we never celebrated my birthday."

"Oh, okay, cool."

A moment of silence befell the room.

The next song on the LP started to play.

John breathed a heavy sigh. "Long day," he said, sitting on the arm of the couch.

"Yeah," Kasey said, staring at the floor.

"Yeah."

Tapping his fingers, he looked around the room. Kasey was lost in thought, deeply contemplating the events that had transpired.

"John?"

"What's up?"

"I'm really sorry about tonight," she faintly spoke.

"*Ah*, don't worry about it. I'm sure we'll look back on this someday and laugh."

"I don't think I'm ever going to laugh about this, John."

"*Come on,* we're alright now. Shit happens."

"I almost got us killed," she choked out.

"What?" he scoffed, hopping off the arm of the sofa. "No, you didn't," he said, walking toward her. "I'm the idiot that got us lost. I should've just let you put the damn GPS on."

Her voice cracked as she spoke, "I should have just given him the stupid purse."

"Kasey, I'm the one who screwed up, not you," he said, loosely putting his arm around her. "If I would've just listened to you, we would've never gotten lost in the first place."

"I thought they were going to shoot you," she sobbed, struggling to hide her full emotion.

"It's okay," John said, wrapping his arms around her. "We're fine now."

"I thought you were going to die," she cried, burying her face into his chest. "I'm so sorry."

"You don't have to be sorry, Kasey," he said, hugging her tightly. "I'm the one that should be sorry—not just for getting us lost—for everything. I'm a fucking idiot to treat someone like you so poorly all the time. I'm so fucking stupid, it's unbelievable."

The third track of *Mule Variations* began to play.

"I'm glad we're friends, Kasey. I'm glad we didn't die. I'm glad we're safe," he said in a soft panic, stroking her back. "I'm so happy you're okay, Kasey. I'm so happy you're okay. I don't ever want to see you hurt. I'm a God damn fool. I'm so sorry I ever hurt you. I'm so sorry," he sniffled.

Looking up, she became hypnotized by a teardrop sliding down his cheek.

"I forgive you," she exhaled, catching her breath. "I forgive you."

～〜

Their night had gone from fun and excitement to violence and mayhem and all the way to the edge of death. And there, as the Tom Waits song sang melancholy through the stereo speakers, it had brought them into each other's arms. The glass entertainment center glistened with streaks of moonlight through the bay window. Ghostly fragrances of cinnamon candles and fresh flowers floated through the air. She wiped the tear away from his face, looking deep into his eyes. Their heartbeats raced in sync. Without fear of interruption, they inched closer. Drawn together by an inexplicable magnetic force, they collided, to a wild and ravenous, enigmatic embrace.

CHAPTER 24

ENTANGLEMENT

When Kasey awoke in her bed later that morning, John was gone. A note he wrote in her eyeliner sat on the nightstand: *I didn't want to wake you. -John. XOXO.*

Professor Diana Luskovo's 66ᵗʰ birthday celebration began at noon. John planned to attend after his morning appointment with Philippe Álvarez. On his way to *The Dollhouse*, John organized his thoughts. Commentary surrounding the recent event in Washington D.C. swelled in the recesses of the internet. Bradley Hamilton was still in a coma. John rigorously checked for updates, but information on the gunman's motives and targets remained a mystery. If the Anastasia Carval article had provoked the incident, it would have marked two failed assassination attempts elicited by the witch hoax.

Although John would undoubtedly speak of the underworld that resuscitated the witch hoax, his morning appointment was for something less nefarious: breakfast. Philippe Álvarez was turning 57. While the Avalonti Society prepared a celebration for Diana Luskovo, John would be having a birthday breakfast, miles away, at Philippe's residence in the hills of West Virginia. After breakfast, John and Philippe sat in his dilapidated kitchen and talked for a while. Noticing the broken passenger-side window on John's car when he pulled up, Philippe urged him to divulge information about his wild night in Baltimore. Philippe, after spending twenty-five years among hardened criminals in a maximum-security prison, questioned why the two men who drew firearms on them simply walked away when John pulled his gun out. John and Kasey's survival, in the eyes of Philippe Álvarez, was unmistakably a miracle from God. John quite naturally resisted the notion, suggesting that the young men were petty thieves rather than hardened criminals. When he brandished his firearm with confidence, John argued that he had effectively called their bluff and scared them off.

Their disagreement inflamed a theological discussion and John lost track of time. Upon realizing the hour, John bid farewell to Philippe and rushed back to Maryland in hopes of catching the latter half of Professor Luskovo's birthday celebration.

~~

John entered his apartment, turned off the NPR broadcast on his alarm clock radio, took a shower, threw on some clothes, then headed for the university. By the time John arrived, most of the guests had already left. Vandacheler, Kasey, Marcus, Arjun, Diana Luskovo and a couple Avalonti Sages remained.

"Sorry I'm late," John announced, walking toward the remaining guests.

"John!" Kasey shouted, jumping up to give him a hug and a kiss on the cheek. "I missed you!"

John blushed as the guests fell silent. Marcus dramatically raised his eyebrows. Arjun smirked condescendingly. Vandacheler leaned towards Marcus and said, "Lobster bisque—quite delicious."

Marcus grumbled incoherently.

Kasey gathered her belongings, preparing to leave to meet up with a friend.

As the guests resumed their conversations, John pulled Kasey to the side. "Hey, *Kase*," John whispered, "don't you think we should be a little more discreet?"

Kasey scrunched her face, refusing to whisper. "Discreet? I—I don't see why. Unless..." She paused for a moment. "Do you regret what we did?"

"No, no, no, no, not at all. I just—you know—want to keep a little composure, showcase some professionalism. You know what I mean?"

Kasey grinned. "Don't be such a wuss, John," she said, leaning up to kiss him on the lips. "I'm getting ready to head out. Alyssa and I are going to The Red Porcupine in a little while. I'll see you around, okay?"

"Uh, yeah, okay," John said, smiling uncontrollably.

"Goodbye, John," she said, winking suggestively.

John chuckled. "See ya, Kasey."

"See you guys!" she shouted, looking back, walking toward the exit. "Happy Birthday, Ms. Luskovo!"

"Be safe," Vandacheler urged.

"Goodbye, Kasey," Arjun saluted.

"I'll see ya, darling," Diana Luskovo said, waving cheerfully. "Remember, don't take anybody's shit!"

"I won't," Kasey hollered, smiling, walking to the threshold.

In the center of the grand foyer, John gazed upon the double doors, which had been propped open for the event. Marcus quietly joined him, watching Kasey disappear beyond the evergreen hedges.

"Nice welt," Marcus said, glancing at John's face.

"Yeah," John said, "accident in the mosh pit."

"I heard."

"Oh, she told you guys about the show?"

"Yep. Doesn't look like she told us everything, though, eh?"

John shrugged.

"So, you guys are a thing now, huh?" Marcus inquired.

"*Uh*, maybe. I don't know. I guess so."

"There must've been some magic at the rock concert last night, eh?"

John continued to face the exit. "You could say that."

"I'd like to say something to you, John, and I don't want you to take it the wrong way."

"Go ahead."

Marcus turned his head, meeting him face-to-face. "Kasey has become like a sister to me. You're a good friend, John, and I'd like it to stay that way. Treat her right, brother."

"I will," John assured, offering a handshake.

They shook hands.

"I know you will," Marcus said with a hint of skepticism.

John took a breath then started to walk back toward the others.

"Oh, hey, John."

"Yeah?" he said, turning back around.

"I—*uh*, noticed KNWRZ picked up a new contributor. Some skeptic—calls himself *Reyal Xaoh*."

John's heart rate accelerated. "I didn't notice."

Marcus squinted. "You should check him out, John. He's really sharp—really *passionate* too."

John swallowed. "I haven't really been paying much attention to the conspiracy theory crap. I need to declare a major soon, ya know, and we got finals coming up. I've been concentrating a lot on schoolwork lately. I'm thinking about taking some physics classes next semester. And now that Kasey and I are a thing—*I guess*—I just don't have time for it."

Marcus nodded. "Yeah, I have a lot going on too. Just stay out of trouble, my friend."

"Yeah, I try."

∽∾

John called Kasey after he left the hall and invited her to have dinner at his apartment. She accepted. Visiting a grocery store near The Marquis, John purchased the necessary ingredients for a curried Thai dish that would accommodate Kasey's recently professed vegetarianism. Lacking confidence in his culinary skill, John bought extra supplies; a decision that would prove saving. While scurrying to finish the replacement batch of tofu, John heard a knocking on his door. Kasey had arrived. He opened the door, greeted her in the threshold, took her overnight bag and hugged her tightly.

"Miss me, John?"

"Sorry," John said, chuckling, releasing her from his embrace. "Come on in."

Kasey looked around and walked over to the little dining room, noticing a rose in a vase on the center of the table. John quickly returned to the stove.

"*Awe*, look, you even got us a flower," she complimented.

"I know you like flowers, especially roses," he said, stirring the curried tofu.

Kasey snickered. "That's so cliché, isn't it?"

"Roses are a beautiful flower," John reassured, continuing to battle his kitchen.

"It's wonderful, John. I really appreciate you doing this for us."

"It's my pleasure, *Kase*. Have a seat, dinner will be ready in a minute."

～～

John activated a classical music playlist on his computer. He lit two candles on the table, poured two glasses of Cabernet Sauvignon and presented his culinary creation. Kasey expressed sincere gratitude, remarking that the Thai curried tofu and steamed rice were delicious. She courteously took a single sip of the wine as they engaged in conversation.

After dinner, they sat together on his 14th story balcony, admiring the evening view of the bustling streets below. A chilly spring breeze prompted John to wrap a light blanket around them. In between the bouts of silence, they talked about life, their dreams and their plans after graduation. Recalling a fleeting memory of visiting a beach in Florida with his family when he was five, John expressed an interest in taking a trip to see the ocean. Kasey showed him pictures of Ocean City, Maryland on her phone and promised to go with him after the school year.

As the night neared its end, John fixed himself a drink and closed the kitchen while Kasey rested on his bed. When he entered his room asking if she wanted to watch a movie, he discovered that she had already fallen asleep. John smiled. He turned the lights off and quietly joined her.

John awoke just before dawn to the sound of two men having a political conversation in his living room. They were talking about the Russian revolutionary, Leon Trotsky. His heart raced as he listened to the strange discussion through his bedroom wall. Gently removing Kasey's arm from his chest, he slipped out of bed and crouched beside the nightstand, grabbing his .357 Magnum revolver.

Creeping through the little hallway toward the living room, John drew back the hammer on the revolver and took a deep breath. Jumping out from behind the wall, he yelled, "Freeze, motherfucker!"

Lowering his gun, he laughed, shaking his head. He'd forgotten that he'd programmed an alarm the day before his meeting with Philippe Álvarez. Turning off the NPR broadcast, he sighed and returned to his room.

Kasey opened her sleepy eyes to find John placing his gun on the nightstand before crawling back into bed.

"What are you doing?" she asked.

He kissed her on the forehead. "Nothing."

Lying on his chest, she fell asleep again in a matter of seconds.

John put his arm around her, stroking her gently as he drifted into deep thought. The alarm clock episode had inspired him to contemplate the Philippe Álvarez debates, which were rapidly approaching. Additionally, John recalled Dr. Ouradnik mentioning something about a bizarre phenomenon observed in the quantum world that would supposedly expand his mind. He wanted to know more, but Dr. Ouradnik hadn't give him any details on what to look for; he merely stated that he would know it when he found it. John planned an afternoon of research after his morning classes.

Unable to get back to sleep, John snuck into the kitchen to surprise Kasey with breakfast. Halfway through cooking sausage and his last three eggs, he stopped, slapped his forehead and called himself an idiot. He opened his bare fridge and searched his lonely cabinets for something vegetarian. Tapping his fingers on his cheek, he improvised. The Marquis' room service always arrived with a complimentary piece of fruit. Since John was never billed for room service, per his Avalonti membership, he had an ample assortment of fruit laying on his countertop.

"Morning!" John greeted Kasey, turning off the blender as she emerged from the bedroom. "I made you a smoothie for breakfast."

Kasey rubbed her eyes and smiled. "Thanks, John."

~~

John returned to his apartment that afternoon ready to delve into the world of quantum mechanics. Alone, he poured himself an IPA and sat at his computer desk. When he entered queries into Google, looking up strange quantum effects, search results bombarded the screen. Almost everything about quantum mechanics appeared bizarre to him. Figuring out which one Dr. Ouradnik was talking about would prove more challenging than he had anticipated.

"All I Have to Do is Dream" by The Everly Brothers played through his Atmos speakers. While he was researching and watching YouTube videos, an unfamiliar, nagging, gentle nausea struck his stomach. Moments later, he called Kasey.

"Hey, Kasey, how are you?"

"I'm good, what's up?"

"I was, *uh*—just thinking about you. Are you doing anything tonight?"

"Well—that's up to you," she said, giggling.

"Yeah?" he chuckled. "You should come over again for dinner."

Kasey happily agreed to join him, allowing him only a couple of hours of research before she arrived. John continued but was fruitless in his endeavor to discover the quantum phenomenon Dr. Ouradnik prompted him to find. In lieu of researching physics, he decided to write a quick article for KNWRZ. John wrote about Bradley Hamilton, the man who was shot by the U.S. Capitol police for brandishing a firearm. His call to sense and reason was quickly ridiculed by the conspiracy theorists. The usual juvenile insults flew in, as expected, but he came across a comment that he had not yet experienced; one that startled him. Someone using a fake account, bearing the name Agnes Sampson, issued a grim threat: *I am going to kill you, Reyal Xaoh.*

Normally, John would have brushed off an online threat, but since there were, presumably, two assassination attempts on Congresswoman Anastasia Carval as a result of the hoax, he took it very seriously. He immediately reported the threat to Facebook; something he thought he would never do.

~~

Kasey arrived an hour later with her overnight bag, containing, among other things, her hairdryer, shampoo, makeup, nail files, tweezers, cotton swabs, several articles of clothing and a bottle of perfume.

"You mind if I leave a couple things here, John?" she asked, unpacking her bag.

"Not at all," John answered fragrantly.

"Thanks," she said, continuing to unpack her things.

John sat on his couch and picked up an issue of the *Avalonti Journal* from an end table.

"Do you think what we're doing is weird?" Kasey asked suddenly, squinting.

"What do you mean?"

"My friend thinks it's weird that I'm staying over at your apartment."

"Who's your friend?" he asked. "Mel?" he grumbled.

"Alyssa."

"Why would it be weird?"

"I don't know. She's Italian. Her parents are really conservative and old-fashioned. She tries to be hip and progressive, but I think it's obviously had an impact on her. She just thinks we jumped into this a little too fast."

"Is that what *you* think?" John asked, closing the journal.

"No," she answered impishly, "I'm just making conversation."

John scoffed. "Just making conversation, eh? Look, Kasey, it's not weird. She's probably just jealous that you have a boyfriend now. These feminists are always talking about how women shouldn't be judged on decisions like this—but then, as soon as a woman does something they don't like, they're all over her shit.

You know, sometimes women oppress other women more than men do. That's what I think, anyway."

"I have a boyfriend now, huh?" she asked, plopping next to him on the couch.

"*Um, I, uh,*" John mumbled, blushing, chuckling, "I guess if you want one."

Kasey giggled. "Okay."

～～

Since The Marquis was a modern, state-of-the-art, four-star hotel, their dinner menu included several vegan and vegetarian options. They planned to order room service and lounge around watching movies. John, in quiet solidarity, ordered Chana Masala while Kasey had the tempeh with white wine mushroom gravy and avocado toast. For dessert, they shared a piece of non-dairy chocolate fudge truffle cake and a dish of mango sorbet. Before they started the movie, Kasey asked if she could take a quick shower.

As soon as he heard the water, John leapt to his computer to see what became of Agnes Sampson. Facebook had suspended the account, but there was another strange comment. The user Zgnes Zampson wrote: *Nice try, Reyal Xaoh, but you can't kill a ghost. You'll never stop me.* John quickly realized that reporting the sock accounts was useless. By the time he worked up the courage to reply, he heard the shower stop.

Against his better judgement, he quickly wrote: *Bring it on, motherfucker.*

His comment was almost immediately "laugh-reacted".

Zgnes Zampson replied: *Mr. Kalashnikov is eager to meet you.*

Reyal Xaoh: *I'll stick that rifle up your ass, motherfucker.*

His comment was immediately laugh-reacted.

Zgnes Zampson: *Promise?*

Reyal Xaoh: *Come find out.*

His comment was immediately laugh-reacted.

Zgnes Zampson: *I shall take great delight in watching you die.*

Reyal Xaoh: *You'll be the one who dies if you fuck with me.*

His comment was immediately laugh-reacted.

Zgnes Zampson: *I hide right in front of you.*

Reyal Xaoh: *Why don't you show yourself then, coward?*

His comment was immediately laugh-reacted.

John cringed, saying, "Why did I type that?"

Zgnes Zampson: *Don't worry, sexy, you'll see me soon.*

"Fuck you, troll," he said under his breath, sneaking back to the couch.

Kasey returned from dressing in his bedroom and joined him on the couch a few moments later. They lounged together in their pajamas watching a movie that she had picked; a romantic French comedy entitled *Amélie*. She repeatedly glanced at him to make sure he was enjoying the film. John would summon a smile every time she turned her head. Halfway through the movie, her scrutiny subsided. John carefully freed himself from her embrace, placing a throw pillow under her head as he stood from the couch.

Ignoring the Facebook comments, John resumed his physics research while she slept. He learned about the quantum leap, Schrödinger's equation, the uncertainty principle, quarks, electromagnetic radiation, gluons, and a wealth of other unique characteristics of the quantum world. While researching, he stumbled across a phenomenon that stood apart from the other weirdness of quantum mechanics. John declared that it *must* have been what Dr. Ouradnik was talking about. Intrigued, perplexed and a bit terrified, John was immediately fascinated by what Einstein had dubbed "spooky action at a distance". The strange, bizarre and mind-bending *quantum entanglement.*

Provoked by the weirdness of quantum entanglement, John pored over theories attempting to explain how two entangled particles could instantaneously affect each other; even if they were separated by billions of light years. Upon delving deeper, John discovered various other experiments, effects, and theories that were, to him, equally as weird as quantum entanglement: the quantum Zeno effect, superposition, the double-slit experiment, vacuum birefringence, the Hong-Ou-Mandel effect, entangled time and the neutrino identity crisis.

"What time is it?" Kasey sleepily asked, peeling herself from the couch.

"After midnight."

She walked over to the computer desk. "*Why* are you still awake?"

John looked up at her and smiled. "I was just getting ready to come pick you up and carry you to the bedroom."

She giggled, rubbing his shoulders.

Retreating to John's room, they crawled into bed. Kasey rested her head on his chest and started to fall asleep again. John, still wide awake, struggled to make sense of his bizarre quantum research. He twiddled his thumbs while his thoughts ricocheted between quantum mechanics, Caesar Avalonti, his brother, his father and back to quantum mechanics. Finally, just after 2 a.m., he fell into a deep sleep, where he was met with a confounding dream:

John found himself standing on an empty beach that stretched for miles. The boardwalk rides were lit up and in motion, but there was nobody else there. A moon in the form of a disco ball spun overhead, maybe fifty feet in the air. There was a building on the boardwalk near the attractions with a giant shark tail sticking out of the side of it. The beach hovered in outer space, but there were no stars or planets in sight. Waves formed out of the sand and crashed away from the shoreline. Beyond the breaks of the backwards waves was absolute nothingness.

John heard himself speaking in slow motion, "What is this place?"

In a first-person gaze, he looked at the giant shark tail. It squeaked as it began to wiggle. The hotels and condos were empty. Gentle carnival music twinkled with the turning of the Ferris wheel. The faint sound of children cheering and laughing was heard from beneath the sand. The far side of the beach peacefully evaporated into a black hole. A shadowy figure approached from a distance, periodically calling out his name. His voice echoed strangely throughout the night sky.

John struggled to yell, "Who are you?"

All the rides stopped at once and the carnival lights went out.

The shadowy figure disappeared.

Bewildered, John stood under the bizarre moonlight, alone.

"John," his dead brother stated in a clear, crisp voice, standing directly behind him.

John slowly turned around. His brother appeared exactly how he remembered him over seven years ago. Noticing his own hand from the corner of his eye, John saw himself as he was when he was fourteen; the age he was when his brother had died.

"Freddy, where are we?" John asked, fighting against the slow motion of his voice.

"This is where I live, John."

"I miss you, Freddy."

"John, we don't have much time. You need to listen to me. They're coming for you."

"What? Who?"

A resounding, deep, dark, diabolical laughter encircled them, and John's brother vanished, like powdery hourglass sand blowing in the wind. The maddening laughter continued as the teenager from the punk rock show emerged from behind one of the lifeguard towers. Lurching toward him, he grimaced in pain, clutching his abdomen. Buckets of blood poured from his stab wounds. The teenager stopped walking and gurgled in hellish agony as the black hole ripped him into shreds.

John awoke at four in the morning, startled to discover that Kasey was no longer in bed. The unusual dream had jarred him, but he remained calm.

"Kasey?"

"Kasey?" he repeated.

He sighed when he heard the toilet flush.

"*Oh*, sorry, did I wake you?" she asked as she returned to the bedroom, gently closing the door behind her.

"No, no, no, no, you're fine," John assured.

Kasey giggled, walking around the bed. "You were making weird noises in your sleep."

"Was I?" John chuckled. "How long have you been up?"

"I just got up to go to the bathroom not even a minute ago," she said, returning to the bed. "I was having a *really* good dream too."

"Oh, yeah? What were you dreaming about?"

She wrapped up in the blanket and smiled at him. "The beach."

"*Oh*," he said. "Awesome."

CHAPTER 25

I SEE YOU

John briefly studied for his final exams the following afternoon while Kasey attended a PSRC meeting for an upcoming protest. Philosophy, English and history, for John, were easy subjects, so he decided to switch over to his physics research. While watching videos on YouTube, John was interrupted by a telephone call; the apartment line. The only time his apartment phone rang was when the concierge was contacting him. He answered quickly. The front desk informed him that a truck was out front with a delivery. John threw on a pair of sandals and hopped on the elevator.

Approaching the front desk, John noticed two men outside unloading a black and orange Kawasaki Ninja 650 sports bike. Someone had sent him an extravagant gift. As he was arguing with the drivers about who sent the bike, his phone vibrated; Philippe Álvarez was calling him.

"What do you think?" Philippe asked over the phone.

"You're the one who sent this?" John begged.

"Sure, John, your 22nd birthday is next month. I figured I'd send it early; let you get some use out of it. I just got notification that the delivery was made. I will only need you to sign off on some paperwork and it's all yours."

"Philippe, I can't accept a fucking sports bike!"

"I'd really like you to have it, John. It'll make those long trips easier on your wallet. Gas is so expensive these days. I remember when gas was 62 cents per gallon."

"Philippe, come on, I can't take this. I appreciate it, I really do, but I just can't."

"Acts 20:35. Please, John, it would mean a lot to me if you accept it."

John paused and looked over the beautiful sports bike for a minute. "Alright," John sighed, "if you insist."

"I do insist."

"Thank you, Philippe. The bike looks awesome by the way."

"You're welcome. Happy birthday, son—*ahem*, John."

"Let me talk to the hotel staff and find out where I can store this thing. Thanks again, Philippe. I'll call you soon."

"Goodbye, John. Glad you like the bike."

John returned to the front desk to ask where he could store the bike. The concierge called for the valet then handed John a letter. "Your mail, sir," the woman said.

"*Oh*," John said. "Who's it from?"

"There's no return address, sir."

Scrunching his face at the letter, John called Philippe back.

"John? Everything alright?"

"Did you send me a letter?"

"*Uh*—no, just the bike. What does it say?"

"I didn't open it yet. Let me get this bike put away, I'll call you later."

"Okay. Let me know if everything is alright. Take care, John."

∾∾

John returned to his apartment after the valet took the bike to the hotel's parking garage. Placing his new helmet on the glass coffee table, he sat on his brown leather couch and opened the mysterious letter. After reading the letter, he sprang to his door and locked it. He grabbed his gun and paced around his apartment. The letter didn't have a return address, but it had a postmark. The threatening letter was sent by someone very close. In a small font, printed on the center of a piece of plain white paper, the typed letter read: *I see you, Hoax Slayer.*

Deciding not to go to the police or to anyone at Avalonti, John contemplated *who* sent the letter, *why*, and *how* he would handle it on his own. Whoever sent the letter knew where he lived and knew that he was Reyal Xaoh. How they obtained his unlisted address was a complete mystery. John hoped that it was Philippe Álvarez playing a prank on him but thought it was unlikely because the postmark was not from West Virginia. His only other suspect was Dr. Ouradnik, but he couldn't think of any reason *he* would have sent it. Still, after examining all the evidence, Philippe and Dr. Ouradnik were the most likely culprits.

John put the letter aside and resumed his research on quantum mechanics. He refused to let the letter derail him. While sifting through YouTube videos, he came across a short documentary on optics and how the eyes worked. The video claimed that color was an illusion; a mere interpretation of how the brain processes reflections of different wavelengths of light. Everything a person saw was simply information taken in by the eyes and processed in a rear part of the brain called the occipital lobe. The video suggested that there was no definite external reality, only interpretations of sporadically existing visual stimuli. If there was a definite external reality, the video claimed that no one would ever be able to see it in its true form. Reality, as the video claimed, was only electrical impulses firing off in the brain, and there was no definitive way to prove that a person existed outside of their own perception. A voice at the end of the video menacingly repeated the words "You do not exist" while the film credits rolled.

John paced his living room. He walked over to a mirror that hung on his dining room wall and stared into it while holding his revolver. Examining every detail of his face for fifteen minutes, John chuckled and spoke to his reflection, "I *see* you." After another few minutes of staring into the mirror, he lifted it from the wall and placed it into the closet.

As he returned to his computer desk, the apartment telephone rang.

"Fuck!" he shouted, aiming his gun at the phone.

Lowering his gun, he sighed, walked over and picked up the receiver.

The concierge was issuing a courtesy call, asking John to rate the valet service. When she asked if there was anything else the hotel could do to make his stay more pleasurable, John blurted out, "Liquor—cognac, send me the biggest bottle you got."

John returned to watching YouTube videos. He watched a video on Anton Zeilinger's research on quantum teleportation at the Canary Islands, utilizing quantum entanglement. The video entertained the idea of human teleportation, citing that it could be possible within the next hundred years or so.

Taking a break from his research, he scrolled through his newsfeed on Facebook and came across a shocking article published a couple days after the show in Baltimore. The teenager had died from his stab wounds. John was in deep contemplation when he heard a knock on his door.

"What the fuck do you want!" he shouted, jumping out of his chair, pointing his gun at the door.

"Room service, sir," the man spoke through the door.

John sighed heavily, hiding the gun.

Apologizing before he had fully opened the door, he offered the room service attendant a twenty-dollar tip. The man gladly accepted and wished him well.

"Get a grip, John," he said to himself, placing the bottle of Courvoisier on his countertop. "I need to get the fuck out of here."

Although John technically wasn't supposed to drive his new sports bike until they finalized the paperwork, he returned to the bellhops near the front desk and asked them to summon the valet, requesting his bike. They complied.

～◦

Deciding to surprise Kasey with his new bike, he took a spin over to Devonshire Heights. Before arriving, he worked out a story that his grandmother recently won a handsome sum of money playing Keno and had instructed him to buy something big for himself, as to not expose his secret relationship with Philippe Álvarez.

Knocking on Kasey's door, he soon discovered that she had not yet returned from the PSRC meeting. To pass the time until she returned, John test drove his bike through her neighborhood. Speeding well over the limits, he cheered and laughed, hoping to avoid any flashing lights from a patrolling officer.

~⁓

Guests at The Red Porcupine were wrapping up the PSRC meeting. Kasey was sitting at a table in the café, packing up her belongings. She was wearing her new navy blue "Liberate Hong Kong" t-shirt. Mel quietly approached, taking a seat next to her. Kasey smiled uneasily, anticipating an interrogation.

"You're dating John now, I see?" Mel asked, scrunching her face.

"*Uh*," Kasey said, "I'm going to give him a shot."

"You know that's a bad idea, right?"

Kasey sighed defensively. "He's made a lot of progress."

"Kasey, he's sexist. He's misogynistic. He's homophobic."

"No," Kasey defended, "his best friend was gay. They were very close."

Mel scoffed. "*Oh, if I had a nickel for every racist who had a best friend who was black.* Come on, Kasey, we've discussed this before. Toxic romances can never end well."

"He's not as bad as you think."

"No, I'm pretty sure he's worse," Mel surmised. "You're making a big mistake by giving him this chance."

"Mel." Kasey paused for a moment. "I saw you and John in the café together before," she confessed with a hint of attitude. "What were you guys talking about?"

Mel squinted, almost smiling. "*Oh*, John and I had a *nice* little talk. John came to me expressing what seemed to be a sincere desire to change, asking *me* for help. We had some *words* last year. Against my better judgement, I gave him the benefit of the doubt and agreed to have a conversation with him. I discussed with him where his problems were and how he needed to address them. One such issue that we covered was his abrasive treatment and attitude toward women. With his hand on his heart, he swore that he was going to immediately remedy his behavior. Less than

243 | P a g e

a week later, you told me that he was screaming in your face in the middle of Manhattan, wishing that you hadn't gone on the trip. Then, after that, he physically assaulted a homeless woman. Remember?"

Kasey's eyes fell to the floor.

Mel leaned towards her sunken posture, attempting to make eye contact. "He's violent, Kasey. He's dangerous. You can't do this to yourself."

"Look, I know he's not perfect," Kasey said, meeting her face-to-face, "but you don't know him like I do. He can be very sweet. He cares about me. He really does. We have something very special together, something real, something that *you* don't understand."

"Kasey, he's a piece of shit," Mel snapped. "Remember when you first met him—during orientation? You told me that he belittled you for taking a summer vacation to France. He whispered *rich bitch* in your ear when the others weren't looking, remember? Remember how you were too afraid to ride with him in the limo? You were right to listen to those intuitions. His abuse will never stop; it'll only get worse. It *will* turn to physical violence. As time goes by, it'll become normalized. You'll start to accept it. You'll build a life around it. Then, escaping it will become nearly impossible. That's how oppression works, Kasey. It's a process of slowly breaking down somebody's will to fight. You have to break up with him. He's no good for you. You have to trust me, Kasey, I know what's best for you."

"I appreciate your concern," Kasey said, standing from her chair, "but *I'll* decide what's best for me. Goodbye, Mel."

Mel's stabbing gaze followed her to the door.

Kasey walked out as her Uber pulled up.

～

Riding at the far end of Devonshire Heights, John passed a young man standing next to a car parked on the side of the road. He turned back around, pulled up behind the car, turned the bike off, removed his helmet and hopped off. Recognizing John, the man immediately took off running. John chased after him. It was the very man who had attacked Kasey months earlier. Despite the backpack he was wearing, he was able to gain on him. Feverishly, they ran towards a wooded area along the edge of the neighborhood.

"I see you, motherfucker!" John shouted, running into the woods after him.

Furious footsteps pummeled the ground in a steady percussion. The woods were vacant, dense and damp from the recent rain. The man tripped over a branch. Quickly standing, he continued his escape but lost his lead. John caught up to him. Pushing him off course, John slammed him face-first into a tree.

"Fuck!" the man bellowed, wincing in pain.

Images of the man forcing Kasey to the ground flooded his thoughts. With immeasurable intensity, John grabbed the back of his neck.

"Motherfucker! Motherfucker!" John shouted, repeatedly bashing his face into the tree, breaking away pieces of the bark. "Motherfucker! Motherfucker!"

With one hand, John unzipped his backpack and pulled out his gun. Grinding his teeth, he turned the man around and jammed the gun into his forehead. "You like chasing women down the fucking street, huh, motherfucker?" he growled, pressing the gun harder against his skull.

The man groaned, urinating, drooling blood as he slipped out of consciousness. The beating had severely disfigured his face. John let him go. With a *thud*, the man hit the ground.

"Shit," John uttered, slowly backing away. "Shit."

~~

When John arrived at Kasey's house on the other side of the neighborhood, she was pulling up in an Uber.

"Kasey!" John greeted her as she exited the vehicle. "Check out my new bike!"

Kasey smiled brightly, closing the car door behind her. Barely noticing the bike, she rushed over to him and threw her arms around him. They stood on the sidewalk, hugging as if they were long-lost friends who hadn't seen each other in ages. Eventually, they disengaged. John showed her the bike and delivered the fabricated story of how he came to acquire it. While they chatted in front of her house, John listened carefully for sirens, but they never came. Before exiting the woods, he noticed the man regaining consciousness, but he never called the police. John rightfully assumed that he would not pursue legal recourse or involve law enforcement, but he did, however, anticipate retribution.

~~~

After his short visit with Kasey, John cruised the business district, showing off his new bike. Kasey agreed to meet up with him when she was finished studying. John offered to return to her house to give her a ride, but she refused, stating that she required a helmet before riding on the back of his bike. Checking online, he saw that motorcycle helmets cost around one hundred dollars. Without hesitation, he entered his debit card number and completed the purchase.

Nearing twenty minutes of driving aimlessly up and down the boulevard, he spotted Marcus, dressed in a suit, exiting his BMW in front of Piacevole's; an upscale Italian restaurant. Marcus and Ashley were en route to Piacevole's to meet up with several others who had attended an Adam Smith lecture at the university, delivered by an economist visiting from the London School of Economics. Ashley Foster, at 5'9", was only a little shorter than Marcus. As a Prophyte in a prestigious sorority, she maintained a conservative choice in attire and always wore a pearl necklace. She had ordinary, shoulder-length blonde hair and had mastered the art of walking in high heels. A devout follower of the Cato Institute and the Hoover Institution, she proudly campaigned for the Libertarian Party and was often a guest speaker at similar functions herself.

John pulled up behind Marcus's BMW as he was helping Ashley out of the passenger seat.

"Sup, man, like my new ride?" John asked, taking off his helmet.

Marcus's eyes widened. "Damn, man, you rob a bank or something?"

"What? A black man gets a new bike and all of the sudden he's a bank robber?" John joked.

Ashley peered at John with an unmistakably offended expression.

"*Ah*—it's an inside joke," Marcus explained to her. "John's cool."

Ashley forced a smile.

"So, you're the infamous *Ashley?* I was starting to think Marcus made you up," John teased. "It's nice to finally meet you," he said in a serious tone, offering a handshake.

Ashley shook John's hand then looked at Marcus. "You ready to go in?"

"One second, babe," Marcus requested. "So, when did you get the bike, man?"

"Earlier today. My grandmother hit it big in Keno last month. She instructed me to buy something nice for myself. Couldn't argue with her. I paid for this with *cash-money.*"

"Sweet, man! She sounds a lot nicer than your pops—*uh*, no offense."

John smiled. "None taken. Well, you guys enjoy your dinner. I'm getting ready to meet up with Kasey soon."

"You and Kasey spending a lot of time together now, eh?"

"Yeah, actually, it's weird—I can't stand not being with her."

Marcus smiled gaudily. "*Oh*, shit, she bewitched your ass, huh? Women will do that to you."

Ashley glared at Marcus.

"Well, *uh*," Marcus said timidly, "I think we're gonna head in. I'll see ya, John."

John chuckled. "Take care, guys."

"Behave yourself, John," Marcus said, smiling, opening the restaurant door for Ashley.

"What's the fun in that?" he asked, revving his engine.

～✺

Kasey met up with John at his apartment a little later that evening. She never told him about her encounter with Mel, and he never told her about his encounter with the man who chased her down the street. They ordered room service and planned to watch another movie. Kasey chuckled and told him that he didn't have to keep ordering vegetarian meals. John happily refused, even though he didn't agree with vegetarianism. After dinner, they sat on his couch, laughing and throwing grapes at each other, attempting to catch them in their mouths.

Before starting the movie, Kasey took a shower. John threw grapes one by one into the air, attempting to catch them in his mouth while he waited for her to finish getting dressed. When he heard the bedroom door open, he positioned himself to playfully launch a grape at her to see if she could catch it in her mouth from a distance without warning.

Kasey returned to the living room, stopping at his computer desk. John drew back his arm, preparing to hurl the grape.

"John, what's this?" she asked, picking up a piece of white paper.

John retreated, lowering his arm.

"I see you, Hoax Slayer," she slowly read, squinting at the paper.

His eyes widened.

"What's this mean?" she asked, looking up from the letter. "And where's your dining room mirror?"

John took a deep breath. "*Um*, the mirror was crooked. It was driving me nuts. I think I have OCD. It's in the closet. I put it in there so it wouldn't get damaged. I'm gonna have the hotel hang it properly. 'I see you, Hoax Slayer' is the name of a dissertation I'm planning to write, chronicling various clashes between hoaxers and skeptics throughout American history."

John held his breath, awaiting her response.

"Oh, cool. Yeah, that mirror was a little crooked."

He exhaled slowly.

Kasey walked to the couch and sat next to him. "You're not still into that witch hoax stuff, are you?"

John tapped his fingers on the arm of the couch. "Well, I think hoaxes are interesting. I don't concern myself with the project that we did at Avalonti anymore, if that's what you're asking me—but I do still find conspiracy theories and that *whole world* to be interesting. I will say, however, that quantum mechanics and physics are slowly starting to push all that to the backburner. I might not even write the essay on hoaxers. I might write something on quantum entanglement instead."

"Cool," she said, nodding. "I'm curious about something else, John. What prompted you to become so interested in physics?"

"*Uh*, I met a theoretical physicist who thinks that evil could be a quantitative force."

Kasey chuckled.

John grinned. "Yeah, I disagreed with him and stumbled into a debate war with him and his friend. When I remembered I didn't know jack shit about physics, I texted you and asked if you could tutor me—because I liked you. I wanted to get to know you better and I'm glad I did."

She smiled. "I'm glad you did too."

He leaned over and hugged her. "I'm really glad I did."

"John?"

"Yeah?"

"Who was the theoretical physicist that you met? Is he at Avalonti?" she asked, continuing to hug him.

John gritted his teeth behind her back. Pulling away from the hug, he wore a smile. "Just someone I met online when all that crazy hoax stuff was going on. I'm not even sure if he's really a physicist. I'm just stubborn and I like competition. So, *uh*—how did your meeting go today? You never told me how that went."

∿

Successfully derailing Kasey's inquisitiveness, John listened attentively as she told him about the controversial far-right guest speaker who was scheduled to do a lecture the day after the school dance. John disagreed with PSRC's tactic of shutting down events but applauded Kasey for her passionate refusal to go unheard. Kasey, who agreed with John that events shouldn't be shut down, argued that their demonstration was merely to showcase opposition, which was imperative to maintaining the free marketplace of ideas. John didn't know it, but after their frequent ideological clashes earlier in the year, Kasey took to reading Nietzsche, John Locke, Voltaire, Jean-Jacques Rousseau, Baruch

Spinoza, Immanuel Kant, Albert Camus and the philosophies of freethinking that he so vocally espoused.

CHAPTER 26

WITCH FEVER

John entered his apartment and threw his keys on the coffee table. He poured a glass of whiskey and sat at his computer to write another article for KNWRZ. "Alright, you stupid fucks," he said, grabbing the computer mouse, "time for another dose of reality from Dr. Xaoh."

He opened his internet browser. The first article that appeared on the home page was about Anastasia Carval. John squinted, shaking his head as he read the headline. "This is a fucking joke, right?"

The headline read: *Casualty at the Capitol: Congresswoman Anastasia Carval Shot Dead.*

He read half of the article.

"No, no, no, no, no, no, no."

Breathing heavily, he brought his forehead to the desk. His body tensed up. Growling, clenching his jaws, he clutched the glass of whiskey. Wincing, trembling, he squeezed it with stupendous force. Shaking, rattling, the glass shattered in his hand.

"Fuck!" he erupted, throwing the shards against the wall. "You God damn fucking idiots! She's not a fucking witch, you fucks! You fucks! You fucking fucks! There's no such thing as witches!" John wailed at his computer screen, cracking the monitor with his fist. Sweat poured from his face. Veins bulged from his neck. Smashing the keyboard against the monitor, fragments flew across the room. His face was turning purple. Lifting the monitor above his head, a twitch of satisfaction met his face. He slammed it to the ground. "Fuck! Fuck!" he screamed, stomping on the monitor. "Fuck!"

~⁓

John's rage, which had reduced dishes and glasses to shards and his computer monitor and keyboard to rubble, endured for about eleven-and-a-half minutes; about the same amount of time his father's rampages would last. His father, after *his* outbursts, would read the Bible and pray for hours, citing that the devil's legions flocked to those who demonstrated "great weakness". Pastor Hallman found calming strength in the Lord's word, and protection in prayer. John's mother constantly worried about her husband's safety. Pastor Hallman had recently turned 61. For years, he struggled with high blood pressure and heart issues. John's mother prayed equally hard after his outbursts, fearing the next one may have been his last.

Anastasia Carval, along with two congressmen and a police officer, were shot near the U.S. Capitol building during a lunch hour. The officer and two congressmen survived but were in critical condition. The gunman, sixty-five-year-old Jacob Buchwald, was shot dead by the United States Capitol Police. Authorities searching the gunman's Virginia home after the shootout found a cache of weapons and explosives stored in his basement. Along with a stockpile of ammunition, they found documents detailing his plan, his targets and his motives. Jacob Buchwald had fallen ill to the witch hoax propaganda that festered in the underbelly of the internet. He wrote an undelivered letter to his grandchildren, promising them that he would "expel the evil that was invading the most sensitive institutions of power in their country". Intrigue surrounded Buchwald. He was a loving husband, an honorable community leader and a devout Christian who had no criminal record or history of mental illness. He also possessed a bachelor's degree in psychology and had an IQ of 141. His family claimed they were unaware of his deep involvement with conspiracy theories. In Buchwald's mind, his murderous actions were righteous and godly. Every news outlet in the country was covering the bizarre story. The witch hoax found its new home on a national stage. The 21st century debate over "evil witches" commenced and permeated social media.

John sat in a corner on the floor of his apartment, observing the disaster he caused while smoking a cigarette. Surprising to John, none of the surrounding guests contacted the hotel security over his outburst. He suspected that may have been the result of the type of people who frequently rented the suites on his floor. One night, returning from Francesca Hall, John saw a businessman unlocking the suite next to his while a prostitute caressed his shoulder. The girl was younger than John. Another night, just before Kasey started tutoring him, a young man staying on his floor offered him a bump of cocaine in the elevator. John accepted, sniffing a lump of cocaine off the tip of a stranger's car key. Walking through the hallway on a different night, John passed a group of women in their late twenties returning early from a bachelorette party. A drunk woman wearing a "Bride to Be" tiara grabbed him by the arm as he was walking by. She commanded him to join them in their room for sex. John pulled away from her. They all laughed as he ran back to his room. John's floor was known to some as The Devil's Floor. There were eighteen floors at The Marquis. John's floor was labeled as the 14th floor, but it was really the 13th. When The Marquis was built, it was popular for hotels to omit the 13th floor to accommodate superstitious guests.

~~~

An outcry from the Wiccan, pagan and various nature-based spiritual communities surfaced, pleading for the public to research the real history of witches. Only hours after the murder of Anastasia Carval, copycat crimes were being reported all over the country.

A woman's car was torched in Greenwood, Mississippi for having a "Blessed Be" bumper sticker and a decal of a witch silhouette.

A witch museum in Salem, Massachusetts fell to vandalism.

In Phoenix, Arizona, a homosexual couple who identified as Druids were robbed of their clothes, beaten and left on a sidewalk.

In Billings, Montana, the home of an interracial Wiccan couple was spray-painted with swastikas and anti-witch graffiti.

A gang of teenagers in Provo, Utah beat a man within an inch of his life for wearing a pentagram pendant on his necklace.

The reports were flying in. Pandemonium was on the horizon. The outcome appeared bleak, but many rallied against the violence and intolerance. A Jesuit priest stood in solidarity and called for an end to the "madness". Several religious leaders followed suit, reminding their congregations that violence and destruction were not their way. But the crimes continued. Those who sought to take a "righteous stance against the darkness" recoiled from the call to reason. All across the nation, news of Anastasia Carval's murder was wreaking havoc.

～

Leaving an electronics store after he purchased another keyboard and monitor, along with an MP3 player, John decided he would take a drive in his car to West Virginia to sort out his thoughts. On his way to see Philippe Álvarez, John calculated that *he* was just as responsible, if not more, for spreading the witch hoax that led to the murder of Anastasia Carval. John and Philippe talked over coffee in the kitchen of *The Dollhouse*. Before they delved into the witch hoax discussion, John finished the paperwork for the ownership of his new sports bike. Philippe was distracted. He was, as well, disturbed over the death of Anastasia Carval.

"I posted the retraction," Philippe said, staring into his coffee. "They didn't believe me." Philippe heaved a sigh. "They thought I was publishing the retraction because I was being intimidated by the government. There was nothing we could have done, John. Once you open the cage, you'll never know where the bird will fly— and you sure as hell ain't ever getting it back."

"Everyone is talking about witches now," John softly spoke. "This is all our fault, isn't it?"

Philippe sighed. "We're involved, true—but we're not guilty. If I sell a man a gun and he shoots his neighbor with it, should I go to jail? When somebody blows up a building, should William Powell be posthumously responsible because they received bomb-making knowledge from the book he wrote?"

"That's a complicated philosophical question," John asserted. "Should we be put in jail for the murder of Anastasia Carval? No, of course not—but should we feel guilty? You better believe we should."

"Of course—but I fear we have a much bigger problem on our hands now, John."

"A bigger problem? What's that?"

Philippe swirled his finger around the lip of his coffee mug. "This evil—the devil, the witches—they know about us. They see us. The demons will come for us."

"There are no *demons* or *witches*, Philippe. It's all nonsense. I read the history. Witches were just pagan sects who were vilified by the church. It's all folklore and religious indoctrination. And demons—that's just a metaphor. Lilith, Beelzebub, Ravana, Tengu—they're just representations of people. I hate to tell you this, but God—*God* is not real, Philippe."

Philippe slowly stood from his chair. "You really believe that, John?"

John nodded. "Yes, you know I do. We've had this conversation before."

Philippe placed both hands on the tabletop and gazed into John's eyes. "I don't believe you."

John chuckled forcefully. "Well, that's your problem."

Philippe paced toward the refrigerator. "You prayed that night—didn't you, John?"

John grimaced. "What? What night?"

Philippe returned to the table, sitting in a chair in front of him. "Baltimore. When you saw them guns. When you felt that barrel licking the back of your head. You prayed—*oh, yeah, you prayed.* You asked God for help."

"Bullshit," John snarled.

"Every man prays before he dies, John," he said, tapping his brow, smiling. "You can see it in their eyes."

John leapt out of his chair. "You sent me that letter, didn't you!"

Philippe raised his hands defensively. "Relax, John. I didn't send you any letter."

"You're going to kill me, aren't you?"

Philippe gasped, standing from his chair. His eyes started to water when he realized that John was serious. "John. I would never think of it. You're—you're like a son to me. I love you like family, John."

John's face writhed in disgust. "That's preposterous, Philippe, we barely know each other."

"Like I said on the day we first met, John, we're kindred spirits. God has brought us together for a reason. What that reason is, I'm not exactly sure. But what I do know is that God is the only one who can save us now."

John shook his head angrily. "*No*, this is crazy. This isn't even happening. It's *uh*—it's a bad dream or something."

Philippe approached and put his hand on John's shoulder. "The nightmare has yet to begin, John. They *will* come. You antagonized the agents of Lucifer and now they have your scent. They see you weakening. They'll hear you weeping at night. They'll eavesdrop on your prayers. They'll hear every word you say. They'll hide in the darkness and feed off your fears. At your weakest, they will take you."

John gritted his teeth, breathing heavy. "How do I know *you're* not the fucking devil!"

Philippe paused and took a deep breath. Calmly, he walked to the other side of the room, removed a crucifix from the wall and placed it on his kitchen table. John silently watched him. Philippe opened a kitchen drawer, removed a sharp knife and, without warning, plunged it into the center of his own hand. John jumped back against the kitchen counter, watching in horror.

With his profusely bleeding hand, Philippe took the crucifix, closed his eyes and held it into the air. "First Corinthians 9:27," he recited, "I chastise my body and bring it into subjection, in the name of the Holy Spirit. It is to our Lord Jesus Christ, and to Christ alone, that I devote my blood, my life and my soul."

"You're fucking crazy, man," John said, trembling, pressing along the edge of the kitchen toward the threshold.

Blood poured from his hand.

"Before you go, John," Philippe gasped, "take this, you're going to need it."

John looked down at Philippe's unharmed hand. "I don't want that."

Philippe dangled the object in front of him. "Take it!"

John snatched the item from Philippe's hand then escaped to the front door. As if running for a Hail Mary pass with six seconds left in the fourth quarter, he dashed to his car. A cloud of dust rose into the air as he sped along the dirt driveway.

~~

Returning to The Marquis, John found Kasey sitting on a chair in the hotel lobby.

"John! Hey!" Kasey shouted, smiling, jumping from the chair. "I texted you a bunch. Why didn't you text me back?"

"Oh, sorry, I didn't realize."

"No worries."

Looking at his phone, John saw that Marcus had called dozens of times as well.

"Whatcha got there?" she asked bubbly.

"This? *Uh*—it's a computer monitor and a keyboard," he answered, lifting the bag.

Kasey squinted, still smiling. "Your monitor and keyboard looked fine to me."

John sighed. "You heard about Anastasia Carval, right?"

The smile ran away from her face. "No, what happened?"

John huffed. "What, do you live under a fucking rock or something?"

"John," she whimpered, recoiling, taking a half-step back.

"I'm sorry, Kasey," he said. "Congresswoman Anastasia Carval is dead."

Her eyes widened. "What?"

"She's dead, Kasey. The man who shot her—he was—he believed she was a witch."

Kasey pressed both of her hands over her gaping mouth.

John's face contorted with grief.

"Let's go upstairs," she whispered, hugging him consolingly.

"We can't," John softly spoke.

"Why not?"

"I had an episode when I heard that she was murdered. I lost my temper. The apartment is a disaster. I destroyed my monitor and the keyboard. There's broken dishes and glasses all over the place."

Kasey paused. "It's—it's okay, John. I'll help you clean."

"You'll help me?"

She smiled. "Of course, I will."

John chuckled relievedly.

～⌒∽

John and Kasey took the elevator to his apartment. Kasey located a broom, a dustpan and a vacuum in the storage room on the balcony; a room John had never looked in. No matter how messy, he let housekeeping clean up after him and tipped them according to how dirty the apartment was, if he had any money at the time. The disaster wrought from his explosive outburst, however, would be kept secret from the hotel staff. They worked together cleaning his apartment. Kasey found every key from the busted keyboard except for the number 3. John occasionally interrupted her, hugging her and kissing her on the cheek, telling her how lucky he was to have her in his life.

While John was setting up his new monitor, Kasey repeatedly vacuumed the carpeted areas, fearing that remaining glass particles would be discovered later by one of their bare feet. Eventually, she took a break and turned on the television. The news was covering the story of Jacob Buchwald's assassination of Anastasia Carval and the recent events surrounding it. Everyone in the country was talking about guns and witches.

John closed his eyes tightly. "Turn it off."

"Oh, I'm sorry," Kasey said, picking up the remote again.

"Thanks."

Joining him at the computer, she helped him program his MP3 player and mischievously added a few of her favorite punk songs to his playlist. While they were searching for songs to download, a frantic knocking arrived on the apartment door.

"John! Let me in!" Marcus shouted through the door.

"Fuck," John said, gritting his teeth.

"Want me to get it?" Kasey asked.

John nodded.

Kasey stood from the chair, walked over and opened the door.

"*Oh*—Kasey—you're here," Marcus said.

"Nice to see you too," Kasey said sarcastically.

"I'm sorry, Kasey," Marcus said, walking a few feet into the apartment. "I just wanted to talk to John for a second. But since you're here, you need to know this too. I talked to Vandacheler. Avalonti has a close eye on us right now. The society is going to be scrutinizing our every move. We can't say anything about the project to anyone. They'll shove those membership certificates directly up our asses if we do. I know there's some fucked up shit going on right now, but we can't lose all this. If any of us three say anything, they're going to shit-can all of us. I can't lose all this. I just can't."

"I see," John agreed. "I get it. I'm with you, Marcus."

"Yeah, I'm not going to say anything either," Kasey said.

Marcus nodded slowly. "Alright. Cool. I'll uh—let you guys get back to your night then. Call Vandacheler and let him know that I talked to you, okay?"

"Yeah, sure," John agreed.

Marcus stared into John's eyes. "Remember, they'll be watching us."

Kasey chuckled. "We get it, Marcus."

"I know," Marcus said with a tint of skepticism, walking to the threshold.

"Goodbye, Marcus," Kasey said, smiling, reaching for the door.

Marcus looked at John again, holding his hand against the door. "Hey, John. *I see you*—guys later." He winked at John before walking away.

Kasey shook her head, still smiling, closing the door behind him. She turned the deadbolt and fastened the latch.

John stood perfectly still, staring at the door.

"John? You okay?" she asked.

John snapped out of his gaze. "*Uh*—yeah, I'm good."

Kasey chuckled, walking to the other side of the room. "Our apartment is pretty clean now—you wanna get some dinner? Call room service?"

"*Our?*" John said to himself, smirking, looking at the back of her. "*Um*—I'm not sure that's a good idea, *Kase*."

She turned around. "Why do you think that?"

"Well, Marcus just said they'll be watching our every move. Maybe it's not a good idea to keep running up room service bills. I know they own the building, but they still gotta pay for it."

"Oh—yeah, that's a good point."

John massaged the back of his neck with one hand. "Is there anything going on tonight? I don't really want to be stuck inside. I need to get out of here for a little while."

Kasey pondered tongue-in-cheek. "*Uh*—there's an open mic at The Red Porcupine. We could get some coffee and some food and listen to some *slam poetry*. It might be a good distraction. I'll pay for everything."

"Is *Mel* gonna be there?" John grumbled.

"She's in Philly."

John nodded enthusiastically. "Then, yes, absolutely. We should *definitely* do that."

Kasey smiled. "Cool. I'll grab a quick shower. It starts in a little while."

"Thanks, *Kase*. You're awesome."

CHAPTER 27

OPEN MIC NIGHT

When John and Kasey entered the dimly lit café, a woman with short brown hair wearing thick retro glasses was welcoming everyone to the event. They had arrived just in time. They proceeded to the last three open chairs at a table in the back. John used the extra chair to occasionally prop his feet up. Most of the crowd were sitting in the middle of the floor where the bookstore met the café.

As John carefully navigated his way to the café counter to fetch coffees, he noticed several of the attendees on the floor holding 40oz beer bottles in their laps. The Red Porcupine did not serve alcohol and did not possess a liquor license. Although they discouraged drunkenness, they permitted guests to bring alcohol to the open mic events provided they were discreet and respectful. The establishment would have faced penalization and possibly be shut down if the county knew they were allowing underaged drinking on their premises. There was a liquor store across the street, but John decided not to drink any alcohol while he was there.

John surveyed the audience while the man with the microphone spoke of his challenges of being black at a predominately white university. Aside from a few aging hippies, most of the guests were young, progressive college students. John raised an eyebrow when they snapped their fingers, in lieu of clapping, when the man finished his speech.

John leaned toward Kasey and whispered, "I don't know how to snap."

Kasey giggled.

John returned to the café counter to fetch vegan "chicken salad" wraps for them after Kasey said she was getting hungry. Waiting for the wraps, he listened to the third speaker; a nineteen-year-old English woman with cyan hair. She offered a diatribe against corporate America, European imperialism, colonization and white hegemony. While she was speaking, Kasey used the restroom reluctantly, thinking it was disrespectful, but she couldn't wait any longer. John ventured back to the table, stopping near the amplifier on his way.

"Are you having a good time?" Kasey whispered, returning to the table.

"Yeah, very interesting stuff," John replied softly, pushing the vegan wrap a little closer.

∾

John listened attentively to each speaker, occasionally tapping his foot under the table. Kasey's friends Karen and Joy arrived late. They saw that she was with John and sat on the opposite side of the coffeehouse. Up at the front, a student finished reading her poem on the harms of cultural appropriation then retook her seat on the floor. The host reached into a top hat and pulled out a little piece of paper. She read the name on the paper and announced, "Our next speaker is John Hallman."

Kasey's jaw hit the floor.

John kissed her on the forehead, standing from his chair. "You're gonna love this."

The crowd warmly snapped their fingers as he approached the front.

John took the microphone and spoke into it, "I fucking hate you."

The crowd gasped.

John continued in a slow, poetic tone, "People say that to each other all the time. I wonder—do they *really* know what they're saying? Let's all just kill each other. Why not? Just get it over with, right? And I wonder—how hard is *God* laughing at us right now?

While we bleed to death on the ideological battle ground, he's popping more fucking popcorn."

The audience looked around at each other.

Ignoring the murmurs from the audience, John continued to improvise. "We're all devils and witches—gods and saints. We should be hunters and gatherers and live primitively with our beautiful planet that gives us everything we need. But we build vast worlds instead. Then we put it all under the microscope. What's there? Strings vibrating? Billions of neutrinos whizzing through you at every second, unnoticed, infinitesimally small? Reality isn't real. You don't exist. There's nothing here. If there is, it's just waiting to be devoured by a black hole or engulfed by the sun that *will indeed* explode someday. All proof that we ever existed—all our knowledge—gone in the blink of an eye. We're a tiny blip on the cosmic radar. A mere droplet in the endless sea of time. And how will we spend this insignificant amount of time? *I know*—we'll fucking kill each other. We'll hate each other. We'll throw each other into the fire—like Giordano Bruno, or the countless men and women we burned at the stake in the name of God or Allah or whatever the fuck you want to call it. Where did you go, Voltaire? Where is reason and logic? Where is enlightenment? There are no happy endings. We live our entire lives knowing this and we're still surprised by the end. My father hates me. I've only seen my mother cry once. My brother died of a heroin overdose. My father blamed himself. He couldn't understand why it happened—how he failed him. Now *she's* dead—not my mother, someone else. They call her a *witch*. Do witches still fly on broomsticks, or do they ride in Boeing 737s? How will I sleep at night knowing they die because of me? How will I live now? What am I going to do? I'm so glad I have you, Kasey. Maybe you can save us—because *God* has forsaken me."

The host inched towards him, smiling cautiously.

"Thank you," John said, handing over the microphone.

Kasey stood and started clapping. Most of the crowd glared at her in disgust. Karen and Joy kept their attention on the floor, refusing to look in her direction. John took a deep breath, scanning the silent audience.

A large Caucasian man with brightly colored red hair, sitting in the corner of the bookstore, snapped his fingers ironically. "Yay,"

263 | P a g e

he shouted sarcastically, "let's all hear it for the able-bodied, heterosexual, cis-gendered white guy and his awesome sob story! *Whoopee!*"

The crowd laughed. They began to unleash their comments and criticisms.

"*Aw*, poor white guy," a blonde-haired woman mocked, making a pouty face at John.

"Islamophobic much?" another student jeered.

A teenaged girl started to sing monotonically, "We don't care how you sleep at night."

John shrugged.

A woman snarled, "Saying 'you don't exist' from your position as a white male is harmful to the people of color in the audience. You don't *get* to say that."

John nodded, accepting her criticism.

"Nice clothes, dude," a young man criticized. "So, you're cool with sweatshops?"

"Fuck Voltaire!" a teenaged student hissed.

"Bigot!" another student hollered.

Isolated booing sounded from the audience.

"*Okay*," the host admonished over the microphone, "that's enough, please." She pulled another name out of the top hat. "Our next speaker is…"

John cut through the center of the café and headed straight for the door.

Kasey quickly followed him out.

"John," Kasey said, taking his hand, "I'm sorry about that. I thought your speech was really good."

John smiled at her but didn't speak. They held hands, walking to his car, ready to call it a night.

～～

Returning to John's apartment, they sat on the brown leather couch watching an apolitical documentary on Netflix. Halfway through the nature documentary, Kasey fell asleep. John paced around his apartment, periodically looking at his phone but refusing to search anything regarding Anastasia Carval *or* the witch hoax. It was almost one in the morning. He noticed that Marcus's Facebook status was showing "active 8 minutes ago." Marcus was awake.

John snuck out of his apartment and took the stairs down to the 9th floor where Marcus's room was. He gently tapped on his door.

No response.

He tapped a little louder.

No response.

He waited a minute then knocked louder.

John heard a faint grumbling.

The chain-link door guard unlatched.

"John?" Marcus said, opening the door a hair. "What the fuck are you doing, man?"

John forced the door open and walked in, discovering Ashley sitting on the couch with a throw blanket over her naked body. He quickly covered his eyes.

Marcus pushed him into the hallway. "What do you want, man?"

John gritted his teeth, speaking with restrained anger, "Why the fuck did you send me that letter?"

"Why?" Marcus aggressively whispered. "Because you're a fucking idiot, John, that's why."

"Are you Agnes Sampson?"

Marcus snarled his face. "Who?"

"Did you threaten to kill me?"

"What!"

"Did you threaten me online?"

Marcus looked inside of his apartment to see if Ashley could hear them. He closed the door then turned back to John and whispered, "Man, what the fuck are you talking about?"

John calmed a little, realizing that Marcus was not the one who made the online death threat. "Avalonti. Do they know I'm Reyal Xaoh too?"

"I don't think so, but who knows? *I knew it*. I was just trying to let you know how obvious it motherfucking was. What the hell are you doing messing around with this Álvarez guy?"

"I guess because I'm a fucking idiot. I'm done with him, though. I was just trying to stop the hoax, man. I was desperate. That letter you sent—it scared the fuck out of me by the way, asshole."

"*Good*, that's why I sent it. You're gonna fuck this up for yourself, man. They're gonna throw you out. They're gonna throw me out, too. It ain't worth it, man. It ain't—it ain't fucking worth it."

John looked at the floor then back up at Marcus. "Carval, what about *her*?"

Marcus raised an eyebrow. "What about her?"

"I mean—she's dead. It's because of us. That doesn't bother you?"

"Listen, John. It sucks. It really does. I feel for her family and *all* of her loved ones, I really do, but I didn't pull the fucking trigger."

John faintly scoffed. "No, you didn't—did you?"

"Nope. Neither did you. Goodnight, John."

Marcus abruptly reentered his apartment.

John heard the door latch being applied belligerently.

He sighed and returned to the stairwell.

Emerging onto the 14th floor, John saw a man in a black suit standing in front of his door. When he saw the man opening his apartment door, he raced down the hallway shouting, "Hey! What the fuck are you doing!"

Grabbing the man and slamming him against the corridor wall, John shouted in his face, "What the fuck do you want! Who the fuck are you! You Agnes? You Agnes *fucking* Sampson?"

The man's cheeks were bright red and his eyes were barely opened. He hiccupped.

"John," Kasey said sleepily, opening the door, "what's going on?"

"This motherfucker was trying to break into our apartment," John said, pressing him harder against the wall.

Kasey picked up a room key from the floor and read the number on it. "Is this yours?"

"That's mine. I'm—really sorry," the man slurred.

John released him slowly.

Kasey handed him his key. "It's okay. Your room is across from ours. You're just on the wrong side."

"*Oh*, I'm—I'm so sorry guys," the man said, wobbling, swaying.

John sighed heavily, rubbing his temples while Kasey helped the man unlock his apartment door. The man thanked Kasey repeatedly and apologized eight more times.

Kasey rubbed John's back as they reentered their apartment.

"John," Kasey asked as the door closed behind them, "where did you go?"

John looked at the floor. "I was, *uh*—feeling a little antsy—just wanted to take a walk. Sorry, I didn't realize that guy was just drunk and confused. I came up the stairs and he was opening our door. I didn't want him to hurt you."

Kasey smiled. "It's okay, John—you didn't know."

"I'll make sure I lock the door next time."

"Okay."

They sat together on the couch.

"John?"

"Yeah?"

"Who is Agnes Sampson?"

John sighed heavily.

~

After he cooked up a story to explain why he asked the drunk man if he was Agnes Sampson, John sat on the edge of his couch and contemplated. Kasey curled up with a blanket and fell asleep. To him, it seemed like no one else cared about Anastasia Carval. Kasey expressed regret, but she didn't feel as responsible because she didn't want to do the project in the first place. Álvarez claimed to care, but John lost faith in his mental stability after he pierced a kitchen knife through his hand. There was, however, someone else who felt deeply responsible for the atrocity in Washington D.C.; someone linked to the witch hoax project.

CHAPTER 28
BLOW THE WHISTLE

While John was destroying his keyboard, computer monitor and half of the dishes in his apartment, someone else was contacting the media. John watched an interview on the news the following afternoon, after his ill-received open mic performance at The Red Porcupine. A shockwave of disbelief pulsated throughout the Avalonti Society when they learned of Professor Diageo's whistleblowing.

The newspaper headlines all read: *University Society Hatches Witch Hoax.*

Professor Diageo scoffed at the Avalonti Society's refusal to offer clarification to the public after the *first* assassination attempt. A prerequisite for Diageo lending his assistance was the promise that it would be a maintained experiment with published results. He couldn't understand why Caesar and the High Council had shut the project down. Their silence was maddening to him. As a result, Diageo took a leave of absence after being released by his Caribbean kidnappers. His rage would quietly fester. After news of Anastasia Carval's murder fell upon his ears, he issued a full exposé to the public, beckoned by his remorse.

In the interview, Diageo explained precisely how the witch hoax began, informing the public that large expense accounts were used to rapidly bolster a fake news publication to spread misleading information on Anastasia Carval. He confessed to providing his team with the leaked email that fueled the conspiracy theory, and to orchestrating the plan to hire a foreign advertising and digital marketing company to spread propaganda videos throughout the internet. In explaining how they constructed their refined targeting profiles, he divulged that social media giants were mining, accumulating and selling their users' personal data. He showed how their two-pronged attack persuaded carefully selected targets; one vessel striking as an apparently reputable news source while a covert battalion flanked them with blatant propaganda. Philippe Álvarez's publication, the influential KNWRZ, was also named as one of the independent news outlets that carelessly recirculated the misinformation. Diageo concluded by insisting that the original plan for the social experiment included revealing the documents and the data to the public. He maintained that the society never expected anything serious, like murder, to occur.

After the televised interview, the Avalonti Dukes immediately sanctioned Diageo and filed a petition for an expulsion hearing. Before any member was terminated, their case would be presented to a committee of Avalonti Judges. The Judges were solely responsible for inducting new members, as well as voting on revocation of memberships. Occasionally, Apprentices demonstrating an unsatisfactory performance would be summoned before the tribunal, but it was extremely rare for an established Sage to face an expulsion hearing. The last Sage to face an expulsion was Edwin Shumner, the editor-in-chief of the *Avalonti Journal* in 1963. Shumner, a proud leftist, covertly desecrated Francesca Hall with anti-communist graffiti, attempting to radicalize the society and incite a war with jingoist anti-Soviet hardliners of the day. The false flag attack was uncovered and Shumner was expelled.

Rallying the Avalonti Dukes to sanction Diageo was one of the most esteemed members of the High Council, Dean Robert Rafalski. Since his promotion to Duke, Rafalski routinely scrutinized lower-ranking members to weed out subversives. According to Rafalski, Professor Diageo was a dubious character and had been since his induction into the society over fifteen years prior. Diageo's whistleblowing was all the proof Rafalski needed to pin him as an infiltrator. The initiative to oust Diageo, however, was not unanimously agreed upon. Professor Diageo was a protégé and long-time friend of the most notable Avalonti Judge, Diana Luskovo.

The High Council operated democratically, affording each of the three branches specific responsibilities and powers. Under normal operation, the branches worked in tandem, ensuring the smooth function of the society. The Diageo affair, however, wrought controversy, confusion and disorganization. The ordeal sparked a schism at the Avalonti Society between the Dukes and the Judges. Aside from those who chose to stay neutral, roughly half of the society were supporting Diageo's continuation while the other half sided with Dean Rafalski and wanted him expelled for his "treacherous whistleblowing".

There was only one man who could overturn a decision made by the Judges, but Caesar Avalonti almost never interfered with their process. The hierarchy of the Avalonti Society was established and solidified in the early 1950s under the direction of the founder. Phineas Avalonti bestowed upon the branches their specific responsibilities and powers and decreed that they were immutable. In Caesar Avalonti's forty-year reign, he had never interposed or contradicted the branches, except for one time; when he bypassed the Judges and inducted John, Kasey and Marcus. Regarding the Diageo affair, Caesar would not interject. Whatever their decision was would be final.

Aside from offering clarification, Professor Diageo's whistleblowing had pushed the Avalonti Society into the limelight. Among the intelligentsia, Avalonti was well-known, but many people in the country had never heard of the society. The *Avalonti Journal*, published monthly or bi-monthly for eighty years, retained an elite, academic readership throughout its life and did not grace the newsstands. Two days after Professor Diageo's public confession, Don Vandacheler requested a meeting at Francesca Hall with John, Kasey, Marcus and a couple of other recently inducted members, to offer coaching. The students sat around on the antique furniture in front of the grand fireplace.

"As we approach the end of the school year," Vandacheler addressed the students, "we are reminded of the fragile stability of order. We are, as you may know, undergoing a process of adjusting to newly acquired fame and some rather unexpected tension within our walls. I shall like to say that your perseverance and cooperation will prove to be rewarding in this matter. I assure you this will all pass. This is not the first controversy we've endured and likely will not be our last. We shall grow, evolve and learn from our mistakes. It is my recommendation to you not to worry yourselves with the bureaucracy of the society. Instead, concentrate on studying for your final examinations and do look forward to a rejuvenating summer break as well. I believe..."

A loud *thud* against the door interrupted him.

"Odd that," Vandacheler remarked.

Mr. Budwin proceeded to open the double doors to investigate. The students raced to the entryway. John shielded Kasey. As Mr. Budwin stepped out onto the front porch, four undergraduates took off running, one of them shouting, "Illuminati whores!"

Mr. Budwin picked up a busted plastic bag that contained sand, rocks, and a piece of paper that read: *Fuck the NWO.*

"Never mind," Vandacheler said, calling the students back to the couch. "Pranksters is all."

The students gradually returned to the furniture in front of the fireplace.

Vandacheler took a deep breath. "As I've said, this will all blow over very soon and things will return to normal. You need not worry yourselves over hype and sensationalism."

"Why would they call us the Illuminati?" Kasey asked.

Vandacheler sighed. "My dear Kasey, they're merely choosing words that they believe are impactful or damaging rather than employing any thoughtful insight or inquiry. Rational discussion, as we've observed throughout the ages, is far less appetizing to those hungry for controversy and war. As we are now in the national spotlight, we can expect an occasional performance from the amateur-hour intellectual. But—remember this, my dear pupils—you are in the big league now. Pay no attention to the *mindless chatter*."

John leaned back in his chair, crossed his legs and keenly observed Vandacheler. The meeting continued for another fifteen minutes. Most of the students were hopeful that Vandacheler was correct, and that the plague of fame would pass over them quickly. John wasn't sure what to make of it all.

∽∾

After the students left, Don Vandacheler and Mr. Budwin stood on the porch, looking out across the quad.

"You have enemies," Mr. Budwin stated.

"Friends of yours?" Vandacheler joked.

Mr. Budwin chuckled. "No, I don't believe so."

"Yes, of course," Vandacheler said humorously, "you would need at least *one* friend for the pluralization to be anything but flattery."

Mr. Budwin snickered. "Will you report this to the council?" he asked, lifting up the plastic bag.

"No," Vandacheler answered, "we'll play it by ear."

∿∾

John and Kasey returned to The Marquis. Neither of them said much at the meeting or during the trip back to his apartment. With permission from the sun sinking below the horizon, John went straight to the kitchen toward his stash of liquor bottles.

"Why would they call us the Illuminati?" Kasey asked, placing her backpack beside the coffee table. "I honestly don't know much about this *New World Order* stuff."

"The Illuminati," John said, caressing a bottle of whiskey on the kitchen countertop, "was a Bavarian secret society forged in 1776 by university professor Adam Weishaupt. Their goal was to weaken the grip of religious authoritarianism, monarchism and superstition. Through reason, secularism, science and philosophy, they sought to preserve and expand the Enlightenment. The society retained many influential intellectuals, writers, philosophers and powerful people as members. The name Illuminati is derived from the Latin plural *illuminatus*, which translates roughly to *the enlightened*."

"That *does* sound a lot like what the Avalonti Society is," Kasey reluctantly confessed, "but why would they think that knowledge and enlightenment are bad?"

"The Prince-Elector and Duke of Bavaria, Charles Theodore, with the encouragement of the Catholic Church," John explained, "outlawed the society, along with others like the Freemasons, in subsequent years following their zenith in the late 18th century. The society allegedly continued to operate underground after their suppression in 1785 and endured vilification from religiously conservative organizations as a result. They believed the Illuminati were responsible for the French Revolution and The

Reign of Terror. This vilification gave rise to conspiracy theories that exist to this day. Some believe the Illuminati grew into a much more powerful secret society who are trying to establish an authoritarian global government: the New World Order. In short, they think the Illuminati are controlling the world. Because Avalonti resembles the *original* Illuminati, they think we're with them—or that we *are* them."

Kasey scoffed. "That's crazy, right?"

John nodded. "The Avalonti Society is wealthy and influential, but we aren't a secret society. We're not the *New World Order*. Even if Avalonti was a resurgence of the original Illuminati, so what? The original Illuminati were Lockean, Voltaire types—like liberal freethinkers who believed in sense, justice, freedom and autonomy. They opposed despotism and totalitarianism rigorously, just like the Avalonti Society does. Why would any society, whose members believed in true liberalism, seek to establish an order of tyrannical fascism? It's contradictory and doesn't make sense. Also, Avalonti isn't hellbent on destroying all religions like some may think. There was a bishop at the Thanksgiving charity gala. Avalonti gives money to all kinds of church-sponsored community programs. Avalonti has its own theologians; Christians, Catholics, Jews, Muslims, etcetera. All great members—all coexisting with atheists and agnostics in the pursuit of truth. We all just have a different idea of what that truth might be. These conspiracy theorists don't understand who we are, so they make up bullshit. It's all fear-mongering delusional hogwash."

"We're the good guys, right?" Kasey softly asked.

"Of course, we are, Kasey," John assured. "We fucked up with the witch hoax crap, but that can't erase eighty years of excellence. Haven't you read the journals? I started reading them before I was a member, during my freshman year. It's an incredible publication. The philosophers, scientists, theologians—the writers and academics who contribute—they are among the most respected in the world. We are the pedigree of university societies. We're the good guys—*they're* the lunatics—jealous of our status. We are fucking *kick ass*."

Kasey smiled. "Yeah, we are pretty awesome."

John left the unopened bottle of whiskey in the kitchen and joined her on the couch. "You're especially awesome, *Kase*."

"Well, thank you," she said bashfully, looking at the floor.

John kissed her hand, looking into her eyes. "I mean that." He smiled, then a moment later stood from the couch.

"I know you do. I'm glad we're together, John. You make me feel safer. This whole thing has me on edge. It's all so weird and scary."

John walked over to his computer desk on the other side of the living room. "I think Vandacheler might be right. Maybe we all need to calm down and proceed rationally."

"Yeah, Don is *usually* right about everything."

John opened his desk drawer and carefully picked up his .357 Magnum revolver, hiding his actions from her. He opened the cylinder to make sure the gun was fully loaded then placed it back in the drawer. "We have nothing to worry about, *Kase*. We have nothing to fear. All this crap is going to blow over, like Vandacheler said. We'll go dancing next weekend in Baltimore. Me, you and your friend will have a great time. Everything is going to be okay. I promise."

"Yeah, I'm looking forward to Xapà's. I just hope my parents don't freak out over this witch stuff."

"They won't," John said, returning to the couch. "If they do, we'll, *uh*—tell them you're pregnant—they'll forget *all* about witches."

Kasey chuckled, poking him. "Yeah, but they'd still be burning *someone* at the stake."

John laughed, kissing her on the cheek. Kasey turned her head, kissing him on the lips.

As they began kissing on the couch, John's phone vibrated; Don Vandacheler was calling.

"Who is that?" she asked.

"No one," he replied, rejecting the call and tossing the phone to the floor.

They started kissing again.

A loud knocking arrived on the apartment door.

John sighed heavily. "Jesus *fucking* Christ, now what?"

275 | P a g e

Kasey giggled.

"Yeah?" John shouted at the door. "Who is it?"

"It's Marcus."

"*Oh* my God, he's killing me," John said, standing from the couch.

Kasey sat up straight, gently fixing her hair.

John quickly unlocked the door and opened it. "This better be good."

Marcus walked in. "I just got some news."

John shook his head. "*Now* what?"

Kasey looked at her phone. "*Uh*, Don's calling me."

"Call him back in a minute. He's going to tell you what I'm about to tell you," Marcus said.

"What?" Kasey asked.

Marcus clicked his tongue. "Diageo quit."

John's eyes widened. "What do you mean he quit?"

"Professor Diageo resigned from the Avalonti Society. He renounced his membership earlier today. They're already processing the paperwork. We just found out."

"Th-th-that's crazy," John said. "Why the hell would he do that?"

Marcus shrugged. "I don't know. Maybe it was out of spite or anger—they did sanction his ass. They temporarily revoked all his privileges. They barred him from Avalonti property—including subsidiary properties—until his hearing next semester. I guess I can't blame him, I'd probably do the same shit. Pride will fuck you sometimes."

"That's so sad," Kasey opined. "Diageo is a good man. This really sucks."

Marcus nodded slowly. "Yes, yes it does. So that leaves me to wonder—what's going to happen to us? He quit, so now all his supporters are going to be looking at us—resenting us. They're going to blame us, I know it."

John sighed. "Is that all you ever think about, Marcus? Yourself?"

Marcus nodded vigorously. "You're God damn right it is. Did you read Dr. Thomas Sowell's book I gave you? What about that Ayn Rand book *Bo* gave you?"

"I read some of it—been a little too busy for leisure reading," John said.

Marcus smirked. "Well, you need to learn your ass about the *virtue of selfishness*. The only motherfucker on this planet that matters is *you*. If you forget that, then you've sacrificed yourself to the *shit pits* of society."

John shook his head. "Why do you care so much about getting kicked out of Avalonti? I mean—one of their big things is philanthropy. Didn't Ayn Rand hate charity?"

"I got nothing against charity, John. If I get stuffed on filet mignon and lobster tail, I'll gladly throw some potato scraps to the dogs."

Kasey scrunched her face. "The dogs? Really, Marcus?"

Marcus chuckled. "I know, Kasey, you're a liberal—you're not allowed to see reality. Sweep it under the rug. Throw a Band-Aid over it. Do whatever it takes to lessen your unbearable, unnecessary guilt. But we're no different, Kasey. If *you're* starving and *they're* starving—who's eating first?"

"We could eat together," Kasey answered proudly.

"Yeah!" John said, putting his arm around her.

"Yeah, John?" Marcus questioned. "Like the pizza at the bar that night? *Shit*, you already know about the virtue of selfishness."

"I was drunk that night," John snarled. "I used to give half my lunch to a homeless guy when I was in middle school. I barely had any to give away to begin with. Everyone thinks pastors are these Joel Osteen types, but my dad didn't make that much money. We lived modestly. Do you know what that's like, *Mr. Fancy Boarding School?* I'm not selfish. Fuck selfishness."

"Listen," Marcus said, modifying his tone, "I love you guys. I didn't come here to fight with you. I just need to know that my ass ain't gonna be next on the chopping block. They're still ordering silence on the witch hoax ordeal, even though it's already public knowledge. I think they're going for plausible deniability. The media might try to contact you, but you can't say anything to 'em. If you do, we're toast. I need to know that you two are gonna keep your damn mouths shut about this witch hoax bullshit. Diageo was a *hero*—and look where he's at now."

"Why would we say anything?" John huffed.

Marcus peered at him. "You *really* want me to answer that?"

John looked at the floor and quickly answered, "No."

Kasey squinted at John.

Marcus clasped his hands together. "I need you guys to promise, promise, promise me that you aren't going to say anything about this witch hoax shit to anyone."

Kasey scoffed. "We already told you before, we're not going to say anything. You're just going to have to trust us. Now, we're busy, so if you don't mind—we'd like to get back to our evening."

Marcus snickered. "Cute. I see the feminists are teaching you well. Standing up for yourself and everything. I like it, I like it. Just don't be getting too righteous like Diageo did. It ain't gonna do you any good. Don't be a fucking hero, okay?" He looked at his watch. "I gotta get going. You guys have a good night. No hard feelings, eh?"

John bit his tongue. "Yeah, it's all good, man—you got nothing to worry about. No hard feelings."

Marcus smiled. "Alright then. Goodnight, *John Boy.* Goodnight, Kasey."

"Goodnight," they both replied.

After Marcus left, John opened the bottle of whiskey and poured. Kasey softly sighed when she saw the scotch glass nearly overflowing. John leaned his head over the glass and slurped down enough to make carrying it to the living room a manageable task. He sat on the couch, set the drink down, kicked his feet up on the coffee table and stared blankly at the television.

"You okay?" Kasey asked, affectionately rubbing his shoulder.

"No, not really," he answered, bringing the scotch glass up to his mouth. "Something isn't right about all this."

"What do you mean?" she asked.

John sighed. "Like—me, you, Marcus, Don. Zach. Arjun. Diageo. Mr. Wilcox. Dr. Arnold. The journal writers. The journal. You know—that's the society to me. That's the society that *I* know. Then you have Caesar and these guys in New York and that miserable bastard Dean Rafalski. I don't know. Something doesn't feel quite right about them."

Kasey took a deep breath. "Do you think that there may be some truth to this New World Order stuff after all?"

John closed his eyes for a moment. "No. No. No. No. No. No. No. There's no truth to the *New World Order* stuff. That's just crazy conspiracy theory shit. I'm not making any assertions; I'm just saying that something seems a little odd about them. I can't put my finger on it. It's not a conspiracy theory, it's just—logical deduction. There's a difference."

"Is there?"

"Yeah," he insisted, "there's a big difference. Remember the society dinner? Remember how when the gunshots went off, Van just sat there talking to Professor Diageo? He could tell—just by the *way* they were shooting the gun—exactly what they were doing. Based on the evidence around him, he knew he wasn't in danger. That's a logical deduction. He pieced a puzzle together to reveal a true picture of what was happening. Now, when I think about this whole ordeal—with Diageo, Caesar, the social experiment, the High Council—I just don't see any picture coming into focus. It just doesn't make any sense to me."

"John, what are you talking about?"

"It's just—you know—this silence. It doesn't make any sense. Diageo went to the media and he told them everything. The whole world knows what we did. Why is it still such a big deal that we all keep quiet?"

"Plausible deniability," Kasey suggested, "like Marcus said."

"I don't know about that," John said, shaking his head. "And there's more. Like—why did it take so long for them to cancel the project? Why did Caesar show up the day *after* we published the defamation article? Why did he hand-deliver the certificates? Why not just mail them? And why a social experiment at all? I mean, for eighty years the induction process was the same. The

279 | P a g e

probationary members just did some stupid debate in front of the panel of society Judges. Then, all of a sudden, they change it. Why?"

"Caesar is experimental. That's what Don said."

"Yeah. Caesar's been running this society since the late '70s when his father got sick. Why now? Why change things? If they're so concerned about the image of prestige—why a social experiment? Why try to fool people if you're all about truth and knowledge and enlightenment?"

Kasey shrugged. "I guess people just like to try new things sometimes. They *were* testing the idea of letting undergraduates in. He probably just wanted to run with that momentum of being experimental. Maybe he just got a little carried away. Once he realized that he had made a mistake, he tried to do the right thing and cancel the project. He gave us the certificates and apologized. It's not that hard to imagine. Sometimes people just make mistakes and want to try to fix things, that's all. They want to try to make things right again."

John sighed, rubbing his temples, resting his head against the couch. "Yeah, I know all about that. I don't know. Maybe I'm just talking out of stress. All this shit is giving me a fucking headache. Let's just talk about something else, okay?"

Kasey smiled. "Okay. So, *uh*, what are you wearing to the Greektown dance?"

John chuckled. "I guess my tux."

CHAPTER 29

GREEKTOWN

Xapà's was a two-story, upscale, authentic Greek restaurant in Baltimore. The building's décor and interior design was heavily influenced by ancient Greek architecture and art. The floor level housed a formal dining area and a fully stocked bar with top-shelf and exotic liquors. The second story was a reception hall that was often reserved for corporate events, weddings, parties, as well as themed dance nights hosted by the restaurant. A smaller bar greeted guests as they emerged from the stairwell into the upper level hall. The upper level had an open floorplan with twenty-four round tables covered with white tablecloths. Purple, black and red polyester carpeting with an abstract floral design rested under the tables. On the right side of the hall there was a long rectangular buffet table, sometimes used as a head table during weddings. The left and back walls were made of glass, offering a romantic view of the city streets below. In the center of the hall there were two ancient Greek-styled pillars. Near the bar was a DJ table and a professional sound system owned by the restaurant. Between the bar and the tables was a polyurethane-coated hardwood dance floor.

John had offered to drive Kasey and her friend Alyssa to the '50s & '60s themed dance party at Xapà's that Friday night, but Alyssa politely protested. Although she had never seen his car before, she refused to ride with John because his 1989 Buick LeSabre had "inadequate safety features". Since Kasey had already agreed to go with her, Alyssa offered John a ride as a compromise.

In spite, he refused and drove his own car, meeting up with them at the restaurant shortly after they arrived.

Expecting a stiff, upper-class turnout, John smiled when he scanned the second floor of Xapà's from the stairwell. Men who once worked at Bethlehem Steel shared the hall with men who retired from Domino Sugar, the shipyard, H&S Bakery, Cloverland Dairy and A&P. They were veterans, mechanics, electricians, plumbers, forklift operators, truck drivers and laborers; men who wore old scars as badges of honor and still believed in chivalry. They sat with their loving wives with whom they adored and weathered the ages with. They didn't wear $12,000 suits or designer apparel, but they dressed to the nines with what they had.

"John!" Kasey shouted, running across the dance floor to greet him.

John hugged her, saying, "I think we're the youngest ones here."

Kasey chuckled. "By far."

Nodding to the music, John joined Kasey and Alyssa at their table. They had a front row seat where the carpet met the dance floor. A nice couple in their seventies had joined them. Several in the crowd clapped along with the music while a few people danced.

"Alyssa, right?" John asked, shaking her hand.

"That's correct," Alyssa said. "You look sharp, John," she complimented.

"Thanks," John said, modestly adjusting his collar. "You both look great as well."

"Thank you," Alyssa said.

Kasey smiled, kissed John on the cheek and rested her chin on his shoulder.

Kasey wore a tight white embroidered floral backless midi dress, and Alyssa wore a heavy-laced black cocktail dress. John wore the only formal attire he owned: the cheap tuxedo he bought for the Thanksgiving charity gala. Instead of wearing his tie, however, he had purchased a bow tie.

Promising not to drink any hard liquor, John ordered a Bud Light and gradually started making friends with the elderly guests in attendance. Kasey watched him under the ambient lighting, occasionally smiling and waving at him. Wandering from table to table, he innocently flirted with old ladies and confidently engaged in conversation with the other men. They immediately liked him, and he immediately liked them. Kasey saw John and a group of old men sharing a hearty laugh, presumably from one of his inappropriate jokes that he was too afraid to tell at the university.

Standing from their chairs, Kasey and Alyssa kicked off their heels to hit the dance floor. John snuck up behind Kasey and kissed her on the cheek. Kasey turned around to give him an affectionate hug.

"Hey, John, did you want to dance with us?" Alyssa asked politely.

"He doesn't know how," Kasey said. "I'm sorry, John," she quickly apologized.

John smiled. "No, no, no, you're fine. You girls knock 'em dead."

After Betty Everette's "Shoop Shoop Song", Claudine Clark's 1962 hit, "Party Lights", began to blare through the hall's speakers. John lounged in his chair, smiling, watching Kasey and Alyssa dance together. A few people joined them, trying to keep up. The crowd clapped and cheered as they took center stage. Focusing on Kasey, he sipped his beer in awe. The old man at his table leaned in and announced that she was an "incredible dancer". John nodded enthusiastically, taking another sip of his beer. The others who were dancing cleared the area. The floor belonged to them. John gazed admiringly at her as if she was the only woman in the world.

When the song was over, John stood and clapped, louder than anyone else in the room.

Kasey rushed over to give him a hug and a kiss.

"You're amazing," John conferred.

Kasey smiled bashfully. "Thank you, John." She looked at Alyssa. "Alyssa was pretty awesome, too."

"Yeah," John said, nodding in polite agreement.

"Nowhere near as awesome as you," Alyssa gushed, gently punching her in the shoulder.

She snickered.

Kasey and Alyssa started talking amongst themselves.

With apprehension, John leaned toward Kasey and carefully said, "*Tu danses très bien.*"

Kasey paused, slowly returning a bottle of water to the table. "*Merci*," she replied softly.

"I didn't know that you knew how to speak French," Alyssa said to John.

"I didn't know it either," Kasey said, maintaining eye contact with him.

"I'm still learning. I got a long way to go until I'm fluent. I've been learning it on my own."

"That's awesome, John," Alyssa complimented.

"Thanks. It's Kasey's favorite language," he said, winking at Kasey.

Kasey exhaled, wearing a bewildered smile.

The crowd *oohed* as the lights dimmed. The disco ball cast its reflections on the walls and the dance floor. As the Elvis Presley song "Can't Help Falling in Love" started, the DJ grabbed his microphone and said, "Let's slow things down a little."

"Let's dance," John urged, taking Kasey by the hand.

"But you don't know how," she said, gently pulling away.

John grinned, beckoning her to the floor with a nod.

Kasey squinted, scrutinizing his confidence.

John walked her to the center of the dance floor. Several elderly couples joined them. John took a deep breath, pondering his dance rehearsals with Pierre and Bo in his living room. With summoned grace, he moved in a mirrored symmetry with Kasey.

"I thought you didn't know how to dance," she said, smirking.

John turned her delicately. "I didn't."

"When did you learn how to do this?" she asked, smiling wider.

"Right after you said it was a shame that I didn't know how."

Kasey chuckled, shaking her head. "You're something else, John Hallman."

A Korean War veteran pensively watched them from his table as they slow danced to the Elvis song. Losing his darling wife to cancer two years prior, he would go to Xapà's to remember better days. Discreetly, he peeked at a photo of them that he kept in his wallet, taken in 1956. His wife resembled Kasey in that picture, and he resembled John. Watching them closely, the old man touched his face as tears welled up in his eyes, reminded of a time long ago; when he was once there; once young and fearless.

John and Kasey locked eyes. Their body language radiated a fierce intensity. They stood as friends; as rivals; as equals. They were lost, found only by the madness of passion; still casting its ready victims so willingly into its fire. They were alone on the crowded dance floor. The world outside those walls had vanished. As the Elvis Presley song neared its end, she looked deep into his eyes and spoke something that she had never said to him before: "I love you, John."

John swallowed nervously. Staring blankly, he slowly let go of her hand.

The music stopped.

"John," she asked, "are you okay? What's wrong with you?"

John looked at her and opened his mouth but couldn't speak.

Kasey gasped sharply as John abruptly ran to the stairwell. He tripped once but immediately picked himself up and started running again. Down the fifteen steps to the lower level of Xapà's, his dress shoes grazed only four of them. Alyssa quickly joined her on the dance floor. Kasey listlessly walked to the window and looked out at the street below. She and Alyssa watched John running full speed toward the parking lot at the far end of the block. Among the ample assortment of cars, they watched a pair of headlights turn on. The car peeled out of the space and raced off into the night.

CHAPTER 30

THE BROKEN WINDOW FALLACY

Kasey ignored a text from John, claiming that he ran off as a result of stomach pains. She knew exactly where to find him the following afternoon. A group of Avalonti members gathered at Francesca Hall for their mandatory Saturday meeting. John sat in a parlor chair, keeping to himself, reading an old article written by Caesar Avalonti. He had not mentioned Kasey or Xapà's to any of the members. Kasey had not told anyone from Avalonti either.

When Kasey pushed open the doors of Francesca Hall that afternoon, she brought with her fire and brimstone. "Johnathan Hallman," she yelled out, "you better get over here *right now!*"

All the members in attendance gasped in astonishment. They gazed at the foyer where Kasey stood with her hands clenched into fists. Calmly placing a journal on the coffee table, John stood from his chair.

"What in the *hell* do you think you're doing!" Kasey shouted as he stepped towards her.

Vandacheler and Marcus looked at each other, sloping their eyebrows.

John didn't speak.

Kasey put her hands on her hips. "Stomach pains, John? Really? You *really* must think I'm stupid, don't you?"

Faint laughter from one of the grad students was heard in the background.

John began to speak, "I—*uh*..."

"How could you do that to me!" she cried. "I was humiliated! Everyone was staring at me in disgust, like *I* did something wrong. How could you do that to me, John? I thought you cared about me!"

"Kasey, it was a mistake," he calmly spoke.

"A mistake!" She laughed boisterously. "You ran out of a dance hall and left me standing there looking like a *God damn* fool—and that was just *a mistake*?"

"No," John said dismissively, "me and you."

Kasey froze in shock, as if she had just been electrocuted. "Me and you?"

John nodded coldly.

Kasey's chin began to tremble. "What do you mean, John?"

"I mean—I'll have the concierge mail your stuff to your house," he said, maintaining a stern look on his face.

"What?" she exhaled. "I can't even believe I'm in reality right now. I can't believe you're serious, John."

"Well, I am," John said, turning away from her, returning to his chair.

"You're a coward, you know that, John! You're a God damn coward!"

"I know," John uttered, too low for anyone to hear.

She turned around, pulled open one of the doors and ran out of the hall.

"Kasey!" Marcus shouted, running after her.

"Let her be," Vandacheler instructed.

Marcus stopped. He looked at John then back at the entranceway then back at John again. His nostrils flared as he shook John's chair. "Get out of that fucking chair, motherfucker!"

"Marcus," Vandacheler scolded, shaking his head, "don't."

Marcus stood in front of John, who had calmly returned to reading. "Man, what the fuck are you doing? I—I—I don't get it. What happened? Why are you doing this!"

"It's none of your business, Marcus," John said, keeping his focus on the journal, turning a page.

"It's my business, man. I care about her."

John scoffed. "Then you take her. You always had a thing for her anyway."

"Man, she's like a sister to me."

"Yeah, right."

The guests jolted as a twelve-foot-tall, stained-glass window behind the library shattered. A large rock slid across the marble floor towards them.

"*Oh*, my goodness!" Arjun shouted. "She's thrown a rock through the window!"

"Crazy bitch," Zach uttered.

Several members rushed to the entranceway, investigating the outside.

"*Uh*—I don't think it was *her*," one of the grad students stated cautiously.

"What do you mean?" Arjun questioned, approaching the doorway.

The grad student pointed at Kasey on the other side of the quad.

Murmurs filled the hall when they realized it wasn't Kasey who threw the rock. John continued reading the journal as if the attack had not taken place. Marcus gritted his teeth at John while the others clamored for answers. Don Vandacheler called Dean Robert Rafalski, who was not in attendance that afternoon, and alerted him of the situation.

"Doesn't this place have cameras?" the recently inducted grad student asked.

"Unfortunately not," Vandacheler answered, returning his phone to his pocket.

"The university might," the grad student suggested.

"We can check their cameras, but it's highly unlikely we'll get a positive ID. There are trees and shrubbery all around the building.

I can assure you; this will be our loss alone to manage," Vandacheler declared.

"Well," the grad student said, "you know what they say—a broken window is good for the economy at least."

Vandacheler rolled his eyes, walking over to John.

Marcus peered intently at the grad student. "What?" he scoffed. "Physicists don't read Frédéric Bastiat anymore?"

The grad student raised an eyebrow. "Who?"

Marcus sighed. "A broken window does *not* help the economy. If that window costs $850 to replace, then sure, it's good for the window guy, but it doesn't add anything to the economy. That $850 that we spend on the window would've gone towards bottles of expensive champagne or scientific research or whatever. There is no net gain in the economy as a whole. It's—ironically in this case—called the broken window fallacy. Look it up."

"You're right about the broken window fallacy," an Avalonti economist said to Marcus, "but that window is *a lot* more than $850."

Marcus closed his eyes and shook his head for a moment. Opening his eyes, he turned to look at John, who was ignoring Don Vandacheler's words of wisdom, flipping through pages of the journal while he spoke. Vandacheler reminded John that cordiality and respect were imperative, and that his affairs were not to disrupt the balance. Eventually, he acknowledged Vandacheler with a slight nod.

~~

John returned to The Marquis to gather Kasey's belongings and box them up for mailing. The concierge provided him with a large flat-rate priority USPS box and a roll of clear packing tape. Entering his apartment, John stopped and looked at the dining room table where he and Kasey had their first romantic dinner together. He remembered how her face lit up when she saw the roses. Making a fist, he gently struck himself on the center of his forehead in a vain attempt to block out thoughts. Taking a few more steps, he looked on to the balcony where they would sit for hours and talk about life. He glanced away. Next to the coffee table was a motorcycle helmet; the one he had recently purchased for Kasey. "Just don't look at it," he said, folding and taping one end of the box. "I'll send it back Monday."

Walking across the living room, he looked at the brown leather couch where they watched movies, cuddled and playfully threw grapes at each other. He sighed. Continuing down the hallway, he made it to the bathroom, where most of her belongings were. Packing her shampoos and conditioners, he remembered how scared she was to take showers at her own house, fearing that someone would break in and attack her while she was vulnerable and stood little chance of escape. He breathed heavily. When he picked up a bottle of her perfume from the cabinet, he sniffed it intensely and started to sob. Placing the bottle on his bathroom sink, he caught his reflection in the vanity mirror. Watching a tear rolling down his cheek, he clenched his jaws until veins popped out of his forehead. "Don't fucking cry, you fucking pussy!" he screamed, punching the mirror, shattering it into various sized shards of jagged glass. Droplets of blood fell into the sink.

He heard his cell phone buzzing on the coffee table out in the living room.

"Kasey," he said, rushing out of the bathroom.

Picking up his phone, he grumbled. Philippe Álvarez was calling him. He didn't answer it.

He finished packing up her stuff. Blood stains covered the box. "I should get a new box," he said to himself, picking up the remote control. He looked at his still bleeding hand. "And a bandage."

∿∾

After bandaging up his hand and cleaning the glass out of the bathroom, he sat on his couch and contemplated the witch hoax. It wasn't over. More and more suspects were named every day. John dove hopelessly into the underground, searching for answers. Upon researching, he found a myriad of allegations against the Avalonti Society on the ZzzChan message board. Professor Diageo's public confession had pushed them firmly into the crosshairs of the conspiracy theorists. John stumbled across a militant anti-globalist organization called The Georgia Deathstone Society that published a widely circulated blog. Utilizing a series of proxy servers, their true location was unknown. GDS was inexorably convinced that the Avalonti Society was a garrison of the New World Order. They claimed that the National Archives and Records Administration had no legal records of an Avalonti family being in the United States prior to

1785, contrary to the early 19th-century history books that claimed they were early settlers. GDS believed that the Avalonti family had successfully altered history books to cover their involvement with the Illuminati. Their belief was that Avalonti was an anagram for *Lavation*, conjecturing that the society was preparing to "cleanse the world of autonomy and establish an elite, global oligarchy". The plan for world domination that the Avalonti family were allegedly involved in, according to GDS, had been in the works for centuries. They vowed to burn Francesca Hall to the ground with all the members inside of it. John believed that the rock thrown through the hall's window was no act of petty vandalism. He suspected that it was a warning; a preamble to the greater destruction that most certainly awaited them.

Thinking of Kasey's safety, John called Don Vandacheler and pleaded with him to press for heightened security at Francesca Hall. John wouldn't divulge any of the information he reviewed on the ZzzChan message board, out of fear he would face disciplinary action just for meddling, so he disguised his concern as a hunch; a *feeling* that something worse would happen. Vandacheler appeared to John as complacent when he assured him that no additional security was necessary.

John's phone started to buzz.

"Damn it," he said, seeing that it was Philippe Álvarez again.

He declined the call.

"Just fucking call her," he said to himself.

Picking up his phone and putting it down repeatedly, he finally plucked up the courage to hit the call button, dialing Kasey's number. It went straight to an automated voice message.

He sent her a text message: *Hey Kase, can we talk?*

Unable to Send

John threw the phone across the room. "She fucking blocked me!"

～

Deciding to take his anger out on the hotel staff, John pried the shattered vanity mirror from the wall and concocted a story that it had fallen as a result of a loose screw. He took the drywall anchors and stashed them in his pocket. When the maintenance man arrived, John screamed and yelled at him, telling him, "Next time try putting some fucking drywall anchors in there before this piece of shit hotel gets somebody killed!"

The maintenance man apologized repeatedly and, within an hour, installed a new vanity mirror with new drywall anchors. The hotel manager sent John a gift basket full of fine cheeses, imported meats and olive oils, and a handwritten apology letter. John called the concierge asking for the hotel manager. When she got him on the line, John said, "Nice cheeses, asshole, they'd go great with a bottle of your finest Cabernet—get on it, motherfucker!"

Within fifteen minutes, a room service attendant presented to John a $549 bottle of Cabernet Sauvignon. John took the bottle and slammed the door, shouting, "I said your *finest* Cabernet!"

∿

John plopped on the couch, placed the wine on the coffee table and began to sob. Moments later, he uncorked the wine bottle and dumped it down the kitchen sink. Figuring that to be a waste, John stuffed the cheeses and imported meats into a plastic bag and set out on his sports bike in search of the homeless veteran that he met on Christmas Eve. Unable to locate the man, he dropped the food in a donation box designated for clothing, outside of the Basilica of Divine Hope.

∿

John had no intention of returning home after he dropped the imported meats and cheeses into the cathedral's donation box. Halfway to West Virginia, he realized he had forgotten his gun, but proceeded to *The Dollhouse* anyway. Upon arriving in front of the long dirt driveway leading to Philippe's house, John decided not to visit after all. He filled up his Kawasaki Ninja with unleaded regular gas and rode aimlessly through the hills of West Virginia.

After a couple of hours of riding, John didn't know where he was. He rode for another hour before attempting to activate the GPS on his phone but couldn't get any service. Close to midnight, he elected to stop at a bar in the middle of nowhere to have a beer.

Pulling into the dirt and gravel parking lot, he stopped to survey the vintage muscle cars, pickup trucks, motorcycles and custom choppers. As he advanced toward the entranceway, a muscular man wearing a leather vest offered him a dirty look as he walked out. A middle-aged woman with long black hair wearing cutoff jean-shorts, leather boots and a tank top accompanied the biker. The man's Harley Davidson revved loudly as John entered the honky-tonk.

Scanning the bar, he heard Johnny Paycheck's song "I'm the Only Hell My Mama Ever Raised" playing on the jukebox. Cigarette smoke, country music, rambunctious laughter and the sound of billiard balls *cracking* against each other filled the evening air. John cautiously proceeded to the bar and sat on a stool, staring at the large Confederate flag that hung on the wall behind the liquor bottles.

"Whatchu want?" the old bartender asked him.

"*Uh*—just a Bud Light bottle," John answered nervously.

John laid a few dollars down, waiting for the bartender to bring him his bottle of beer. He lit a cigarette and rested his forehead on his left hand, looking at the bar top with a gloomy expression. John took a drag of his cigarette with his right hand, maintaining his troubled gaze. As the old bartender returned with his beer, a man approached the stool next to him.

"I know *that* look," a forty-two-year-old blond-haired man wearing tight blue jeans, beige cowboy boots and a tucked-in, red flannel shirt said in a thick southern accent. "*Hell*, there ain't a *son-of-a-bitch* in this world who ain't had *that* look on his face before." He sat down next to John. "What's her name?"

Taking a sip of his beer, John looked at the man, then answered, "Kasey."

"Kasey? *Ooh-wee*, she sure does sound pretty," he said, pulling a cigarette out of his pack. "So, why'd she dump your ass?" he asked, lighting his cigarette.

John chuckled. "Because I'm a dumbass."

"Dumbass?" The man howled like a wolf, laughing boisterously as he slapped the bar top with the palm of his hand. "*You's* in good company," he said, winking.

John smiled.

The man took a deep drag from his cigarette and spoke as he exhaled, "I'll tell ya whatchu need to do. *Getchu* the ugliest broad you can find and fuck her six ways to Sunday. Don't even let that bitch cook you eggs in the morn'n. *Hell*, you'll forget *all* 'bout her—least for a night."

John laughed, taking a drag of his cigarette. "Name's John," he said, extending his hand.

"Teddy," the man said, smiling, shaking John's hand.

"Nice to meet you."

"Say, Buck!" Teddy hollered for the old bartender. "How's about a shot of whiskey for my new friend here?"

Buck nodded.

"Putta foot on the gas pedal there, Buck—I ain't got *all* night," Teddy joked, looking at John. "Slugs move faster than this *son-of-a-bitch*."

Buck slowly returned with two shot glasses and a bottle of whiskey. He placed the shot glasses on the bar top and carefully poured. Teddy and John each slid a shot closer to them.

Teddy raised his shot glass in the air and shouted, "Here's to all the fat, ugly, three-toothed white women and the dumb sons of bitches who can't get enough of 'em!"

John clinked his glass against Teddy's, tapped it on the bar top then downed the whiskey in one swift gulp.

Teddy howled.

"Thanks," John said, "I needed that. Let me get the next one, eh?"

Teddy paused and looked at him for a moment. "*Hell*, the world looks like it done took a shit on you, boy—I got us tonight, partner."

∾

Teddy and John sat at the bar talking for nearly an hour. John told dirty jokes and Teddy told stories of his days as a roadie for a hair metal band in the late '90s. He offered John numerous life lessons and various "words of wisdom". Periodically, Teddy would buy John a fresh beer when he ran out and a shot of whiskey to go with it.

As the hour grew late, tension near the billiard tables boiled up. Two small groups of men were having a dispute over a pool game. Teddy took out a wad of cash, mostly one-hundred-dollar bills, and called for the bartender, "Say, Buck—what'd I owe ya?"

"Hold on," Buck said, slowly putting on his glasses to retrieve Teddy's bar tab.

"Mercy!" Teddy shouted, dropping $200 on the bar top. "Keep the change, Buck—get something *real nice* for Darlene."

Buck nodded gratefully.

"I, *uh*—really appreciate this," John said with a happy slur in his voice.

Teddy looked over John's shoulder at the men who were arguing by the pool table. "Say, John—it's about to get *real* ugly in here. What do you say we take the party outside?" he asked, inconspicuously revealing a large baggie of cocaine.

John nodded enthusiastically. "Hell yeah."

～✿

In the parking lot, John sat in the passenger's side of Teddy's souped-up, black 1969 Z28 Chevy Camaro, watching him cut lines of cocaine on a small square mirror with a razor blade. Bon Jovi played softly through the car speakers.

Teddy snorted a line with a hundred-dollar bill then passed the mirror to John. "*At'll* put some hair on your chest."

John took the rolled-up bill from Teddy, held it to his nose and lowered his head to the mirror. In one strong snort, he cleared a line.

"*Hell*, you almost look like you know *whatchu* doing, Sweet Pea," Teddy joked.

John squeezed the bridge of his nose. His eyes widened and he began talking vivaciously about quantum mechanics, conspiracy theorists, black holes and String Theory. Teddy occasionally chuckled at him in between taking lines. He had no idea what John was talking about but found his animated behavior amusing. A few people ran out of the bar, but they didn't notice.

John took a second line and perked up even more, talking about the witch hoax, quantum entanglement and Philippe Álvarez. Teddy, in a supportive gesture, discouraged him whenever he brought up Kasey. John snorted a third, then a fourth line. Teddy flicked a cigarette onto the gravel parking lot and rolled up his window. While quietly watching John ramble, Teddy licked his teeth, fidgeted for a moment then started to unbuckle his belt.

John paused confusedly. "What the fuck are you doing, man?"

Teddy breathed heavily, sweating, stroking himself gently. "You didn't think all them drinks was free, now, did ya?"

"*Oh*, Jesus *fucking* Christ," John said, reaching for the door handle.

"Hang on, Sunshine," Teddy said, pulling a gun on him. "*Theys* only one way you getting out of this alive. Devil's gotta get his dues." Teddy glanced down at his lap. "My *friend's* gonna need a little kiss. Pucker up, Buttercup."

John glared at Teddy, who waited in sweaty anticipation. "Just fucking shoot me."

Teddy scowled. "What the fuck did you just say?"

John crossed his arms and shrugged. "Just shoot me. I'm not doing it."

Teddy pulled the hammer back on the single action .45 Colt revolver. "You really are a dumbass, ain't *cha*?"

John looked into Teddy's wild eyes. They weren't the eyes of a petty criminal; Teddy was going to kill him. John didn't know if it was from the drugs, the whiskey or the heartache, but he just sat there and quietly waited for it. His mind wandered. He remembered shooting a .45 Colt revolver with his uncle when he was twelve. The men at the firing range referred to it as a Long Colt. Smiling, he remembered the recoil being so powerful that the gun nearly leapt from his hands when he pulled the trigger. They were good times. Everyone he loved was still alive. In the background, Teddy was saying something, but he tuned him out. He thought of Kasey and the attacker who had climbed on top of her, trying to kiss her neck while she lay helplessly on her back, trapped. John glanced at Teddy's gun. Closing his eyes, he wondered if Teddy was really going to shoot him inside of his Camaro, or if he would take him outside in the parking lot instead.

"Shit," Teddy said, turning his head, still pointing the gun at John. Three cop cars pulled into the parking lot. A vicious fight had erupted inside of the bar over the pool game and Buck had called the police immediately.

"Fuck you!" John cried, attempting to disarm him.

Vying for control of the gun, John caused Teddy to reflexively pull the trigger. A bullet zipped inches from his head, instantaneously shattering the Camaro's tinted passenger-side window. John's ears went completely, temporarily deaf.

"Son of a bitch!" Teddy bellowed out.

Within seconds, police surrounded the vehicle.

Teddy and John both threw their hands into the air.

John heard the officer shouting, muffled in his ringing ears, "Get on the ground! On the ground!"

John's face scraped against the gravel as an officer threw him to the ground. Holding him down with a knee, the officer handcuffed him. John didn't move a muscle.

∿∾

At the police station, an officer held a rotary telephone in front of John and instructed him to make his call. The phone *chimed* as it landed on the desk. John asked the officer where he was as he picked up the receiver. The officer laughed and said, "Jail."

John refused to call anyone from Avalonti, and he didn't have any friends who would drive out to unincorporated West Virginia to pick him up. Reluctantly, he decided to call Philippe Álvarez, but there was a problem; John didn't know Philippe's number from memory and the officer wouldn't let him retrieve his phone to get it. John waived his right and never called anyone. He spent the next thirty-one hours in custody.

∿∾

Teddy had a rap sheet that stretched from Alabama up the east coast to West Virginia and beyond. His crimes ranged from petty larceny to illicit gambling, pimping and drug dealing. He was also wanted for a murder in Mayfield, Kentucky. Teddy would be held for bail proceedings. John was released on his own recognizance Monday morning and charged with possession of a controlled substance; a misdemeanor in West Virginia. After his release, John walked nine miles to the bar to retrieve his Kawasaki Ninja sports bike, refusing a courtesy ride from an officer. The commissioner had informed John that the District Attorney's office would likely drop the charge against him, which was levied only as a "matter of protocol". In time, he would be required to return to West Virginia for a court hearing. The long walk afforded John ample time to evaluate his life. Checking his phone for text messages and missed calls, he saw that the only person who attempted to contact him was Philippe Álvarez. No one knew he was arrested, and he intended to keep it that way.

CHAPTER 31

FINALS WEEK

Returning from West Virginia to his apartment early Monday evening, John poured a glass of whiskey, sat on his brown leather couch and stared blankly at the wall in complete silence. He had three final examinations scheduled that week for Tuesday and Thursday; one on Tuesday and two on Thursday. He had not invested a significant amount of time into preparation, although he claimed preparation was not necessary.

He dumped the whiskey down the kitchen sink. There was no way he was going to miss his final exam in the morning. Knowing that one single taste of whiskey would have likely thrust him into another night of drinking, he ardently abstained. His hands trembled at the mere thought of walking into the gymnasium to take the test. Looking down, he noticed beads of sweat forming on his arms. A rush of cold pulsed through his body, followed by an intense sensation of heat. He felt sick, almost like the flu, but he didn't have the flu.

Fidgeting on the couch, he struggled to lay comfortably, hoping to get some sleep. His eyes refused to stay closed. With a cold rag on his forehead, he battled his mind and body. Every time he started to doze off, his body would jolt, waking him up again. He endured the process repeatedly. Gently convulsing, he pulled a blanket over himself, or removed it, accommodating the sudden changes from intense chill to unbearable heat. The hour grew late.

~~

John didn't remember calling Dr. Ouradnik after what seemed like an eternity of talking on the phone with him.

"John, you just have to remember something about my dear friend, Philippe," Dr. Ouradnik explained over the phone. "He's an ex-con. Many inmates who serve long prison sentences develop strong spiritual convictions. It's not a bad thing. Their relationship with God helps them find new meaning in their lives, and it keeps them out of trouble a lot of the time. You should show some sympathy, John."

"He pierced a kitchen knife through his hand, though," John argued, sitting on his couch in moonlit darkness.

"Yes, I understand, John. Many times, their convictions will be devout. It's the stigmata he aimed to replicate. You questioned his loyalty to God, and he passionately felt like that was his only way to prove he wasn't of evil character. He cares about you, John—he really does. You should give him another chance."

"I don't know, Dr. Ouradnik, it was quite a grisly sight to bear."

"Well, think it over, John. Don't be too hasty in your decision to cast people from your life. Anyway, you should try to get some rest. Your big final examination is tomorrow at ten-thirty. You need to sleep."

John paused, removed the phone from his ear and gazed upon it. Nervously, he put the phone back up to his ear. "Dr. Ouradnik—I never told anyone what time my test was. How did you know?"

Static hissed over Dr. Ouradnik's voice.

"Dr. Ouradnik?"

The static continued.

"Hello?"

He lost reception.

"Damn it."

Hanging up, he stood from the couch and walked to the living room light switch near the kitchen. The lights wouldn't come on.

"Shit," he said, looking through the sliding glass door, noticing that the entire town was experiencing a blackout.

"What the hell," he uttered, inching closer to the balcony. Opening the sliding glass door, he was met with a howling, subzero wind. Snow covered the surrounding buildings. "It's May," he said, touching the frozen railing. "What the fuck is going on?"

John surveyed his surroundings. "This can't be real," he said, peeking over the railing. The streets below had vanished. Darkness, for miles, fell into an abyss. Leaning over the railing, he looked up. The hotel stretched beyond the heavens. "I must be dreaming." A drop of liquid fell from the balcony above him, landing on his arm. It was blood. "This can't be a dream," he said in a panic. "I'm not speaking in slow motion."

Behind him, there was a faint sound of digging coming from the kitchen. Stepping back into his apartment, he closed the sliding glass door. "This isn't right," he said, kneeling down, plucking a blade of grass from his floor. The carpeting was gone, replaced with a damp soil. Feet stuck out from behind the breakfast bar. "Who is that?" he asked, walking toward the kitchen. "Come on, John, wake up," he said, covering his eyes. Bo's naked, severely decomposed body laid on a pile of dirt in the middle of his kitchen floor. Chain from the silver pocket watch that he was buried with stuck out of his mouth, as if somebody had crammed it down his throat.

His bedroom door closed.

"Who's back there?" he asked, sharply turning his head.

Faint voices came from the hallway.

Kasey's voice, giggling: "He doesn't know how to dance."

Marcus's voice: "Treat her right, brother."

Liam's voice: "He's dead, John."

"Kasey," he said, breathing heavily, slinking down the hallway, "is that you?"

A black raven fluttered its wings, perched on the landline telephone.

"How did *you* get in here?" he asked the bird, leaning toward it.

Meeting the bird eye-to-eye, they stared at each other for a time.

A knock on the sliding glass door disrupted his showdown with the raven.

John's dead brother stood on the balcony, blue, frozen, cradling a baby boy in his arms. Gently rocking him, Freddy cooed, kissing the baby with his lips encased in tiny icicles. "I *wuv* you *so* much," Freddy said to the baby, holding him over the railing.

"Freddy, no!" John shouted.

Freddy turned his head, smiling devilishly at John.

"Oopsie," Freddy said, dropping the baby over the railing.

"No!" John gasped, cowering against the living room wall.

Kasey's voice, giggling: "Newton's Third Law."

Marcus's voice: "Treat her right, brother."

Freddy froze into a statue, still holding his arms over the railing.

The apartment telephone rang.

"Hello," John said, quickly picking up the receiver.

"Good evening, sir, this is the concierge," a woman spoke. "We're issuing a courtesy call to make sure that everything is okay with your room, and to see if you needed anything to make your stay with us more pleasurable."

"Yeah, there's something wrong," John said, trying to catch his breath.

"Oh, okay, okay," the concierge said in Kevin's voice, "we have a maintenance man on the way."

"What?"

A dalmatian darted past him and into the kitchen.

"I said we have a maintenance man on the way," the woman spoke in her voice.

"No," John exhaled, "I'm only dreaming."

A demonic growl replaced the woman's voice. "You're not dreaming, John."

A menacing laughter blared through the telephone.

"Fuck you!" John shouted, slamming down the receiver.

The Atmos soundbar powered up by itself. A disco ball dropped from the ceiling, casting the moonlight's reflections on the walls as it spun. "Then He Kissed Me" by The Crystals played as he crept through his apartment. Elderly couples danced all around him. John spoke to them, begging them to listen, but they refused to acknowledge him.

"Fine, I'll just read then," John said, laughing maniacally, grabbing a journal from the coffee table. "I'll just fucking read then!" The *Avalonti Journal* was indecipherable, with scrambled words on every page. "What's happening to me?" John sobbed, gasping for air. "What's happening to me, God damn it!"

The disco ball giggled.

John raised his head.

"I've seen you in my dreams before," he said, standing from the couch, pointing at the disco ball. "I've seen you before! I've seen you before! I've seen you before!" he screamed, reaching back, punching the disco ball with all his force. Lightning flashed for a millisecond. He grunted, backing away. Coughing, he spit four of his teeth into the palm of his hand. Blackish-red blood dripped onto the floor. The unharmed disco ball giggled once more. Dropping the teeth, he inspected his mouth with his opposite hand. He raised his bloody hand to continue searching. All of his teeth remained intact.

"What the fuck is this! What's happening!" he heard himself crying out from the bedroom.

"Who is that?" he whimpered, proceeding down the hallway.

Papers rustled from behind the bedroom door. Cautiously, he pushed the door open.

"It's not in here!" his doppelgänger cried, throwing a newspaper into the air. "It's not in here! It's not in here!"

Sweat poured from his face as he watched his double sitting on the bed, repeatedly throwing the same newspaper into the air over and over. Whenever he threw it, it would instantaneously reappear in his hands.

"It's not in here! It's not in here!"

"You're being lied to," Dr. Novini said, strolling down the hallway. Ignoring the real John, he walked into the bedroom and sat next to his doppelgänger.

"What is this?" the real John uttered, standing in the threshold.

"Reality isn't what you think it is," Dr. Novini explained to John's double, placing his arm around him. "You know when you're in bed at night and it feels like someone is lying next to you? It's not just paranoia—there really *is* somebody there. There's an infinite number of parallel universes and they're all merging into one. *He's* trying to kill you," Dr. Novini said, looking up, pointing at John.

John yanked the bedroom door shut and raced back to the living room, heading for the exit.

Thunderous knocking arrived, so hard it splintered the front door. "Maintenance man!" someone shouted theatrically, sounding as if he were a carnival announcer. "Maintenance man! Maintenance man!" he yelled, repeatedly kicking the door.

The elderly couples disappeared with the music. A low rumbling above him began, increasing in volume with every tick of the clock. The hotel was collapsing, starting at the 2,750th floor. Voices encircled him, reverberating hauntingly as he braced himself against the living room wall.

Kasey's voice, happily: "Our apartment—I'll help you clean."

Marcus's voice: "Treat her right, brother."

Vandacheler's voice: "You're in the big league now."

The old woman in New York's voice: "Great evil is coming for you."

His own voice: "A witch hoax."

Chad Wilcox's voice: "We stand on the shoulders of our great predecessors, Dr. Arnold."

Vandacheler's voice: "Mindless chatter."

Clint's voice: "Nice bracelet, poser."

Arjun's voice: "Everything is connected in ways we are unable to comprehend."

Marcus's voice, fading: "Treat her right, brother."

His father's voice: "Both my sons are dead."

The robber in Baltimore's voice: "Your money, motherfucker!"

Teddy's voice: "You think all them drinks was free?"

Dr. Ouradnik's voice: "Theoretical physics."

His own voice: "A witch hoax."

Philippe Álvarez's voice: "At your weakest, they will take you."

Professor Diageo's voice: "Propaganda. Propaganda. Propaganda. Propaganda. Propaganda. Propaganda. Propaganda. Propaganda. Propaganda. Propaganda."

Exploding into fragments, the door shot across the room with a burst of freezing wind. John closed his eyes. Something powerful had entered his apartment. He felt their breath upon his face. Trembling, he cautiously opened his eyes to find out who it was.

Unable to scream, John shivered in petrified horror.

The devil peered deep into his eyes, grinning, chuckling, growling. Flames from the abyss shot up over the railing. The sky outside cracked like glass. Grabbing John's throat, the devil forced him against the wall. He pulled a .357 Magnum revolver out of thin air, cocked it and jammed the gun into John's forehead. The wall turned into a tree and his apartment vanished into blackness.

John and the devil flew through space nearing the speed of light on a meteor with a tree growing out of it. Nika Godec's electric violin music erupted in a fiery fantasia. Slowly, as they whizzed through space at tremendous speed, the devil's face changed into his own. He could see into his own icy eyes, pressing the gun harder and harder against his forehead. The meteor raced towards a black hole. The universe was imploding. Smiling, with a bizarre sense of virtue and satisfaction, he pulled the trigger.

~∾

John awoke to the phantom sound of a gunshot and his own bloodcurdling screams. Saturated in sweat, he jumped from the couch and flipped on the light switch, grabbing the wall as if it were a life preserver rescuing him from the darkness of eternal waters. The lights came on. It was four-thirty in the morning.

Though the nightmare was over, there was no relief. John had never experienced a dream so real before.

Convulsing, he splashed cold water over his face in the bathroom. Looking into the mirror, he slapped himself several times to make sure he was truly awake. He was. John returned to his living room and sat on the couch, weak and trembling. Lacking the courage to pull back the curtain from the sliding glass door, he imagined that his dead brother was still standing on the balcony. The nightmare was burned into his mind. Checking his smart phone's log, he saw that he never called Dr. Ouradnik. Sometime during his earlier struggle, he had managed to fall into a deep slumber. Too afraid to sleep again, he skimmed through the material that would be on his test in a few hours.

~~

Ten-thirty had arrived like a cloaked executioner on his way to deliver some poor soul their final breath. Students chatted as John sat in isolation, looking at the decorations on the walls for the upcoming school dance that Friday night. Desks cluttered the gymnasium. The basketball court was shiny, recently buffed. Shoes *squeaked* agonizingly over its surface. The bleachers on either side were empty, aside from a few straggling students who had not yet taken their seats.

Silence befell the gymnasium as the test began. The nightmare had an enduring effect on him. John would sweat and find it difficult to focus. Anxiety, though not from the test, encompassed him. Touching his face, he realized he hadn't shaved. Neglecting to shower, he wore the clothes that he was arrested in early Sunday morning. The smell of alcohol welled up in his nostrils. He wasn't sure if anyone else could smell it, or if it was really there at all.

Finishing the exam before anyone else, he rested his head on the desk for a minute. Closing his eyes, he thought he might take a little nap. Under his head was a test that would receive a score of 99.7%.

~~

After the exam, John walked across the quad toward Francesca Hall. Scaffolding on the left side of the building climbed to replace the towering stained-glass window vandalized by the unknown assailant. Marcus was way off in his assessment of $850. The replacement window, with labor, would cost the Avalonti Trust Association $6560.41.

John stood on the cobblestone pathway, looking at Francesca Hall as if he had slipped backwards in time to the days before he received his invitation; days when he would stare in awe and envy, wishing that he was a member. He pondered inescapably over Kasey. Remorse churned in the depths of his tortured mind, remembering a time before he savagely ripped her still-beating heart from her chest and crushed it right before her eyes. He would've given anything to return to Xapà's restaurant that night and finish their dance; anything to hold her one more time.

One of the grand cherry wood doors opened.

"Marcus!" John shouted, running towards the building.

Marcus peered at him with keen disinterest, standing beside a Corinthian column.

"Marcus!" John repeated, dashing up the stone stairs.

"What do you want, John?" Marcus asked dismissively.

"Look, I apologize for my behavior," John said, nearly out of breath. "I screwed up. I don't know what to say."

"Don't apologize to *me*," Marcus snarled.

"Kasey won't talk to me. She blocked me. I need your help. You have to talk to her for me."

Marcus studied the imprint of a pendant under John's shirt with perplexed curiosity.

"Please, man," John implored, "you have to help me."

Marcus imprudently reached down into John's shirt and pulled out the pendant. John quickly snatched it away and stuffed his golden necklace back under his shirt.

"John," Marcus asked forebodingly, "why the *fuck* are you wearing a crucifix?"

"*Uh*—it was just a gift," John blurted out.

"A gift?" Marcus questioned intensely. "From whom?"

"Don't worry about it," John said, backing away from Marcus's glare.

"What the fuck is going on with you, John?"

"Nothing—I gotta go," John said, running away.

Taking a long walk, John found himself standing in front of the Basilica of Divine Hope, where he, days prior, had dropped off imported cheeses and meats into a donation receptacle. Reluctantly, he walked into the cathedral and sat on one of the aged, dark brown oak pews. Sitting, observing the spectacular architecture around him, his eyes grew heavy. Gentle organ music slowly lulled him to sleep. Guests sporadically visited the altar as he rested. Nearly an hour later, John awoke to a handsome young priest standing in the aisle beside him.

"Are you okay?" the young priest asked him warmly.

John, half asleep and in a daze, answered, "My dream was good."

The priest smiled, sitting beside him. "There can be no bad dreams in the house of God."

John rubbed his eyes. "Is *that* where we are?"

The priest chuckled. "Something troubles you?"

"Are witches real?" John asked.

The priest relaxed his posture. "Believe it or not—you're not the first person to ask me that question this week. It seems to be something that's on everybody's mind."

"Some more than others," John said, sitting up straight. "I'm an atheist—well, agnostic. I don't know. I don't what's true or false anymore. Witches can't be real. The devil can't be real—can they, Father?"

The priest took a breath of air. "If it were winter and you were lost in the woods and discovered bear tracks in the snow near a disemboweled, partially consumed animal—yet you saw no bear— what would you do?"

"I'd get the hell out of there," John answered.

"Why?" asked the priest. "You don't see any bears around."

"Well," John said, looking down, "I guess if there's tracks in the snow and a dead animal—something was there—and that *something* might be on its way back."

The priest nodded slowly. "When we observe the world around us, we don't see the devil—but we see his tracks in the snow. The evidence of evil is upon us. Evil that we must acknowledge and prepare against—or be consumed by. The bear is always there. The bear is always watching."

"But the *uh—uh*," John stuttered, "the science—what about science?"

"The electron," the priest explained, "has never been observed by human eyes. The mass of the subatomic particle is so low that it's impossible. But we know that the electron exists because we can measure how it affects its surroundings. The devil is like the electron; negative electricity that's all around us."

John rubbed the pendant under his shirt.

"Would you like to pray with me?" the priest asked.

"I—*uh*, gotta get going," John said, standing from the pew. "Could you—*uh*—do something for me if it's not too much trouble?"

The priest nodded faintly.

"Could you pray for my friend Kasey? She's—I don't want anything bad to happen to her."

"I'll pray for her," the priest promised.

"Thanks, Father," John said, walking away.

"I'll pray for you as well," he said, raising his voice a little.

John paused. Turning his head, he looked over his shoulder. "Just her."

∼⌒

Wednesday morning arrived with a burst of relief. John managed to get a few hours of consecutive sleep without having any mind-shattering nightmares. He had two final exams the next day but was confident enough in his ability that he didn't need to study for them. Instead, he isolated himself in his apartment and read a book on pacifism and non-aggression, seeking balance and tranquility.

The book was written by a martial artist who spent eleven years meditating, eating only fruits and nuts, in near isolation inside a temple atop the Himalayan mountains. After reaching enlightenment and an epiphany, the man instructed his disciples to kill him. He allowed them sixty seconds and would not defend against the attacks. If the onslaught had killed him, he believed humankind was not yet ready to hear his words. If he survived the thrashing, he would reveal the secrets that he had learned to all those who wished to obtain them.

After reading the book, John decided that he would traverse the great American open road with only a backpack and his sports bike. He planned to camp at the Rainbow Gathering in one of the country's wild national forests during the Fourth of July. Entertaining an improbability, he thought he might meet up with Clint somewhere and they could travel from city to city together, drinking cheap beer at punk shows, talking unconventional philosophy. Escape was inevitable. John resolved to never return home to Missouri, and without Kasey, there was no reason for him to stay on the east coast during the summer. Once the school year was officially over, he would set out for California.

∼◡∽

Jubilation soared across the university by Thursday afternoon. Most of the students, including John, had finished their final exams. While other students prepared for the school dance and the celebratory weekend parties, John planned his cross-country adventure. Before leaving, he wanted to make peace with Kasey, but she still wouldn't accept his calls. He sought her out at the PSRC meeting that was being held that afternoon at The Red Porcupine for Saturday evening's campus protest.

Arriving outside of The Red Porcupine, John met an ample turnout. The facility overflowed with guests. Looking through the windows from the outside, he searched for Kasey who may have sat somewhere in the café or the bookstore area. When one of the men inside took his seat, he saw Kasey and Alyssa, sitting next to each other near the checkout counter. His heart skipped a beat when he gazed upon her smiling face. While he stood outside contemplating whether to go in or not, Mel, wearing her military green bandana and a screen-printed Emma Goldman t-shirt, walked toward the entry door with one of her friends.

"Hey, Mel—how are you?" John asked, rushing over to her.

"What do *you* want?"

"I, *uh*—know we haven't been the best of friends, Mel, but I'm wondering if you could help me talk to Kasey?"

"She can't talk to you," Mel said, turning her back to him.

"Hang on," John said, blocking her from entering the café. "Please. Could you just tell her to come out here? Tell her I come in peace."

"You can't pursue your victim like this," Mel stated firmly.

John raised an eyebrow. "My *victim*?"

"Yes, your victim. She was intoxicated and emotionally incapable of consenting to sex that night as a result of her being under a high level of stress after the robbery in Baltimore," Mel explained.

"What!" John argued, "She only had two fucking beers the whole night!"

"Doesn't matter, John," she said, "you raped her."

"Are you fucking serious!" John shouted. "Get the fuck out of my way!"

"Listen, *dude*, you need to back the fuck off," Elsa snapped, throwing herself between him and Mel.

"Fuck you, bitch! I need to talk to Kasey," John barked, attempting to enter the café.

Mel and Elsa grabbed him, pushing him back out onto the sidewalk. A six-and-a-half-foot tall man with dreadlocks, wearing army fatigues, assisted Mel and Elsa after realizing John was being aggressive. John continued, trying to force his way through. They pushed back. The crowd inside directed their attention to the entranceway where they struggled.

"Kasey!" John cried out. "Kasey, I need to talk to you!"

More people assisted, trying to remove John from the threshold. The entire building began shouting at him, demanding that he leave at once.

Kasey looked at John for a moment, then turned away. Alyssa and her friends shielded her in case he managed to break through the barrier.

"Kasey! Come on! I need to talk to you! I'm fucking sorry!" John begged.

John's arms were held so he couldn't retaliate against the mob. His face was bright red with anger, fighting with all his might to break free. The coffeehouse was subsumed in the ruckus.

Kasey stood up and took a step towards the entranceway.

"John!" she shouted.

The commotion de-escalated slightly.

"John!" Kasey repeated as a hush fell over the crowd. "I don't ever want to see you again. I need you to leave me alone."

"You can't mean that," John whimpered.

"Just get out of here," Kasey commanded.

"You don't ever want to see me again? Well *fine*, then you'll never fucking see me again! Fuck you! Fuck all of you!"

The PSRC members let him go when they felt him pulling in the opposite direction. John stormed off down the sidewalk, shouting indistinctly. Kasey watched from inside, shaking her head, refusing to show any emotion.

CHAPTER 32

DANCE WITH ME

Arriving at the dance in the university gymnasium on Friday night, Alyssa grabbed Kasey's arm, preventing her from running out. Apprehensively, Kasey stayed for a little while, drinking punch served from a glass bowl and sifting through appetizers in search for one that was vegan. The gymnasium was decorated in an intentionally banal theme resembling a middle school dance. The music playing was all retro pop hits from the 2000s and early 2010s; music they would've heard while they were in middle school. Several young men asked Kasey to dance, but she politely declined. Not long after she had arrived, she told her friends that she wasn't feeling well and would be catching an Uber home as to not compromise the dance for anyone else. Alyssa offered to take her home and stay with her, but Kasey refused.

∾

Don Vandacheler was attending a yearend symposium comprised of chemists and scientific researchers that night. Many of the attendees were Avalonti members. Originally, they had planned to have their reception at Francesca Hall after the seminar but decided to relocate after the recent vandalism. Someone had returned to the hall on Wednesday and spray-painted DIE ILLUMANTI WHORES across the front of the building. Since there would have been outsiders in attendance, the society thought it too embarrassing to proceed while the graffiti remained.

While sipping champagne at nine that evening on the university's cosmic observation deck, Vandacheler received a disgruntled voicemail from Mr. Budwin, who was mistakenly never alerted of the cancellation. The reception was originally scheduled for 8:30. The grouchy phone call was, however, not in reference to the lack of guests at Francesca Hall. When Vandacheler played back his voicemail, Mr. Budwin had simply said, "You better get over here and deal with this."

∿

Vandacheler, who was informally in charge of Francesca Hall, sighed with aggravation as he knocked on the doors, discovering that Mr. Budwin had already left.

"That scoundrel," Vandacheler grumbled, opening the door for himself.

Walking through the cherry wood double doors, he noticed that half of the lights were still on. By the vintage record player, Kasey danced alone to the dreamy harp music that played, twinkling softly throughout the hall.

"Don Vandacheler!" she shouted at the entranceway. "Have you come to dance with me?"

Vandacheler, on edge from Mr. Budwin's vague yet alarming voicemail, proceeded slowly. His dress shoes tapped lightly across the marble floor. As he walked by the Victorian couch near the grand fireplace, he observed droplets of red wine scattered around on the floor.

"As a matter of fact, I have," he diplomatically answered.

"Then dance with me!" she shouted, lunging towards him, spilling wine from her glass.

Vandacheler leapt to catch her.

Gently taking the wine glass from her hand and setting it on the mantlepiece, he stabilized her and they began to dance.

Slow dancing to the light classical music, Vandacheler stepped with kingly posture, debonair in his tailored suit. In her white embroidered dress, Kasey beamed as if they were nobility, dancing the waltz 200 years in the past under the dazzling chandeliers of Chatsworth or the Winter Palace. Pain was evident in her mascara-swollen eyes.

"What's been on your mind, my dear?" Vandacheler asked thoughtfully.

"Men *fucking* suck," Kasey answered. She cackled at the sound of herself using an unfamiliar swearword.

Vandacheler smiled brightly, speaking in an understanding tone, "Yes, that certainly can be true. Especially when they're young—and afraid—with all the world telling them that they're not allowed to be. John cares for you. He just hasn't learned how to express himself."

Kasey rolled her eyes. "What makes you think I'm talking about *him*?"

Vandacheler turned her, keeping her stable as she spun in a circle. "A wild guess—or a foolish assumption, perhaps," he said with a note of sarcasm.

"It's not him," she said, frowning.

"Understood," Vandacheler said, nodding.

"I just don't understand why he would do this to me," she slurred. "What's wrong with me?"

"It's not you, Kasey. He's afraid to let *anyone* in."

She sniffled. "I told John that I loved him, and he just ran away from me," she cried. "John doesn't love me. He'll never say it. I'm a loser."

"We both know that's not true," Vandacheler reassured. "You're a remarkable human being, Kasey. Nary have I met a kinder soul. You're a truly good person—a rarity in this world as we know it today. A loser, my darling, you will never be."

With an unexpected giggle, she jokingly asked, "Would *you* marry me, Don Vandacheler?"

"Of course, I would, my dear," he answered, chuckling softly. "John will see that he loves you. It's unmistakable that he does. It's a matter of *logical deduction*. Just give him time."

"He came looking for me at the café. I told him that I never wanted to see him again."

"We all speak out of hurt from time to time. A couple of days from now, talk to him. You'll work it out, I promise."

Through her teary eyes, she looked up at him and smiled. "Okay. I will."

She rested her head on his shoulder.

Vandacheler patted her on the back, holding her close, and they continued to dance.

After a minute, she fell asleep in his arms.

Chuckling, he lifted her and carried her, placing her gently on the Victorian couch.

Sitting in one of the parlor chairs across from her, he contemplated how he would resolve the situation at hand. Looking at Kasey's phone sitting on the coffee table, he calculated a plan.

"Hey, Kasey, how ya doing?" Alyssa asked, answering Vandacheler's call.

Vandacheler exhaled slowly. "Good evening," he said, "my name is Don Vandacheler. I'm a mentor at the Avalonti Society. This is highly unorthodox—*I know*—but I have your dear friend Kasey here at Francesca Hall and I'm wondering if you might be of service. I'm afraid she's gotten into a bit of wine."

"Is she drunk?" Alyssa giggled.

Vandacheler looked at her passed out on the couch. "Terribly so."

∽∾

Alyssa and Vandacheler took Kasey home and helped her to bed. Alyssa promised to stay and watch over her. Before he returned to Francesca Hall to clean up Kasey's mess, Alyssa gave him a hug and told him that he was "one of the good ones". Vandacheler smiled and spoke with an Italian accent, "*Non esiste una cosa del genere, mia cara.*"

Vandacheler locked up the hall and raced back to the university's cosmic observation deck to rejoin an old friend at the reception who had recently moved back to Maryland; a brilliant chemist by the name of Dr. Lucille Smith, the thirty-six-year-old daughter of Joseph Brent Smith.

∽∾

While Kasey was slow dancing with Vandacheler at Francesca Hall, John was pacing his living room at The Marquis, listening to

Hank Williams, Johnny Cash, Merle Haggard, Patsy Cline and various classic country artists, occasionally standing in front of his mirror to adjust his tuxedo. Accompanying him was a bottle of whiskey and a bottomless glass.

Frequently taking sips from the glass, he struggled to finish a handwritten letter. After he finished writing it, he set the paper next to his gun that was resting on the countertop. He called his mother and told her to tell his father that he loved him, citing the martial arts philosophy of filial picty.

Smoking a cigarette at his breakfast bar, he gradually increased the volume of the music. The country music played, crystal clear with a booming presence. On the other side of his dining room wall was the neighboring suite of the hotel. Banging arrived, indicating that his new neighbor was dissatisfied with the loud music. John gave "the finger" to the wall theatrically, turning the stereo up even louder with the remote control.

Dolly Parton's song, "If You Ain't Got Love", came up next. While the song played, John contemplated the materialism that was pervasive among the members of the Avalonti Society. He sought to understand Caesar's amalgamated philosophies of wealth and philanthropy. In a journal published in 1992, Caesar wrote a praise piece on Andrew Carnegie, even though his wealth was largely bequeathed through primogeniture, whereas Carnegie's was self-made. Caesar wrote about fine art and the craftsmanship that existed and survived as a result of a demand for luxury from the upper class. According to Caesar, if there weren't wealthy people to purchase them, then objects of profound artistic beauty might not exist in the capacity in which they did. Paying exorbitant amounts of money, to him, was simply telling the artists and crafters to "please continue to amaze us with your talents". Caesar's philosophies carried weight through his convictions. Since 1981, he'd donated sixty-seven billion dollars to charity, research and membership benefits.

John heard the banging on the wall again. Ignoring the demand, he paced around his living room, listening to the loud music while drinking whiskey from his glass. He imbibed the liquor in ample gulps, pretending like he was back at Xapà's dancing with Kasey under the ambient lighting of the banquet hall. Dancing alone in his living room, he could almost hear her saying, "*I love you, John*", behind the music.

Interrupting his melancholy dance was the furious banging on the wall, returning louder than before. John clenched his jaws so hard he nearly cracked his teeth. "Fuck you!" he shouted, throwing the whiskey glass against the wall. "Fuck off! Fuck off! Fuck off! Fuck off! Fuck off!"

He lurched forward and sank to a stool, hanging on to the breakfast bar, sobbing.

The last entry on his playlist began to play Conway Twitty's 1958 recording of "It's Only Make Believe."

Recovering from the emotional breakdown, he began to pace and sway, singing with the music as he periodically took a chug of whiskey straight from the bottle. The amount of alcohol in his blood was rapidly approaching levels of deadly toxicity, yet he endured and continued to sing. Toward the end of the Conway Twitty song, he sang the final verse loudly at the wall in a fit of defiant passion. He chugged the remaining liquor from the bottle, stumbled backwards and collapsed in the recliner.

～◌

When the hotel security knocked on John's door, they noticed that the music was no longer playing and dismissed their advance. They were unaware that he was in there lying unconscious next to an empty bottle of whiskey.

CHAPTER 33

MERCY OF THE DICE

When Kasey woke up with Alyssa sleeping in her bed next to her, she was momentarily confused until memories of the night before came rushing to the forefront. Before Alyssa awoke, she texted Don Vandacheler and apologized feverishly. He texted her back, easing her mind some: *You have nothing to apologize for. We've all been there. Do not worry about it a minute longer.*

She texted Marcus and divulged to him that she had gotten drunk the night before, seeking further reassurance. In a sympathetic gesture, Marcus offered to bring her a nice plate of food from the Bemastra Yacht Club after his dinner with Ashley that night. Claiming that it would be an inconvenience for him, she modestly declined. Marcus insisted. She informed him that she might get some food with Alyssa at the campus rally if she could make it. Marcus said that, either way, he was bringing her dinner. Reluctantly agreeing, she closed the message app and began searching online for hangover remedies. She desperately wanted to attend the campus protest that evening.

The Progressive Student Rights Coalition were gearing up for a showdown. Vincent Novak, a controversial far-right speaker, would lecture at the university auditorium that evening. The decision not to rescind Novak's invitation to speak was ultimately left to Dean Robert Rafalski, who maintained that controversial speech was protected by the First Amendment. Rafalski aimed to uphold that right even though it was a private institution. PSRC rebutted, claiming that Novak's words incited real violence and posed a threat against marginalized students on campus. Maintaining his decision, Rafalski urged students to protest and speak their minds if they disagreed with what was being said, so long as it was a peaceful demonstration. Beyond that, he would not intervene.

Vincent Novak was invited to speak, astonishingly to some, by the Mid-Atlantic Black Conservative Alliance. It was surprising because Novak was routinely accused of being a white supremacist; a claim denied by both Novak and MABCA. The conservative alliance argued that the allegations were unsubstantiated political rhetoric aimed at defamation rather than genuine assessment. PSRC responded, slamming Novak for his traditionalism, Christian fundamentalism, anti-feminism and hardcore nationalist views, arguing that they were "part and parcel" to white supremacy. A campus constitutionalist organization chimed in as well, warning their fellow conservatives not to attend the lecture, insisting that Novak's views were "misguided" and "anti-libertarian".

Novak seemed to have very little support at the university, but strangely the tickets sold out. Some would attend the lecture even though they had no interest in what he was saying, just to antagonize the protesters. Other students hid their reasons for purchasing their tickets. At any rate, it would be the biggest non-sporting event of the year. Electricity was in the air well before Novak had arrived. Campus security reinforced in preparation. The local police were also made aware of the situation. It was likely that outsiders would piggyback the peaceful rally to levy physical attacks against the patrons of the event; an outcome observed during past demonstrations. The doors would open that night at 8, while most of the students were enjoying parties celebrating the end of the school year. Kasey was left with the decision to either fight through the hangover or give up her chance at voicing her opposition at the demonstration.

∽

By six that evening, John's Kawasaki Ninja sports bike had not moved from The Marquis's parking garage. Don Vandacheler, after the previous night of witnessing Kasey's emotional drinking at Francesca Hall, attempted to contact him but he wouldn't answer. Worriedly, he asked Marcus to check in on him. Marcus reluctantly complied and knocked on his door on his way out with Ashley. Since John was typically mysterious in his day-to-day activities, Marcus didn't pay any mind to the fact that he didn't answer the door. He texted Vandacheler back, insisting that John was most likely fine.

~~~

Around 7, Kasey arrived at the painful conclusion that she was not going to attend the demonstration that evening. She sat alone in her living room watching foreign films and reruns of British comedies in her pajamas, occasionally receiving updates from Alyssa about the protest. Novak had arrived at the university and was preparing for his lecture. Patrons of the event were lining up in front of the auditorium.

~~~

While Kasey was lounging on her couch eating blueberries and drinking seltzer water, John was prying himself from his empty jacuzzi bathtub, fully clothed and wreaking of alcohol. Sometime during the morning, he woke up from the recliner in his living room, lit a cigarette and drank two glasses of whiskey. He had no recollection of how he ended up in the bathtub afterwards.

Drinking another glass of whiskey, John slowly recovered and developed the urge to attend Liam's "End of the School Year" party at Carnegie Village. Before leaving the hotel, he stopped by The Marquis bar and choked down an IPA, transitioning from liquor to beer in the interest of surviving the party without passing out. To assist with readjusting to normalcy, he snorted two lines of cocaine in a bathroom stall inside of the bar. During the next hour or so, he would nurse beer until his BAC returned to a "nominal" level.

~~~

Walking into Liam's place, John met a full house of people and nearly left quicker than he had arrived. "Like a G-6", by the hip-hop group Far East Movement blasted through the speakers. The floor rumbled with the bass. Cigarette smoke and the sound of rambunctious reveling filled the air. He had not been to a Village party since he and Bo were viciously beaten at the New Year's Eve blowout.

From a distance, Liam spotted John standing by the entryway.

John twiddled his thumbs.

"Hey, John," Liam said, raising his voice above the music as he approached. "I wasn't expecting to see you here."

John shrugged defensively. "I can leave if you want me to. I just felt like getting out of the apartment."

"Chill, man," Liam said in a softer tone, reaching into his six-pack of craft beer. "Have a beer. Relax. Enjoy the party, *mi amigo*." Using a key chain bottle opener, he popped the top off a beer and handed it to John.

"Thanks, Liam."

"No problem," he said, patting John on the shoulder.

John took a sip of the beer.

Liam nodded to the music.

"Hey, Liam," John said, dropping his eyes to the floor, "I apologize for fighting in your house. You and Lucas are awesome guys to throw parties like this all the time. I didn't mean any disrespect."

Liam paused, searching for words. "It's *uh*—cool, man. Don't worry about it. Shit happens. Those guys were assholes that should've never been here."

John nodded, still looking at the floor.

"They were douchebags, John."

"Yeah." John took another sip of his beer.

Liam tapped his fingers against his thigh. "Listen, John. I know it's been rough losing Bo—and I get that we don't really know each other that well—but if you need anything, just let me know."

With the beer in his hand, John pointed at him and nodded. "Thanks, man, I really appreciate that."

Liam glanced at a young woman who called out his name on the other side of the room. "No problem, John. Enjoy the party. If you get hungry, we got a grill going out back," he said, walking backwards, raising his voice with every step. "Plenty of food up in this motherfucker—just hurry up before Fat Fuck Mike gets here." The young woman rushed over and jumped up for a piggyback ride. He caught her and shouted to John over the music, "And, hey, if you can find a chick who can put up with your ass for fifteen minutes, just remember to wrap that shit up!"

"You bet," John chuckled, raising his bottle in the air. He quickly lowered his arm, noticing that two students were watching him salute Liam, who was no longer paying him any attention.

John sat on a lonely couch near the back of Liam's place, watching the delighted partygoers dancing and carrying on. Thinking of Kasey, he inwardly sulked, occasionally taking a sip from his bottle while inattentively watching a beer pong match. Not long after he inflicted isolation upon himself, Ritchie's ex-girlfriend approached and sat next to him, holding a red plastic cup full of keg beer.

Hailey was one of the most sought-after sorority girls on campus. With professionally manicured nails, salon-pampered blonde hair and pearly white teeth, she was described by many of her classmates as being "perfect". After she announced her breakup with Ritchie on Facebook, she received over 300 direct messages from boys who wanted to date her; all of whom she rejected.

John tensed up as he glanced at her sitting next to him on the couch. She wore white, open-toed shoes, tight blue jeans and a slouchy, hot pink top.

"Hi, John," Hailey said in her bubbly, high-pitched voice.

John sniffed disinterestedly. "Hey."

"You and Ritchie still fighting?"

"Nah, we squashed it. He still fucking hates me though, I'm sure."

Hailey grinned. "Yeah, he does."

"Right. So, I'm sure he wouldn't want me talking to his girl."

"His girl, huh?" she chuckled. "You're out of the loop. We broke up last week. Bastard cheated on me."

"Oh. I'm sorry."

"Eh, it's *whatevs*."

John forced a smile, raising his bottle of beer to take a sip.

Hailey inched closer to him. "I'm sorry he beat you up," she said, seductively twirling his dirty-blond hair with her index finger. "I know a way we can get him back," she whispered in his ear.

John raised an eyebrow, recoiling.

"Are you dating that little *oriental-looking* girl I saw you with?" she asked condescendingly.

John peered at her. "Her *name* is Kasey—and no, we broke up."

"*Oh*, that's too bad," she said, pressing up against him. "But I have some good news for you."

John swallowed hard. "What's that?"

"You get to be my boyfriend now," she said, confidently placing an arm around him.

John looked at Hailey through the corner of his eye. Memories of Ritchie punching him while he lay helplessly on his back raced through his mind. Hallow revenge was only a smile and a nod away, but he drifted. He thought of Kasey and how *her* arm around him felt like a bridge connecting two souls. He thought of quantum mechanics and childishly imagined building a time machine to return to the days before he broke her heart.

"Fuck off," John said, leaping from the couch.

Hailey's eyes widened in shock.

John advanced toward the exit.

"You fucking faggot!" she screamed, throwing her plastic cup of beer at him.

John snickered, walking through the door.

∼∽

The following Saturday was the official end of the school year. Deciding that there was no reason to wait that long, John packed for California. He left his apartment virtually undisturbed from the night before, leaving his apology letter to Kasey on the kitchen counter. He revved up his sports bike and hit the highway.

Listening to Dion and The Belmonts on his MP3 player, John soared along the interstate with nothing in mind except fleeing the confines of university life and the relentless, torturing thoughts of Kasey. The nighttime spring air wistfully beckoned him to travel west to San Francisco. Heading for the Pennsylvania turnpike en route to I-80, he stopped and sat on a guardrail near the diesel pumps on the outskirts of a travel plaza. The smell of gasoline and exhaust permeated the atmosphere.

"You okay, boy?" a seasoned Louisiana truck driver with short, peppery black hair asked from a distance, returning to his rig from the rest area bathroom.

John nodded lethargically.

"You sure, now?" he asked, walking over to him.

John flicked a cigarette butt into the woods behind him. "I'm fine, sir. I'm just taking a rest."

The faint sound of cars whipping by on the interstate whispered in his ears.

The man approached. "Where ya headed?"

"California—or anywhere but here."

"*Ah*, okay," the old man said, sitting next to him on the guardrail.

John glared at him.

"Did you try taking her flowers?" the man asked.

John chuckled. "I'm that obvious, huh?"

The man laughed. "I was your age once, boy. See that woman over there?" He pointed to his tractor-trailer where his wife sat in the passenger side of the cab. "We've been married forty-two years next month. Lord knows I almost lost her a couple of times."

"She rides with you?" John asked, popping the cap off a bottle of beer.

"She didn't always ride with me. Kids are grown," he said, divagating. "I'm an OTR man—*over the road*. I've been out here many years. Should've retired two years ago. Loneliness is an awful thing, now. One day out of the blue she asked me if she could ride along with me. I told her I'd think about it. A second later I gave that woman there a hug and a kiss and she's been riding with me ever since. I love her—and I'm gonna keep on loving that woman 'til the end of time."

John took a sip of his beer, hiding his remorse.

"What happened with you and your little lady?" the man asked thoughtfully.

John sighed heavily. "I screwed up. We were at a dance over in Baltimore. We were dancing to an Elvis song. She told me that she loved me, and I panicked. I ran out of the building and left her there. The next day she came to the clubhouse at the university— it's, *uh*, an academic society we both belong to. She was furious and humiliated. I had the chance right then and there to apologize to her and make things right, but I didn't. I kicked her out of my life like a God damn idiot. Biggest mistake I've ever made."

"Oh, Lord."

"Yeah, it's over now."

"You gotta talk to her," the man suggested in a regal tone. "If she cares for you and you care for her—you gotta talk to her."

"I tried. She blocked my phone number."

"Your *phone number*?" The man chuckled. "*Boy*, women don't want you calling on the damn telephone. You gotta show her that you're a man. You gotta *go* to her."

"I tried that too. She told me she didn't want to see me again. The whole place was laughing at me," John explained.

The man raised an eyebrow. "The whole place? What place?"

"It's like a café bookstore outside of our university."

"*Oh*, no—can't do it there," the man said, shaking his head. "Can't be in public like that. It's gotta be in private. Just you, her and the good Lord. Where is she at now?"

"She's probably at the campus rally—but she should be at her house soon."

"You need to go to her."

"*Nah*, I blew it. I'm heading to San Francisco. I'll stop in Ohio to sleep tonight, then I'll ride I-80 and sleep near the Council Bluffs tomorrow night..."

"She a pretty lady?" the man asked, interrupting him.

John chuckled. "Yeah."

"A pretty lady ain't gonna sit around waiting for you forever, now. You gotta get over there. Get in that travel plaza gift shop, buy you up some roses. Put that beer away. Woman don't wanna smell no beer on you—it's cowardly. Take your bike, show her them roses and tell her that you made a big mistake by letting her go."

"I can't," John said, looking at the ground.

"If you need help with them roses—I'll buy them for you."

"It's not that. I just—I can't."

The man looked over at his wife, who exited the tractor cab and stood with her hands on her hips. He turned to John, authoritatively saying, "You're wearing a tuxedo. A man doesn't leave town on a motorbike wearing a tuxedo. Listen to what I told you, boy. Go to her. I'm gonna get on out of here. You take care of yourself, now."

"Yes, sir. Thank you."

The man shook his hand firmly then returned to his tractor-trailer.

John went into the travel plaza general store as the man pulled away.

~⁓

John returned to sitting on the guardrail. On his MP3 player, the songs Kasey had mischievously programmed on his playlist began to play. He listened to an uplifting song entitled "We're Coming Back" by the English punk band Cock Sparrer. After taking a whiff of Kasey's bottle of perfume through his backpack, he finished his beer, tossed the empty bottle into the woods, took a bump of cocaine and revved up his sports bike. Instead of heading west to San Francisco, he reversed course and sped off back toward the university. Before leaving for California, he had something he needed to tell Kasey that could not wait until the following semester.

~⁓

On a three-lane interstate en route to Kasey's house, John spotted a gridlock in the distance; brake lights as far as the eye could see. The right-hand shoulder was blocked by vehicles attempting to exit the highway. There was no left-hand shoulder, only a concrete road divider. Squinting, he thought about the kids riding bikes during the traffic jam in Baltimore. "Janie Jones" by The Clash played. He turned it up as loud as it would go.

John peeked down at the speedometer as he approached: seventy miles per hour and climbing. Two cars were taunting him in the distance; the first two vehicles he had to pass before lane-splitting over three miles of bumper-to-bumper traffic. They were the point of no return. The space between them seemed to shrink as he drew near. Their taillights met as devilish eyes in the darkness, peering sharply into his soul. For a moment, blackness enshrouded the highway. Below the brake lights, a mouth formed between the cars, grinning, snickering, calling out to him in a deep and haunting voice, "Do you feel lucky, John Hallman?"

With mere seconds remaining before his field-goal passing of the first two vehicles, he calculated his chance of clearing the jam. Although a seasoned rider was perfectly capable of handling the feat, John's inebriated condition and overall lack of riding experience had placed him firmly at war with the odds. It was a total gamble. Zooming between the first two cars, John threw himself at the mercy of the dice. Furious drivers blared their horns. John laughed, riding faster and faster through the jam. Looking down, he saw the speedometer climbing over one-hundred miles per hour. The stakes were high. One false move would've been the end.

Speeding between the cars, he was enveloped with a unique serenity; one achieved only by casting aside any shred of reason or logic and jumping over the edge with no hope of landing safely at the bottom. He thought of Kasey. The wind crashing against his face inspired images of him standing on a beach in California, holding her hand by the lonely sunset, gazing upon the infinite splendor of the wide Pacific Ocean. Philippe Álvarez's words landed heavy on his mind: *every man prays before he dies*. John thought of heaven and what it might be like to stand again in the grand company of those who fell before him; to see his grandfather and brother smiling as he walked towards them on a majestic sea of clouds; or to once again share a laugh with Bo, overlooking the plains of eternity from a sparkling veranda of gold. John glanced down to see that he had nearly doubled the speed limit. Passing the vehicles at tremendous velocity, the drivers became a shadowy blur. He wondered who they were; where they were going; who *he* was and how he had gotten to that point in his life. On his first day of college, he did not know the taste of whiskey or the sting of cocaine. He was a bird, set forth from its cage to wander the unexplored terrains of youth. His path had led him there; soaring inches away from certain doom in the middle of an interstate highway traffic jam.

Ahead, a motorist was inching over the line, hoping to gain access to the middle lane. In under three seconds, he would've stuck out just enough to block John's path completely. John had to think fast. Soft deceleration would've guaranteed collision. Hard braking might've hurled him over the handlebars. John's only other option was to keep the throttle open and ride full speed through a gap with less than an inch of space on either side of him. Grinding his teeth with a maniacal glare, he stared death in the face, refusing to let off the accelerator.

One.

"Don't slow down, motherfucker!"

Two.

"Holy fucking shit!"

Three.

The motorist slammed on his brakes as John zipped between him and the other driver, narrowly avoiding a devastating crash. Looking in his side-view mirror, he saw the man exiting his vehicle, standing behind the car door, shouting in a rage. John smirked. With the clearing in his sights, he breathed a hearty sigh.

"I did it!" John cheered, raising a sweaty fist into the air. "I fucking did it!"

In the distance, cars merged into a single lane on the left-hand side of the interstate. Miraculously clearing the traffic jam, John blazed by the accident that had caused the congestion. Paramedics and police were on the scene. A demolished motorcycle sent a chill down his spine. Shrugging off the shock, he sped along the nearly empty highway reaching speeds of over 120 miles per hour.

◈

Arriving at Kasey's house, John pulled up into the grass and parked his bike. Her living room lights were on, indicating that she was home. Reaching into his backpack, he retrieved the crumpled roses and proceeded up the walkway. Too intensely focused on what he would say, he didn't pay any mind to the billowing smoke that was rising over the treetops from the university. People were curiously exiting their homes and standing on their lawns.

Earlier in the night, Vincent Novak's lecture was disrupted by a group of protesters who had purchased tickets for the event. In the middle of his talk, they began shouting, chanting, swirling vintage noisemakers and setting off confetti bombs. The disruptive students were eventually removed after a bout of struggling. A roar of solidarity resounded outside of the building as they were escorted out. The commotion was so loud it could be heard by the nearby residents of Devonshire Heights. As such, the neighbors were convinced that the fire at the university was coming from the auditorium. Their deduction, however, was inaccurate. Minor scuffles had broken out between the Novak supporters and protesters throughout the evening, but police and campus security were able to restore and maintain order at the demonstration. The smoke was *not* coming from the auditorium.

"Fire," a young man said.

"I bet it was Antifa," another man said.

John knocked on the door without any response.

"Come on, Kasey!" John shouted through the door. "I know you're in there. Please, open the door, I just want to talk for a minute before I leave for California."

No response.

John knocked louder, pressing his forehead against the door. "Please, Kasey—just open the fucking door. I'm leaving forever, I just want to say one God damn thing before I go."

No response.

John kicked the door. "Come the fuck on! Open the fucking God damn door!"

No response.

Kasey's neighbors, Dave and Jennifer, ran into the yard. They were both grad students living together in Devonshire Heights. After the attack she experienced earlier in the year, Kasey had developed a close friendship with them. Jennifer was slightly taller than Kasey and only a little shorter than Dave. Although they occasionally threw quiet parties, Dave and Jennifer were serious students who had few interests outside of academics. Dave proudly referred to himself as a nerd and would've likely lost an arm-wrestling match against Jennifer; should he have ever mustered the desire to compete in one.

John punched the door. "Come on, Kasey!"

"Hey, dude, what the hell do you think you're doing!" Jennifer demanded.

"Fuck off, bitch," John blurted out.

"Dude, come on," Dave said. "Not cool, man."

"Come the fuck on, Kasey!" John cried, pounding on the door.

"I'm calling the police, asshole," Jennifer threatened.

Dave nodded. "Yeah, go ahead and call 'em."

John threw the roses against the bay window. With brazen determination, he kicked the door until it began to splinter. "Why the fuck are you doing this! I said I was fucking sorry! Kasey! Come on! Open the fucking door! I swear to fucking God I'm gonna break this fucker down!"

"Whoa! Whoa! What the fuck, man!" Dave shouted, inching toward the porch.

"Stay back, Dave!" Jennifer begged. "He's fucking nuts!"

"Open the fucking door, bitch!" John erupted, puffing up his chest.

"Help us!" Jennifer cried, calling out to other neighbors. "Help!"

"That's it! Fuck you!" John detonated, lunging shoulder first into the door.

Kasey *shrieked* as the door burst open.

John froze like a deer in headlights when he saw Marcus holding on to her in a dashing black suit. Kasey looked at John with fearful eyes, still wearing her pajamas.

"I fucking knew it!" John exploded, grabbing Marcus by the collar, pulling him out of the house.

"Fuck you!" Marcus roared.

Marcus grabbed him by the throat and slammed him against the wooden porch post, nearly splitting it in two. "It's not what you think, you dumb motherfucker!" he shouted. Spit flew from his mouth. Veins popped from his forehead. He strangled John with all his might.

"Guys! Stop!" Kasey screamed, standing at the door.

John gurgled and hissed, struggling to pry Marcus's hands from his neck. His face was bright red and turning purple. Reaching down, he straightened his arm and clenched his hand into a fist. Snapping like a spring, he launched an uppercut, striking his jaw with a resounding crunch. Marcus stumbled backwards, falling from the porch. His head smacked the concrete at the bottom of the stairs.

"John! No! Stop!" Kasey pleaded, throwing up her hands.

"Fucking traitor!" John declared.

Leaping from the porch, John's remaining sense of reason and rationality was replaced with a vacant barbarity. Flying through the air, his knee stretched toward the sky, chambering his leg to deliver a devastating assault. Onlookers froze into a solidified glare as he descended upon him. Marcus weakly rolled out of the way, barely dodging his foot, crashing against the pavement with a heavy *thud*.

"Stop, stop, stop!" Dave begged, grabbing on to John.

"Fuck off!" John barked, whipping around a fist.

Dave's fragile body jolted with a wave of shock. His eyebrow split into a waterfall of blood. Jennifer wailed with an ear-piercing screech, lunging towards John in a fit of retaliation. With unfamiliar savagery, John wrapped his hands around her neck and slammed her face-first against the porch railing.

"Fuck you, bitch," John snapped.

"Fuck *you*, John," Marcus wept.

"Fuck me? Fuck me?" John growled, kicking him in the ribs. "Fuck you!"

Marcus coughed and winced, staring blankly at the clouds that were expanding with the smoke rising from the university. Kasey and the other neighbors were too afraid to physically intervene. Their pleas for him to stop were the trumpets of a battleground bugle, falling on the ears of a deranged soldier whose lust for combat had survived long after the last days of the war.

"Stop! Leave him alone! Don't hurt him!" Kasey cried, cowering on the porch.

John glowered, drooling vitriolic rage. "Don't hurt him? Don't hurt him? I fucking knew it!"

John's rapacity for revenge was inflamed to the melting point. Emptiness filled his eyes as he climbed on top of Marcus and unleashed a ferocious series of punches and strikes. Marcus slipped out of consciousness. With every powerful blow, his head *thumped* against the pavement. Displaying no intention of stopping, John was on the verge of killing one of his only friends.

The petrified onlookers turned their heads to see a blonde-haired woman wearing pearls and a formal dress racing to the scene. As if punting a football sixty yards to the end zone, she kicked John in the face. John grunted with a roar. The powerful kick rattled him immensely. Dazed and disoriented, he struggled to stand to his feet.

"You fucking piece of shit!" the woman screamed.

John's nose was shattered. Stunned and no longer able to defend himself, the ensuing onslaught was a harrowing victory for the blonde-haired woman. With a fist full of his hair, she held him at his knees, repeatedly punching him in the face. Her diamond engagement ring dug into his open wounds with a passionate fury.

"Stop!" Kasey bellowed out.

The blonde-haired woman looked up on the porch. Distracted by Kasey, John was able to push her away. Woozily, he lurched towards his bike. Blood poured from his nose. The blonde-haired woman grabbed him from behind, refusing to let him go. With the last bit of his strength, he cocked his elbow forward and *cracked* it against her temple. She fell unconscious to the ground.

Collapsing on his bike, John feebly put his helmet on and started up the engine.

Two stout, middle-aged men hastily approached the scene from a few houses down. They were close neighbors as well as hunting buddies. One of the men drew a nine-millimeter pistol.

"Shut it off!" the man commanded, tramping into the yard, aiming the pistol at John.

The other neighbors rallied behind the men, positioning themselves to capture John before he could escape. Kasey squeamishly watched from the porch, holding on to the railing. With silent tenacity, John hoisted his backpack from the ground, reached into it, pulled out his .357 Magnum revolver, pointed it toward the sky and popped off two warning shots. The man with the pistol stopped dead in his tracks. Most of the neighbors scattered at the sound of the gunshots. Examining John's confident yet unstable demeanor, the man sank to a knee and diplomatically placed his pistol in the dirt. With newly summoned courage, Kasey leapt from the porch.

"John!" she cried, fearlessly rushing over to him. "Wait!"

John peered deep into her teary eyes.

"John," she wept, shaking her head, "what in the world are you doing?"

John leaned in close. "Look what you did, you fucking whore!" he yelled, spitting blood onto her face. "Fuck you!"

Kasey stood motionless under the pale of the moonlight, weeping with spatters of his blood on her face. John revved his engine and peeled off into the night. The paramedics and police arrived one minute after he had vanished. Once they received information that he had fled, the police raced off to pursue him. Paramedics were assisting Marcus, Dave and Jennifer. A gurney was immediately deployed for Marcus. An additional EMT arrived for Dave and Jennifer. Not significantly injured, a small group of neighbors were able to stand Ashley to her feet. Disoriented from the fight, John didn't realize who it was he had knocked to the ground. Exhausted from the Bemastra Yacht Club dinner, Ashley had elected to wait in the car while Marcus delivered the carryout food to Kasey. Dozing off, she had missed an important text message from Marcus: *John's banging on KC's door. We called the police.*

∾

Numb, bleeding and detached, John escaped, riding his bike toward the I-270 en route to West Virginia. John knew he couldn't return to his apartment. While he didn't know the status of Marcus, or the others, he was fully aware of the critical damage he had caused. A gentle rain began to fall. Under an overpass, he waited for a moment to see if the rain would stop. Adding two bullets to his gun, he passionately vowed, "I'm not fucking going to jail."

~~

State police radio dispatched an APB on John, poising every officer in Maryland to be on the lookout for a black and orange Kawasaki Ninja 650 sports bike. Serendipitously, he had managed to cross the state line without being apprehended. He threw his bike to the ground, leapt onto the porch and pounded furiously on Philippe Álvarez's unlocked front door.

"Let me in! God damn it, let me in!" he shouted.

"John!" Philippe gasped, opening his door to find him soaking wet and covered in blood. "Get in here for heaven's sake!" He pulled him inside of his candlelit living room. The storm had knocked the power out.

John took off his backpack, staring at Philippe with a vengeful glare.

"John, what has happened?"

John didn't speak, pulling out his double-action .357 Magnum revolver.

"John?"

"It's over," John said, pointing the gun at Philippe.

A flickering bolt of lightning illuminated John's sincerity.

Philippe surrendered, raising his hands into the air.

"This is all your fault," John declared, attempting to steady his trembling hand.

"John, this is not our fault," he said, inching closer to him.

"Back up, motherfucker!" John ordered.

Philippe complied, taking a step backwards with his hands remaining in the air.

"This is a fucking nightmare," John cried. "None of this should have happened. My brother died, I just wanted him to be proud of me. I wanted to make something out of myself. That's never going to happen now. It's all over now—it's all over."

"John, it's not over," Philippe stated. "We can fix whatever happened."

"It's all over."

"We can fix this," Philippe promised.

"It's all over. It's all over," he sobbed, backing into the corner, sliding down the wall. He sat on the floor, shivering, crying, opening his mouth.

"No, John!" Philippe roared.

John closed his eyes tightly. "I'm sorry, Mom," he cried, wrapping his finger around the trigger. "I'm sorry."

"No!" Philippe screamed, lunging desperately toward him.

John pulled the trigger.

Befuddled, Philippe grabbed the gun out of John's hand and darted backwards to the center of the room. The gun had misfired. John drooled and cried, laying his head on the unfinished hardwood floor. Philippe opened the cylinder and pushed the ejector rod, releasing six fully intact high-velocity center-fire rounds. The bullets clanked heavily in succession against the hardwood floor, rolling away in random directions. Philippe gazed at John in whimsical disbelief.

CHAPTER 34

THE GREAT WAR

John endured a heavy silence from the outside world, isolated within the walls of *The Dollhouse*. Philippe cared for him, drawing his baths and bringing him breakfast, lunch and dinner while he recovered on an old couch in a little altar room next to his office. Philippe's West Virginia property was surrounded by woods, miles away from any neighbors. In his backyard he had assembled a makeshift shooting gallery. On Monday, when some of John's strength had returned, Philippe asked him to join him outside. With him, he brought the .357 Magnum double-action revolver and the six bullets that were in the fully loaded gun on the night of John's suicide attempt.

"Why are we out here?" John asked listlessly with his hands in his pajama pockets; attire that belonged to Philippe.

"We have to find something out, John," Philippe said, loading the bullets back into the gun.

"What are we finding out?"

John tensed up as Philippe abruptly fired all six rounds into a paper target attached to a stack of hay at the edge of the yard.

"I'm sorry, John, I should've given you ear protection," Philippe said genuinely as he turned to find him defensively covering his ears, cowering from the blasts.

"What are you trying to find out?" John asked, slowly bringing down his hands.

Philippe released the spent casings on a gun-loading table and picked one up. "Don't you see, John?"

"See what?"

"You shouldn't be alive right now, John. Those bullets I just fired were the same ones that were in your gun that night. They were perfectly fine bullets—perfectly fine gun."

"I thought it was a dud," John said, inspecting the bullet casing. "What does this mean?"

"It means God has a plan for you."

John scowled. "What?"

"Who are you, John Hallman?" Philippe asked.

"I don't know. I'm nobody."

"Well," Philippe said, placing his arm around him, "we need to figure who you *really* are. Come on, let's go inside. I'll make us some lunch and we'll talk."

"Okay," John timidly agreed.

∿

Philippe's Queen Anne kitchen was dingy, weathered, and contained little food outside of a stockpile of MRE packs and an assortment of canned goods with faded labels. For fresh food, he occasionally purchased bread, cheese, butter and unpasteurized milk from a local family who also sold methamphetamines, tranquilizers, chloroform, heroin and gallons of 190-proof moonshine. When he cooked, there was an unmistakable aroma leftover from the old gas stove; one that Philippe swore did not exist.

John took one tiny bite of the grilled cheese sandwich, staring blankly at the wall.

"The book of Revelation," Philippe said, taking a bite of his sandwich, "speaks of the end of days—the apocalypse."

"I've read it," John said.

Philippe chewed and swallowed. "It's my belief that we are on the precipice of war. Armageddon. The great war is coming. The final battle in this ancient war will decide the fate of the universe forever. In this war, God will call upon his angels; his soldiers."

"What does this have to do with me?"

Philippe smiled ominously. "You've been called upon."

"I have?"

"Yes, you have, my dear boy. You don't know who you are. You're lost. God will call you home with golden trumpets. It was not an accident that we met, John. I am summoned by God to lead you into the light so that you may find yourself once again. You've been chosen."

John pulled out the pendant from under his shirt and held it close to his heart.

"This evil," Philippe explained, "must be contained. These demons and witches *will* come for us. They know who you are, John. They seek out soldiers of Christ to incapacitate them, in hopes of weakening the front lines of the great war before the battle commences. They are saboteurs."

"What do we have to do?" John asked, clutching his crucifix.

"We have to figure out who the servants of the devil are. You see, Lucifer himself does not have the power to incapacitate a child of God until the war begins—nor can his demons. He needs mortal beings to assist him. He needs those who have surrendered themselves in temptation, lusting over his ill-fated promises. Those of whom I speak are the witches—the worldly foot soldiers of Satan. Witches can harm us; they're human, or humanoid. With witches, there are essentially no rules. We must stop them before they kill us—and they are coming."

"How do we figure out who they are?"

"I'm going to find out, John. I will figure it out—believe me. You will rest, and I will begin piecing the puzzle together."

John looked around at his dilapidated kitchen. "Philippe?"

"Yeah, John?"

"What do you do with all the money that you make from your website?"

Philippe snickered. "That was random, John. Well, I do the right thing with it. I donate whatever I don't need. I do not seek riches or worldly pleasures. I seek only the glory of God."

John sat back in his chair, beaming up a smile.

～✎

On the following day, John worked up the courage to check social media to see if anyone was talking about the fight between him and Marcus. After looking on Twitter for a minute, he threw his phone to the floor and vowed never to open the app again. Liam had tweeted about the fight, calling John an "alcoholic", a "cokehead", a "sexist", a "racist" and a "Nazi". He announced that John was officially banned from all future Village parties and called upon the university to expel him. Liam's Twitter post was *loved* and *retweeted* by dozens of people, including Arjun, Zach, Pierre, Lucas, Hailey, Ritchie, Brian, Jennifer, Dave, Alyssa, Mel, Elsa, Joy, Lakesha, Karen, the chapter president of Kappa Sigma, and a teacher John had during his freshman year who once remarked that he was an "exemplary student". His phone started buzzing on the hardwood floor. He flipped it over with his foot to see who was calling. Lying back on the couch, he covered his face with his hands and began to weep.

While Philippe worked tirelessly to discover who the witches were, John played back Don Vandacheler's voicemail. His voice was weary and not in the vibrant, regal tone that he so often spoke in:

"John—I—it's difficult for me to make this call, as I'm sure you imagine. Marcus is still in the hospital. He's alive, and hopefully will make a full recovery, but he is not well. Four of his permanent teeth were dislodged. Unfortunately, we are compelled at this time to cooperate with law enforcement, assisting them with your capture. My recommendation to you is that you come forth and turn yourself in. I believe a more favorable outcome will result if you comply. As your former mentor, it is with great anguish that I inform you that your case will go before the High Council, and— given the severity of the situation—will inevitably result in your expulsion from the society. I'm afraid I cannot help you this time, Johnathan. Take care of yourself."

Sickness in his stomach and a sense of vertigo overcame him. Weakly, he dropped his phone, grimacing in nausea. Helplessly, he vomited and collapsed, face-first in the puddle.

"John!" Philippe shouted, rushing into the room. "What's wrong?"

"I knew it was coming—but actually hearing it made me fucking sick," John wept.

"Hear what?"

"Avalonti," John said faintly, "they're kicking me out—and the police are looking for me. I'm a fugitive."

Philippe swallowed. "Marcus—is he dead?"

"No, he's alive, but I'm a goner. I'll never be able to step foot inside that school again."

"You need not worry about them, John. Your allegiance is to God and to God alone. You've been called to a higher purpose. I will protect you. I will house you. I will do whatever I can for you, but you must accept the Lord. You *must* say it."

John trembled, fighting back tears.

"Come on," Philippe said, "let's get you cleaned up first."

~~

Philippe helped him to his feet and walked him to the bathroom. John decided that he would take a shower. Finding it difficult to stand, he sat in the empty tub while the lukewarm water poured over him. Thoughts of violence raced through his mind. Fond memories of Kasey were like a disease without a cure. All his hopes and dreams were far beyond his recall. Closing his eyes, he clasped his hands and lowered his head. The warm water turned cold.

"I accept you, Jesus Christ, as my Lord and savior," he spoke tearfully while the cold water showered over him. "Forgive me—for I am sinner, and I have sinned. Forgive me."

He opened his eyes, letting the water hit his face.

"I'm so sorry, Marcus," he cried, closing his eyes, lowering his head. "I'm so sorry."

~~

In a bedroom converted into an altar room with candles, a statue of the Virgin Mary and a collection of religious decors, John rested on the couch that once sat in Philippe's office. Cozy and peaceful, the little room reminded John of the Basilica of Divine Hope. Rest soon blossomed into a coma-like sleep. Philippe granted him his slumber. Hours later, while he was researching, Philippe stumbled upon a bit of unsettling news.

"John," Philippe said, entering the room. "John, are you awake?"

John opened his eyes, smiling.

"John," Philippe said, "I'm afraid I have some bad news."

The smile ran away from his face.

"I can't take any more bad news," John wept.

"John, Francesca Hall was attacked. Someone torched the building with Molotov cocktails."

"What! Who died?"

"There were no fatalities, but everything inside was destroyed. Someone from GDS is claiming responsibility, but I can assure you it wasn't them."

"When did this happen?"

"Around the same time that you and Marcus were fighting. They used the campus protest as a way to cloak themselves."

John closed his eyes, breathing heavily.

"John, don't you see what's happening?"

John shook his head, mildly disoriented. "No."

"John," Philippe explained, "the forces of evil are drawn to the provocateurs. The witches are the ones who torched the building. Everyone who worked on the witch hoax project is going to die if we don't succeed, including you and me."

"Kasey," John said, sharply raising his head. "We have to warn her. You have to call her and tell her—or let me use your phone, I'll tell her."

"We can't do that, John. They'll know where you are. The police will come here, and we can't have that."

"What are we gonna do?" John cried.

"We have to figure out who the witches are—and we have to be *absolutely* certain."

~~

Philippe took to isolation, trapping himself in his office, desperately attempting to piece together the puzzle that would reveal to them who the witches were. They had not left the property since the evening of John's suicide attempt. Quiet contemplation had encircled Philippe for hours upon hours while John rested, regaining his strength. On the evening of May 19th, Philippe called upon John to answer a series of questions.

"Have a seat," Philippe instructed.

"What's going on?" John asked drowsily, sitting in a chair across from his desk.

"I need to ask you a series of questions. We must go back to the beginning of all this and take it step by step. Can you answer some questions, John?"

"Sure," John said, attempting to open his sleepy eyes a little wider.

"The social experiment project; who came up with the idea to do a witch hoax?" Philippe asked, holding a pen over a blank sheet of paper.

"I did," John answered. "It was all my idea."

"How did you come up with the idea?"

"I read a book that Marcus gave me for Christmas about witch trials. I also read Dr. Novini's book about conspiracy theorists, corrupt journalism and media propaganda. It just kind of came to me after that."

"What was their reason for shutting the project down?"

"Because we targeted a politician. They didn't want anyone high-profile involved. Caesar realized he fucked up by making us do a social experiment and gave us our membership certificates the same day they cancelled it."

"Okay," Philippe said, writing something down.

John stared at the floor, struggling to keep his eyes open.

"John," Philippe continued as if conducting a police interrogation, "did you ever see your friend, Bo, taking drugs before? Was he a frequent drug user?"

"I mean, we drank all the time when I lived in the dorm—but I never knew him to be a drug user. In fact, he used to lecture me all the time about smoking pot. Which was odd, because his friends were the ones who smoked me up for the first time. They got me drunk for the first time too, during my freshman year."

Philippe nodded. "When you were in New York—where you saw the old woman—what were you doing there?"

"We took the New York trip to see one of Vandacheler's friends at some old theater. She was some crazy violinist chick that does suspension art. The old woman, we saw her the next day. I think she was just a nutty homeless woman. Van paid for all the rooms and the bus ride."

"What does he do for a living?"

"He's a chemist. He gets shit tons of money just for doing scientific research at the university. He used to be an actor though," John added, yawning.

"An actor?"

"Yeah," John answered, "he co-wrote and starred in an off-Broadway musical when he was only nineteen years old. He's like a metrosexual hipster."

"Huh. When you were in Baltimore the night of the rock show, how long were you parked before the two gunmen showed up?"

John looked at the ceiling, searching his memory. "*Uh*, I would say maybe a few minutes. Not long."

"Did you notice anyone following you after you left the venue?"

"No—I mean, I don't think so. We rushed out pretty quick. There was some big fight happening."

"And that was the first night that you and Kasey were, *uh*—involved with each other?"

"Yeah," John said, chuckling, "her friend Mel thinks I sexually assaulted her because Kasey had two stupid beers the whole night. She's like a hardcore feminist in some women's group."

"Women's group?"

"Yeah. *Women's group*. If anyone is a witch, it's probably Mel."

"We'll get back to her in a second," Philippe assured, returning to his questionnaire. "The individual using the fake Facebook account with the name Agnes Sampson—did you ever find out who that was?"

"No. It was probably just some internet troll."

"And the threatening letter you received?"

"Marcus sent it to me. He was tracking me, watching my every move. He found out that I was Reyal Xaoh and thought that I was going to get him kicked out of the society. He was trying to warn me that I was being too obvious."

"That makes sense. Okay—this woman Mel—you say she's in a women's group. What does the group do? Do you know?"

"Yeah," John said, nodding, "they sit around and bash men all day."

"Does Mel have any pets? Have you ever seen her with an animal?"

"Nah."

"You sure?"

"Yeah, I'm sure. Oh, wait, no, no, no. Mel doesn't, but her friend does. Karen. I saw the dog before in the café."

"*In* the café?"

"Yeah," John chuckled, "it's her *emotional support animal*. The Red Porcupine lets these idiot progressives get away with anything so long as it's branded as a social justice thing."

"It might not be an emotional support animal," Philippe said forebodingly, "it might be something different."

"Like what?"

"An animal guide," Philippe said. "A supernatural entity in the form of a dog."

"It's Mel," John blurted out. "She's the witch."

"We don't know that," Philippe discouraged.

"It has to be."

"John, we can't make blind assumptions here, this is important."

"Well, then, do you have any other leads?"

"Not yet," Philippe answered, shuffling some papers, "but I will figure this out. Unfortunately, it's going to be difficult to name any suspects at this time. I'm going to have to dig deeper—but I assure you, I will piece this puzzle together."

"So, I can go lie down now?"

Philippe smiled. "Yes, John. Get some rest. I'll work on this. I'll have some more questions later though, no doubt."

∾

Returning to the altar room, John rested on the couch, staring at a religious painting on the wall that featured clouds and a passage from the bible: *Matthew 7:15*. After a few minutes of pondering, he fell into a deep sleep.

He awoke a couple of hours later to his phone buzzing in his pocket. Philippe's best friend, Dr. Ouradnik, was calling him.

"Hello," John said, rubbing his eyes with his free hand.

"John, are you still at Philippe's house?" Dr. Ouradnik asked.

"How did you know I was here?" John implored.

"I talked to Philippe a little while ago. Listen to me—I have something important to tell you. Keep your voice low during this call, okay?"

"Yeah, okay, what's going on?" John whispered.

"I'm not exactly sure what Philippe is up to, but I am deeply troubled by what he's telling me. He's made mention of an apocalyptic war. He believes that you two are being pursued by evil forces—witches, more specifically."

"Yeah, we are."

Dr. Ouradnik scoffed. "John, listen to me—there are no evil forces. There will never be an Armageddon."

"But you said it yourself—you said evil was a force, like electromagnetism."

"John, those are prompts. They're exercises in critical thinking. They're designed to inspire deeper levels of thinking for theoretical physics and whatnot. Sciences requires—you know—having to question everything. I was under the impression that my prompts were to provoke a more interesting argument from you during the debates. I'm telling you, John, there's no witches.

There's no war. There's nothing coming after you. You haven't been *chosen*."

John shook his head, chuckling. "Didn't Philippe tell you about the gun? I should be dead, but God saved me. He's calling me to a higher purpose."

"Yes, I'm aware of the suicide attempt. I was very sorry to hear about it. But let me ask you this; did you cock the gun before you pulled the trigger?"

"*Uh*, I can't remember. I think I did. Why?"

"The gun Philippe gave you is an old double-action revolver. Those old double-action revolvers misfire all the time if you don't cock the gun first, John. I don't mean this in a bad way, but there's nothing special about you—you just got lucky."

John scoffed. "I'm pretty sure I pulled the hammer back. I should be dead."

"John, Philippe is a brilliant man—far more intelligent than you think—but he does not deal in truths. He'll take coincidences and connect the dots, forming patterns that aren't really there. You've seen his website. He convinces people to see what he sees. From missing pieces of a story, he'll redesign it—he'll make it an entirely new story."

"They're after us, Dr. Ouradnik—great evil is coming for us," John said impatiently.

"Listen to me, John. I love him like a brother, but Philippe is a dangerous man. We have to get you out of there..."

John hung up and blocked his number. He began to stand from the couch to alert Philippe of the call but shrugged it off instead. Smiling and giggling, he kicked his feet up on the couch. "You're just a dream, Dr. Ouradnik," he said to himself, looking at the crucifix on the wall, "and there can be no bad dreams in a house of God."

~~~

Provoked by the torching of Francesca Hall, Don Vandacheler wrote and submitted an opinion piece to the *Washington Post*; something he had never done before. The article was a passionate tirade against the bigotry, violence and intolerance that was plaguing the nation. From his stance as an independent, he conjured a hailstorm of criticism targeting all sides of the political spectrum, including freethinkers. Contained within his fiery diatribe was a sizzling condemnation of the Georgia Deathstone Society; the group claiming responsibility for the arson of Francesca Hall. Scornfully, he rejected the practice of validating hypotheses without substantial evidence and thoroughly endorsed the scientific method, urging conspiracy theorists to do the same.

The article was a scathing onslaught; but it wasn't all fire and brimstone. He had, as well, issued words of wisdom. He called for enlightenment, peaceful coexistence, the rebirth of science and logic and a "renaissance of the intellectual age". He wrote on compassion, understanding and the rigorous pursuit of knowledge. He wrote of egalitarianism, progress and the stunning complexities of human civilization, offering hope for the future. Of the millions of readers of the *Washington Post*, many of them found true inspiration from his booming voice of reason. The article won praise from the academic community and beyond. Of course, naturally, it was not loved by all. Peppered within the screed was Vandacheler's admiration for Professor Diageo, and a gentle castigation against the Avalonti Society for their mishandling of the witch hoax dilemma. He anticipated immediate sanction for his article, but it didn't come. Unlike Diageo, Vandacheler was almost universally viewed as an asset to the society, even though not everyone agreed with his public critique. Dean Rafalski gritted his teeth at his article in the *Washington Post*, but he didn't push for censure. Namely because the society was enduring a critical defeat with the near obliteration of Francesca Hall.

The vandalism of Francesca Hall was a devastating blow to the society, far beyond the substantial monetary loss. All of what was in the left side, and most of what was in the middle of the hall, fell to the fire, including Caesar's Steinway piano, the priceless book collection, the *Avalonti Journal* archives, the grandfather clock, the floor globe, the antique furniture and most of Francesca's paintings. There was, however, a few items that survived. Since the arsonists struck from the left side of the building, some of the contents in the right wing were still intact, or repairable. As such, a salvage mission was scheduled.

Caesar Avalonti arrived for the salvage mission on Thursday afternoon with Joseph Brent Smith and his son, Arthur. Gloom encompassed the atmosphere. Several members, including Don Vandacheler, were in attendance. Mr. Budwin assisted as well.

Diana Luskovo, Caesar's dear friend and old flame, followed him to the hallow doorway. The blackened walls of Francesca Hall were a grievous assault on his senses. When Caesar spotted the charred remains of one of his beloved mother's paintings, he fell into Diana Luskovo's arms and cried hysterically, shaking and moaning no less thunderously than he had on the day she died. Joseph Brent Smith and Arthur had to help him back to the limousine. As he was leaving, Joseph Brent Smith glared at Vandacheler behind his back.

On the return flight to New York, Caesar, Arthur and Joseph Brent Smith conferred about the society's course of action. The decision was hasty, and the news traveled fast. Francesca Hall would *not* be renovated as their clubhouse. The Avalonti Trust Association would donate their plot of land to the university with the recommendation that the hall be demolished to make way for the new dormitories they were seeking. The society's future orientations would be held at the university's media center. Special events and charity dinners would be held at one of their subsidiary properties, such as the Lafayette Banquet Hall or The Avalonti Marquis.

❦

The eerily vacant university glistened under the strange moonlight. The cobblestone pathways were slick with an overlay of rainwater. Pinkish white pedals from the Yoshino cherry trees covered the grounds. As the rest of the salvage team slowly departed, Don Vandacheler said goodbye to Mr. Budwin one last time. They shook hands and hugged like the old friends they were. Diana Luskovo stood with Vandacheler near the old Victorian lampposts, never to be lit again, holding him closely as they gazed upon the ruins of Francesca Hall. The hour grew late. Hypnotized by the haunting surrealism before him, he soon found himself alone.

"Hello there!" an older gentleman shouted in the distance, emerging from the faculty parking lot. His voice carried with a faint echo. The man wore a classic brown trench coat over a white button-down shirt with a red tie, a bowler hat, designer dress shoes, leather gloves and a pair of tailored slacks.

Vandacheler glanced at him then returned to his melancholy observation of Francesca Hall, standing on the cobblestone path under the gentle falling of the rain.

"Good evening, sir," the gentleman spoke in a deep, sophisticated voice, walking down the cobblestone path. The tapping of his dress shoes mocked the sound of a sleepy horse-drawn carriage. "If we could call it such," he said, joining Vandacheler in his observation of the hall.

"Can we?" Vandacheler spoke with a crack in his voice.

The man shook his head. "A priceless three-hundred-year-old book collection. Finely crafted 19th century furniture. A beautiful Steinway baby grand piano—all wrought to ruin. A rare tragedy to say the least."

"Are you a member?" Vandacheler asked, breaking his gaze of the hall for but a moment.

"An admirer," the man declared.

Vandacheler nodded wearily.

"These conspiracy theorists," the man said, chuckling boorishly, "such imagination they possess. Invisible oligarchies, shadow governments, new world orders—such preposterous buffoonery. Their passion for mayhem is matched only by their love of madness."

"Indeed," Vandacheler said, his lip twitching with a fleeting smile.

The man stood proudly. "To them I say, 'A pox on thee. May your damnable misdeeds forever condemn you as the reviled and villainous savages that you are and will undoubtedly always be.'"

"Well said," Vandacheler praised.

"And to you, Mr. Vandacheler," the man theatrically spoke, "I say farewell."

Vandacheler turned his head, squinting, smiling. "Have we met before?"

Vandacheler grunted, wincing, dropping to his knees.

The mysterious man strolled down the cobblestone path, calmly sheathing under his trench coat a gold-plated, intricately engraved .45 caliber pistol with an Octane stainless steel suppressor. He climbed into his 1967 Cadillac sedan and disappeared into the night.

∽

The rambunctious jazz of the early soirees would never again be heard within the walls of Francesca Hall. Those days were gone forever. The architecture, the antiquity, the allure, the profound philosophical discussions of yesteryear; all but a fading memory of the past. Francesca Hall was dead. And there, by the charred remains of its former glory, as he drew his final breath, Don Vandacheler had died alongside it.

~~

Thirteen minutes after the murder, Don Vandacheler's body mysteriously vanished without a trace. Meanwhile, John forced himself to eat some food while Philippe pored over his research documents, trying to discover who the witches were. Barely leaving his office that day, Philippe believed that he was close to piecing the puzzle together. Periodically, he would call John into his office with another round of questions. John divulged practically every detail of his life to Philippe Álvarez.

The buzzing of the pale green circa 1970s refrigerator battled with the quiet hum of the vintage daisy ceiling globe while John sat in isolation, tapping his fingers on the kitchen table. Rain and angry wind battered the lonely house. John kept his ears sharp, listening for movement from Dr. Ouradnik, who was tied up and sedated in the other room. He had made a critical error by not alerting anyone before attempting to rescue John.

John's phone started to buzz.

"Kasey!" he cheered, reaching into his pocket. "Mom?" he said, squinting at the screen.

"Hello," he said, answering the call.

"John," his mother spoke, crying on the other end.

The hair on John's arm stood up. Since his mother rarely cried, he knew something was terribly wrong. Naturally, he assumed the call was in reference to the violence he had enacted against Marcus, and the likelihood of him being expelled from college as a result.

"John, this is your grandma," she said, taking the phone from her daughter. "You need to come home, baby. It's your father, John—he's passed on."

A faint, high-pitched ringing in his ears accompanied a fuzzy vertigo. John stared at the wall, unable to speak.

"Didn't you hear me? You gotta come home, baby," his grandmother said, sniffling.

John did something he never imagined he would do; he hung up on his grandmother.

"I'm sorry, Grandma," he choked out, turning off his phone. "I'm sorry, Dad."

Philippe returned to the kitchen to find John frozen, staring blankly with teary eyes.

"John," Philippe cautiously asked, "what's the matter?"

"My mother just called me," he said, breathing heavily, "my father's dead. The witches must've killed him. They're sending me a threat. They're going to kill me next."

"I'm so sorry, John," Philippe said, nervously rustling the papers of his report.

John looked at Philippe's hands. "Is that the report? Are you finished?"

"Yes, John, I'm finished. I know who the witches are."

Rain slammed against the house.

With the voice of desperation, John asked, "Who are they?"

Lightning struck with a clap of thunder.

A crucifix fell from the wall.

Philippe threw his report on the kitchen table. "We don't have much time."

CHAPTER 35

THE GRAND REVEAL

Chloroform. *Check.*

Lumber. *Check.*

Kerosene. *Check.*

Matches. *Check.*

Rope. *Check.*

Torch. *Check.*

Wooden stake. *Check.*

Holy Bible. *Check.*

~~

Secluded by trees near the Francis Scott Key Bridge, the Fort Armistead city park stood as a relic of the past. Built in 1898, the fort was once owned by the United States military to protect the outer channels of the Baltimore harbor. After becoming obsolete, it was purchased by the city in 1926 with the intent to recreate it as a tourist destination. Over the years, interest in the fort waned, and it was eventually left to disrepair. Aside from the recreational fisher who occasionally spent their morning on the piers overlooking the Patapsco River, the forty-five-acre park was virtually unused. Philippe Álvarez had carefully selected the location. With Philippe's pickup truck, they had delivered their supplies to a small room in the basement of the fort on the night before the kidnapping. At 3:30 a.m. on Saturday, May 22nd, they returned to perform their clandestine undertaking.

"Grab the feet," Philippe whispered, instructing John as they carried the suspect from Philippe's car to a hidden pathway leading to the fort.

Philippe wore a black pinstripe suit. John wore his tuxedo that was recently washed and pressed. They used chloroform-soaked rags to render their suspect unconscious. Carefully, they advanced to the underground corridors of the antiquated fort.

"We have to be quick, John," Philippe reminded, placing their suspect on the concrete floor of the dungeon-like chamber. "Light the torch."

John lit the torch and forced it into a crack along the damp concrete wall, providing them with just enough light to carry out their task.

"Help me, John," Philippe requested, lifting the unconscious person against a large, kerosene-soaked wooden stake; held in place by cracking a portion of the concrete and digging a hole in the ground below.

John tied the ropes, attaching the person to the stake.

"Throw on the wood," Philippe instructed.

John nodded, proceeding to the corner to fetch an armload of lumber. Philippe fortified the stake, ensuring its stability during the immolation. In a teepee formation, John piled the wood around the bottom of the stake.

"W—what," the suspect faintly uttered, slowly waking up from their chloroform sedation.

"Silence, witch!" Philippe shouted, forcefully gagging them with a bandana then tying it around their neck.

"The kerosene, John," Philippe ordered, pointing to the container near the opposite side of the room. "Pour it on, quickly!"

John complied, dousing the lumber below the suspect's feet.

The kerosene container *bubbled* and *gurgled* as he poured.

"It's time, John," Philippe said, retrieving a Bible from his backpack. "We will sever their alliance with the devil and purify their soul."

John stared at the wooden stake. The chilly basement room was pungent with the odor of kerosene and the musty fragrance of the long-abandoned fort.

"Get the torch, John," Philippe commanded.

John nodded obediently.

Philippe recited passages from the Bible.

Pulling the torch from the concrete wall, John turned and looked at the woman tied helplessly to the wooden stake. Ineffectually, she struggled to escape.

"Light it," Philippe instructed.

John stood face-to-face with the woman tied to the stake. He raised his arm above her head.

Reflections of the torch fire danced in her tear-filled eyes. "I love you, Kasey," he confessed intensely, dropping the torch beneath her feet.

A *whooshing* pillar of flames engulfed her.

Muffled screams filled the wicked air.

"Remember, John," Philippe said, inspecting his reaction, "they killed your father. They murdered Bo."

"Yeah," John said, studying her flesh as it began to blister and boil.

"They manipulated you from the beginning," Philippe reassured, speaking with passion and vigor. "Their lies. Their theater. Their *staged* robberies. You fell into their traps like clockwork. They are masters of deception. The witch hoax, John— it was their plan all along. The dark armies know that Armageddon is on the horizon. They were trying to draw out and sabotage soldiers of Christ, like black ops snipers. They wanted chaos. They needed a patsy. They needed to keep their cover. They wanted you to think that *you* were the creator of the hoax, then drive you to *kill* yourself before the great battle commenced. They were weakening you. They knew your fears. You wrote them down in the essay. They were listening when you read it aloud. They *knew* how to get you into Kasey's arms. *She* is Agnes Sampson. *She* was sent to seduce you and drive you mad. You were set up. They wanted to erase you. They wanted you to kill yourself, John, but

God wouldn't let you succumb. God wouldn't let you die. You are chosen. You were a lost angel—but you've been found again. You are a warrior, John. You are a courageous warrior in God's holy army."

John gazed coldly at the crackling red-hot fire, casting his shadow on the walls of the concrete tomb.

"The witch is dead," Philippe announced. "The love spell is broken. Next, we will find and kill Marcus Williams. Then—*all* of the Avalonti witches."

Grinning devilishly, John backed away from the inferno. "Goodbye, Kasey."

CPSIA information can be obtained
at www.ICGtesting.com
Printed in the USA
LVHW090851100520
653765LV00003B/3